CUNARD

◆◇◆

Library

Out of respect for your fellow guests, please return all books as soon as possible. We would also request that books are not taken off the ship as they can easily be damaged by the sun, sea and sand.

Please ensure that books are returned the day before you disembark, failure to do so will incur a charge to your on board account, the same will happen to any damaged books.

PRAISE FOR BARBARA HANNAY'S BESTSELLERS

'It's a pleasure to follow an author who gets better with every book. Barbara Hannay delights with this cross-generational love story, which is terrifically romantic and full of surprises.'

APPLE IBOOKS, 'BEST BOOKS OF THE MONTH'

'Barbara Hannay has delivered another wonderful book . . . For me no one does emotional punch quite like Barbara Hannay.'

HELENE YOUNG

'Gripping tale of outback romance . . . Her most epic novel to date.'

QUEENSLAND COUNTRY LIFE

'Lovers of romance will enjoy this feel-good read. Hannay captures the romantic spirit of the outback perfectly.'

TOWNSVILLE BULLETIN

'Get your hands on a copy of this book and you will not be disappointed.'

WEEKLY TIMES

'Barbara Hannay has delivered a fantastic story with beautiful characters and a lovely backdrop.'

1 GIRL 2 MANY BOOKS

'An engaging story of joy, tragedy, romance and heartache set within the dusty landscape of the Australian outback.'

'In beautiful, fluid prose, Hannay once again puts together all the ingredients for a real page-turner.'

'Everything a romantic reader could want . . . A brilliant piece of work.'

'Bound to become a new favourite.'

'A breathtaking read. Once again, Barbara Hannay manages to knock this reader over with a feather.'

'Barbara Hannay writes beautiful visuals of rural and remote Australia . . . This is a remarkable book.'

ALSO AVAILABLE FROM PENGUIN BOOKS

BARBARA HANNAY

The Country Wedding

MICHAEL JOSEPH
an imprint of
PENGUIN BOOKS

MICHAEL JOSEPH

UK | USA | Canada | Ireland | Australia
India | New Zealand | South Africa | China

Penguin Books is part of the Penguin Random House group of companies
whose addresses can be found at global.penguinrandomhouse.com.

Penguin
Random House
Australia

First published by Penguin Random House Australia Pty Ltd, 2017

1 3 5 7 9 10 8 6 4 2

Cover design by Adam Laszczuk © Penguin Random House Australia Pty Ltd
Text design by Samantha Jayaweera © Penguin Random House Australia Pty Ltd
Cover photography: woman: Getty Images/Moodboard Stock Photography Ltd,
church: Shutterstock/Robert Crum, field: Shutterstock/kwest
Typeset in Sabon by Samantha Jayaweera, Penguin Random House Australia Pty Ltd
Colour separation by Splitting Image Colour Studio, Clayton, Victoria
Printed and bound in Australia by Griffin Press, an accredited ISO AS/NZS
14001 Environmental Management Systems printer.

National Library of Australia
Cataloguing-in-Publication data:

Hannay, Barbara, author.
The country wedding/Barbara Hannay.
9780143783312 (paperback)
First loves–Fiction
Weddings–Fiction
Romance fiction
Queensland–Fiction
Shanghai (China)–Fiction

penguin.com.au

For my daughters, Emma and Victoria, who both
followed their artistic dreams . . .

CHAPTER ONE

Burralea, 1958

The day was a stinker. The sun overhead was blazing and sweat trickled beneath the bridegroom's collar. Unfortunately, the weather wasn't the only cause of his discomfort as he waited outside the quaint white church perched on a rise above Burralea.

'You look like you could do with a smoke, Joe.' His best man, Cliff, shook out a packet of Camels.

Joe hesitated, remembering the aunts he would have to kiss once this ceremony was over. Then he thought about his bride, who was carrying his child, and who was about to head down the aisle in a fancy white wedding dress specially transported over a thousand miles from a Brisbane department store.

Stuff it. He needed a smoke. 'Thanks,' he said, taking a slim cigarette and then ducking his head to meet the flame held between Cliff's cupped hands.

'They reckon every bridegroom gets nervous,' Cliff suggested.

'Yeah. Course.'

'I s'pose the trick is to keep your thoughts fixed on the honeymoon.'

Joe dragged a little harder on his cigarette. Grey clouds hunkered on the horizon, but they offered no relief from the burning sun.

'You'll have a bonzer time on Hayman Island,' Cliff suggested. He'd been Joe's mainstay during the past few weeks, ever since the drunken debacle at Joe's twenty-first birthday party, the night that had started this wedding train rolling. The poor fellow was still doing his best. 'I hear it's really flash.'

Joe nodded, but he wasn't about to confess that the bride's father had coughed up the money for the luxury Barrier Reef resort. Ted Walker wanted the very best for his daughter, of course, and as owner of Burralea's one and only pub, a grand two-storey affair with a splendid fireplace and a magnificent silky oak staircase, Ted could easily afford it. He was footing the bill for the wedding reception, too. It was going to be held in the pub's enormous dining room.

Joe didn't have that kind of money. He ran a cattle property with his dad not far out of town. Kooringal was a modest place compared with the huge stations out west, but Joe and his dad turned out good quality beef, and they kept their heads above water.

He knew the Walkers weren't happy about their daughter marrying 'down', but when Gloria had told them she was pregnant, they'd had little choice. They'd demanded a wedding, and put on brave faces.

Joe knew how that felt. He needed a brave face now as the church's wheezy organ started up and Reverend Gibson popped his head around the vestry door. The minister beckoned to Joe and Cliff.

'Time, gentlemen.'

This was it.

A cold jolt of panic spiked through Joe. His legs felt hollow as he ground the cigarette into the dirt with his heel.

He didn't want to do this. He had no choice.

Cliff patted his coat pockets. 'Still got the ring,' he said with an encouraging grin.

Joe couldn't manage an answering smile. 'Good man,' he said.

Shoulders squared, Joe followed Reverend Gibson into the little church, packed with family and friends all dressed in their wedding finery. He saw his parents in the front pew, his mum looking dewy-eyed and his dad stern but proud. They were both disappointed that Joe's older sister, Margaret, hadn't come up from Melbourne for the big day, but Joe understood why she'd stayed away. Besides, he had bigger things to worry about today.

Now, his collar was choking him, but a whispering excitement buzzed through the congregation, and there was a stirring at the back of the church. No time to ease the knot at his throat. Already, too soon, the organist was striking the chilling chords that announced the arrival of the bride. Joe stiffened like a prisoner facing a firing squad.

He told himself that once the ceremony was over he'd be okay. He'd just get on with the rest of his life as best he could. He wouldn't be the first man to wed out of necessity, and he and Gloria would manage. Romance was supposed to be overrated anyway, although Joe, drowning in the very deepest of regrets, knew this wasn't true.

Uneasily, he turned and saw Ted Walker and a figure in frothy white making their way down the aisle towards him. A rustle of satin whispered at his side, announcing Gloria, looking pretty and surprisingly innocent, behind a misty veil. The music stopped.

Reverend Gibson's voice boomed. 'Dearly beloved, we are gathered here today in the sight of God . . .'

Joe took a deep breath and the time-honoured ceremony flowed seamlessly towards its inevitable end.

Afterwards, they posed on the front steps of the church for photographs. There were photos of the bridal party, photos with parents, with the aunts and uncles, with friends.

More clouds had gathered by this point, now darkening the sky and casting a gloom over the afternoon. Joe was blinking from all the camera flashes when he saw the lone figure in the distance.

From the church's position at the top of the rise he had a clear view down the street. About halfway, a woman was standing beneath a leopard tree, watching them.

His heart stilled.

She was wonderfully slender and wearing a green dress, a dress he remembered too well, with a scalloped neckline that sat neatly against her perfect pale skin, and a narrow belt that circled her slim waist. Despite the gathering clouds, her hair glowed like honey.

Hattie.

For bleak, gut-churning moments Joe stared at her. Helpless. Distraught. She was more than a hundred yards away, and he couldn't read the expression on her face, but he felt her desolation land like a blow, an axe to his heart.

He had tried to apologise to her for this heartbreaking mess, but no apology could undo his stupid, careless, unforgivable mistake.

'Hey, Joe, you're not smiling,' his Aunt Gertrude called rather bossily.

Joe swallowed, tried desperately to dredge up a smile as another flash went off and another cloud, dark as a bruise, rolled over the church's roof. A gust of wind came with it and all the wedding guests looked up, their faces a picture of dismay as they realised they were about to be drenched.

The rain arrived in a sudden, nasty scud that sent everyone scattering. Gloria's father stepped forward with a huge black umbrella held protectively over his daughter.

Down the street, the girl in green climbed into a small white VW and drove away.

* * *

Hattie tried to let herself into the cottage quietly, but she hadn't managed yet to oil the front door hinges and so they squeaked.

'Is that you, dear?' her mother called weakly from the bedroom.

Hattie stopped just outside the bedroom doorway, needing to compose herself before she went in. Closing her eyes, she took a deep breath and then let it out slowly, willing her rioting emotions to calm.

The unthinkable had happened. Joe was married and somehow she would have to find a way to keep going.

When she stepped through the doorway, her mother looked gaunt and sallow against the white pillow. In recent weeks, even her hair had faded, and now it was the colour of withered cornstalks. She was lying just as Hattie had left her, and the level of water in the glass on the bedside table was exactly the same.

'Have you been asleep?' Hattie asked her.

'I'm not sure. I think I might have dropped off.'

The rain was blowing in through a window. The white painted sill glistened with water and streaks of dampness showed on the floral curtains. Hattie crossed the room and closed the window. She would have to fetch a towel to dry the sill.

'Were you caught in the rain?' her mother asked, eyeing similar dark streaks on Hattie's dress.

'Only a few spots, really,' she said. 'I jumped in the car as soon as it started.'

'You went to watch the wedding.' It wasn't a question, but a matter-of-fact statement.

Hattie flinched. 'How did you know?'

'About Joe Matthews's wedding? Jenny Greeves told me yesterday.'

'Oh.'

Their neighbour had obligingly agreed to sit with Hattie's mother on Friday afternoons, while Hattie drove to Atherton to attend to the weekly business of banking, grocery shopping and getting her mother's prescriptions filled.

'You should have stayed well away from that church today,' her mother said now. 'You should have more pride, Hattie.'

'I kept my distance. No one saw me.' This was a lie, of course. She knew Joe had seen her.

Despite the distance between them, she had known the very instant that his careful smile left his face. She'd sensed his distress in the sudden way he'd become ramrod-still as he'd stared down the street at her.

It was no compensation for the unbearable pain he'd caused her.

'Darling, I know you're hurting, but I'm sure Joe can't have been right for you. What's happened is for the best. It has to be.'

Hattie wanted to challenge her mother, to demand how she could possibly know this. How could losing the one you loved ever be for the best? But she couldn't ask such a thing. Her mother was dying.

With a very thin, too-pale hand, Rose Bellamy patted the space beside her on the edge of the bed. 'Hattie, come here, please, darling. Sit here. There's something I need to tell you.'

Suddenly nervous, Hattie stayed where she was. 'What is it? Do you feel worse? Should I call the doctor?'

'No, no, I don't want the doctor.'

'I'll heat some more of that chicken soup.'

'Not now.' Her mother looked even more distressed than usual. 'There's something I need to explain. It's very important, and I don't want to leave it too late.'

A horrible chill crept through Hattie. 'What's this about?' she asked fearfully, as she edged towards the bed and took her mother's frail hand in hers.

'It's about you.' Rose squeezed her hand ever so gently. 'Firstly, I want you to promise that you'll go to England now. When this —'

She gave a small nod to indicate her failing body, the bed, the sick room. 'When this is over, you must go.'

Rose had written to Hattie's grandmother in England when she'd first learned how ill she was. The reply had been sympathetic and, in her grandmother's polite, remote, English way, she'd invited Hattie to come and stay with her. Indefinitely.

'I know you've been resisting, because you were so set on Joe,' her mother said, 'but there's no point in staying here now, is there?'

'I can still get a job.'

'Hattie!' The thin voice was surprisingly sharp. 'I'm not asking you, I'm *telling* you to go to England. I need to know that you'll do this. I'm sure there must still be enough money in the account.'

The last thing Hattie wanted was to distress her mother by arguing, but she didn't want to leave Burralea. This quiet country town was their home. She could scarcely remember anything else. And yet, she knew she would be miserable trying to stay here without her mother or Joe. Besides, how could she refuse her mother at this point?

'Yes, all right,' she said. 'I promise.'

'Thank you.' Rose looked more exhausted than ever and closed her eyes.

'I'll leave you to rest for a bit,' Hattie said.

The faded blue eyes flashed open again. 'Don't go yet. There's something else I need to tell you.'

'But you're tired. Leave it till later.'

This brought a bitter, dismissive little laugh. 'I'm always tired and this is important. It's something I should have told you long before this – about what happened when you were born. I need to explain about – about your father.'

Her father?

Hattie's mind had been preoccupied with Joe and her mother's illness, and she was totally thrown by this sudden mention of a father she'd never known. Her mind flashed to the photograph album they'd brought with them when they'd fled to Australia from China.

Hattie had been almost five when they left, so she had only shadowy memories of Shanghai, but the photos had helped to keep these memories alive. There were pictures of her grandparents' spacious, pleasant house in the French Concession, set back from a tree-lined boulevard behind tall wrought-iron gates.

Another snap showed Hattie aged four with her amah, Ah Lan. Hattie was wearing a party dress with a satin sash and a full skirt, with frilly socks and black patent leather shoes. Ah Lan was dressed simply in plain dark cotton and her hair was pulled back tightly from her round, smooth face to reveal her gentle smile. From beneath her skirt, her tiny, misshapen, bound feet peeked.

There were also photos of Rose, her mother, looking young and pretty, and of Hattie's glamorous Aunt Lily with her bright honey-gold hair cut into a bob and lacquered into waves like corrugated iron. Her Uncle Rudi with his dark, dark eyes and flashing smile. Her very proper and rather distant grandparents.

Then Hattie's mild-eyed father with his pleasantly handsome face and smart seaman's kit.

'My father's dead.' Her mother was well aware of this sad fact, of course, but Hattie felt impelled to repeat it now. 'He died when I was a baby.'

Rose had told her this story many times over the years, speaking of Hattie's father with a fond smile, as if her memories of him were comforting. Her story had never changed and Hattie found it terribly important to repeat it now. 'My father was Stephen Bellamy. He was English, a merchant seaman based in Shanghai, and his ship was bombed by the Japanese. He was terribly heroic, saving the lives of lots of passengers, but he was injured too, and he died.'

Over the years, Hattie had come to cherish a mental image of her father as a handsome and heroic seaman, a veritable knight in shining armour who had nobly sacrificed his life for others.

'I'm sorry, Hattie,' her mother said softly. 'I really am so terribly sorry.' Her pale lips trembled. 'I'm afraid the correct story is rather more complicated than that, and it's time you knew the truth.'

CHAPTER TWO

Burralea, 2015

The cottage was even more charming than Flora Drummond remembered. The enchantment began from the moment she pushed open the front gate, framed by a wisteria-covered trellis, and went up the crazy-paving path to the gabled porch and the white door set with panels of gold and green daisy glass.

Inside, the cottage was simple and small by many people's standards, but for Flora it was perfect. She loved the glowing timber floors, the white walls that must surely have been freshly painted, the yellow cushioned seat in the living room's bay window, and the country-style kitchen with thick timber bench tops and deep windows that looked down into the rainforest bordering the creek.

This was to be Flora's home for the next six weeks or so. In her less optimistic moments, she saw this cottage as her bolthole, a necessary escape.

Her recent, unavoidable decision to resign from the job of her dreams had been a total kick in the guts. After working so fiercely to score a prestigious position with Orchestra Victoria, she'd hated walking away. Sadly, her boyfriend's increasingly disturbing behaviour had left her with little choice.

Flora had come back to the north to lick her wounds, so to speak, but she didn't plan to stay here for long. She wasn't going to let Oliver stuff up her life completely. In the new year, she would audition for a rank-and-file position with the Queensland Symphony Orchestra. If that didn't pan out, she would probably head overseas. She had musician friends in Hong Kong and in Germany. The world was her oyster, really.

These few weeks in the small, far northern town of Burralea, close to where she'd grown up, would be Flora's chance to regroup, to rehearse her audition pieces like crazy and to try to leave her unhappy experiences behind her. As a precaution, she'd bought a new phone and had destroyed her old sim card, so Oliver wouldn't be able to track her. And by a fortunate coincidence in timing, her parents had just sold their family cattle property at Ruthven Downs, which meant that Flora should be even harder to trace.

The owners of this rental cottage, the Woods, who were family friends as well as partners in Burralea's one and only law firm, had made sure there were no records that Flora was staying here. In a final precaution, Flora's good friend Ellen had laid a false trail by dropping hints to Oliver that Flora had gone to the Gold Coast.

Now, for the first time in months, she felt safe and free.

Once again she was in charge of her life, making her own decisions without having to worry about what Oliver might say or do to spoil her plans. Already, she was feeling stronger and more confident. Burralea wasn't simply a retreat, a place to hide. It was a staging post before she set off in a new and exciting direction.

Just the same, when Flora heard a knock on the cottage's front door, she experienced a nasty spurt of fear.

'Who is it?' she called, feeling a bit foolish, but not prepared to take any risks.

'Mitch,' came the cheery reply. 'Mitch Cavello.'

She let out a huff of relief and was grinning as she opened the door to a blue-uniformed figure. 'And a very good morning to you, Sergeant Cavello.' Flora launched forward and hugged him. 'It's so good to see you.'

'You, too, Flora.' His return hug was gratifyingly warm-hearted. 'I only just heard from the Woods that you were staying here.'

'Do you have time to come in? Would you like a cuppa? You can be my first official visitor.'

'That's an honour I won't knock back.'

'Come through to the kitchen.' Flora was pretty certain Mitch wouldn't want to sit in the lounge and be formal. Anyway, she was using the lounge as her practice room so she had her music stand set up in there and sheet music scattered all over the sofa.

Mitch certainly seemed perfectly comfortable as he parked his big frame on a wooden kitchen stool, adjusting his position slightly to make room for the handcuffs and holster attached to his belt.

Years ago, she'd been stupidly coy around this guy. At the time, Mitch Cavello had been a troubled teenager and his widowed father had struggled to keep him in check. After a disturbing incident involving a stolen motorbike, a policeman mate of Flora's father had arranged for Mitch to do a stint of work on Ruthven Downs to 'straighten him out'.

Under her father's watchful eye, Flora's brother, Seth, and Mitch had spent their long summer holiday working in the cattle yards and helping with fencing or mustering, or whatever was on the go. It was around the same time that Seth had stopped being a major pain in the butt and had begun to take on the more pleasing qualities of an okay big brother.

Over that summer, Seth and Mitch had become the best of mates and Flora had merely been the inconsequential little sister who spent a good chunk of her holiday away at a music camp. Mitch had ended up staying on their property for the rest of the year, while Seth went off to uni and Flora returned to boarding school. Each time she'd come home, though, she'd been aware of the changes in Mitch. It was wonderful to see his surly broodiness slip away as he became outgoing and confident. Fun to be around.

No doubt his dark Italian good looks had ensured that Flora paid attention to this transformation. She'd had a silly crush on him at the time. Okay, if she was honest, she'd made a total fool of herself over him, but that was years ago. Buried and, hopefully, forgotten.

These days Mitch was quite the man. Totally reformed, a policeman, in fact. And knowing that he was stationed just a few doors up the street was incredibly reassuring.

'Cute place,' he said, looking about at the attractively rustic interior.

'I know. I'm going to love staying here.' Flora filled the kettle and freed yellow-and-white striped mugs from hooks.

Mitch grinned as he let his dark gaze follow her movements. 'So that's the Melbourne look, is it?'

She supposed he was referring to her purple nail polish and the asymmetrical haircut with a few purple streaks.

'It suits you,' he said.

'You've certainly changed,' she quipped. 'Once upon a time you would have teased the life out of me. Asked me if my hairdresser was drunk or on drugs when she took to me with her scissors.'

Mitch grinned at this and looked ridiculously attractive.

Flora hastily changed the subject. 'I suppose you've been out to see Seth's new place? That's all very exciting, isn't it?'

'Yeah, I'm glad he bought the Matthews's property. Kooringal's a good piece of dirt.'

'He's very happy. He's going to breed stud bulls. Droughtmaster and Senepol.'

Mitch nodded. 'I reckon he'll do very well.'

'I hope so. He deserves to. Not that I'm biased,' she added, smiling as she dropped teabags into their mugs.

On the way to the fridge, she asked over her shoulder, 'What about you, Mitch? I haven't heard any gunshots or sirens or screams for help, so you're obviously doing a great job of keeping law and order in Burralea.'

'Last month we had kids on ice breaking into the pharmacy, but it's mostly overloaded trailers, speeding tickets and little old ladies locking themselves out of their homes.'

Flora found the milk. 'Do old ladies lock themselves out on a regular basis?'

Mitch shrugged. 'Your neighbour, Edith Little, is a corker. I think her memory's failing. Twice now I've had to pick the lock on her front door. Saves her the trouble and expense of calling a locksmith, of course.'

'Aww, that's so sweet of you,' Flora said, half-teasing. 'But I think I might be in for a bit of trouble with her, too. I don't think she likes living next to a muso. She made quite a business of closing her windows when I started practising yesterday.'

'Ouch.' Mitch frowned, looked sympathetic. 'Edith's a bit of a loner and she can be a tad touchy.'

'I haven't met her yet,' Flora admitted. 'I guess I'll have to bite the bullet and speak to her, but I'm not sure what I'll do if she really hates my practising.' She looked out through the bank of windows to the tall trees along the creek bank. 'I thought I'd be private enough here at the end of the street and near the bush, but if the violin really upsets her, I might have to try to find somewhere else.'

'I could speak to Father Jonno,' Mitch offered. 'He might be able to help.'

'*Father* Jonno?'

'The vicar. I've had a fair bit to do with him. Coppers and clergy often get called in when there's a problem. He's a good bloke. Not much older than me. Anyway, he might be able to let you use the church hall.'

'Well . . . thanks. If you think he wouldn't mind, I'd really appreciate that.'

The kettle came to the boil and Flora reached for it. 'So apart from work, what else is happening in your life?'

'Haven't you heard? I'm getting married next week.'

Flora came to such an abrupt stop she almost scalded herself on the kettle. Immediately, she felt foolish and embarrassed. Talk about an overreaction.

She wasn't sure why she was so surprised by Mitch's news. He was an obvious catch, and a country town like Burralea wasn't exactly brimming with eligible bachelors. It was more surprising that he'd lasted this long before someone snapped him up.

'Hey, that's wonderful,' she finally remembered to say and she flashed him an extra-bright grin. 'Who's the lucky girl?'

'Angie Browne.' Mitch's smile was a tad goofy as he said her name. 'She's a chalkie. Originally from Townsville. Teaches Year Two at Burralea primary.'

'Oh, that's perfect, isn't it? A teacher and a policeman.'

He looked over-the-top happy. 'I thought Seth might have told you. He's going to be my best man. If I'd known you were going to be in town, I would have made sure you got an invite.'

'No worries,' Flora said lightly. 'There's been so much going on in our family lately, what with selling and buying properties, and Mum and Dad taking off for overseas.' And she'd deliberately kept contact with her family businesslike, mostly because she'd wanted to share as little about Oliver as possible.

Now, she also realised, somewhat uncomfortably, she wasn't breaking her neck to watch Mitch be married to his school teacher.

He accepted the mug she slid across the bench. 'Thanks.'

'Milk?'

'Just black, thanks.' But Mitch helped himself to a hefty spoonful of sugar. 'It's a shame that your parents can't be there,' he said as he stirred his tea. 'I would have liked them to see me get hitched.'

Her parents were having a great time travelling in Canada, combining sightseeing with hunting down first-class cattle semen for Seth's new stud business. 'They didn't offer to fly back?'

'Oh, sure, Hugh did offer. But they had a cruise up the Alaskan coast booked and I didn't want them to miss that.' Mitch shrugged. 'We couldn't really change the date. Next week's the best time for Angie. Then she can make the most of the school holidays.'

Mitch grinned again. Man, she'd forgotten that devilishly hot smile. Very deliberately, she shifted her gaze and took a huge interest in her tea. Mitch seemed suddenly awkward, too. He fiddled with the handle of his mug. 'Actually, Floss, I have a favour to ask.'

She rather liked being called Floss again. Like old times. No one in Melbourne had ever called her by her nickname. Oliver had called her Drumbeat, a corruption of her surname, Drummond, and she'd thought it was cute at first. She'd thought everything about Oliver was cute. At first.

Quickly, she steered her thoughts away from that unhelpful track. 'What's the favour?' she asked.

'Well, I know it's very last-minute, and it's a big ask, but Angie's got her heart set on having a string quartet to play at the wedding. In the church.'

'Oh.'

'Yeah.' Mitch gave another small shrug. 'She's managed to round up three musicians – mostly other teachers – from around the Tablelands, and they were on the hunt for a fourth when I heard that you were back in town. They're dead keen to have you.'

'Are you sure these other musicians would want a last-minute ring-in?'

'Of course. They know all about you. In fact, Peg Fletcher, your old music teacher, recommended you.'

'Peg? Of course. Right.' Flora wasn't sure why she was being cautious. She loved Peg and she loved playing in quartets. She was also very familiar with the popular repertoire for weddings.

'I think they want you to play first violin,' Mitch added.

Flora nodded.

'What do you think?'

There'd been a time when Flora would have given her eye teeth to play in Burralea's little church, and she knew it was ridiculous to hesitate now. She was lying low, but not *that* low.

'If people want me, then I'd be happy to,' she said quickly.

'Great.' Mitch looked totally delighted and Flora experienced a small pang. It was very sweet of him to be trying so hard to make his bride happy. 'Angie wants traditional classical music. I think she's made a list.'

Again, Flora nodded. 'I suppose there'll be a rehearsal,' she said. 'I'd better give you my new phone number.'

'Sure.'

As Mitch pulled his phone from his pocket, she felt a bit nervous about handing over her new number. She didn't want to have to explain to Mitch about Oliver. Not when he was so happy. Besides, no one up here was likely to be in contact with Oliver. No one knew him.

Wouldn't know him from a bar of soap, she could hear her dad saying.

With the number recorded, Mitch gave his customary easy smile and he stood. 'I'd better make tracks. Thanks for the cuppa and for saying yes to the quartet. Angie will be over the moon.'

'It will be my pleasure,' Flora assured him as she followed him back down the short hallway.

'It's good to see you again, Floss.'

'You, too. And if I don't see you before the big day, all the best.' She had to reach up, almost on tiptoes, to kiss him on the cheek.

'Thanks.' With a parting smile, Mitch left.

*

As Flora closed the door she felt flat. Like a toad on the road. It was annoying, but somehow she couldn't help it. Everyone she was close to – her parents, Seth and now Mitch – seemed to be especially happy and she wanted to feel happy too.

Unfortunately, her life had turned to rubbish. After heading off to Melbourne with such high hopes and with the knowledge that all her family and friends were proud of her and had huge expectations for her brilliant career, she had crashed and burned. Instead of the wild success everyone had envisaged, she'd made a really dumb choice by falling for a rising operatic star, who had turned out to have a massive insecurity complex beneath his superficial layer of charm.

What was it with her and guys? She never seemed to pick the right one. In her teens, she'd fallen for Brett, but he'd always had a bit of a reckless streak and he'd ended up being killed in a quad bike accident on his parents' farm. Then there'd been the time she'd embarrassed herself over Mitch, but that had been thankfully brief and they'd both pretended it never happened.

At the Conservatorium, she'd dated a double-bass player called Ethan. They'd been going out for six months when he suddenly told her he wanted to be Eve. In lipstick and high heels, Eve had looked stunning. Flora had been totally deflated.

Then Oliver. Flora had been relieved when he seemed so suitable. Not reckless, or an extrovert. Just an impressively handsome guy with a magnificent tenor voice.

Of course, she should have smelled trouble when Oliver presented the idea of moving in with him as a kind of ultimatum. Flora had known this wasn't quite normal, but she'd been completely smitten at the time, and frightened of losing him.

So they were established as a couple before she recognised his cruelly manipulative streak, and not long after that he'd revealed his even scarier tendencies to violence. When she'd come home for her father's birthday, she'd tried, unsuccessfully, to cover her bruises.

This was when Kate Woods had taken her aside, given her a stern lecture and offered her this cottage as part of her escape plan. But now, after accepting that she had to move clear away from the man, Oliver's impact was hard to shake off. His last phone message on her old phone still rang in her ears.

You're a pathetic loser, Drumbeat. You might run away, but you've no staying power and you know you're never going to make it. You should give up now, you hopeless bitch.

Flora shuddered. No wonder her confidence was shaky.

Don't. Don't let your mind go there.

She took the mugs to the sink and looked out through the windows to the tall, graceful trees. She watched a bush turkey pecking its way through the undergrowth.

It was time to truly grow up, she told herself. Thanks to bloody Oliver she'd had to resign from a job she loved, but her task now was to prove to him – and to herself – that she could do even better.

She had to get over this. Put it behind her. Everyone knew that life was always a matter of ups and downs.

So what if her parents and Seth and Mitch, one of their oldest friends, were all blissfully happy at the moment. Their lives hadn't always been roses and sunshine. Her parents had been through quite a deal of stress before they set off tripping around the northern hemisphere.

And sure, Seth had just bought a new farm and found a lovely new girlfriend, Alice, who was shaping up as someone pretty special. Before this, however, Seth had been through a really shitty patch. He'd had to mature super-fast when an English backpacker dumped a baby son on him and then calmly announced that she was heading back to the UK to marry her fiancé.

As for Mitch Cavello, he might be on the eve of marrying his school-teacher sweetheart and cementing his own role as a pillar of the Burralea community, but he'd certainly had his share of unhappiness. His mother had died when he was only five and he'd never had brothers or sisters. More recently, his dad had passed away, leaving him quite alone in the world in terms of family.

It made sense that Mitch was keen to settle down and start a family of his own.

Just be patient, Flora told herself. *You'll be okay. You're on the right track.*

With a heavy sigh, but new resolve, she went through to the lounge room and opened her violin case. She picked up her bow and tightened it, then tucked her violin under her chin and checked the tuning.

She was already smiling as she began to play Aaron Copland's 'Hoedown'. The wild, Kentucky-inspired folk music could always be relied on to cheer her up.

CHAPTER THREE

Mitch couldn't believe he was in danger of being late for his own wedding.

Not again. Not Edith Little.

'I'm sorry.' Despite these words, the elderly woman sounded quite unapologetic when she called him from an even more elderly neighbour's telephone. 'I just stepped outside to water my pot plants and the door shut behind me. There must have been a gust of wind.'

Mitch was halfway through getting his bow tie to sit right, and he sighed as he tried to think of a way out of this dilemma.

If only Edith was a little friendlier, she could sweet-talk a kid from her street to climb through a window for her. Unfortunately, Edith was a crusty old thing and she didn't make friends easily.

If she had family, she could call on a son, or a son-in-law, but Edith, like Mitch, was quite alone in the world.

At least Mitch was about to remedy his own situation.

He grimaced at his reflection in the mirror. When he'd first joined the police force he'd had dreams of becoming a gritty and brilliant city detective. Yet, here he was, still a small-town cop, at the beck and call of little old ladies.

The last time Edith had called him, he'd suggested that the locksmith was only ten kilometres away, and she'd reminded him about
the locksmith's charges and the difficulties of managing on a pensioner's income. Mitch had relented and helped her out again.

Clearly that had been a mistake.

A rod for your own back, mate.

He grimaced again as he considered Edith's options now. Apart
from his mates, who were probably already at the church, he
couldn't think of anyone who could be called on to pick the lock on
an old woman's front door at short notice. Not without having to
offer awkward explanations.

Even the constable on duty today was likely to give Mitch an
earful. Newly arrived from the city, and super-conscientious about
sticking by the rule book, he wouldn't sanction breaking into anyone's home, certainly not for such a pissant reason as Edith's.

Mitch checked the time again. He should be able to swing by
Edith's and still make it to the church in good time. At least in a
small town there wouldn't be traffic hold-ups.

'You're all dressed up.' Edith's tone was accusatory, as if she didn't
approve of a formal suit in the middle of an ordinary Saturday.

'Yeah.' Mitch grinned as he slipped a penknife into place to ease
her front door open. 'I'm getting married.'

It was gratifying to see the way the woman's jaw dropped.
'Today?'

'Yep.' Most of the Burralea residents were well aware that this
was Mitch's wedding day. He'd been getting messages of congratulations and best wishes all week.

Edith looked a bit put out that she hadn't heard. She was a
dumpy, plain little thing and now, stooped and clutching her walking stick, she frowned up at him from beneath a limp grey fringe.

'What's that thing around your neck?'

Mitch gave a heaven-help-me roll of his eyes as he pushed her door open. 'It's a bow tie. I was in the middle of trying to get it right when I got your call.'

Edith eyed him with quivering disapproval. 'Why is it pink?'

Good question. Wearing pink was the one aspect of this wedding that Mitch wasn't too thrilled about. 'It matches the bridesmaid's dress,' he told her.

The woman didn't look impressed.

'Look, I've gotta go. You need a doorstop, Edith. I'll buy you one as soon as I get back from my honeymoon.'

At this, Edith appeared instantly mollified. 'That's awfully kind of you.' She actually smiled. 'Well, good luck, Sergeant.' She lifted a bony, arthritic hand as if she wanted to pat his arm. 'I hope the ceremony goes well for you, and I'm sure you'll have a very happy marriage.'

'Thanks.' Mitch was used to her mood changes. He gave her a smile and held her hand as he dropped a kiss on her papery cheek. He would have to kiss a lot of cheeks today, so he might as well get into practice now.

Edith's pale eyes shone and, for a moment, there might even have been a tear in her eye as she stood, clutching the door knob, and waved him off.

* * *

The members of the quartet, dressed discreetly in black and white, had arrived early at the wooden church perched at the top of Burralea's gentle slope. The church was quite small, so they'd needed time to work out how to squeeze their chairs and music stands into one corner of the nave, and they'd wanted this done before the guests showed up.

In the end, they'd had no choice but to arrange themselves around the baptismal font, which had been filled for the occasion with a huge pink and white bouquet.

'As long as we leave plenty of room for the minister and the wedding party, we should be okay,' suggested Lisa, who taught at Malanda High and, as a friend of the bride, was also their unofficial leader, even though she was playing viola.

Flora was to play first violin and Peg Fletcher, her old music teacher, was on second. Peg was a tough old biddy, but she was a fine musician, and she'd been the first to kindle Flora's love of music. She'd given Flora a wonderful foundation before she went away to boarding school.

Another of Peg's protégés was on cello. Josh, a shy, lanky Year Twelve student from Ravenshoe had an impressive talent and he was heading for Brisbane's Conservatorium in the new year. The poor fellow had to keep ducking his head to avoid a dangling spray of orchids, though, and Flora had no qualms about rearranging the flowers to make things easier for him.

She'd been in the middle of doing this when the first guests arrived. A woman in turquoise lace, possibly the person in charge of arranging these flowers, had sent her a rather severe look of disapproval, but Flora hadn't let it bother her.

The only thing that bothered her today was the thought of Mitch standing just metres away on those chancel steps. A bridegroom.

Not that Flora wanted Mitch for herself, or anything ridiculous like that. She'd stopped thinking of him in that way years ago. And after Oliver, she was, quite definitely, over men for the foreseeable future. She just hoped she wouldn't get foolishly emotional today, particularly as Seth would be there, too, as Mitch's best man.

At least she would have the music to concentrate on for a good deal of the time, but there was still the ceremony. And those goosebump-inducing words.

Do you take this woman . . . to have and to hold . . . to love and to cherish . . .

'So, we're still starting with Pachelbel's Canon?' Flora asked the others.

Lisa nodded. 'And then "Ave Maria". If there's time, we can also do "Air on the G String", but we'll only play "I Dreamed a Dream" if we're really stretched. I know we're a bit shaky with that piece, but I doubt we'll need it.'

After a last-minute check that their music was in the right order, Flora lifted her bow and played an A, and the others responded, tuning their instruments carefully and quietly. As the chords blended, she felt a little flutter of pleasure, a shimmy of excitement deep down. It was the way she always felt at the beginning of a performance, no matter how big or small the occasion.

Today she was going to enjoy the music without worrying about any unpleasant aftermath. Oliver was two states away and she wouldn't have to endure his cutting critique and postmortem of her performance.

Looking out at the congregation, she saw that about half the pews were filled already and by the sound of the voices outside, there were still plenty of people arriving. Through a small side door, she caught a glimpse of Seth looking ultra smooth and GQ in a dark suit and pink tie.

Clearly pink was Angie's favourite colour. The ribbons on the ends of the pews were pink and white.

'Okay,' Flora said with a smile when everyone was satisfied with the tuning. 'We're sounding great, guys.'

Lisa smiled. 'I think we should start.'

'Righto.' Lifting her violin into position again, Flora nodded to Josh, who began to play the slow, steady opening cello bars that

would continue throughout Pachelbel's famous canon, providing
a steady heartbeat for the other instruments.

Flora's spine tingled as she joined him with the melody. She
sensed a subtle change in the congregation, too, and she could feel
their anticipation building, as she was echoed by the second violin
and then by the viola.

The group had decided at their rehearsal to take the piece quite
slowly, giving it a deep, romantic, vibrato-filled sound. Now, the
familiar tunes wove and built, signalling the approach of a special
occasion.

Flora thought of Mitch waiting patiently outside for his bride
and she hoped he was enjoying the music.

By the time the canon reached its conclusion, quite a few more
pews were filled. Flora saw Seth's girlfriend Alice, looking gorgeous in a grey silk dress that was a perfect foil for her rich auburn
hair. Alice was sitting with Tammy, Burralea's popular hairdresser,
who had probably spent the morning looking after the bridal party.

And the Woods were sitting further back, along with a fellow
she recognised as a local butcher. Another man in the back pew, tall,
with a head of dark shaggy hair and a five o'clock shadow, had an
impressive looking camera on a solid strap around his neck.

The little church was almost full to bursting by the time they'd
finished playing 'Ave Maria'. Flora suspected there wouldn't be time
for 'Air on the G String'. The bride was bound to be there by then.
She was marrying Mitch Cavello, after all, and according to Lisa,
Angie's place was only a couple of blocks away.

And now, Flora could see Mitch, looking even more handsome
than she'd imagined, and surprisingly comfortable and relaxed as
he waited with Seth at the little side doorway opposite her. At any
moment, the men would file inside the church and take their places

in front of the quietly expectant congregation.

She drew a sharp breath. *Don't be an idiot. It's just another wedding gig.*

'Angie should be here at any moment, but let's start on the "Air",' suggested Lisa. 'As soon as she's here, we'll stop. Flora, you'll give us the signal?'

'Sure.'

'Right. And then Father Jonno will let us know to begin the Bridal March. Okay, everyone?'

'Absolutely.'

'Got it.'

So the quartet was off again, playing Bach's beautiful 'Air on the G String'. The acoustics in the small, high-ceilinged space were fabulous and at one point, Flora looked across to the little doorway opposite and caught Mitch's eye. He sent her a smiling thumbs up.

Damn. His smile gave her a wobbly moment and she almost fumbled her bowing. She would be glad when this wedding was over.

By the time they'd played this piece all the way through, there was still no sign of the bridal party.

Mitch was no longer looking relaxed. He was standing unnaturally straight with his shoulders back and his head held stiffly high. Flora was sure he was worried, but trying to hide it.

Poor man.

A young clergyman in a long white surplice appeared at Mitch's side. By now Flora had met Father Jonno who'd happily agreed for her to practice in the hall. He was chatting with Mitch and there was a little shrugging going on, some forced smiles.

After giving Mitch's shoulder a reassuring squeeze, the priest came into the church and went to the lectern, checking the Bible, no doubt to make sure that the right readings were bookmarked. He was an interesting looking guy, quite different from any Anglican priests Flora had known in the past.

No more than mid-thirties, with a slim, wiry build, Jonno had freckles and straight, rusty-coloured hair, rather long for a priest. He smiled at the musicians and at the assembled wedding guests and then stood calmly at the chancel steps, as if he wanted to reassure everyone that all was well.

On the far side of the church, Seth was chatting to Mitch as they continued to wait. No doubt her brother was doing his best to keep his mate cool and calm. Judging by Mitch's careful smile, he was doing his damnedest to hide his inner tension, but Flora wished the poor guy didn't have to wait like this. She was beginning to feel rather annoyed with his Angie.

At the back of the church, the dark-haired fellow with the industrial strength camera rose and went outside.

'He's the editor of the *Burralea Bugle*,' whispered Peg.

Unhelpfully, Flora imagined this week's headline – 'The Bride Was Late'. Hastily, she scratched that thought. 'Do you think we should make a start on "I Dreamed a Dream"?' she asked the others.

Lisa shrugged. They hadn't spent much time rehearsing this piece. 'There's no sign of Angie yet, so I guess we'd better give it a go.' She looked to Peg and Josh with a nervous smile. 'Will you be okay?'

Josh nodded.

Peg looked a bit worried. 'I can probably fudge my way through it. What the heck? We might not have to play it all.'

'Right then. Good luck, everyone.'

Again they began to play. There was a section in the middle of the familiar music from *Les Misérables* where Lisa got a little lost, but they managed to keep going smoothly enough.

They were playing the final phrase, and Flora was wondering

about taking them back to the beginning, when she heard voices outside. They seemed rather agitated. Or were they merely excited? This had to be the bride at last, surely?

The church was silent as midnight when the music stopped. Everyone turned to the back, their eyes expectantly riveted to the empty doorway where a vision in white was about to appear.

Flora felt unaccountably nervous as she waited along with everyone else. She was about to dig out the tissue she'd tucked into her sleeve in case she needed to wipe her nervous hands, when she was distracted by a new arrival at the side door.

A grey-haired man, dressed in a formal dark suit with a pink carnation in his buttonhole, seemed very distressed.

'That's Angie's father,' hissed Lisa.

The conversation in the wings was very agitated. Angie's father was shaking his head and throwing up his hands, and his message was clearly *not* good news. Mitch's Mediterranean complexion paled. Seth looked shocked and his hands curled into fists.

Father Jonno, aware that a problem was afoot, quickly joined them.

'This is looking bad,' whispered Lisa. 'I hope there hasn't been an accident.'

'What's happening?' Josh had to turn right around to see what was going on.

Hushed whispers rustled through the congregation like wind in river reeds. People strained forward in their pews, trying desperately to see what was happening.

Eventually, Father Jonno nodded and patted both Mitch and Angie's dad's shoulders. Looking solemn, he came back into the church with the two grim-faced men following him. Flora's stomach churned. It was like watching a procession to the gallows.

In the middle of the chancel steps, where the bride and groom should have been standing, ready to be bound in holy wedlock,

Angie's father stepped forward. His face was red and contorted, his hands shaking.

'I'm so sorry, everyone. I – I – just —' The poor man seemed too upset to speak.

'It's all right, Charlie.' Mitch placed a steadying hand on the other man's arm. 'I've got this.'

Pale, but with a resolute jaw and squared shoulders, Mitch turned to face the anxious congregation.

Flora thought how brave he looked.

'I'm sorry, folks,' he said. 'There's – there's – not going to be a wedding.'

A collective shocked gasp burst from the guests, and Mitch's throat rippled as he swallowed.

Flora, as stunned as everyone else, was frozen to her chair.

'I know this is hard, coming out of the blue,' Mitch said, and then he had to pause again, and Flora couldn't bear to think how difficult this must be for him. Standing stiffly to attention, he pressed on. 'I'm afraid Angie's made her decision and she doesn't want this wedding to proceed.' He sounded wooden now, like a policeman giving an accident report. 'I'm sure you'll understand, Angie needs privacy, and to make sure of that, she's left town.'

Oh, my God.

Flora couldn't believe the woman wasn't even going to face Mitch. How could she be so selfish and cruel as to run off without giving her bridegroom an apology? An explanation?

How could she do this? She had to be out of her mind, surely?

'I'm really sorry,' Mitch continued, white-faced. 'I know a lot of people here have put in a big effort with – with the flowers and decorations. You've bought beautiful gifts —' He stopped and swallowed again, took a deep breath. 'And of course I'll return them.'

Angie's father stepped forward now. 'Please, everyone, don't forget there's a fabulous meal all prepared for you at the Lake House.

Your choice of salmon or rack of lamb. Plenty of drinks and good wine. I hope you'll still head over there and enjoy the spread.'

The poor man's voice broke over the words and his lips trembled as he struggled with tears. 'I was so looking forward to this. Mitch is a great —' He had to stop while he pulled a huge damp handkerchief from his pocket and mopped at his eyes.

Father Jonno stepped in and kindly led the poor man away, leaving Mitch alone. But there was obviously little else that he could do or say. With a formal nod, he also turned on his heel and walked out.

After that, there was a shocked moment or two of silence, before a distressed babble erupted. Flora didn't wait to hear what Lisa or the other musicians had to say. Setting her violin and bow on her chair, she edged past them and flew across the nave to find Seth, who had already disappeared out the side doorway.

By the time she reached the doorway, Seth was halfway across the church's carefully mowed grounds. She called to him, 'Seth!'

He turned, but didn't respond. He simply pointed to Mitch and continued hurrying after him. Flora hurried too, close at her brother's heels.

'Mitch, wait for a sec, can't you?' Seth called as they caught up to him at the corner.

Mitch turned slowly. His bridegroom's suit seemed incongruous with the rigid set of his face and body. He gave no answer.

Seth stepped closer and spoke gently. 'What the hell's happened, mate?'

Mitch merely glared at them and then shook his head. His eyes were wild, his hands clenched and he was clearly not prepared to discuss this.

Flora couldn't bear it. 'Mitch, we just want to help. Can't you tell us —'

But Seth was frowning at her now, shaking his head to signal that she should shut up. He stepped a little closer to Mitch and spoke quietly. 'We just want to know you're okay. Are you sure you're okay?'

Mitch gave an irritated shrug. 'I'm not going to do anything stupid. I just need some space —'

'Okay,' responded Seth, backing off. 'Where are you going?'

'Home.'

Flora hadn't realised that Mitch's car was parked nearby. Now, without another word, he climbed into it and gunned the motor.

As he roared off, Flora and Seth stood together on the footpath, watching his car charge around the corner too fast. 'If he's not careful, he'll have to give himself a speeding ticket.' Seth failed to smile at his own weak joke and Flora felt totally gutted. She couldn't begin to imagine how Mitch must feel.

'There you are, Seth.'

A young woman in a long pink dress came rushing up to them. Her blonde hair was in ringlets dotted with rosebuds, her carefully made-up eyes huge.

'Oh, Rachel, hi.' Seth turned to Flora. 'This is Rachel Holmes, Angie's – uh – bridesmaid.'

'*Ex*-bridesmaid,' Rachel corrected miserably.

'Well, yeah.' Seth quickly introduced Flora. 'What the hell happened, Rach? How could Angie change her mind?'

Rachel rolled her eyes. 'You have no idea. It was unbelievable. Her old boyfriend turned up.'

'When?' demanded Flora. 'Not just before the wedding?'

'Well, yes, he did come to the flat this morning, but he actually arrived in town two nights ago.'

A low growl broke from Seth and he gritted his teeth. 'What sort of prick would do that?'

'Kevin, apparently,' Rachel said with a shrug. 'He's been working in America.' She was obviously keen to expand on her story.

'He broke Angie's heart when he left her about a year ago, and she hadn't heard from him. Then he suddenly turned up here. Out of the blue. He came to our place, saying he wanted Angie back. It was like she'd seen a ghost. Honestly. She was so upset. She told him no, of course, but she's been in a terrible mood ever since.'

Rachel shook her head, making her ringlets bounce sadly. 'Last night was dreadful. Angie was in tears. She was so torn and messed up. She kept saying that Kevin was the love of her life, but of course she was still going to marry Mitch. Mitch was such a nice guy. She couldn't hurt him.'

'So what went wrong today?' demanded Flora and Seth together.

Rachel's eyes widened even further with the importance of her story. 'She seemed fine this morning. Quite composed. We went to the hairdresser's and everything was back to normal. We went home, changed into our gowns. Angie's parents arrived. And the photographer. It was all systems go. The photographer was about to start snapping when Kevin turned up again.'

'The bastard.' Seth looked horrified.

'Yes, he was dreadful. Frantic. He begged Angie, in front of everyone, pleading with her to change her mind. It was such a low trick.'

'Disgusting,' said Flora, appalled.

'Angie's dad was furious. He was shaping up. Honestly, I thought he was going to punch Kevin, knock him out, but Angie stood between them.' Rachel started to cry. 'It was just horrendous. Angie was in hysterics.'

'But she said yes to Kevin?' prompted Flora.

Rachel nodded, swiping at tears. 'In the end, she just couldn't say no to him.'

'What's wrong with the woman?' Flora cried vehemently.

Rachel gave a helpless shake of her head. 'Angie's mum, Sandra, actually fainted. I've never seen anyone do that before. Her eyes kind of rolled back in her head and she collapsed. At first I thought she'd dropped dead. I splashed water on her face. She was okay, thank God.'

'But Angie's definitely left town?' Seth was flexing his fingers as if he was ready to wring someone's neck.

'Yeah. When she went into her bedroom, I thought she just wanted some privacy, to compose herself. But she threw off her wedding dress, changed into shorts and a T-shirt, and grabbed the bag she had packed for her honeymoon. And next minute she was jumping in Kevin's car.' Rachel paused, took a breath. 'I'm telling you. Angie. Has. Gone. I guarantee she'll be resigning from the education department next.'

'Un-bloody-believable.' Seth let out a heavy sigh. 'Poor Mitch. I mean, you sometimes hear of stupid grooms not turning up for their wedding, because they're too drunk from the bucks' party. But this is ridiculous.'

'That Kevin guy must have some kind of hold over Angie,' Flora said thoughtfully. 'And I don't mean in a good way. He sounds totally manipulative and selfish.'

Seth shot her a searching, worried look. He only knew the sketchiest details about her breakup with Oliver, but he was clearly bothered that she might be speaking from experience. Which, of course, she was, and she had a nasty suspicion this intervention from Kevin might not end happily for Angie.

'Anyway,' she said quickly, not wanting to dwell on those thoughts. 'Thanks for filling us in, Rachel. I suppose you'll still go to the reception dinner at the Lake House?'

Rachel nodded. 'I feel as if I should. Angie's parents are so gutted. They'll need support.'

'Yes, they will, and it's good of you to be there for them. You were there when Kevin turned up. You shared the shock of it all.'

'Yeah.' Rachel sighed.

'I'd better get back to the church and rescue my violin,' Flora said. 'What about you, Seth?'

'First up, I need to speak to Alice. She might still go to the reception with Tammy, but I reckon I'll head over to Mitch's place. I know he wants to be on his own, but I'm not sure that's a good idea.'

'No.' Flora was pleased that her brother had made this decision. 'Actually, I have a couple of steaks in my fridge. You should take them as well.'

'Steaks?' Seth looked at her like she'd lost her marbles.

'Well, you shouldn't turn up there with a couple of sixpacks and nothing to eat, Seth. And Mitch was planning to head off on his honeymoon. He's probably cleared out his fridge.'

'Yeah. Guess you're right. Getting him drunk on an empty stomach certainly won't help.' Mitch smiled sadly. 'When did you get so practical?'

She shrugged. 'I'll throw in a couple of onions, too. I don't suppose Mitch will feel like eating, but the smell of fried onions is hard to resist.'

'Good thinking.'

They shared wan smiles, and Flora supposed Seth was remembering, as she was, the lost, angry teenager who had turned up on their property all those years ago. Mitch had overcome the legacy of a lonely childhood with a widowed father who didn't know how to show love to his only son. Since then, he'd turned his life around.

And now, here he was again, facing yet another major kick in the guts.

Sometimes, life really sucked.

CHAPTER FOUR

Mitch swung the axe hard and the log split with a satisfying crack. His satisfaction was only momentary, though. Almost immediately, the pain bit back.

Angie was gone.

There would be no wedding.

And none of what had happened today made sense.

He couldn't believe Angie had bolted. Even though their relationship was only six months old, he'd thought he knew her pretty damn well, and she'd never given him any sign that she wasn't as keen as he was. As far as he was concerned they'd been great together. Sympatico. The perfect couple.

Everyone had commented on what a great team they made, the cop and the school teacher. From the start, the idea of marrying Angie had felt absolutely right.

A good portion of Mitch's life had been messed up, but with this marriage he'd felt as if he'd finally hit the sweet spot. The road ahead was straight with a clear view of the future – him and Angie riding into the sunset, sharing their lives together.

Instead?

He'd been jilted. At the altar of all places.

Whack! Mitch's axe came down again, shattering a piece of ironbark into flying pieces.

He'd been fucking jilted. Hell, he'd experienced some low blows in his time, but he'd never known this gut-wrenching humiliation and pain.

Angrily, he set another log on the block, lifted the axe high and smashed it down. *Crack!* Grey bark flew and the timber's red heart split in two.

Again, the satisfaction was fleeting and Mitch reached for yet another log. He would chop wood all night if he had to. Anything was better than pacing the floor, or slumping in a heap on the sofa. Thinking. *Dwelling* on the pain of Angie's rejection. Her treacherous fucking defection.

With another log in place, he swung the axe again. Thump. *Crack.*

The afternoon was growing darker, sliding quickly towards sundown. Even though it was November, it still grew cooler in the Tablelands with the onset of dusk.

The terrace in front of the tractor shed that Mitch had converted into his home offered a fabulous view stretching and rolling all the way to the western hills. Already, the sky above the hills' darkening rim was glowing a rosy pink.

Pink. *Fuck.* Mitch split another log in two. He'd never been happy about wearing that pink bloody bow tie. Now, pink was officially his least favourite colour.

Damn it, he was as mad as he was sad. He was mad with Angie. Mad with her bloody crazy ex-boyfriend, who was no longer an ex. Mad with that crazy bitch, Fate. Mad with himself for being such a —

'Hey, Mitch!'

Swinging abruptly around, he saw Seth approach from the

corner of his house, burdened with a couple of sixpacks and a super-market shopping bag.

Mitch stiffened. An instinctive reaction. He wasn't looking for company. He didn't need sympathy. What he needed tonight was to be left alone, to suffer in silence, to let the pain in his heart crack wide and deep, like this timber.

He scowled at Seth, who was still dressed in his best man's trousers and shirt, although he'd removed the coat and frigging pink tie.

'Flora sent you a couple of steaks,' Seth said.

Flora? Guiltily, Mitch remembered. 'I forgot to pay the musicians.'

'Hey, don't sweat it, man. They won't be chasing you for payment. Certainly not tonight.'

'But I had the money with me at the church.' It had been in the inside pocket of his coat. 'I'll get it for you now, Seth, before I forget it again. You can give it to Flora.'

Seth looked at him strangely, but he shrugged. 'Yeah, sure. Whatever.'

Mitch hurried inside. He'd left the money in an envelope in the brand-new, expensive suit coat that was lying where he'd dumped it, hanging over the arm of the sofa.

'Here,' he said to Seth when he returned to the terrace with the envelope. 'Can you give this to Flora? She won't mind passing the others' share on to them, will she?'

'No, I'm sure that's fine.'

'Good.' With this small duty despatched, Mitch wanted to feel relieved. But he only felt numb. Like there'd been a death. Maybe his death.

Seth set the beer and the shopping bag on the rustic outdoor table that Mitch had constructed in happier times. Then he looked rather deliberately at the pile of chopped wood and the fire pit that Mitch had also created last winter and set in the middle of the paved terrace.

'If you get that fire going,' Seth said, 'we could cook the steaks out here.'

'I wasn't planning to eat.'

'No, I don't suppose you were.' Seth snapped the top off a beer and held it out to him. 'But why don't we throw these steaks in a pan anyway? You never know, you might change your mind.' He smiled as he stood with his arm outstretched, offering the beer. Offering the hand of friendship. Mateship.

Mitch hesitated, but he was pretty sure Seth wouldn't push where he wasn't wanted, drowning him with well-meant advice. Or alcohol. Seth Drummond was a steady bloke, like his old man.

Mitch owed the Drummonds so much, and he didn't want to be rude now. Besides, he'd asked Seth to be his best man, and the guy was simply following though on that duty even though things had turned to shit.

If he could trust anyone, it was this bloke. With Seth, there'd be no pressure. No awkward questions. No deep and meaningful probes.

'Thanks,' Mitch said, accepting the beer. He felt the awful tightness in his gut loosen a notch.

They didn't talk much as they got the fire going and then sat on logs fashioned into seats, watching the last of the daylight disappear and the stars come out in the inky blue sky. Mitch set a long-handled cast-iron pan on the fire and they fried the steaks and onions, more or less taking it in turns to flip or to stir, while they sipped at their beers. When the food was done they stuffed it into the hamburger buns that Seth had brought.

They tasted good. They tasted great, actually.

Mitch realised he hadn't eaten since breakfast and that meal had been a simple piece of toast with coffee.

Shit. He didn't want to think about this morning.

This morning he'd still been innocent and ridiculously happy. Looking forward to a honeymoon in Phuket.

Phuket? Damn it, why hadn't he remembered before this? Angie had their plane tickets and all the booking info. What had she done with them?

She wasn't still heading for Thailand with this other fucker, was she? Could this situation get any worse?

'I'll have to apply for a transfer,' he said suddenly.

'Why would you want to do that?' Seth didn't try to hide his surprise. 'You're doing a great job here, Mitch. You're Burralea's favourite cop.'

'And every damn person in this town knows I was supposed to be married today.' He closed his eyes as he thought about all the back-slaps and handshakes and messages he'd received over the past couple of weeks.

'That reminds me.'

Without another glance Seth's way, Mitch rose abruptly, strode inside the house once more. In the kitchen, he snatched up the pile of wedding cards from the bench, all of them filled with best wishes and glowing tributes.

I've got too close to this community. A copper shouldn't get as involved as I am. If he thought too hard about the goodwill expressed in those damn messages he'd lose it.

Hurrying outside, he tossed the cards onto the fire and felt a ferocious stab of satisfaction as he watched the cardboard catch light, curl and blacken.

The fire was the best place for these things now.

Beside him, Seth watched in silence, following the bright flames, but making no comment as he took an occasional sip of beer. Mitch wondered what his mate was thinking, and it was then, with a slam of shock, that he remembered Seth had been through this.

At least, Seth had been through something very similar, when a chick he'd known briefly had dumped a surprise baby son on him and then hightailed it back to England to a fiancé she'd forgotten to mention.

'You know what this is like, don't you?' he said as the final card blackened and turned to ash.

In the firelight, he saw Seth's frown. 'How do you mean?'

'This happened to you,' Mitch said. 'When Charlie's mother took off back to England.'

'Well, yeah, kind of. But it wasn't quite the same. Joanna and I were only ever casual. I wasn't planning to marry her.'

'You weren't in love with her?'

Seth didn't answer at first and Mitch turned to him, staring through the darkness, trying to catch his mate's expression in the flickering firelight.

Eventually, Seth shook his head. 'As I said, it was only casual.'

'But you're with Alice now and I guess that's different?'

'Well, yeah. I mean, Alice and I have only just moved in together, but being with her is light years away from what happened with Joanna.'

The change in Seth's voice, the extra warmth, seemed to come spontaneously as soon as he spoke about his girlfriend. *Bloody hell.* Mitch's throat was suddenly aching as if he'd swallowed a burning cinder, and the pain wouldn't go away even when he took a deep swig of his beer.

'You're in love with Alice?'

'Yeah.'

Even with that single syllable, Mitch could hear the depth of affection in Seth's voice.

Fuck. He couldn't believe he was asking these crazy personal questions. Why the hell had he brought up the subject of relationships? The very topic he'd been desperately hoping to avoid?

A groan escaped him, and he might have apologised for his brainless lapse, but he was distracted by the sound of another car coming up the track.

'Someone's here,' said Seth.

Sure enough, a car door slammed and footsteps crunched on the gravel path at the side of the house. Mitch tensed, bracing himself. He didn't want to see anyone else. Not tonight.

The footsteps got closer and Jonno Gray, the priest, loped around the corner. He'd changed into battered old jeans and a loose grey sweater that sported the odd hole, and he was carrying a bottle of wine in each hand.

Mitch let out the breath he'd been holding. Okay, so this was the one other person he wouldn't send packing. He and Father Jonno were well acquainted.

As priest and cop, he and Jonno had both been called to attend the same crisis a few times now. Burralea was a peaceful, law-abiding country town on the surface, but its citizens still had their fair share of troubles. Recently Mitch and Father Jonno had been trying to help two teenagers who'd been the first on the scene when their mate was killed in a tractor accident.

Mitch had been impressed by the priest's down-to-earth common sense and compassion, as well as his lack of preachiness. It probably helped that Jonno had grown up in the bush, spending years as a stockman and even doing a stint as a rodeo clown.

Of course, he'd also studied theology, philosophy and whatever else was involved in becoming a man of the cloth, but around these parts, he fitted in easily.

'Am I intruding?' Jonno asked now, politely, as he set the bottles down on the table.

Mitch shook his head. 'It's good to see you.'

He held out his hand in welcome, but instead of a handshake, he received a warm hug. It was a surprise, but the close contact felt good. In the three decades that had comprised Mitch's life so far, comforting hugs had been in short order.

'How are you?' Jonno asked as he released him.

Mitch hesitated, unwilling to tell the truth that he felt like crap, that he wanted to clear out of this shit-hole town and never come back.

'He's doing pretty well,' Seth volunteered. 'He hasn't punched me yet.'

They all had a chuckle at this, even Mitch.

'Well, I've got to say, I've performed a lot of wedding ceremonies, but I've never had this happen before.' Jonno gave a slow shake of his head. 'It's tough, Mitch. Damn tough.'

Mitch nodded, blinked hard.

'I would have been here earlier,' Jonno continued quickly, 'but I heard Seth was heading this way, so I knew you were in good company, and I was worried about the bride's parents. I wanted to make sure they were okay too, so I headed over to the reception.'

Mitch was a little ashamed that he'd been too caught up in his own sorrows to give much thought to Angie's parents. 'How are they?' he asked. 'Did many people turn up at the Lake House?'

'Almost everyone, I think.' Jonno smiled. 'This community is remarkable, really. People are entertaining themselves over there. Kate and Brad Woods have been marvellous as MCs and they've organised little impromptu acts. A couple of songs, some bush verse. All things considered, it's going really well, and Angie's folks are bearing up gamely.'

Jonno picked up the bottles he'd brought and his smile widened as he held them up. 'And I thought I should try to raise the tone of this party. I reckon a night like this could use some serious, good-quality red.'

Mitch couldn't help smiling again. 'Thanks, mate.'

'And I've already eaten,' added Jonno. 'So you don't have to feed me. Oh, and Seth's lovely Alice has offered to call by here when we're ready and she'll drive us both home.'

'I'll get some glasses.' Mitch was already on his way. 'Jonno, pull up a pew.'

It shouldn't have been a beautiful night. It was November, thunderstorm season. The heavens should have been black with rain and split by lightning, befitting Mitch's inner turmoil. Instead the sky was cloudless and clear with a silver half moon and a spectacular splash of stars.

The air was pleasantly cool and the guys opted to stay outside on the terrace, around the fire, which had reduced to brightly glowing embers.

Mitch found some olives and the end of a piece of pecorino, and by a lucky miracle, he also unearthed an unopened packet of crackers in the pantry. He assembled these, plus a knife, on a platter, which he set on an old milking stool that served as a small table.

As the trio settled into more comfortable deckchairs, the silence of the country night seemed to amplify the small sounds, the gentle crackle of the fire, the buzz of insects in the grass, the gurgle of wine being poured into glasses, the occasional distant shrieks of a fruit bat.

Jonno's wine, as promised, was extra good, and it slipped down smoothly. They sat, staring at the fire or at the stars, and they talked quietly, carefully skirting around the topic of the non-wedding. Jonno asked Seth about the new property he'd bought and about his plans for building a stud herd. Seth told them he had a contractor coming on Monday to dig a new dam. They discussed the chances of a decent wet season.

To Mitch's surprise, he was the first to break the unspoken taboo. He found himself needing to talk, to ask questions, to dig into the very tender spot he'd sworn to avoid.

'I take it you've never been married, Jonno?'

'No,' came the careful reply. "Fraid not.'

'But you can marry, can't you? You're not like Catholics? Sworn to celibacy?'

'Sure, I can marry if I want to, but I've never taken the plunge.'

'Sensible man,' Mitch replied glumly, and he wondered if the wine on top of beer was loosening his tongue. He would have to be careful, or he'd say something stupid, or ask a really dumb question.

Changing the subject, he said, 'I saw Finn Latimer prowling round the church with his camera. I hope to hell he's not going to put something in the *Burralea Bugle* about today's fiasco.'

'He wouldn't,' said Seth quickly. 'He's a good bloke.'

'Yes,' agreed Jonno. 'I like the man.'

'But you like everyone,' Mitch challenged. 'It's part of your job description.'

Jonno smiled. A piece of wood on the fire spat and crumbled into glowing red-gold coals. Seth picked up another piece and poked it into place. They watched as its edges caught and flickered.

'Mitch, you know there's no way of avoiding the pain,' Jonno said, surprising him. 'It's good to do this, for us to have a few drinks tonight, but there's no going around it. At some point, eventually, you just have to stand still and feel the crack.'

'Funny you should say that,' Mitch said. 'That's how it feels, you know. Like a crack.'

A crack filled with anger and hurt, he added silently, although to admit that was going too far.

'A crack that's not going to heal,' he said instead.

'But it will heal, of course. In time.'

Mitch eyed Jonno warily. He didn't look like a priest tonight in his old jeans, a holey sweater and dusty riding boots, sitting in a deckchair with a wineglass in one hand, an ankle propped on a knee. Mitch supposed this talk of wounds and healing was probably a sly warm-up for a chat about God.

'I'm afraid I'm not much good at praying,' he warned, hoping to head Jonno off at the pass.

'Prayer's not for everyone.' Jonno smiled and gave an easy shrug. 'I can always pray for you. That's what I'm paid to do.'

This was why Mitch liked the guy. He acted out his faith without ramming it down your throat. 'Thanks,' he said. 'I'd appreciate that.'

He knew Jonno was right. It wasn't possible to avoid accepting what had happened today. He'd lost the woman he loved. All his dreams had crashed in one fell swoop and in the most public and humiliating way possible.

'Just before you arrived, I was telling Seth that I want to apply for a transfer,' he said.

He didn't know what kind of reaction he'd expected, but he was surprised when Jonno turned to look back over his shoulder to the house. Mitch had spent two years remodelling this place, transforming it from an ancient tractor shed into a comfortable home. The completed project had earned him plenty of compliments, and he was pretty sure he could guess what Jonno was thinking.

Yeah, it would be a wrench to leave the house.

But he needed to get away. Somewhere completely new, where nobody knew him. Maybe he could hang onto the house and rent it out. Just in case . . .

'I told Mitch he'd be sorely missed,' chipped in Seth.

Jonno nodded. 'No doubt about that.'

'But I feel like I need a fresh start,' said Mitch.

'Fair enough,' said Jonno. 'And I didn't come here to give advice. I wouldn't try to talk you out of leaving town, Mitch. Not if that's what you want.'

'It is.'

Jonno gave another nod. 'But I guess you can't put in for a transfer till Monday, and you never know, you might feel differently by then.'

'Not a chance.' Mitch stuck his jaw stubbornly forward as he refilled their glasses.

CHAPTER FIVE

By Monday, after the shittiest of shitty weekends, Mitch had not changed his mind. He still needed to get out of Burralea and he needed to get out fast.

He'd never really intended to stay in the bush for his entire life, but somehow he'd slipped into a cosy zone where he was on top of his work and everything felt comfortable and familiar. He'd quite liked knowing a large proportion of the locals by name and he'd been happy enough to help out old ladies like Edith, or to deal with low-key disputes no other agency wanted to touch, such as weed killer being used on a fence line and destroying a neighbour's precious plants.

Damn it, for the past two years, he'd even dressed up as Santa Claus for the community's Christmas concert.

Now, though, after his non-wedding's savage kick in the balls, the scales had fallen from Mitch's eyes. He couldn't believe he'd never noticed he was living in a rut. Going nowhere. Hell, he was barely in his thirties, and he'd been living the safe and steady life of an old codger on the verge of retirement.

Angie's bombshell had well and truly flattened him, but one

thing was certain. He sure as hell wasn't going to hang around here licking his wounds.

On Monday morning, dressed in civilian jeans and a T-shirt, he drove to the police station straight after breakfast. Jim O'Reilly was out on highway patrol, and Mitch was pleased there would be no one looking over his shoulder as he logged onto his computer and pulled up the application for transfer.

Unfortunately, he wasn't alone for long. He'd barely begun filling in the basics on the form when a knock sounded at the door.

The door opened a crack to reveal Flora peering worriedly in at him, and Mitch was instantly tense. Once again he was reliving the lump-in-the-throat music at the church, the wedding guests in their fancy clothes. The gut-gnawing shock and shame.

'Hey,' Flora said softly and she pushed the door wider open. She was wearing purple shorts and a black strappy top. Beneath a sweeping wing of dark hair, her grey eyes looked wide with concern.

'Hi,' Mitch responded gruffly.

'I thought I saw you pull up outside.'

'Did you get your money?' he asked. 'I gave it to Seth.'

'Oh? Yes. He dropped it off yesterday. Thanks. But I wasn't chasing the quartet money, Mitch.' Flora looked uncharacteristically shy, almost out of her depth. She fiddled with the door knob. 'I – I hope you don't mind me popping in. I just wanted to say how sorry I am about – everything.'

There was too much emotion in her eyes. Mitch had to look away. 'Yeah,' he said. 'Thanks.'

'I guess I just wanted to remind you that I'm here,' she pushed on, almost as if she'd set herself a mission and she wasn't leaving until it was successfully accomplished. 'I'm just down the road – as you know – if you want company or anything.'

Mitch frowned. The last thing he wanted was a female dishing up tea and sympathy, especially a girl as kind-hearted and friendly as Flora Drummond.

'I cook a mean curry,' she added and, even though he wasn't looking, he could hear the hint of a smile in her voice.

'Thanks,' he said again.

Problem was, Flora's kindness would only remind him of how selfishly his bride had behaved. 'I'm not really feeling very social at the moment.' He kept his voice gruff, willing her to get the message.

'That's okay. That's fine. I understand. Maybe – well, anyway, I just thought I'd let you know the door's open. If you change your mind – or whatever.'

Looking up, Mitch saw a suspicious sheen in her eyes, but she quickly smiled. Maybe he'd imagined the tears.

'Bye,' she said, then she disappeared, pulling the door closed behind her, leaving him to feel crazily bad, as if he'd kicked a kitten.

Mitch sighed. He was entitled to feel pissed off and angry, but it wasn't in his DNA to be rude to Flora. He was scowling as he turned back to the forms he'd been filling in and he welcomed the steadying task of answering routine questions. Full name. Date of birth. Current address. The date he'd entered the police force. He'd only completed the first page when the office phone rang.

Damn. He was supposed to be off-duty.

'Good morning,' he said cautiously.

'Mitch? I didn't expect to speak to you. That's lucky, it's Seth here. Are you back at work?'

Was this a Drummond conspiracy? Mitch suppressed another sigh. 'Just filling in my transfer application.'

'Oh.' There was a brief pause from Seth. 'So you're still going ahead with that? You're determined to leave us?'

'Yup, 'fraid so.' Mitch scowled impatiently at the screen in front of him. 'Now, how can I help you?'

'Well, I'm actually calling on police business and it's kind of urgent. I've got Danny Holmes, the dozer guy, here. We started excavating the dam first thing this morning, but Danny's hardly begun and he's turned up bones.'

'Bones?' Mitch sat straighter. Seth had his full attention now.

'Yeah,' Seth said. 'Human bones.'

'Are you sure they're human?'

'They certainly look human to me. There's no skull so far, but we've stopped digging.'

'Yeah. Don't touch a thing. If you think they're human, I'll come straight over.'

'I'm no expert, obviously, but I've seen plenty of animal bones. Cattle and horses. Dingoes. I reckon these are different. They're old, I'd say, but I reckon they've got to be human. Gave poor Danny a fright.'

Mitch was already out of his chair. This kind of work hardly ever came up in Burralea. The transfer application would have to wait. Sergeant Cavello was recalling himself to duty. 'I'll see you soon.'

Mitch had to race home first to change into his uniform, but luckily his small acreage, once part of a much larger farm, was on the outskirts of town. He changed in record speed, buckling the belt that carried his sidearm as he hurried out the door.

Seth's place, Kooringal, was about five kilometres further on. The property comprised sixty hectares of prime grazing land edged by the Barron River and had belonged to the Matthews family for several generations.

Joe Matthews had been the end of the line. His daughters and sons-in-law hadn't been interested in cattle, so Joe had hung on, still running the place well past retirement age, until he recently sold to Seth and moved to a house in town.

The road to Kooringal took Mitch through pockets of ancient rainforest and past fields of legumes and open grazing paddocks, but it wasn't long before he was turning in through the white gate posts that marked the property's entrance and following the winding track up to the old Queenslander homestead.

Alice, Seth's girlfriend, was waiting at the bottom of the homestead steps to meet him, and Seth's son, Charlie, was with her.

'Morning, Mitch.' Dressed in jeans and a checked shirt, Alice was very much the country girl these days. She was quite a looker. Slender, with long, curly auburn hair and soft, creamy skin that hinted at Celtic origins.

By contrast, Seth's son, Charlie, was a sturdy little chap and his hair was dead straight and white-blonde. Charlie wasn't Alice's biological child, but Mitch could see by the trusting way the kid held her hand that the pair had formed quite a bond.

'Morning, Alice,' he said. 'And how are you, Charlie?'

Charlie grinned and Alice smiled and, to Mitch's relief, she made no mention of the wedding. 'Seth's waiting for you,' she said. 'I think he's quite anxious. He got a shock when they saw the bones.'

'Yeah, I can imagine.'

'I hope it's not —' Alice stopped and looked down at Charlie. 'Anyway,' she went on, 'you follow that track.' She pointed to a two-wheel dirt track, heading off past the machinery shed. 'I don't think you'll have any trouble finding them.'

'Thanks.'

'Catch you later, maybe.'

'Bye bye!' called Charlie, waving with the wonderfully gleeful enthusiasm of a happy toddler.

The kid was damned appealing, and Mitch had to squash the stupid pang of regret that spiked when he remembered there would be no little family for him now. He'd had dreams of giving his kids the kind of happy family life he'd never had.

Yeah, right.

He drove on, past the old three-door machinery shed made of corrugated iron, past the cattle yards that were a combination of old weathered timber and new metal fences, through a patch of acacia and eucalyptus scrub. Emerging from the trees, he arrived at a big open grazing paddock which would, no doubt, soon be home to a herd of impressively deep-chested and thickly haunched stud cattle.

In the centre of the paddock where the land naturally made a slight dip, he saw Seth with Danny Holmes, both wearing broad-brimmed hats and squatting in the shade of a bright yellow bulldozer.

They got to their feet as soon as they saw his vehicle. Right next to them were fresh cuts in the ground and a hillock of newly scooped red earth.

'So,' Mitch said as he shook their hands. 'Let's see what we've got here.'

Seth led him to the pile of earth. 'I cleared the dirt off a couple of the bones, trying to work out what they were.' He pointed to two long grey and very worn bones lying beside the dirt pile. 'I reckon they're leg bones, don't you?'

Mitch frowned at them. 'Maybe.'

'But then, look here. I reckon this is the clincher.' Seth was moving behind the tractor now, pointing to the freshly scoured earth.

Following him, Mitch saw the flat clean cut the dozer blade had made and then the bones lying, half-buried. These were smaller bones, similarly grey and weathered, lying loose, but in the unmistakable pattern of a human hand.

'Jeez.' Mitch's chest tightened.

'Gives a shiver down your spine, doesn't it?' Seth said.

Mitch nodded. 'I'd say they've been there a long time.'

'Yeah. Probably. I don't know if it was a grave,' Seth said. 'There was no mention of graves when I toured the place with Joe Matthews and nothing was marked.'

'Well, that's our job to ascertain, of course.' Mitch was already reaching for his phone. 'Sorry, guys, I'm sure you understand you'll have to hold off on this dam project for a day or two. I'll have to declare this area a crime scene and you'll need to leave everything as it is until we know more about why these bones are here.'

'Yeah, we were expecting that.' Seth didn't look happy, though.

'What about my dozer?' Danny piped up. 'I've got other jobs to get on with.'

'Don't move that dozer until forensics have photographed everything,' Mitch told him. 'I'll get onto it straight away, though. The scenes-of-crime officers will be coming from Mareeba, so they can probably get here pretty quickly. You shouldn't be held up for too long.'

Danny didn't look too excited, but he accepted this with a shrug.

Mitch went back to his vehicle to put through the call to police communications, who would in turn make calls to detectives from CIB, as well as the forensic officers from Scientific and from Scenes of Crime. And, of course, the Inspector had to be notified.

'I'll have to tape off this area,' Mitch said when he'd finished.

'I was expecting that, too.' Seth cracked a lopsided grin. 'I've watched enough TV crime shows.'

'Good,' said Mitch. 'So you'll understand that once the tape goes up, the only people who can enter the crime scene will be the officers necessary to the investigation. Forensics, detectives, the Inspector and so on.'

Seth nodded and gave a mock salute. 'Got it.'

'It's going to get pretty busy here,' Mitch warned. 'As well as the forensics from Mareeba, there'll be detectives and scientific officers from Cairns crawling all over this. They'll look at any material around the bones and try to identify how long they've been there. Then they'll probably send the bones off to Brisbane to get DNA and run it against the database.'

'I guess you'll be hoping that a skull turns up as well,' said Seth.

'That would certainly be handy. It might give a clearer picture of how this person died, and we can use dental records to check against missing persons.'

Narrowing his eyes against the glare, Mitch looked towards the pile of scooped earth. 'We'll probably get a bobcat driver to dig gently around there. Brisbane may even decide to send a forensic archaeologist.'

Seth's smile faded as he stood, hands on hips, staring solemnly at the curved pattern of finger bones embedded in the red earth. 'You have to wonder, don't you?' he said and then let out a heavy sigh.

Mitch couldn't help feeling sympathy for his mate. Seth had been so excited when he'd bought this property. After years of working for his dad on Ruthven Downs, he'd finally scored his own place, and he was champing at the bit to start his stud-breeding program. The possibility of a crime committed here wasn't just a time suck, it cast a nasty taint on those happy dreams.

Not that Seth was prone to feeling sorry for himself. 'You want a hand with that tape?' he asked.

'Sure, thanks.'

They were in luck, finding handy saplings, more or less suitably spaced, that could be used as corner posts, and it didn't take long to stretch the blue-and-white police tape between them.

'I daresay you'll have to tell Joe Matthews about this,' Seth said when the job was done.

Mitch nodded. He'd been thinking about Joe Matthews from the moment he'd got Seth's phone call. The old fellow had to be close to eighty now, and until he'd sold Kooringal to Seth, he'd spent his whole life here, living and working on this peaceful stretch of country. As far as Mitch knew, Joe was a gentle, law-abiding old-timer, a retired cattleman as honest as the day was long. He'd lived quietly and worked hard, and now he enjoyed pottering in his vegetable garden in his twilight years.

Mitch wasn't looking forward to stirring Joe up with the news of this unsettling discovery.

Joe's house was right in the heart of Burralea, in a pretty street with a strip of terraced garden down its centre. The cute factor was high in this town and the garden strip was well tended with carefully pruned weeping bottlebrush and lilli pilli trees as well as all kinds of daisies, lilies and bright flowering ground covers spilling over a low rock wall.

Joe's house was on the lower side, and his front fence was also made of rock, set with a small green paling gate. His cottage was called Rosegum, no doubt named after the huge tree that shaded its yard. The front door was shut, but there were windows open, so Joe was probably home.

When Mitch knocked there was no sound from inside at first, but it wasn't long before he heard footsteps and the door opened.

Joe was a tall man, thin, but still quite wide in the shoulders and showing no sign of a stoop. He was wearing faded old jeans and a pale-blue shirt with the long sleeves rolled back to just below his elbows. He had snow-white hair and keen hazel eyes behind rimless glasses.

'Good morning, Mr Matthews,' Mitch said politely.

Joe nodded, frowning slightly. A dog appeared at his heels, slim, with an intelligent, black-and-white face and pointy ears. Mitch guessed it was a kelpie–border collie cross, an old working dog, now retired, like its master. Mitch had seen the two of them going on regular walks together, using the track that followed the creek.

'What can I do for you, Sergeant?' Joe asked.

'I'd like to have a word, Joe. There's been a discovery on Kooringal, and as you owned the place until recently, I need to ask you a few questions.'

'A discovery?' Joe's frown deepened. 'What kind of discovery?'

'Can I come inside, please?'

Joe Matthews stood for a moment, staring at Mitch from beneath stern white brows. Then his craggy shoulders lifted in a resigned shrug. 'Of course.'

Dog at his heels, he led Mitch down a short central passage before turning into the lounge room, which was furnished predictably with old-fashioned furniture, but also, somewhat to Mitch's surprise, with loaded bookshelves crammed into every available wall space.

'You're quite a reader,' Mitch couldn't help commenting.

Joe nodded. 'Always have been.' He offered Mitch an armchair by the window and then had to clear a pile of books from another chair before he could sit down. He set them on the rug beside his chair.

Mitch glanced at the books' spines. Hemingway, Raymond Chandler, Gabriel García Márquez. Mitch was more of an action guy than a reader, so he was quite impressed.

'So,' Joe said, once they were seated. 'What's this discovery? Don't tell me Seth Drummond's found gold on Kooringal? Or sapphires?' He smiled at this remote possibility.

'I'm afraid it's nothing exciting like that,' said Mitch. 'But Seth started excavating a new dam this morning and he's turned up bones.' There was a beat before he added, 'Human bones.'

There was no missing the flare of shock in Joe's eyes. 'Where was this?'

Mitch shrugged. 'You're more familiar with Kooringal's layout than I am, but it was in the middle of one of the big grazing paddocks.'

'I see.'

'I was wondering if you could shed any light on this, Joe.'

The old man was frowning deeply now, and he seemed to stare

at a spot on the faded oriental carpet. 'No,' he said, looking worried. 'No, I can't.'

Mitch remained silent, waiting in case Joe had something more to add, but the man simply continued to frown at the carpet.

'You don't know of any family graves on the property?'

Joe shook his head and this time he looked directly at Mitch as he answered. 'I'm almost certain that everyone from my family's been buried in the Atherton cemetery. My wife was cremated.'

'Right. And you've never heard of Kooringal land being used as an Indigenous burial site?'

Again, Joe shook his head. 'No, nothing.' He was sitting with his elbows propped on the arms of his chair, his hands tightly clasped in front of him.

From the little Mitch knew of Joe, he'd always been a fairly serious kind of guy, but he seemed extra tense now. Mitch had a gut feeling there was something the man was holding back.

'So you can't think of anything that might help us identify these bones?'

'No, nothing,' Joe said with an air of quiet but determined finality. 'Sorry.'

'Very well.' Mitch took his time getting to his feet. He wanted to give Joe a chance to reconsider his statement. 'Obviously, we'll have a team of detectives and forensic experts checking this out. So if you think of anything that might be useful, you'll ring me, won't you?'

'Yes, of course.' Joe was rising somewhat stiffly from his chair.

'Don't worry about getting up,' Mitch told him. 'I can see myself out.'

As he left, he wondered if he would hear from Joe again. Mitch suspected the old guy wouldn't volunteer any further information. Just the same, he felt pretty sure there was more to this story.

As the front door clicked shut behind him, Mitch's skin prickled, deepening his suspicion that something about Joe's story wasn't right. He wasn't an expert on reading body language, but he knew Joe had been tense.

Pondering this, he squared his shoulders and took a deep breath. Damn it, he had a mystery to solve.

It felt good.

CHAPTER SIX

Hattie thoroughly enjoyed her mid-morning coffee habit. Her doctor had warned her that she should limit her caffeine intake, so apart from a cup of tea as soon as she woke, this cappuccino was her daily indulgence, and she'd made it into something of a ritual.

At around ten-thirty each morning, she left her apartment with its satisfying views of the Brisbane River and took the lift to the ground floor. Then she walked – quite briskly, since her successful knee replacement – to her favourite café, stopping to buy a copy of *The Australian* from a newsstand on the way.

Anton, the rather charming and good-looking Macedonian barista, liked to tease her. 'Hattie, you know that a flat white is trendier than a cappuccino.'

Hattie simply laughed. 'I've never been worried about being trendy and I'm not likely to start now at my age.'

Her coffee came with a tiny piece of shortbread, or some other miniature delight, tucked on the saucer. Depending on the weather, she sat in the shade or in a patch of sunshine. Today, in November, it was excessively hot and humid, so she chose a table inside the air-conditioned café.

Once she'd taken a little of the froth with her spoon and had downed the first blissful sip of coffee, she skim-read the headlines on the newspaper's front page. The headlines were, as usual, quite depressing. She turned over to the puzzle page next, mainly to check out the letters in the Circuit Breaker, and to see how many words she would have to find before she could be deemed 'Excellent'.

Hattie wasn't very good with numbers so avoided Sudoku, but she liked the word puzzles and conscientiously tried to keep her little grey cells active. Planning to come back to this page later, she turned to the meatier inside pages.

Before she had retired, she'd worked in publishing. Her area had been novels, commercial women's fiction mostly. Perhaps because of this, when it came to news, she'd always preferred the arts and human interest pages to those that concentrated on politics, although she did like to follow one or two of the columnists.

Occasionally, there were interesting snippets from regional areas that most of the metropolitan papers tended to skip. Today, she was browsing this section when a headline caught her eye.

TABLELAND BONES SPARK MURDER INQUIRY

Goodness.

It was a story about the Atherton Tablelands. A lifetime ago, Hattie had lived there. Intrigued, she took a closer look.

> Police in Far North Queensland suspect that a gunshot wound caused the death of an unknown man whose skeletal remains were found on a cattle property on the Atherton Tablelands last week.
>
> Property owner Seth Drummond unearthed the bones on his stud cattle farm near the town of Burralea while excavating a dam. Inspector David Johnstone, head of

the Mareeba CIB, said yesterday that forensic tests had
confirmed evidence of violent trauma and that the shallow
grave was now being treated as a crime scene.

'At this stage we are checking missing persons lists in
an attempt to identify the deceased person, but the forensic
report also indicates that the remains have been in the
ground for many years,' Inspector Johnstone said.

'We are also confident this property known as
Kooringal is not an old Indigenous burial site and we
will be using all our police resources on the Tablelands,
with the scientific backup from Brisbane, to identify the
victim and further our inquiries into what we now believe
was a shooting and the deliberate disposal of a body.'

Hattie was so shocked she felt quite breathless and dizzy.

Surely, this couldn't be . . .

Her pulse raced giddily as she forced herself read the story
again. She wasn't mistaken. It was all there. Burralea. Kooringal.
Gunshots . . . and a body being buried . . .

It had been years since she'd had a hot flush, but she experienced
one now as she tried to think straight. She'd almost forgotten that
long-ago afternoon from her childhood. Now, sitting in a Brisbane
café, this news story brought everything rushing back.

It had happened in the early months after she and Rose had first
arrived in Australia from Shanghai. At that time, they were still living in a cottage on Kooringal, which belonged to the Matthews
family. Hattie and Joe Matthews had been almost the same age, quite
young. Joe was no more than six or seven and they used to spend
nearly all their spare time together. They'd become great mates.

Joe had taught Hattie how to ride a pony and to catch rainbow fish to keep in a glass jar. On the afternoon she was remembering now, Joe had asked her if she wanted to help him to trap finches.

Thinking back, she could picture the simple aviary at the back of the Kooringal homestead, built in the shade of the tank stand. In today's modern enlightened climate, trapping finches would be very un-PC, but back then in 1942, no one raised an eyebrow at people catching birds and keeping an aviary.

Besides, when Hattie had lived in Shanghai, she'd been to the markets with her amah and she was used to seeing all kinds of poultry kept in bamboo cages. After the noise and bustle of that crowded, war-torn, cosmopolitan city, she had been completely fascinated by the new world in Australia, living in the quiet and peaceful bush with a tall, friendly boy as her closest neighbour.

She had no idea what trapping finches involved, but Joe had his heart set on collecting more crimson finches, and she'd readily said yes. Joe had given her a wooden box with several lidded compartments to hold, while he put his hand into the aviary and gently caught a flustered little bird with a bright red face.

'This will be the caller,' he told Hattie as he cupped the little fellow in his hands and then carefully slipped it into one of the compartments in the box she held.

Joe shut the door on the finch and the children headed off together, following a dirt track through the scrub till they came to a barbed wire fence. Here, Joe held down the wire for Hattie to climb through and then she did the same for him. They were in an open meadow of knee-high grass now, in a big curving bend of the river.

Remembering that day after so many years, Hattie was surprised by the details that were suddenly so vivid. The afternoon had been sunny, but the grass was still damp after several days of rain and the hem of her striped cotton skirt was wet as it brushed against her calves. She remembered the smell of damp earth, and the insistent high-pitched call of the trapped finch, the low buzz of insects singing, the chomp and rip of cattle tugging at grass nearby.

Joe set the box down in the middle of a clearing and deftly lifted the spring-loaded doors on the empty compartments. Of course the poor distressed finch twittered and peeped more loudly than ever.

'It's frightened,' Hattie told him.

'But its call will bring in the others,' Joe said with the certainty of one who had done this before, and then he showed her where to hide behind a clump of bottlebrush.

And so they'd squatted quietly in their hiding place and Hattie hadn't minded the wet skirt or the ants climbing over her bare ankles, because she was there with Joe.

Watching through the branches of the bottlebrush, she saw several little finches arrive, glowing crimson and twittering and fluttering, curious to check out their noisy mate.

As one little bird inched towards an open compartment door, Joe and Hattie waited, tense, holding their breath, willing it to take just a few more hops and trigger the door's catch.

Hattie could remember leaning forward to peer more closely through the branches, not wanting to miss a moment. Even though she felt sorry that a bird was about to lose its freedom, she was also caught up in the thrill of the hunt. And, well, she liked Joe.

Even at that early age, she'd liked his quiet, serious manner, warmed by his occasional bright-eyed smiles. There'd been something about him that made her feel tingly and super happy. If he wanted this bird, so did she.

The children were poised, watching, breathless with anticipation when the loud crack of a gunshot rang out, making them flinch. And then another shot, splitting the afternoon stillness.

Of course, the finches instantly disappeared. Even the caller bird fell silent. Joe and Hattie stared at each other.

'What was that?' she whispered.

Joe was frowning. 'I'm not sure. It didn't sound like my dad's rifle.'

Scared that the gun might go off again, they stayed crouched behind the bottlebrush for some time. But there were no more shots. Once again, the bush fell silent and still.

Eventually, Joe and Hattie got to their feet and Joe was about to step out from their hiding place when a new sound stopped him. A motor. A truck was rumbling down the track and as it emerged from the forest they ducked down again quickly and crouched in their hiding place.

The truck belonged to strangers. It was khaki with a big white star painted on the side. Neither of the children had ever seen it before.

'I think it's the Yanks,' whispered Joe.

Hattie looked at the newspaper again, remembering Gabriel, the man who had disappeared on the same day they'd heard the gunshots. She couldn't be sure the events of that afternoon were connected to this story about the discovery of bones, but the coincidence was difficult to ignore. How incredible that it should surface again now, after all this time. More than seventy years.

There was no mention of Joe Matthews, though.

She checked the story again. No, Joe definitely hadn't been named. Someone called Seth Drummond owned Kooringal these days.

Thoroughly shaken, Hattie sat very still, needing to compose herself. Unfortunately, the story had stirred too many memories – not just of that fateful afternoon, but of other aspects of Hattie's past that she'd tried to forget. Now the memories kept tumbling like beads spilling from a broken necklace. Most of them centred on Joe.

He had been her neighbour and first friend in Burralea, but later, after Hattie and Rose had moved into Burralea township, Joe had been relegated to being just another boy in Hattie's class at school. They'd sometimes exchanged a word or two and careful smiles, but like all primary school children of that era, they'd become a little self-conscious and shy, aware that the opposite sex was 'other'. Joe played cricket and footie with the boys, while Hattie played hopscotch and skipping with the girls.

It wasn't till they were nearing the end of their high school years, really, that their childhood friendship had resurfaced and gradually blossomed into an achingly sweet romance.

Rose hadn't been happy that Hattie was forming a close attachment to a local boy at such an early age. Her English family's class snobbery came to the fore.

'We've spent far too long in this little country town. It was a mistake to stay here all this time. I should have seen that long ago.'

Rose had talked of them moving to Cairns, or even to Brisbane, where Hattie would have the chance to mix with a 'better class of young man'. Hattie had hated the idea of leaving. She couldn't imagine anyone better than Joe.

To her relief they hadn't moved. Perhaps, even then, Rose hadn't been well and lacked the energy for such a change. Meanwhile, Hattie and Joe had grown closer, certain they would spend their whole lives together. Then Rose became seriously ill.

In the year Hattie turned twenty, her whole life had fallen apart. Joe had broken her heart and Rose had died, and as if these catastrophes weren't shattering enough, Hattie had heard an incredible story that turned everything she'd believed about herself and her parents on its head.

By the time Hattie had left for England after Rose's death, she'd been a mess. She'd not only lost her mother and the man she'd loved, but her own understanding of who she was.

In England, she'd wasted the best part of a decade trying to come to terms with all of this. Eventually, she'd managed to put that phase of her life behind her and she'd pushed on, undertaking extra study and forging a successful career, and embarking on two successive marriages.

Now, all these years later, Hattie didn't welcome being reminded of that darker time in her early years. Perhaps she could forget it. If she hadn't bought this newspaper she would never had read the story about Kooringal. Besides, Joe was probably dead. That was more than likely the reason there was no mention of him in this news story.

But what about the bones? And the police investigation?

Uncomfortably, Hattie wondered if a woman nearing the end of her seventies was obligated to share a long-suppressed childhood memory that might or might not be relevant to this case.

At the time, Joe's father had sworn the two of them to secrecy.

But now . . .

'Hattie, are you all right?' Millie, one of the friendly wait staff, was hovering and looking concerned.

'Oh, yes,' Hattie assured her. She tapped the newspaper. 'Just mulling over something I read in the paper.'

The girl rolled her eyes. 'I hardly ever read the news. It's always bad. I find it so depressing.'

'You're right. It's very depressing,' Hattie said faintly. She finished the last, now cold, sip of her coffee and folded the paper. She wasn't in the mood for the puzzle page now. Perhaps she would tackle it later when she felt calmer.

If she felt calmer . . .

She put the newspaper into her copious handbag and stood slowly, giving her stiff joints time to cooperate. She needed to walk for a bit and to think about what she must do.

And a little research on the internet was in order.

*

By evening, Hattie had discovered that there was a Joe Matthews still listed as a committee member of the Agricultural Show Society in Burralea and she had found an address and phone number in White Pages Online. She could only assume it was the same man she'd known and she supposed he must still be alive, although she had also found a funeral notice for Gloria Matthews, which meant that Joe must have been a widower for quite some time.

She was surprised by how unsettling this discovery was. Surely, after more than fifty years, she didn't still care about Joe?

She wondered if the police had spoken to him. It was possible that Joe was helping them with their inquiries even though he hadn't been named in the paper.

Then she pondered the possibility that his memory might be failing. Regrettably, her own memory was only too sharp and it was bothering her, pricking her conscience, prodding her towards uncomfortable action.

She wouldn't be rash, of course. She wouldn't jump in and telephone the police just yet. She would feel much happier if she could speak to Joe first. She needed to know if Joe had spoken to the police. If he hadn't told them about that day when they'd gone to trap finches, she wanted to know why.

Alternatively, if Joe had spoken, she was very keen to know what he'd told them. She thought about dialling Joe's phone number, but it would be a very strange business to try to conduct a long-distance conversation with him after decades of silence.

It was only a matter of time before Hattie realised the inevitable. If she wanted to have her mind settled about any connection between these bones and those gunshots and Gabriel's disappearance, she should make the journey north.

Fortunately, thanks to two marriages in different parts of the world, she had become quite an accomplished solo traveller. Now it would be a relatively simple matter to fly to Cairns and then take a bus up to the Atherton Tablelands. There was a guesthouse in Burralea that she dimly remembered, and it still looked quite all right in the photos on the internet.

Once she was in Burralea, she would set about finding Joe. If it was absolutely necessary, she would hire a small car. Her priority was to find Joe and to speak to him before she spoke to the police.

Of course, Hattie had rather mixed emotions about going back to that small country town and seeing Joe again after all this time, but she was reassured by the fact that their reunion would, under the circumstances, be businesslike.

First off, she wanted to know whether Joe even remembered her, or the events of that fateful, long-ago afternoon. And, if he did remember, how closely did his story match hers?

Really, there were so many questions.

To calm herself, she poured a glass of white wine and took it out onto her balcony. Her apartment was on the seventh floor, and she had a rather lovely view of the lavender dusk settling over the river. The lights of the bridge and the busy traffic and buildings glowed in the soft twilight. In the west, the last blush from the sun showed as a faint shimmer above the dark ridge of Mt Coot-tha.

It was a scene that usually soothed Hattie, but this evening she still felt stirred up, almost excited. She told herself she was being a ridiculous old woman, but she couldn't help it. Apart from the disturbing business of the bones, finally, after all this time, she was going to see Joe again.

CHAPTER SEVEN

Flora woke with a start. Her skin was crawling, her heart pounding. For a moment, caught between sleeping and waking, she thought Oliver was in bed with her again, his hands under her nightgown, touching her intimately while she slept.

To her relief, she realised she was alone, but the unpleasant sensations lingered. Oliver's uninvited groping had become a huge source of tension when she'd lived with him in Melbourne.

Not at first. Oliver had been clever enough to be charming at first, a dream boyfriend. He had taken Flora to interesting restaurants, to art galleries and concerts, and for romantic walks along the Yarra River. There'd also been quiet evenings of listening to music together, with the two of them sharing a bottle of wine along with their hopes and dreams. They'd seemed so perfectly in tune, both planning brilliant musical careers.

The changes had been gradual. He'd started by criticising her wardrobe or the way she wore her hair, or the choices she'd made for their dinner.

There'd been occasional bursts of anger. Sometimes Oliver had sworn and abused her for no apparent reason, but afterwards he'd apologised profusely and Flora had forgiven him, because she'd known he was on edge. It was hard for him, trying to balance his part-time career as a tenor with the Australian Opera and his day job in the Commonwealth Bank. She'd told herself he was a sensitive artist and he found the banking work dreadfully tedious.

But then had come the night when she'd woken to find him lying on top of her, pushing his way between her thighs.

She'd protested and ordered him to stop.

'I don't want this now. I was asleep, for God's sake.' Sex was supposed to be consensual and she could hardly give her consent if she was sound asleep.

'You're in my bed,' Oliver told her with his typical arrogance. 'That counts as consent as far as I'm concerned.'

It was enough to ensure that Flora slept very badly after that night, but this hadn't bothered Oliver. His control over her was even stronger when she was tired and nervous.

Then, perhaps inevitably, his abuse had become violent, which was when Flora had left, escaping at first to a girlfriend's flat and then later, with the help of Kate Woods, here to Burralea.

Shuddering now at the awful memories, she switched on her bedside lamp. It was a relief to see the familiar bedroom in the little cottage. The plain timber chest of drawers and the wardrobe painted a full gloss cream. Fresh floral curtains, an old-fashioned, mirror-backed dressing table and a bowl of bright yellow and tangerine nasturtiums that Flora had picked from the garden.

Oliver was two states away.

He can't find you. It's okay.

There was no need to panic.

Feeling slightly more together now, she got out of bed and padded through to the kitchen. She hadn't drawn the curtains, and light streamed through the windows from the almost full moon. Outside in a mango tree, a rusty-coloured possum made its dainty way along a narrow branch, its long tail curling.

Flora watched it until it disappeared among the glossy leaves and then she switched on the kettle. She would make a cup of tea and read for a bit. She needed to clear her head before she tried to get back to sleep.

In bed once again, with a mug of well-sugared tea, she found it difficult to concentrate on her novel. Thoughts of Oliver kept intruding. With a deliberate effort, she switched her thoughts to Mitch instead.

The poor guy had looked shattered when she'd seen him at the police station.

Flora had wanted to tell him that she knew how it felt. She knew what it was like to discover that the person you'd fallen in love with could be selfish and cruel.

Mitch wouldn't have welcomed her comments, of course. He was still in that dark place where no one else's situation could ever be as bad as his own. Besides, Mitch wasn't used to sharing his emotions. Flora knew from the time he'd lived with her family that he found it hard to talk about the heavy stuff. He'd grown up alone with a withdrawn and uncommunicative dad, and he'd kept everything bottled up, which was how he'd ended up a troubled teen.

Flora could only hope that Mitch had more inner reserves to draw on these days. At least Angie had cleared out of his life, and she would almost certainly leave him alone now. Whereas Oliver —

No, stop it. You're not allowed to think about him.

She willed her thoughts elsewhere. Music. Thinking about her music nearly always calmed her. She should contemplate her audition for the QSO.

As well as various orchestral excerpts from composers such as Brahms, Beethoven, Strauss and Elgar, she was expected to play the first and second movements of a Mozart concerto, and a romantic concerto of her own choice. The Mozart was the No 3 in G major, which Flora actually hated. She'd been playing it since high school and she'd done it to death. Unfortunately, the very fact that Mozart's music was so well exposed and fiddly meant that she needed to work even harder at her practice to make sure she still delivered the music with a pure, clean technique.

The concerto of her own choice was the Tchaikovsky, which she adored. It was lush and emotional and packed with the Russian's typically exciting tunes and show-off violin gymnastics. It was a devilishly hard piece, but it was often the yardstick by which good violin playing was measured. If she could pull it off, it would be quite a coup.

It was some time since she'd played the Tchaikovsky – back before Oliver had messed with her head and her confidence – so it was going to take quite a bit of polishing to get the piece back up to scratch, but Flora had decided to set herself a big challenge. Luckily, the priest, Father Jonno, had been very good about letting her practise in the church hall several times a week.

He'd been very understanding. He got that her practice wasn't just a matter of playing through the pieces, but of playing scales and technical exercises, as well as going over and over some sections of the music with tedious repetition, and he'd been very accommodating about making the hall available.

Flora was grateful. She had her heart set on this new job in Brisbane. A fresh start.

With the tea finished, Flora closed the neglected novel and set it back on the bedside table. She turned out the lamp and lay in the dark, listening to the silence of a country town at night. So different from the constant hum of traffic and trams in Melbourne.

She remembered lying like this in her bedroom as a child at Ruthven Downs, listening to the absolute quiet of the bush, broken only by the occasional muffled snorts of cattle or the lonely cry of a curlew.

Until a few years ago, the country life was all Flora had ever known. Even her boarding school had been at Charters Towers, which was just another country town. It wasn't until she'd gone away to study at the Conservatorium in Brisbane that she'd lived in a city, and yet she'd taken to the life of a young city musician like a black duck to Lake Tinaroo.

Funny how she'd chosen such a different path from the rest of her family. On pensive, lonely nights like this, Flora thought back to the day in primary school when a specialist music teacher from Brisbane had visited their school in Mareeba, and her ambition to become a classical musician had been born.

The teacher's name was Dr Stern, and Flora could still picture exactly how he'd looked – small and neat with a bald head, fringed with curly black hair and the whitest hands she had ever seen on a man. He gave a workshop for the string students, and he was wonderfully inspiring and encouraging, even though they'd probably sounded dreadful.

Each child was required to play a short piece. Flora had played Brahms' Lullaby and she'd given it her best. When she'd finished she'd looked up and caught a subtle change in Dr Stern's expression – a lift of his eyebrows, a heightened brightness in his intelligent eyes. He'd dipped his head to her in a small bow, and afterwards, her school music teacher had told her that Dr Stern had been very impressed.

His interest was all it had taken to light the spark. Flora had already loved music, but from then on, she believed she'd found the one thing in her life that could make her unique, different from her big brother Seth who seemed to be good at so many things. She'd worked hard for her next AMEB exam and had gained an A+.

Her mother was so proud. Over the moon.

'It seems we have a violinist in the family,' she'd announced at dinner that evening.

Flora had glowed with happiness. The word violinist sounded so refined and foreign and poetic. But then she'd worried. Would her father approve? What use was a violinist to a grazier who spent his days dealing with dust and heat and cattle?

To her relief, her dad smiled. 'I'm not at all surprised. There's a creative streak in the family,' he said. 'Your Aunt Deborah's an exceptional artist. She never stopped drawing when she was a kid and still hasn't stopped.'

'So you wouldn't mind if I wanted to play in an orchestra?' Flora asked.

'Why would I mind, love? I'd be proud as punch.'

Flora and her mother had exchanged excited grins, and her mum had become her champion, encouraging Flora at every turn, and possibly becoming a tad pushy. She'd found Peg Fletcher who'd given Flora private violin lessons over at Burralea. By then Flora hadn't needed pushing. She was chasing a dream.

And she still wanted that dream now, even though Oliver had dented it severely.

Snuggling deeper into her pillow, Flora sighed. There were still times – especially times like this in the middle of the night – when she felt disillusioned and somehow ashamed for getting herself into such a mess with Oliver. She worried, too. Worried that he would hunt her down and find her if she was working with a high-profile Australian orchestra.

He had such a tenacious streak. In Melbourne, the constant barrage of his text messages had invaded her every waking moment.

Where are you? Hurry up. What's for dinner? Ring me. How long will you be? What are you up to now? I'm waiting on the corner.

His texts hadn't even let up when she'd come home to Ruthven Downs for her father's birthday.

Even now, with a new phone and so much distance between

them, Flora feared she might be safer to get out of the country.

Then, in the next breath, she reassured herself that Oliver wouldn't be interested in trying to find her. He would be too busy stroking his own ego. She, Flora, was being neurotic.

And wouldn't he love that?

It would make Oliver's day if he thought he'd made her paranoid.

CHAPTER EIGHT

The walk from the bus stop to the guesthouse was rather longer than Hattie had imagined. The way wasn't especially steep, but it was mostly uphill, and she was carrying a heavy shoulder bag and wheeling her suitcase. She didn't get very far before she regretted not having hired a car.

The climate here in the mountains wasn't as pleasant as she'd remembered either. Certainly, now in November, it was distinctly tropical and humid.

Plodding on, Hattie passed a butcher shop and a barber, a retro café with tables and chairs squeezed onto the footpath, along with pot plants and lush hanging baskets. A row of quirky little shops sold pre-loved clothing, old furniture and second-hand books. Then she had to lug her suitcase across the wide hot street that was divided in the middle by neatly mown parkland set with colourful flowerbeds. By the time she arrived on the far side at Burralea Lodge, she was quite tired and sweaty.

At least the lodge seemed to be well maintained, and it looked much the same as she remembered, built of white weatherboards with a gabled roof line and dark green trims, and surrounded by attractive, shady trees.

The woman who met her at the guesthouse's reception had a mass of salt-and-pepper curls and a beaming smile. She was probably in her fifties and Hattie thought she looked like a friendly gypsy with silver hoops in her ears, a frilly white blouse and long patchwork skirt.

Her smile turned to a worried frown when she saw Hattie. 'Oh, you haven't walked all this way in the heat, have you, love? You should have rung me. I would have sent Barry down to the bus stop to collect you.'

'Oh, well.' Hattie could be philosophical now the exertion was behind her. 'I daresay the exercise was good for me.'

'Not in this heat,' the woman tut-tutted. 'I'm April, by the way.' She extended her hand and silver bracelets tinkled.

'Pleased to meet you, April.'

'Now, we have you booked in for two nights. Is that right?'

'Yes, thanks.' Hattie couldn't imagine needing any more time here. 'I'm only here on —' Hattie hesitated. She'd been about to claim that she was here on business, but that could become complicated if she was expected to elaborate on what kind of business. 'I just wanted to take another look at the town,' she said instead. 'I used to live here many years ago, when I was a girl.'

'How lovely!' April was thoroughly delighted now. 'So you'll be catching up with old friends?'

'That's the plan, yes.'

'Well, let me know if I can be of any help.'

'I will, thank you.'

April rose from her chair at the computer. 'Will you be all right taking the stairs up to your room? I'm afraid we don't have a lift.'

'Yes, yes, thank you. I'll be fine.'

'I'll bring your bags.'

'Thank you.'

Hattie took the stairs slowly while April bounced ahead, as if the luggage was feather-light.

'Here you are, darling.' April pushed open a door to a room that was quite spacious and clean with attractive aqua and white accents in the decor. 'There's your bathroom through there,' April said pointing. 'And you have air conditioning if you want it. The remote's in a drawer beside the bed.'

'Lovely.'

There were also French doors that had been opened to catch a breeze. The doors led to a private shaded balcony with a small table and two chairs.

'We serve the evening meal downstairs in the dining room,' April explained, almost apologetically. 'But you're welcome to have your breakfast up here, if you'd prefer, wherever suits you. I can bring some afternoon tea up for you now, if you like.'

'Oh, that would be perfect,' Hattie told her gratefully.

She had just enough time to freshen up before April returned bearing a tray with a floral teapot, a matching milk jug and sugar bowl, and a pretty plate of scones with jam and cream.

'There, I'll leave you to it,' April said as she set the tray on the verandah table. 'Ring me if you want anything else. Anything at all, and I'm only too happy to help.'

Hattie thanked her sincerely. April's willingness to please was reassuring, as was her outgoing friendly manner, often in short supply in the city. 'I'm sure I'll be very comfortable.'

Hattie enjoyed her afternoon tea very much. The verandah was shaded by a huge old jacaranda tree that was fully in flower, and the tree was so utterly majestic with its beautifully romantic canopy of delicate mauve flowers, Hattie stopped feeling hot and tired and began to look forward to her stay.

She would wait till tomorrow, however, before she started making inquiries about Joe.

*

April was at the reception desk, doing something on her computer, when Hattie came downstairs. She flashed Hattie another of her huge smiles.

'Just taking a little walk in the cool of the evening,' Hattie told her. She'd had a short nap and felt quite recovered from her journey, and she was keen to see how much of the town she remembered. She would like to see the house where she used to live and she might even be brave enough to walk past Joe's house, just to cast a curious eye over the place.

She thought about asking April if she knew Joe Matthews. The woman was sure to know him in a little place like this, where everybody knew everybody else. But then she decided it was wisest not to mention him, or to ask about the latest news regarding the bones. Heaven knew where or how the conversation might be reported.

'Off to do a little exploring,' she said instead.

'Lovely. Dinner's at seven.'

Hattie waved. 'I won't be late.'

It was cooler now. The sun was retreating behind the tall stand of rainforest that ringed the town. Everything was quiet; the only sounds were birds, calling to each other at the end of the day. She'd forgotten how the birds did that. She'd lived in the city too long.

She remembered living here as a girl all those years ago and listening to birds at dusk. She used to wonder what messages they were communicating.

Come home, it's almost dark.

See you tomorrow.

You want to sleep at my place?

Hattie was smiling at the memory when she saw the small wooden church, set back in a smooth lawn with clumps of agapanthus beside the wooden front steps. It looked almost exactly the same as it had on the day she'd watched Joe posing for photographs with his bride.

She came to a standstill, surprised by the hurtful sting the memory brought. She'd got over him long ago, hadn't she?

For a moment, Hattie wondered if she'd made a very serious mistake in coming back to a place from her past that she'd so resolutely set behind her. Then she gave herself a mental shake. The only aspect of the past that she needed to resurrect with Joe was a single event from their childhood on that afternoon when they were trapping finches. Nothing more. Besides, her life hadn't turned out so badly, and the pain wasn't anywhere near as bad now as it had been back then.

Old age did have its advantages.

About to walk on, she was arrested by music coming from the little hall beside the church. Violin music.

Once again, she came to a complete halt, standing on the footpath in a gentle breeze. The music was beautiful. Exquisite and hauntingly familiar.

Tchaikovsky, if she wasn't mistaken. His violin concerto was the last thing she'd expected to hear being played now in this tiny Far North Queensland country town. How wonderful. Not only was it being played, but played extremely well.

It brought an aching tightness to Hattie's throat.

She loved this piece and she'd listened to it many times over the years, but now she found herself remembering the very first time she'd ever heard similar music being played. Perhaps it was an affliction of old age to be so assaulted by memories?

First, a simple news story about bones had woken such strong and unsettling recollections from her childhood that she'd made her way north to find Joe. And now, a few bars of music had aroused another flood. This time she was remembering Shanghai, walking with her amah, holding tight to her hand.

Despite the decades in between, vivid pictures flashed of Shanghai in those turbulent days. Hattie could see the burnt-out fields and flattened buildings, alongside the colour and confusion of busy city life. Trucks and rickshaws and bicycles, and quiet gardens behind high brick walls. Car horns, bicycle bells, pedlars calling their wares, people yelling at each other in half a dozen languages.

The afternoon walk with Ah Lan. And the music.

Hattie's grandmother had insisted that Hattie and her amah take long walks in the afternoons. She'd claimed they needed the exercise, but neither of them had liked walking much. Hattie was rather afraid of the Japanese bombing in the distance, even though it was part of normal life in Shanghai in the late 1930s, and it was all happening 'over the river'.

Ah Lan could only totter on her tiny bound feet, so she didn't like to go very far either. Instead of walking long distances, Ah Lan often visited her relatives and took Hattie along. Hattie could remember the small room with a low ceiling and a pervading smell from an open drain that ran the length of the alley outside. In one corner of the room, Ah Lan's old, wrinkled grandmother stitched embroidered slippers to sell at the markets. In another corner, a group of men played mahjong.

A charcoal stove in the middle of the room filled the space with smoke, and sometimes Hattie was offered food – eel stewed in oil and garlic, strange vegetables and dumplings. On one occasion, Ah Lan's grandmother allowed Hattie to try on a pair of white embroidered slippers. She'd danced for them and everyone had stopped what they were doing to watch her, their gazes expressionless – inscrutable – and she'd had no idea whether they were pleased or angry.

On other afternoons, Ah Lan had taken Hattie to visit her own relatives. Hattie's Aunt Lily and Uncle Rudi lived on Avenue Joffre, and it was at their place that she'd first heard this music.

Now, in Burralea, as the skilful, unseen violinist continued with the lush, soul-stirring strains, more of Hattie's childhood came flooding back.

She could see herself and Ah Lan approaching the apartment block set back from the street behind a row of liquid ambers. And incredible music, just like this, came tumbling and floating through a window and down the street. Before this, Hattie had heard her uncle play simple tunes on his violin, but this time the music was even more beautiful than usual – sad, but exciting too – so she had assumed it was coming from a radio.

Eager to see her aunt and uncle, she had run ahead and poor Ah Lan had no hope of keeping up. When Hattie reached the doorway she saw her Uncle Rudi standing in the middle of their tiled lounge room and it was he who was making these wonderful sounds.

He stopped playing when he saw Hattie and simply stood there smiling, holding his violin in one hand and the bow in the other. He was a wonderfully handsome man with big broad shoulders and wild dark hair, and his white shirt front open low to reveal his powerful chest and curling dark hair. His lovely dark eyes were gentle as he smiled at her.

Then her Aunt Lily, wearing red lipstick and a long, floaty silver dress, came hurrying forward, her thin white arms outstretched, the high heels of her jewelled sandals clicking on the tiles.

'Hello, my dearest duckling.' She kneeled down and hugged Hattie, holding her close and enveloping her in her flowery scent.

Hattie wasn't quite sure how she'd arrived at the door of the little church hall. She'd been so caught up with the music and her memories she must have drifted across the grass like someone in a trance.

Now she was suddenly inside the doorway, and face to face with the person responsible for the music, a young woman with dark hair cut in a trendy style, and dressed in a simple singlet top, shorts and sandals. In these clothes, she looked little more than a girl.

Then she saw Hattie and the music stopped abruptly, a startling echo of her memory when Hattie had interrupted Rudi.

'Oh, hello,' the girl said now with a smile. 'Can I help you?'

Hattie felt very foolish. 'I'm sorry. I heard your lovely music and I was so entranced —'

'Well, thank you.' The violinist smiled again, this time making an attractive dimple in one cheek. 'I'm glad you liked it.'

'It's Tchaikovsky, isn't it?'

'Yes.' The girl looked pleased. 'I'm just rehearsing.'

'It's wonderful. You're very good.'

'Thanks.' She smiled again. 'You're welcome to listen if you like.' She nodded to rows of plastic chairs stacked against a wall.

Hattie hesitated. For a moment she thought how much she would enjoy sitting here and having a private concert, but then she remembered. This wasn't a performance. The poor young woman was trying to rehearse. 'No, I don't want to impose,' she said quickly. 'I – I should have kept walking.'

But already the girl had set down her violin and bow on a folding card table, and she was lifting a chair from the nearest stack. 'Here you are,' she said. 'You might have to put up with some mistakes and scratchy bits, but you're welcome to sit for a bit.'

'Thank you.' Hattie didn't really want to refuse. The walk around Burralea could wait.

'I'm Flora, by the way,' the girl said as she picked up her instrument again. 'Flora Drummond.'

'Lovely to meet you, Flora. I'm Hattie.'

Flora nodded, and Hattie sat as directed, and the rehearsal continued.

Hattie thought how strange it was that this church should bring such a coincidence of memories for her. On the very same day that she'd stood here in the rain, heartbroken as she witnessed Joe with his bride, Rose had also told her the truth about those tumultuous days in Shanghai.

CHAPTER NINE

Shanghai, 1935

Rose pushed through the jostling crowds on the busy wharf, desperate for her first sight of her sister, Lily. In front of her loomed the magnificent P&O liner that had brought her sister from England, while beyond, a string of Japanese warships stood to attention and a host of little bamboo-roofed sampans crisscrossed the crowded Huangpu River like a flock of purposeful fishing birds.

'Rose! Rose!'

She heard an excited shout, saw a waving, white-gloved hand, the flash of a gold bracelet around a thin, pale wrist. Lily, at last, looking glamorous in a smart new crimson hat, and yet, just as Rose remembered her. Extraordinarily pretty and super excited.

The sisters hadn't seen each other in two years, but it felt longer, as if several centuries had passed.

'Oh, Rose, it's so good to see you at last.' Lily hugged her hard, almost squeezing the breath from her. 'I'm quite sure I would have died if I'd had to spend another day at sea. It's so good to be here. Isn't this place wonderful? It's all so thrilling!'

Lily's blue eyes were huge as she looked around her, trying to take everything in. She didn't seem nearly as overawed by the exotic chaos of the Shanghai docks as Rose had been when she'd arrived two years earlier. Like Lily, Rose had made the journey east to join their parents as soon as she'd finished the two-year college course that would provide her with the requisite 'polish'.

Their father worked for the Bank of England here in Shanghai.

'It's too good a chance to pass up,' he had assured them. 'Landing a solid position in this bank is like getting into Eton.'

Their parents had been in Shanghai for over five years now, while their daughters had remained in England at boarding school and then college, spending their term holidays with their grand-parents in Devon. At the end of her college course, Rose hadn't been at all keen to leave her homeland to live in faraway China. At least, she hadn't been keen until she'd met a certain handsome English merchant seaman called Stephen Bellamy.

'I have a car and a driver waiting at the customs jetty,' she told Lily now. 'It shouldn't be too long before we can fight our way clear of here.'

Lily didn't seem to be in any kind of hurry to leave. She was too busy staring about her at the teeming humanity on the wharves. Chanting coolies in dark-blue pantaloons and muddy straw sandals hauled bundles of dockside cargo. Passengers, sailors and traders of various nationalities dodged dangerously overloaded bicycles. And beyond this was a backdrop of tall, neoclassic banks and office buildings that lined The Bund, running from Sir Victor Sassoon's landmark Cathay Hotel at one end to the Hong Kong and Shanghai Bank at the other.

'This end of town is crazy,' Rose warned her sister. 'It's much quieter in the French Concession.'

'Who wants quiet?' asked Lily. 'I've been on a boat for almost two months. I love all this madness. It's wonderful.'

'How are you, anyway?' Rose asked her quickly. 'How was the voyage? Did you manage to enjoy yourself?'

'I did, actually. There were the usual boring "pudding" types on board, but there were some jolly interesting people as well.'

Rose waited for Lily to expand on this. When she didn't, she asked, cautiously, 'Any shipboard romances?'

'Well, I wasn't like you, Rose. I didn't get myself engaged to be married to the very first Englishman I met.'

'Any more talk like that and I'll ban you from being my bridesmaid,' Rose retorted.

'Oh, Rosie, you know I'm only teasing.'

This was true. Rose was well acquainted with Lily's teasing. Just the same, she didn't appreciate having her cheeky little sister make judgements about her engagement to Stephen before she'd even met him. And anyway, she'd been in Shanghai for at least six months before she'd fallen in love.

To change the subject, she asked, 'Where's Mrs Pemberton?'

'Zara?' Lily shrugged. 'I'm not exactly sure. Why?'

'Shouldn't she be with you? Glued to your side? Didn't Mother arrange for her to be your chaperone?'

'Well, yes. We shared a stateroom and I think Mother did have some sort of chaperone arrangement.'

'Some sort, Lily? What on earth do you mean?' Alarmed, Rose peered about her, standing on tiptoes to see over shoulders. 'What's happened to Mrs Pemberton? Where is she?'

Lily laughed and gave another careless shrug. 'Heavens, darling, don't get in a stew. I didn't need a chaperone. And if Mother believed that I did need one, she should have researched more carefully before she made her selection. Most of the time Zara was too busy with her typewriter. She's far too intent on becoming a famous authoress to keep watch over silly little me every second of the day and night.'

Rose frowned. 'I don't think we should share that information with Mother.'

Lily gave yet another shrug and a silky little laugh that sent an unwanted ripple of disquiet through Rose. She had the disturbing suspicion that her younger sister's adventurous spirit had become even wilder during the past two years. She hated to imagine the mischief Lily might have found herself in during a long, mostly unsupervised sea voyage. It was going to be a challenge to keep an eye on her now in Shanghai, with its glamorous hotels and nightclubs, its endless stream of parties and dinners, but it was important that Lily learned the dos and don'ts of Shanghai's international world.

At last they cleared through Customs, Lily's luggage of wardrobe trunks, shoe boxes and dressing cases were safely stowed, and the Challinors' number-one boy, who was chauffeuring, carefully steered their car away from the busy docks.

Lily sat forward in her seat with her nose almost pressed against the window glass, straining to see every detail in the crowded streets – the riot of signboards with huge gilded characters hanging on metal framework, the beggar children crouched in gutters, the barefooted rickshaw pullers and the trams hurtling past.

They came to a busy intersection where bicycles jostled with shiny black American cars and with carts loaded with fruit and vegetables. A street vendor hawked steaming buns and sweet cakes. A Sikh policeman in a red turban blew his whistle to let two Chinese girls run through the traffic in *cheongsams* that flipped open to the hip.

'Ohhh,' cried Lily, her eyes and mouth open wide. 'Aren't those girls lovely?'

Now it was Rose who gave a deliberate shrug to show her lack of interest. Like her parents, her only contact with the Chinese came via their servants. Their servants were *very good*, admittedly, but while the Chinese were industrious and even-tempered people, they weren't a society that the British folk openly admired.

There'd been plenty of disparaging comments from her father's friends at dinner parties.

'Frankly, once you've seen one pagoda, you've seen them all.'

'Yes, of course I've tried eating Chinese food, when I had no other option. I don't think I've yet recovered from the experience. It felt like going native.'

There had been nods of approval around the dinner table and while comments like these had made Rose uncomfortable, she'd accepted that this was the best way to survive the veritable hotchpotch of nationalities in Shanghai. As well as the British and Chinese, there were American, French and Portuguese businessmen, and huge numbers of refugees, especially White Russians and German Jews.

Also, Rose had read in newspapers that many more Chinese were arriving in the city each day, desperate to escape the raging battles between Chiang Kai-shek and the communists. Added to this mix, large numbers of Japanese had remained a menacing presence ever since their bombing of this city, which most people referred to these days as 'the trouble in '32'.

The balance of cultures was complicated and delicate, and Rose felt it her duty to make sure that Lily understood all of this. Life would be much easier and safer for her sister if she accepted the fundamental rule that most British expats seemed to know instinctively. There was only one sensible way to cope in this incredibly international metropolis and that was to remain deliberately aloof and to mix almost exclusively in safe, familiar circles. *British* circles, of course.

If you followed this common-sense rule, it was possible to thoroughly enjoy life in the Far East. Shanghai provided a wonderfully glamorous lifestyle. Their parents' three-storey house on rue Cardinal Mercier was much grander than their old house in Sussex.

Here there were huge and spacious reception rooms and several lovely bathrooms tiled in black and white, as well as bedrooms equipped with Irish linen bedsheets, monogrammed by hand. And so many servants you never needed to lift a finger.

The social life was hectic and fun, too, with fierce competition between hostesses all vying to put on the best dinner parties. Of course, the Chinese boys did all the cooking, so an ordinary dinner could be ridiculously lavish with two kinds of soup, followed by fish and then an entrée of some sort, a bird, beef, and three or four different puddings.

They really did live very well and there was plenty to amuse them – Russian orchestras and ballets at the Lyceum theatre, films from all over the world, summer garden parties with two bands playing and women in flowing silk dresses of every pretty hue. They even had a racetrack right in the centre of the city and a country club on Bubbling Well Road that provided sixty-five acres of landscaped gardens, as well as a ballroom, tennis courts and a swimming pool.

Rose knew Lily would love the life here as long as she wasn't too distracted by its exotic underbelly. She just needed to keep a close eye on her little sister until she settled in.

Rose and Stephen moved into a place of their own soon after they returned from their honeymoon. Their apartment in the French Concession wasn't nearly as big or grand as Rose's parents' house, but it was well designed to catch plenty of sunlight, and the young couple didn't mind its smallness in the least. They were too excited about setting up their home and embarking on the huge fun of selecting furniture. There was a wonderful range in the huge, multi-storey department stores on Nanking Road.

With everything in place, including Axminster carpets on the floors, gold-framed paintings on the walls and palm trees growing in porcelain tubs, Rose invited her parents and Lily to dinner.

She was very proud of her conscientious preparations. Shopping on Nanking Road she'd chosen special cuts of beef from the dignified British butcher at Dombey's, and she'd gone to Lane Crawford, a British emporium that specialised in imported cheeses, Danish butter and powdered milk. Finally, she'd bought delectable macaroons and chocolates at Bianchi's, the Italian bakery.

To Rose's relief, her first little attempt at hostessing went well. Their newly furnished rooms were duly admired and their Chinese boys produced an excellent four-course meal. Stephen was a considerate host, making a fine selection of wines, and the dinner conversation was very pleasant. The evening was an undoubted success.

She and Stephen were happy and felt quite 'established' as they stood in the front doorway waving the Challinors off.

'That went well,' Stephen said.

Rose slipped her arms around her brand-new husband and kissed his jaw. 'You were a perfect host.'

'Your parents were at their charming best. They made it easy.'

'But you were very good with Lily, too. You smoothed things over when she got Mother on edge by insisting on talking about that supposedly interesting Chinese fellow she's met.'

'Chu Yuan?' Stephen smiled as he closed the door and they came inside. 'Your mother did make a fuss, didn't she? But I have no doubt the fellow is interesting. He was educated in Paris, you know, and he's been to America.'

'Yes,' Rose said with a sigh. 'I know.'

'What's the matter?' Fondly, Stephen tucked a wing of Rose's hair behind her ear.

'I'm worried about Lily.'

'Darling, when have you *not* been worried about your little sister? You know you nearly ruined our honeymoon by worrying about her.'

Rose was appalled. 'Don't say that.' She'd adored every moment of their honeymoon. Stephen had surprised her with a cruise to Australia, where they'd stayed on a tropical island and were driven by coach into rainforest-covered mountains where they'd spent three nights in a beautiful, lakeside hotel.

It was incredibly romantic. Each day, Rose had fallen more deeply in love with her husband. She hated to think she might have done anything to spoil that precious time. 'Stephen, tell me I didn't ruin our honeymoon.'

'Well, no, of course you didn't, sweet girl.' Cradling her hands between both of his, Stephen kissed her fingers.

They smiled at each other over their clasped hands. Stephen's light brown eyes shone with special warmth, just for Rose, and she thought, for possibly the ten-thousandth time, how lucky she was to have married such a lovely man.

From the kitchen at the back of the house came the clatter of dishes being washed. Rose and Stephen went through to their bed-room and closed the door, and Rose sat on the stool in front of her dressing table. She took off her pearls and her earrings and stowed them in a crystal bowl. Stephen slipped off his tie, hung it neatly on the rack inside his wardrobe door.

'You have to admit you were worried about Lily while we were on that cruise,' he said as he sat on the end of their new double bed to untie his shoelaces. 'But while we were away she wasn't arrested or kidnapped or shot. She was absolutely fine.'

'Yes, I know she *seems* fine. On the surface.'

'On the surface?' Stephen dropped a shoe onto the carpet and his gaze narrowed. 'What do you mean? What's the problem?'

'Well, for one thing, Lily's far too easily influenced by Zara Pemberton. I don't know how Mother ever imagined that woman would be a suitable chaperone. On the voyage out here, she put all sorts of dangerous ideas into Lily's head.'

Her husband frowned, but he didn't look convinced as he began to unbutton his shirt.

Rose tried to make her point clearer. 'Zara Pemberton lives by different rules from the rest of us. She's completely Bohemian. Mixes with absolutely anyone. The latest news is, she's taken up with a Chinaman – the same one Lily was raving about at dinner. Can you believe it? He has tons of money, of course, but that's not the point. Zara's moved in with him. She's living with him as his lover, bold as brass. I haven't dared to tell Mother, but I suppose she'll hear soon enough.'

'But that doesn't mean Lily's going to copy her, Rose. You have to give the girl some credit.'

Rose shook her head. 'There's worse. Lily met a chap while we were away in Australia. A White Russian.'

'Ah.' This time Stephen's expression was gratifyingly serious.

'He's called Rudi Vas . . . I don't know, Rudi Vastinov or some such thing. She's quite smitten.'

'What is he? A former Russian prince? The son of a university lecturer? A musician?'

'A musician, I understand. A violinist.'

'And a handsome devil, no doubt.'

'Frightfully handsome if Lily is to be believed. Handsome and romantic and wonderfully talented.'

Stephen nodded. 'That's the White Russian dilemma, of course.'

'If Lily takes up with him, it will be our dilemma too.'

Rose frowned at her reflection in the dressing-table mirror. She and Stephen were both aware of the tricky situation this new liaison might pose. While the White Russians had once been members of Russia's upper and middle classes and pledged loyalty to the Czar, they had been forced to flee for their lives when the communists took over and now they were refugees.

In Shanghai and other parts of China, the White Russians now lacked Russian citizenship, but they also missed out on the benefits of extraterritoriality that had been granted to the British and most other foreigners. While they hadn't been completely rejected, they hadn't been fully accepted. Even in the middle of the 1930s, they were still stateless and their position in society was uncertain. Precarious.

Rose had heard her father talking about how the White Russians had long since used up any money they'd smuggled out of Russia. These days, they weren't welcomed into business circles and, while many of them were well educated and came from backgrounds very similar to the British, it was generally understood that they weren't to be trusted.

'They're unstable and corrupt,' he'd declared. 'Hopelessly sentimental and romantic.' Of course, the older generation of British still thought of themselves as entirely superior. Only an English public school could produce an English gentleman, and only an English gentleman could be trusted.

Stephen got up from the bed and stood, shirtless, behind Rose. She watched him in the mirror as he gently massaged her shoulders. 'Are you sure you're not jumping the gun here, darling? I mean, Lily's only just met the chap.'

'She's quite taken with him, Stephen. And she can't understand why she shouldn't be allowed to fall in love with him.'

'Does he have a job?'

'Well, yes, he plays in the Shanghai Symphony Orchestra.' Frowning, Rose turned from the mirror and looked up at her husband. 'But that's not the point.'

Stephen stopped massaging and let out a sigh. 'What do your parents have to say?'

'I'm not sure. I haven't broached it with them yet. I'm confident they'll try to pull Lily into line. But she already knows the dangers. She certainly knows about the fellow at Father's bank who was sacked because he married a White Russian girl. I tried to explain it's like marrying a Eurasian. It's simply not done.'

'This shouldn't be your problem,' Stephen said.

'Maybe not, but Mother and Father have such busy social lives they don't really pay proper attention. You heard them tonight, all atwitter about an invitation to the ambassador's place for the King's birthday. Anyway, I think Lily believes that our parents surrendered their authority years ago, when they came out here and left us at home. That's certainly how she behaves.'

'Rose.' Reaching for her hands, Stephen pulled her gently from the seat. 'We've had a lovely evening. Let's not spoil it by worrying about Lily.'

He slipped his arms around her waist and drew her against his bare chest. 'I'm sure this will work out. Lily might be impetuous, but she's no fool. She'll be fine. Besides, you do know what they say about Russian men, don't you?'

'I'm not sure. Do I?'

'They're reputed to be exceptional lovers.'

Rose looked up to check her husband's expression. 'You're pulling my leg, aren't you?'

'Not at all. I've heard all sorts of incredible stories about the Russians' amazing powers of seduction.'

Rose shrugged. 'I've only heard stories about the French and Italian lovers.'

'Oh?'

Tracing a line with her fingertip over his chest, she smiled. 'But I don't listen to gossip. I prefer to have firsthand knowledge. And I happen to know, from blissful personal experience, that at least one British chap is unbeatable in the bedroom.'

'Well, there you go.' Smiling, Stephen nuzzled the curve of her neck. 'And you and I are wasting precious time.'

He kissed her chin, the soft swell of her lower lip. 'I'm going to sea again soon and I'll miss you so much.'

Oh, Stephen. An ache of longing bloomed in Rose. Why on earth was she obsessing about Lily when Stephen would soon have to leave her? She was going to miss him too. Dreadfully.

Winding her arms around his neck, she kissed him, savouring the texture of his lips, the warmth of his bare skin, the firm muscles that rippled as he tightened his embrace. Tonight her kiss was even more fervent than usual, tinged with both longing and fear.

In just a few weeks of marriage, she'd discovered so many special depths to this man, including his kindness and steady good sense. And she'd been honest when she'd praised his bedroom skills. She adored the special, exciting intimacy that flowed so spontaneously between them.

She hated to let him go.

Of course, she had known from the start that it wasn't going to be easy to be married to a merchant seaman, but until this moment she'd really never allowed herself to think too hard about what it would be like when Stephen was away at sea.

Now, she had no choice. The honeymoon was over. Stephen was returning to his work, and the reality of life as his wife was about to begin.

CHAPTER TEN

Burralea, 2015

Flora felt decidedly upbeat as she walked back to the cottage through the gathering dusk. The practice had gone well. No doubt she'd tried extra hard to impress the interesting, elderly Hattie, who had become her impromptu audience, but whatever the cause, Flora was feeling quite satisfied with her progress.

She reached her front gate as her phone rang. Her immediate reaction was a spike of fear, but, of course, it couldn't be Oliver. She'd given a few carefully selected people her new number and now she recognised her old music teacher's name in the caller ID. The swirl of panic settled.

'Hello, Peg,' she said as she pushed the gate open.

'Is that you, Flora?'

'Yes, how are you?'

'I'm . . . okay.'

The 'okay' didn't sound very confident. Flora heard a disturbing quiver in Peg's normally cheery voice.

'But I'm ringing from the hospital in Atherton,' Peg said.

Flora frowned. 'You're not a patient, are you?'

'Well, yes, I'm afraid I am.'

'Peg, what's happened?' Flora's mind raced through possibilities. Peg didn't sound desperately ill, but perhaps she was being brave.

'Nothing too drastic,' Peg quickly reassured her. 'I'm fine, really, or at least I *will* be fine. It's just that I've had a bit of a fall. I've managed to bruise my shoulder and ribs rather badly, and I've broken my ankle.'

'But that's terrible. You poor thing.'

'I feel so foolish. I missed my footing going down the stairs. I'm not used to my new multifocal glasses, you see. Anyway, it's no great drama, but they're keeping me here overnight.'

'Can I bring you anything?' Flora asked. 'What do you need? Clothes? Something to read?'

'No, I really don't need anything, thank you, dear. My neighbour has been very helpful and I'm being very well looked after.'

'Right. I see. But is there anything I can do to help?' Flora knew Peg lived alone and she would almost certainly need help at home after she was released. 'I could cook up a few extra meals,' she suggested. 'You'll need someone to help you with cooking and —'

'It's all right, Flora,' Peg cut in almost brusquely. 'That can all be arranged quite easily. You really don't need to worry about feeding me. That's not why I'm ringing, dear. My main worry is the Burralea Christmas Concert.'

'Oh.' A new edge of wariness had crept into Flora's voice. She knew nothing about a Christmas concert.

'I usually produce quite a lively show, but I can't see how I'll be able to cope with it now. They're telling me I might need to be in a wheelchair at first. I can't use crutches because of the bruising.'

'You poor thing,' Flora said again.

'I was wondering if you could possibly help, Flora.'

'Oh? I – I see.' Flora was a little ashamed of the way her spirits took a dive. She'd been fine with the thought of whipping up a few meals for Peg, or offering to do her shopping. But a Christmas concert?

Flora had no plans to become involved with the local community. These few weeks in Burralea were all about focusing on herself. Her audition.

As she wrestled with these thoughts, a curtain flickered at a window next door. It was bound to be Edith Little keeping an eye on her. Flora had only spoken to her elderly neighbour once so far and the woman hadn't been particularly friendly.

She mounted the front steps, felt in her pocket for the key and pushed it into the lock.

'Are you still there?' Peg asked.

'Yes, sorry, Peg. Just letting myself into the house.'

'I've caught you at a bad moment.'

'No, no, I'm inside now.' Flora eased the strap of her violin case from her shoulder, set the case on a chair and pushed the door closed behind her. 'Okay, where were we? What was that about a Christmas concert?'

'It's a children's concert. I've been doing it for the past few years and it's become very popular in the town. People are looking forward to it, especially the children. I know it's a lot to ask of you, Flora.'

'Well, I have my audition.'

'Yes, I know, dear, and that has to be your priority. But the concert's only a few weeks away – early, so it doesn't clash with all the parents' Christmas dos, and I'm sure you could manage it beautifully. There's a choir and a nativity play and a little orchestra.'

Flora gulped as she sank quickly onto the arm of the sofa. A choir, a nativity play *and* a little orchestra? *Really?*

It all sounded totally terrifying. She had absolutely zilch teaching experience, and she didn't need this kind of pressure. She really needed to get this orchestra position. Among other things, it would prove to Oliver that he hadn't browbeaten her into helplessness. She didn't want anything to upset the heavy rehearsal schedule she had planned.

'I know it's a huge thing to ask when you're already so busy rehearsing.' Peg sounded worried and a little nervous now.

Well, yes, Flora wanted to tell her. *It's a huge thing to ask. Enormous. Too much. I'm so sorry.*

She took a deep breath. 'Do you normally look after all of those projects by yourself?'

'Father Jonno is a big help with the nativity play. I'm sure if I spoke to him, he'd take on full responsibility for that. But I can't really think of anyone else who could look after the musical items, particularly the orchestra. Both Lisa and Josh are heading off as soon as the school term finishes.'

A stone seemed to have lodged in Flora's throat. She swallowed, but it didn't help much.

What could she do?

If this request had come from anyone else, she would have found it perfectly easy to give a polite but flat refusal. But this was Peg. How could she refuse Peg? The woman had been her inspiration, her tirelessly patient and insightful teacher. Her greatest cheer squad.

Flora knew she would never have achieved her musical dreams without Peg's guidance and support.

Closing her eyes, she tried to think about this calmly, but her brain immediately flashed up discouraging pictures of kids running amok while she frantically tried to call them to order. She opened her eyes again, banishing the unhelpful scene, and took another, deeper, breath.

'Well, I – I guess I could give it a go, Peg.' *Oh, God, had she really said that?* 'But I have to warn you, I honestly have no experience in this sort of thing. I've never worked with children.'

'Oh, that's okay, dear. You'll be wonderful. Thank you so much, Flora. It's such a weight off my mind.' Peg was bubbling now. 'They're good children. They'll love you, and you'll love them, too, I'm sure. And I'll give you as many pointers as I can.'

'I'm sure I'll need all the advice you can think of.'

'Of course,' Peg said firmly. There was a small silence before she asked, almost querulously, 'You don't mind, do you, dear?'

It was too late to go back. 'No, of course not.' Flora was glad Peg couldn't see the way she was wincing. 'I'm sure it will be a good experience for me. Now, you stop worrying. You need to get all the rest you can. Make the most of your night in hospital.'

After she disconnected, Flora sat staring glumly at her violin case. As a child, she'd enjoyed playing in school orchestras, but then she'd always been painfully obedient and eager to please. She had memories of other kids mucking up, never paying attention, playing hopelessly out of tune and with all the wrong timing. She was sure she wouldn't have the patience to deal with all that.

She thought about this afternoon's practice and the luxury of having the church hall to herself, apart from an appreciative audience of one.

Now. This.

She hadn't thought to ask Peg how much time might be taken up with rehearsals. She hadn't even asked exactly when the concert was to be held. What if —

Bloody hell. There were so many what ifs.

Flora didn't want to feel stressed. *Damn.* She was still trying to put the turmoil of her final months in Melbourne behind her. Now, just thinking about how she might manage a hall full of children made her break out in a sweat. She'd never been a bossy type.

She began to gnaw on a thumbnail and quickly stopped herself.

She'd learned, when she'd first left rural Far North Queensland to study at the busy, big city Conservatorium, that her best way to de-stress was to go for a run. That was what she needed now – a run down to the lake and back. There was no point in sitting here fretting.

*

It was close to dark, and nice and cool. Having changed into shorts and joggers, Flora set off, running through the quiet streets. Everything was very familiar as she ran past the hairdresser's and the bakery that were now shut, past the quaint rows of timber cottages where scents lingered from a flowering creeper that was growing over someone's chook pen.

From gardens came the tinkling voices of children playing in the last of the light, and the hiss of a sprinkler. Further on a lawnmower was still roaring away.

The road wound out of town past a new housing development with larger, brick homes looking very new as they sat in the middle of bare, unlandscaped blocks. Then, on Flora's right, open green fields rolled down to a narrow finger of water, one of the lake's many deep-reaching tentacles.

She saw a row of ancient and twisted fir trees that looked as if they belonged in a Tolkien tale. She went past the boat shed that belonged to the rowing club and the caravan park where retirees put director's chairs in front of their vans and sat drinking wine from plastic glasses as they enjoyed the view of the lake. Finally, she arrived at the picnic grounds with a memorial to soldiers who had died in Afghanistan.

At the lake's edge, she stopped, panting a little from the exercise. The sun had almost disappeared now. All that was left was a narrow golden rim along the low hills on the far side of the water. Faint pearlescent tinges of pink and gold remained, a soft shimmer on the mirror-like surface of the lake. So pretty, so still and peaceful.

Flora stayed for a moment or two, thinking about all the years she'd lived in this district, but further out in the bush at Ruthven Downs. Now, having sold the family farm, her parents were planning to retire here near this lake, and she thought how pleasant it would be for them.

She watched a couple paddling a canoe, and followed a flotilla of ducks as they glided in and out of the reeds near the bank. A pelican came into land on the water, like a high-precision jet, touching down smoothly, making hardly a ripple.

A dog from one of the caravans scampered down to the shore, barking madly. The ducks took off in fright, but the pelican merely glided off into deeper water.

Flora smiled. There was no doubt she felt calmer now, and she turned to run back. It was completely dark by the time she reached the village again. Streetlights cast their beams over quiet, dark gardens. The children had disappeared inside. The mower was silent. Lights shone from windows. She saw a family sitting at a dining table and caught the flicker of an occasional television screen as she jogged past.

She was almost home when Edith's front door opened, spilling yellow light down the front steps. A tall, masculine figure appeared, framed in the doorway, dressed in a policeman's uniform.

Mitch.

'Just remember to use that doorstopper now, Edith,' he called, waving to the small figure, silhouetted behind him.

Edith's door closed and Flora waited for him on the footpath.

'Hey, there,' he said as he came through the gateway.

At least he sounded happier to see her than he had the other day when she'd gone to his office. In the light from the street lamp, Flora actually saw him smile.

'I promised I'd get Edith a doorstop,' he said, 'so now it's safely delivered.'

'That's a good idea. Hopefully it will solve the door-slamming issues.'

'Yeah.' Mitch stood, shoulders squared, hands on hips, letting his dark gaze run over Flora's skimpy attire. He grinned. 'Been for a run?'

'Yep.' It was silly to feel self-conscious. 'Brushing away a few cobwebs. I practised for ages this afternoon and I could feel my shoulders getting tight. Thought a run might help to loosen things up a bit.'

'How far'd you go?'

'Just down to the lake and back.'

Mitch nodded. The overhead streetlight caught the sheen of his black hair, the flash of his dark eyes. He had the face of a movie star and the shoulders of a front-row forward.

What the hell had Angie been thinking when she walked away from this guy?

Carefully, perhaps *too* carefully, Flora asked, 'How are you, Mitch?'

His jaw hardened. 'Yeah, I'm good, thanks.'

Clearly, it was the wrong question. Now he was on edge. Flora supposed he was dead scared this conversation was going to turn personal and hark back to last weekend and his wedding debacle.

She grabbed at a safer question. 'I suppose you've been pretty busy since those bones turned up on Seth's property?'

'It's been full on,' Mitch agreed. 'The poor bloke's had detectives and forensics crawling all over the site.'

'I suppose you're heavily involved as well.'

'That, too.'

'I hate the idea of human bones turning up on Seth's property,' Flora said softly. 'It's kind of spooky, isn't it?'

Mitch nodded. 'He certainly didn't need that complication.'

He smiled at her again and looked relaxed now, and it was on the tip of her tongue to invite him in to her place. She had been planning to make a nice mushroom risotto tonight. It wouldn't take long to cook and they could enjoy a glass of wine and a chat.

Too easily, she could picture Mitch perched on a stool in her kitchen, wine glass in hand, while she, after a hasty shower and change, was at the stove, stirring the risotto and generally keeping an eye on things. Damn it, she'd been on her own in this deadly quiet little town for over a week now. She would enjoy a little company, especially the company of someone who was under seventy.

'Look,' she said, as casually as she could, 'I was about to throw a meal together. Why don't you come in? Have a bite to eat and a glass of vino?'

Almost immediately she could sense the tension in him.

'Ah,' he said and then stopped as if he, the friendliest, chattiest cop in the district, was totally lost for words. He gave her an awkward half-smile. 'I – ah – thanks, Flora, but I really should head home.'

Which meant he still wasn't ready for company. Not her company, at any rate.

'Okay.' Flora gave a shrug and was careful to keep her tone offhand. 'That's cool.' She smiled to prove how very cool she was about this, then she lifted her hand to wave as she turned in at her gate. 'Take care, Mitch. Hope you solve the mystery of those bones.'

'Yeah, thanks.'

She was no longer looking his way, but she sensed his slight hesitation, almost as if he was having second thoughts.

Well, that was okay. That was fine.

Holding her breath, Flora walked up the path super slowly, giving him time to change his mind, stupidly hoping. She didn't look back until she'd reached the front door.

When she did turn to look, Mitch was three doors away and getting into his car.

'The poor man's taking it very hard.'

Flora blinked, unsure at first where the voice had come from, until she saw Edith standing on her front step. She had assumed the old woman had disappeared inside when she closed her door, but now it was clearly open. Had she been watching all this time?

The houses in this street were very close together, close enough for neighbours to talk to each other from their front steps. What had Edith heard?

From down the street came the sound of Mitch's car taking off.

'The poor man,' Edith said again. 'It's just terrible.' She sounded quite devastated, as if she was almost in tears.

Flora crossed the small yard to the side fence, so she could speak more quietly. 'Mitch will be all right,' she told her. 'He just needs a bit of time.'

Edith gave a doleful shake of her head. 'Some people never get over these things.'

The old lady looked pathetic, standing there, huddled in the puddle of light coming through her door. Her limp hair hung unattractively around her face and her skin was dragged down into lines of deep sorrow, almost as if she had taken Mitch's pain into herself. Flora wondered if Edith had experienced her own broken heart that had never mended.

On impulse, she found herself saying, 'Have you had dinner yet, Edith?'

'No. I was just going to boil an egg. Why?'

'I thought you might like to have dinner with me.'

The woman was clearly taken aback. She stood with her mouth gaping, as if she didn't know what to say.

'I'm making mushroom risotto,' Flora said.

Edith's eyes widened even further and Flora was already asking herself why she'd made such a crazy suggestion. What was it with her and old ladies? In one afternoon, she'd invited Hattie to hear her play, she'd told Peg she would take on her concert duties, and now she'd offered this impulsive invitation to Edith.

Maybe she was channelling her gran? Right up until she'd died, Flora's grandmother, Stella Drummond, had always been feeding others and fussing over her elderly friends, even when she herself was quite old and frail.

'If I don't help them today, it might be too late tomorrow,' her gran used to say.

Now Edith seemed to recover from her shock. 'That sounds very nice,' she said. 'Thank you, Flora. I'll just get a cardigan and shut my door.'

'Don't forget your door key,' Flora reminded her.

Edith responded with a light-hearted sound that might actually have been a laugh.

It wasn't quite the same as having dinner with an old friend like Mitch, but Edith was surprisingly good company, sitting at the kitchen table with half a glass of chilled white wine – *I don't drink, but maybe just half a glass* – while Flora stirred her risotto. To Flora's relief, Edith didn't go on for too long about Mitch, who was clearly her hero. She was distracted by all the renovations the Woods had made to the cottage.

'All I ever heard was a lot of noisy hammering and banging and drilling,' she said. 'But it's come up lovely, hasn't it?'

'It has,' Flora agreed. 'I love it.'

'This kitchen looks like one of those pictures in a country style magazine.'

They ate at the kitchen table. Flora lit a couple of candles and selected background music – an old ABC *Swoon Collection* CD that she'd found in the TV cabinet.

Edith was delighted – or perhaps it was the wine that put a sparkle in her eyes and a pink flush in her cheeks. She confessed to being a meat and three-veg cook. She'd never eaten risotto before and she rarely bought fresh mushrooms or parmesan cheese because they were so expensive. After a few careful mouthfuls, however, she declared the meal delicious.

'Phew.' Flora grinned at her. 'I'm glad you like it. It's Italian.'

'I suppose Italian food is all the rage down in Melbourne.'

'Actually, Melbourne is so multicultural these days, you could have just about anything you like. Korean, Moroccan, Greek, Vietnamese.'

'Hmm. Not sure I'd like that spicy stuff, but this is lovely.'

They talked convivially as they ate. Flora mentioned that she was practising in the church hall to give the neighbours a break, and was surprised to hear that Edith hadn't minded the music once she got used to it.

Flora found herself off-loading about the children's concert and her total lack of experience.

'Oh, you'll manage,' Edith declared with the confidence of the innocent. 'All you need to do is play a bit from one of your fancy pieces and the children will be stunned into silence.'

'Gosh, I hope it's that easy.' Flora had her doubts. Changing the subject she asked, 'How long have you lived here, Edith?'

'I've spent my whole life in this district. I was born in the Atherton hospital and my parents owned a dairy farm over near Butchers Creek. Such hard work, dairying,' she added dolefully. 'All that milking, morning and night, seven days a week. Getting up in the early hours when it's freezing cold or raining. Mud everywhere, and always a struggle to make a living. I'm sure it was better for your folks, having beef cattle over Mareeba way.'

'Do you know my family?' Having grown up at Ruthven Downs on the other side of Mareeba, Flora only knew a few of Burralea's worthy citizens, so she considered herself an outsider.

'I knew Stella, your gran, and I know *of* your father,' Edith clarified. 'And I've met your mother, Jackie, once or twice, when I've gone to CWA functions. I don't go out much, but your mum's quite a livewire.'

'Oh, yes, that's so true.'

'And now your brother's bought Kooringal.'

'That's right. You're very well informed, Edith.'

'I read the *Burralea Bugle* from cover to cover.' Flora's guest shot a searching glance across the table. 'What do you think of the bones that turned up on your brother's property?'

'So you've heard about that, too?'

'They were talking about it in the butcher's.'

Flora supposed she shouldn't be surprised. This was a small town, after all, and everyone knew everyone else's business. The discovery of the bones had almost certainly been reported in the bigger papers, and no doubt there would be extensive coverage in the little weekly paper tomorrow.

'I feel pretty sorry for Seth,' she admitted. 'He's got such exciting plans for breeding stud cattle and he's really keen to get started on this new place. I don't suppose the business of the bones should hold him up too much, but it casts a nasty shadow.'

Edith nodded and took another scoop of risotto onto her fork.

'Seth reckons the bones have been there a long time,' Flora felt compelled to add. 'I don't think he's under suspicion. It's quite a mystery.'

This brought another, more emphatic nod from Edith. 'I told Sergeant Cavello he should be talking to Joe Matthews.'

'Oh?'

'Joe used to own Kooringal.'

'In that case I'm sure Mitch will have spoken to him by now.'

Edith gave a knowing shrug, picked up her glass and downed the last of her wine. 'Now *that* was another tragic wedding day,' she said rather dramatically.

'I'm afraid you've lost me, Edith.'

'I'm talking about the day Joe Matthews married Gloria Walker, the publican's daughter. We all knew he should have been marrying Hattie Bellamy.'

Flora frowned. Hattie was the name of the woman who'd come into the hall to listen to her music.

'Hattie was *such* a lovely girl,' Edith said in a way that suggested Gloria Walker could never compare favourably. 'She and Joe were high-school sweethearts.' She crossed her middle and index fingers, somewhat awkwardly, because of her arthritic joints, and held them up. 'Like that, Joe and Hattie were. So suited. But then there was a drunken birthday party and Joe went and got Gloria Walker in the family way.'

Leaning forward, Edith's eyes were huge with the importance of her story as she lowered her voice to an impressive hush-hush. 'They had to have a shotgun wedding. Mind you, Joe was a good husband. Poor man.' She gave a slow shake of her head. 'The mistakes you make when you're young can throw a long shadow.'

Edith said this with such convincing solemnity that Flora wondered if the woman was regretting something from her own youth.

We all make mistakes, Flora thought, unhappily recalling an embarrassing incident that had haunted her on and off for the past six years.

A small shiver ran through her. She quickly banished the memory and switched her thoughts back to Hattie, the rather elegant woman she'd met this afternoon. Tall and slim, with pretty, wavy silver hair, smart clothes and a love of Tchaikovsky. Perhaps she'd been better off without this Joe fellow?

'What happened to Hattie?' she asked.

'Who knows?' Edith gave an expressive shake of her head. 'It was all very sad. Not long after the wedding, her mother died, and Hattie took off. Word was, she went to live with family in England. She was certainly never seen in these parts again.'

Until this afternoon? Flora wondered, but it was a question that, for the moment at least, she was sure she should keep to herself.

CHAPTER ELEVEN

Hattie hadn't expected Joe's house to be quite so charming. Set back behind a stone fence and a paling gate, the house had a storybook quality that she instantly liked.

She was, however, almost paralysed by nervousness, which she knew was perfectly understandable, but she was disappointed. She had hoped to be stronger. She reminded herself that this wasn't a social visit. There was no need to discuss any aspect of her past with Joe, except that one fateful afternoon from seventy years ago.

No sentimental journey, this. It was a matter of conscience and possibly of justice. Nothing more.

Hattie crossed the footpath and the gate opened easily without creaking. No doubt Joe was good at maintenance – he'd always been handy – and her comfortably-soled walking shoes made no sound on the stone path.

Her first attempt to knock was rather feeble and she tried again, more forcefully, then she held her breath as she waited. Unfortunately, when she heard footsteps inside, her heart took off at a dizzying pace and she had to clutch the stair railing for support.

You're being a very silly old woman.

She was prepared for this encounter, she told herself, and that was an advantage she had over Joe. She also knew what he would look like. She had seen a recent photo of him on the internet and she was ready for his white hair and glasses, the age-softened lines of his once strong jaw and cheekbones.

When the door opened, however, it was the eye contact with the man that undid Hattie. While the years had made their predictable changes, Joe's eyes were still the exact hazel she remembered, and the personality shining through them was the man she'd once loved. The man who had broken her heart.

'Hattie?'

Of course, he looked shocked.

She was surprised that he'd recognised her. 'A good guess,' she said, trying, unsuccessfully, to smile. 'It's been a long time, Joe.'

He was dressed in a long-sleeved shirt and jeans and he looked every bit the retired cattleman as he stood, clutching the door handle with one hand, clearly coming to terms with the unexpectedness of this. Nice looking still, he'd aged well.

'Do you mind if I come in?' Hattie was surprised by how much courage this question required.

'Of course, of course.' Joe stepped back politely to allow her entry into the long narrow hallway that ran down the middle of his house.

Sunlight from the open door highlighted the richly toned carpet runner and the hall stand, which held a delicate flowering orchid in a pot. Everything looked rather tasteful and well cared for and Hattie wondered if Joe had a housekeeper. Or a new wife?

A black-and-white dog came padding down the hallway to sit at his master's feet. He looked up at Hattie with wary benevolence.

'How are you?' Joe asked and he seemed worried. She couldn't tell if he was shocked or angry or nervous. 'You look very well,' he added.

'Do I? Thanks.' So silly of her to be pleased, although she had taken special care with her appearance, choosing to wear a stylish black-and-white top over cherry-toned slacks, with the addition of simple earrings and a string of jet beads. 'I'm quite well, actually, all things considered. And you?'

Joe nodded. 'I can't complain.' He pointed to the doorway leading to the lounge room. 'Let's go in there.'

'Thank you.'

Stepping into this room, Hattie wasn't prepared for the books that filled it, crammed into shelves and stacked on the coffee table. She'd spent the best part of her working life deeply immersed in books and to think that Joe —

Abruptly, she stopped herself from commenting on the coincidence. This was no time for nostalgia or regrets.

'Can I offer you tea or coffee?' he asked.

'Not now, thank you.' She didn't want him to think this was a social visit.

They settled into well-cushioned armchairs, the dog sprawled on the floor next to Joe's chair.

'He's a nice-looking fellow,' Hattie remarked. 'What's his name?'

For the first time, Joe smiled. 'Marlowe.'

Marlowe pricked up his ears when he heard his name and Hattie shifted her gaze to the rows of books on nearby shelves.

'He wouldn't be named after Raymond Chandler's Detective Marlowe, would he?'

This brought another smile from Joe. 'He would indeed. Have you read Raymond Chandler?'

'My second husband was a fan,' she said smoothly. 'I watched *The Big Sleep* and a couple of the other Marlowe movies with him.'

Joe's smile wavered. Disappeared. 'He *was* a fan,' Joe repeated. 'Is he —?'

'He died,' Hattie said bluntly, not wanting to go into details.

Joe gave a slight, possibly sympathetic nod.

'I understand that you lost Gloria, too,' Hattie said, proud that her voice didn't waver.

'Yes.' Joe made no mention of a new wife as he reached down and gave Marlowe a gentle scratch on the top of his head.

Watching them, Hattie remembered Joe's gentle, long-fingered hands, all those years ago, cradling a little red-faced finch. Other memories surfaced and she quickly scratched them before they had the power to hurt.

Joe said, 'I assume you're visiting Burralea?'

'Yes, I'm staying at the Burralea Lodge for a couple of nights.'

He nodded slowly. 'And where do you live now?'

'In Brisbane, actually. I came back to Australia about five years ago.'

'You went to England.'

'Among other places, yes.' Hattie decided this was not the time to become sidetracked by their personal histories. She dived straight to the point. 'I'll tell you why I'm here, Joe. I read in the newspaper about those bones, the ones that were found on Kooringal.'

From beneath thick white brows, he shot her a quick, almost frantic glance, and then looked away without making a comment.

In the ensuing, awkward silence, Hattie's heart thumped at a rather reckless pace.

'I felt I had to come,' she continued valiantly. 'I had no idea how well you were, and I wasn't even sure if you were able to remember that afternoon all those years ago, when we —' She stopped and swallowed. 'Do you remember that day when you were trapping those little finches, Joe?'

He let out an exaggerated sigh. 'Yes, I remember.'

'Have you spoken to the police about it?'

'No.'

Impatiently, Hattie waited for him to explain himself.

Eventually, he said, 'I really don't think that business needs to be brought up now. Not after all this time.'

'So you don't think that we can offer anything relevant to this case?'

Frustratingly, Joe didn't answer, but he certainly looked uncomfortable as he sat with his long legs crossed and his hands in fists on the arms of his chair, staring fixedly at some point on the floor.

'Were these bones found in a totally different part of the property?' Hattie prompted.

'No they weren't,' he admitted with obvious reluctance.

'But you're happy to leave the police with a mystery on their hands?'

Joe's worried gaze met hers. 'Hattie, you know we never actually saw what happened.'

'The evidence was all there, Joe. You know it was.'

'I promised my father. He made us both promise.'

'But surely your father can't still be alive?'

'No, of course not. But that's not the point.'

Perplexed, Hattie sat for a moment, trying to make sense of this. She couldn't understand why Joe was being so stubborn. She was remembering the boy she'd so admired for his calm common sense and amazing general knowledge. Had he become pig-headed in his old age?

It seemed obvious to her that they should go to the police with their story. Finally get it off their chests and expose a hidden, inconvenient set of circumstances.

She tried to think of another way to tackle this dilemma, but she kept running into the brick wall of Joe's stubbornness. 'I don't understand,' she said. 'What's wrong with telling?'

Joe's jaw tightened. 'What's it going to achieve other than publicity and gossip?

'Justice?'

The word dropped like a stone into the space between them. Across the room their gazes met again. Hattie wondered if she looked as determined as Joe did, but then, without warning, the fierceness in his eyes softened and he simply looked sad.

'There might have been justice if the story had come out at the time,' he said quietly. 'But it didn't, Hattie. Seventy years have passed and it's far too late for any kind of justice now. Not after all these years.'

This was probably true, Hattie realised, but silence still didn't sit comfortably with her conscience.

'So you're happy to leave the police running around in circles?'

'Why not? Fate made us unwilling witnesses. Fate also prompted Seth Drummond to put a dam in exactly the same spot. Why can't we just leave it at that? Leave it as a mystery?'

Hattie felt suddenly quite miserable. She had recovered many years ago from the heartbreak this man had caused her, but perhaps she'd always misjudged him. Perhaps he simply had no conscience.

'Apart from giving the police satisfaction, what good can come of telling our story now?' Joe persisted. 'As far as I can see, more people will be hurt than helped.'

To her dismay, this almost sounded logical. And yet —

'I have to think of my sister, Margaret,' Joe said next. 'She's over ninety. Think what it would do to her to have all that dragged up now.'

Margaret.

Hattie had certainly forgotten about Joe's sister and her involvement in this, but now, finally, Joe's reticence to talk made a crazy kind of sense.

She drew a long, unhappy breath and let it out slowly. 'I need to think about this,' she said quietly. 'I never liked having to keep quiet. As a child it was bad enough, but your father convinced me it was the right thing to do, because of the war and everything.

Over the years, I've tried to live with it, to accept that perhaps it was best to leave sleeping bones lie. Then, when I saw the story in *The Australian*, I was sure the time had come.'

'I know,' Joe said quietly. 'It's been hard for me, too.'

'Perhaps the police wouldn't bother Margaret. She wasn't there on the day.'

Joe gave a slow, solemn nod of his head as if he acknowledged this possibility.

'Or telling the truth might bring her some kind of peace,' Hattie suggested. 'Closure.'

Another sigh escaped him. Pensively, he fiddled with a loose thread of upholstery. 'Look, I'll give it some more thought,' he said. 'And I'll phone Margaret. She hasn't been well and she's in a nursing home in Melbourne. I won't tell her what's happened, but I'll try to ascertain how well she is.'

'That's certainly a good idea.' *And a step in the right direction.* Hattie sent him an encouraging smile.

Joe smiled too and there was a shimmer of a deeper emotion that sent an unexpected flush rippling under her skin. She reached for her handbag. 'Well, thanks for seeing me, Joe. We'll be in touch tomorrow then. Shall I come back here? It's only a short walk from the guesthouse and it's more private here.'

'Yes, yes, thank you. That would be good.' His eyes were still bright with emotion. 'Are you sure I can't offer you a cuppa now?'

Hattie almost weakened, but to stay would involve talking about other things – about themselves – and that wasn't part of her purpose. The past couldn't be undone.

Besides, she had to keep a check on her emotions. She didn't want to risk any more silly reactions. It was unsettling to know she was still susceptible to a simple smile from this man.

'No, I won't have any tea, thank you.' She got to her feet, thankfully without too much stiffness.

Joe rose too and Marlowe slowly followed him, looking up at them both with a hopeful wag of his tail. 'Yes, boy, I'll take you for your walk,' Joe told the dog fondly.

Hattie thought of her daily walk from her apartment to the coffee shop and wondered where Joe and Marlowe went. She didn't ask. She slipped the strap of her bag over her shoulder and headed out of the room.

'It's been good to see you again, Joe.'

'You, too,' he said, following her.

In the hallway, she waited for him to get past to open the front door. Up close, he seemed taller than she remembered. Or had she shrunk a little?

Standing at the open door, he managed a faint lopsided smile, but his eyes were brimming with far too much emotion. 'I've always wanted to apologise to you, Hattie.'

Oh, no, Joe. Don't. Not now. She couldn't bear it. Already she could feel the sting of tears, but she didn't want to cry. She mustn't.

'I've never forgiven myself for what I did to you.'

Now, she couldn't see him through the blur of tears. She could only nod and press her lips tightly together in a desperate bid for control.

Fortunately, there were only three front steps and she made her way down them, blindly, but without stumbling. It was impossible to speak, to say goodbye, so she headed up the path, blinking madly to clear her eyes.

She was fighting images of the last time she had seen Joe, standing on the church steps beside his bride.

I've never forgiven myself for what I did to you.

At the gate, she turned back, and Joe was still standing there, watching her. With a brief, self-conscious wave, she hurried away, along the footpath, hoping that he wasn't still watching as she felt in her handbag for a tissue.

I've never forgiven myself.

Heart-shattering memories crowded in. Memories of Joe as her childhood friend, playing hide-and-seek in a field of sunflowers, or taking her down the creek in his homemade tin canoe. Joe, as her high-school sweetheart, shyly, hopefully, asking her to the school dance, driving her in his dad's ute over to the movies in Malanda. Joe, as the man she was going to marry, taking her in his arms, promising a lifetime of love and commitment, making her happier than she'd ever dreamed possible.

In a sea of panic, Hattie forced herself to think of other things, *any* other thing. Desperately, she fixed her thoughts on Joe's sister, Margaret, remembering all those years ago, when two children had watched from afar while Margaret had fallen for Gabriel.

CHAPTER TWELVE

Kooringal, 1942

Hattie and her mother had been living in the cottage at Kooringal for a few months before Gabriel Wright arrived.

At the time, Rose was still finding everything about Australia very difficult. She and Hattie hadn't been able to stay for very long in the hotel where she'd spent her honeymoon – they just didn't have enough money for that lifestyle – and she was devastated to realise that a cottage on a farm, quite a distance from town, was the only accommodation available.

Away from the bustle and liveliness of Shanghai and without her family or friends, Rose didn't seem to know what to do with herself. Without servants, she could only cook very rudimentary meals – porridge with milk and brown sugar for breakfast, sandwiches with tomato and tinned ham for lunch, or perhaps a heated-up tin of soup. For tea, boiled eggs with toast soldiers, or a tough little chop with watery potatoes and tinned peas.

There were horses, and Rose had once loved horseriding, especially the exciting paperchases in Shanghai, but somehow riding alone in the Australian bush didn't have the same appeal for her. It seemed to Hattie that her mother spent most days sitting at the kitchen table, looking out through the flyscreen door to a view of trees and grass and cows.

Unlike Shanghai, their view at Kooringal was completely devoid of other houses or people and there seemed to be no chance of anyone calling in to invite Rose to high tea or a lively party. Most days, she did needlepoint or read books, or wrote long letters to her sister, while dirty dishes piled in the sink.

For Hattie, it was also a strange new world, with no amah to dress her, to pick up her clothes or tidy her toys. She missed the special treats she was used to, like parties at the Hotel Metropole with children dressed up as flowers and vegetables, or the meals at the Cathay Mansions in the special children's dining room with animals painted around the walls and blue child-sized furniture.

For Hattie, everything at Kooringal got better, though, when the summer school holidays started and she made friends with Joe Matthews. He was tall and slim, with silky brown hair that flopped over his forehead, and he knew all kinds of fascinating things about living in the bush. He taught Hattie how to ride his pony and he showed her where a mother platypus had made a burrow in the riverbank. He even gave her a firefly in a matchbox to take home to her cottage, so she could watch it flickering at night in her bedroom all alone.

'But after you've watched it, you should let it go,' he warned her.

Hattie did as he told her. Standing at her window, she watched the little fairy light flitting off into the darkness and thought how exciting it was to have a friend like Joe. He seemed to know an awful lot.

Rose usually seemed relieved when Hattie asked if she could go and play with Joe. Luckily, Mrs Matthews didn't seem to mind either. She was happy for her son to have company with someone near his own age, as long as he still did his chores.

By the time Gabriel Wright suddenly appeared at Kooringal, the summer holidays were over and Hattie had started school, a year below Joe, travelling into Burralea each day in a rickety old bus. Gabriel worked for Joe's father, helping to build fences and to clear the scrub to make new paddocks.

Gabriel had shiny black skin that made his teeth and the whites of his eyes look extra bright, and he spoke with an American accent like people in movies. At first he seemed to be frightened of the cattle and horses. Hattie understood this – she'd been scared of them, too. After a while he got used to the animals and helped Joe's father in the stockyards with branding.

He ate his meals with Joe's family inside the house, but he slept on the verandah. His bed was a canvas stretcher under a mosquito net and he kept it very neat and tidy.

Sometimes, late in the afternoons, when the shadows were long and the day's chores were over, Gabriel would sit chatting with Joe and Hattie on the back steps of the Kooringal homestead. If Joe's big sister, Margaret, was free, she would come too and sit on the top step, with a colander in her lap and a scrap bucket at her feet, shelling peas, slicing beans or peeling potatoes.

If she was shelling peas, Hattie would help her. Hattie had sometimes helped the Chinese boys in the kitchen in Shanghai, and she liked sitting in the fading light, popping pea pods with her thumb, stripping the round little peas into the colander, catching the scent of their sweet green freshness, while she listened to Gabriel's stories.

Gabriel told them about the city he came from – Chicago, in America, a huge, important country far away on the other side of a great big ocean.

'Even further away than Shanghai?' Hattie asked, with memories of the long voyage to Australia still fresh in her mind.

'Yes, little ma'am,' Gabriel told her, making his eyes extra wide so that the round white parts showed whiter than ever. 'I believe Chicago is, indeed, even further away than Shanghai.'

According to Gabriel, the very best part of Chicago was Bronzeville where his family lived. It was easy to tell that Gabriel missed his family in the same achy way that Hattie missed her Aunt Lily and Uncle Rudi. He talked about them a lot. His father had a city job working for a businessman and his mother worked in a café called Dreamland where famous jazz musicians played. Gabriel's little brother, Robert, was still at school.

Robert was brilliant, Gabriel told them. He always had his nose in a book and their mother reckoned he was going to be a doctor or someone important when he grew up.

'Why don't you go back to them?' Hattie asked naïvely.

Joe, a year older and ten years wiser, quickly jumped in with a sensible explanation. 'Because of the war.'

Of course, the war.

Joe later told Hattie that they weren't allowed to tell people about Gabriel. 'Dad said we especially mustn't tell people he's American. If anyone asks, he said we have to tell them that Gabriel's a South Sea Islander.'

'Why?' Hattie asked.

Again, it was the same answer. 'Because of the war.'

She accepted this without further question. All the adults ever seemed to talk about was the war. It was because of the war that she and her mother had left Shanghai. Wars meant aeroplanes screaming overhead, and bombings and burnt and crumbled houses, and people being taken off in ambulances with sirens wailing. Wars meant soldiers everywhere, shouldering guns, shouting orders.

Wars meant walking away from your home with one small suitcase, saying goodbye to everyone you loved – grandparents, aunt, uncle, amah and friends. Hattie felt very sorry for Gabriel.

She was sure Margaret felt sorry for him too. Sometimes Margaret would look at Gabriel with a tender smile and he would smile back at her. On these occasions, his dark brown eyes would shine with a special glow, just for Margaret, a kind of secret happiness. It made Hattie's throat hurt to watch them.

A few times, when Joe and Margaret's parents were away on business or visiting friends, Margaret would turn the wireless on, tuning in to a special jazz music station and putting the sound up as loud as she could.

'Swing music,' Gabriel called it, which sounded a very fitting name to Hattie. The songs were played on trumpets and saxophones and the beat was very lively. There were funny titles like 'Chattanooga Choo Choo' and 'Boogie Woogie Bugle Boy' and 'I Don't Want to Set the World on Fire'.

In the lounge room, with the furniture pushed back and the carpet rolled up, Gabriel would teach them all how to dance to this music. The movements were very fast and tricky, and Hattie and Joe would usually end up tripping over their own feet and falling to the floor in a laughing, giggling tangle.

Margaret, however, got the hang of it quickly. She was really good at doing the two-step or the three-step with kicks. It wasn't long before Margaret and Gabriel were dancing together, touching, holding hands. Then Gabriel's arm came around Margaret's waist and they started adding special dips and lifts and twirls.

At the end of a fast and exciting number, Margaret looked very flushed and breathless, but wonderfully happy, as if she might burst.

Then came an afternoon after school, when Joe took Hattie to a shallow bend of the river with a reedy bank and lovely flat rocks dotted across the water that made perfect stepping stones. Their plan was to catch tadpoles.

'We can watch them turn into frogs,' he explained.

City-bred Hattie had never heard of anything so marvellous. Joe said these little wriggling creatures would grow legs and lose their tails. It sounded magic, like something in a fairy tale.

Joe sprinkled bits of crumpled lettuce onto the water to bring the dark little swimmers to the surface. Then he and Hattie squatted on the rocks and scooped the tadpoles into their empty Vegemite jars.

Joe had very cleverly tied string around the mouths of the jars with loops for handles, and Hattie was so excited. They would each take a jar home. She would set hers on the chest of drawers beside her bed where she could watch the miracle that Joe promised.

Carrying their precious tadpole cargo, she and Joe were halfway along the track that led back to the house when they heard soft, giggling laughter in the bushes ahead.

Rounding a bend, they came across Gabriel and Margaret in the shade of a big gum tree. They had their arms around each other and they were kissing.

Instinctively, the children slunk back into the shadows without speaking. Hattie glanced Joe's way, but he didn't say anything. He was too busy staring ahead, but for once he looked shocked. His mouth was gaping.

Hattie stared too, fascinated. Margaret's pale arms were wound around Gabriel's brown neck and his hands were linked around her waist, dark against her pale floral dress.

Gabriel was holding Margaret tight against him, which he didn't really need to do, because she was pressing as close to him as she could. Their faces were mashed together. It was almost like they were trying to eat each other.

As she and Joe watched them, Hattie felt a strange sensation inside, like she'd stepped off a cliff into thin air. She forgot all about the tadpoles until her jar slipped from her fingers, dropping to the ground with a plop.

'Oh, no!'

Gabriel and Margaret sprang apart.

'What are you kids doing?' Margaret looked flushed and upset. Maybe angry. 'Are you spying on us?'

'No,' said Joe. 'We were just walking up the track.'

But now Hattie was crouched in the dirt, dismayed by the sight of her lovely fat tadpoles wriggling and squirming in the leaf litter and muddy puddle, doomed to an early death, instead of being transformed, gloriously, into frogs.

'Off you go!' Margaret told them bossily. 'Get home. And no tittle-tattle to Mum or Dad, Joe, or I'll box your ears.'

'But my tadpoles!' Hattie wailed, casting a desperate glance to Joe. 'I have to pick them up. Can I put them in your jar, Joe?'

'Oh, for heaven's sake.' Margaret sounded completely fed up.

To Hattie's relief, Joe kneeled beside her and helped her to pick up the thrashing little bodies. When they dropped them into his jar, they made the water dirty, but Margaret was watching with poorly suppressed patience, so they didn't dare to go back to the river for more water.

Margaret stood beside the shyly smiling Gabriel, with her hands on her hips, foot tapping, waiting for her little brother and his nosy friend to disappear.

They did so, hurrying silently along the track, and when they reached the homestead, Joe deposited his tadpole jar on a shaded desk at the end of the verandah.

'We can get more clean river water tomorrow,' he told Hattie.

'What about water from the tap?'

Joe shook his head. 'There's algae in the river water. It's stuff the tadpoles can eat.'

'How do you know that?'

'I read it in a book.'

Hattie had no doubt that Joe was every bit as clever as Gabriel's brother, Robert.

She waited for him to say anything about his sister and Gabriel.

When he didn't, she said, 'I won't tell about Margaret – you know – kissing.'

'No, I know you won't.'

'She won't get into trouble, will she?'

Joe shrugged and looked uncomfortable.

'They were like grown-ups in a movie.' Hattie couldn't let the matter drop.

'Well, they are grown-up, aren't they?' Joe said. 'Margaret's seventeen. Gabriel's – I don't know – about twenty.'

He sounded so calm. He looked calm too, not ruffled or twitchy, the way Hattie had felt ever since she'd seen that kiss. 'Do you s'pose it's all right, then? Them kissing?'

'I s'pose.'

'What will happen though?' she persisted.

'What do you mean?'

Hattie wasn't sure why she was so suddenly stirred and worried, but in the back of her mind memories lurked, memories of hushed conversations between Rose and her grandparents. She had never really understood the true nature of their concern, but she had sensed the frantic urgency in their voices, and she'd known they were talking about her Aunt Lily and Uncle Rudi – about the war and about them being in love and how wrong it was. And dangerous, because Lily was English and Rudi was Russian. Somehow the two of them being different mattered. A lot.

Gabriel was very different.

She didn't really know how to communicate any of this to Joe, but she was sure that Margaret and Gabriel must also be in danger.

'What will happen to them? If they're still in love at the end of the war?' Hattie's teacher at school had assured her and her classmates that the war would end one day. 'What if they want to get married?'

Joe simply shrugged again. 'I s'pose they'll just go right ahead and get married.'

'But Gabriel will probably want to go back to America. To Bronzeville.'

'Yeah. I s'pose.'

'And Margaret will have to go, too, if she's married.'

'Maybe.'

Then Joe surprised her by asking, 'Is that what you'll do? Go back to Shanghai?'

'I don't know.' It was a question Hattie had never really considered. 'Maybe,' she said, but she was shocked to realise how much she would hate it, if she had to say goodbye to Joe.

CHAPTER THIRTEEN

Burralea, 2015

It rained during the night. Not the usual soft Tablelands mizzle, but a proper November storm. A heavy downpour drummed on the roof and pelted the ground, thunder rumbled and growled. Wind snapped tree branches and sent them spinning. Lightning ripped the sky, splitting the air, disturbing molecules and bringing much needed nitrogen back to the soil.

The farmers would be pleased.

Mitch rolled out of bed and went to shut a few windows. Then he couldn't get back to sleep. He lay listening to the wildness outside and thinking about all the wrong things, like the new leather duffle bag, still packed and ready for his honeymoon. The updated passport and the bank account he'd opened especially to save for a properly lavish getaway.

Damn it, he probably should have taken the leave even though there would be no honeymoon. He should have got out of town, away from the pitying stares and well-meant offers of condolence. He should have taken off to the Gold Coast, Sydney, wherever.

He thought about Angie, wondered where she was now and tortured himself, knowing that she must be happy. He could see her undressing for Kevin, the bastard who'd come back from America, cocked his little finger and brought her running.

Fuck. He had to stop this.

Anger roiled through him. Unhelpful anger. Familiar anger. The same hurt-fuelled rage he'd experienced in his teens, when he'd learned the truth about his mother's death during a visit from his Aunt Maria from Melbourne.

In an after-dinner conversation, when Mitch was in his room, supposed to be doing his homework, Maria, his father's sister, had spoken of his mother's depression. She'd hinted at suicide and Mitch's ears had pricked up.

He'd crept down the hallway to listen. When he was discovered, his dad had been mad at Maria and a very unpleasant argument had followed, with Aunt Maria in tears. She hadn't stayed as long as she was supposed to. After she'd left, still in tears, it had taken Mitch days before he'd got the truth out of his father.

Now, thinking back, Mitch was ashamed of the way he'd harassed the poor man, but eventually Lorenzo Cavello had admitted that yes, his beautiful wife, Gina, had taken her own life with an overdose. A severe case of postnatal depression had spiralled out of control.

'She was never the same after you were born,' his father had said.

Mitch had been devastated and angry to learn that his mother had willingly gone and left him alone, before he'd turned three. He'd felt guilty, too. It was obvious that his birth had led to his mother's death.

In the years that followed, Mitch's dad had retreated even further into himself and Mitch, hungry for love, had resented his father's withdrawal. Now, though, he could almost understand the man's need to retreat, to shut out the world, to escape risking any more hurt.

Mitch sighed heavily. All he had left of his mother were fragile memories, fleeting, like wisps of smoke he could never quite catch or hold on to. On occasions he thought he could still hear her voice calling his name. Or he could see the shape of her hand reaching out to caress him, the fall of her hair, dark and silky, tumbling in waves to her shoulders, her pretty smile and the tiny gap between her front teeth.

Always, the images would dissolve before they'd come properly into focus, leaving Mitch to wonder if the memories were real, or merely imaginings conjured from the few photographs his father had kept.

Gina, his mother, and now, Angie, his fiancée. Two women he'd loved and lost.

Jesus. With another angry groan, Mitch sat up, forced his thoughts elsewhere. To the bones.

It was a relief to think about the Kooringal case.

The bones were now safely in a Brisbane laboratory and they'd been identified as the remains of an adult male, most probably aged in his twenties. They'd been in the earth a long time. Decades.

So far, the DNA didn't match anyone on the known missing persons lists.

There appeared to be a bullet hole in the pelvis, however, which may have pierced the femoral artery and been the cause of death. Finding an actual bullet would be helpful, but so far none had turned up.

Mitch flopped back onto the mattress. For ages he lay, listening to the rain and thinking about it pelting the site on Kooringal, making runnels in the dirt that the forensic teams had so carefully combed. Eventually, he fell into a restless sleep, but he woke early, just as day was breaking.

The rain had stopped. From his kitchen window the world looked newly washed and clean, the sky once more clear and fresh.

He made coffee and took a mug with him while he fed his dogs, Maggie and Midnight. They went outside – the dogs to sniff in the garden, to lift a leg or to squat, while Mitch fed his chooks.

Mitch had a soft spot for the fat, rusty red and fluffy white girls. He liked their gentle clucking and their constant, conscientious pecking and scratching while they ranged free in his yard.

His vegetables were fenced off from the chickens, of course, and he checked the rows, picking the ripe tomatoes, checking for caterpillar damage on the rain-soaked lettuce and rocket. He didn't like to spray, but it was hard to keep ahead of the competition from pests.

Downing the last of his coffee, he looked about him at the gently sloping land, damp with heavy dew, at the distant green hills dotted with cattle. He looked back at his peak-roofed house with recycled doors and windows that he'd chosen so carefully.

Until this week, he'd had special feelings for this place. The chickens and the veggies were part of a lifestyle choice, but the transformation of the tractor shed into his home had been a genuine labour of love. He'd been so looking forward sharing it with his bride.

Damn. Not again. Mitch tried to scratch that last thought. When it clung on, he marched inside the house, dumped his mug and the tomatoes on the sink, and less than ten minutes later, showered and shaved, he was driving to Kooringal.

He didn't stop at the homestead. By now, Seth and Alice were used to police vehicles driving out to the site without stopping. This morning, Mitch continued on down the track till he arrived at the area still sectioned off with tape.

The newly saturated bush smelled dank and earthy. Muddy puddles had formed in some of the deeper tyre tracks. They would probably evaporate before the day was over.

Ducking beneath the tape, Mitch stepped purposefully forward, keeping his eyes peeled for any changes in this now familiar ground.

As he'd expected, some of the hills of pushed-up soil had been eroded by the rain, their sides now sunken or pitted by silty crevices. He covered the area slowly, methodically, crouching every so often to peer closely at a surface, looking for anything new that the rain might have exposed. He had the uncanny certainty that there should be a bullet here. Somewhere.

He had almost given up when he saw the wink of sunlight on metal.

CHAPTER FOURTEEN

Flora was planning her day's practice when Seth rang, inviting her to dinner at Kooringal.

'It's a bit of a spontaneous thing,' he said. 'It's been a kinda weird week here, with the bones turning up and everything. Alice and I thought we'd have a few people over. Chill out.'

'Fantastic. I'd love to come. To be honest, I've been starting to worry about cabin fever.'

'Then we'd better rescue you,' Seth said. 'Alice is working in Burralea today, so she can give you a lift over here.'

Seth's girlfriend Alice restored and sold second-hand furniture, and she had a shop in Burralea's main street. Since she and Seth had become an item, she'd moved the restoration side of things to a shed on Kooringal and only worked part time in the shop. Between them, they shared caring for Seth's little son, Charlie, although Charlie also spent some days with Brenda James, a day-care mum in Burralea.

'Tammy and Ben should be able to give you a lift home,' Seth added, referring to Burralea's hairdresser and baker, who were now another recognised Burralea couple. 'But if that doesn't suit for any reason, we'll work something out.'

'What can I bring?' Flora asked.

Seth laughed. 'Now you're sounding like Mum.'

Too true. Their mother and her friends were always compelled to contribute an extra cake or a handy salad to any social gathering, no matter how small.

'Don't worry,' Seth said. 'It's just a casual, no-fuss barbecue.'

'Perfect. I'll bring wine.'

Flora felt extra happy as she practised. Her meeting with Peg, who was now home from hospital, wasn't scheduled till the next day. For now she could put the challenge of the Christmas concert out of her mind and stay focused on all the technical details of the Mozart and Tchaikovsky pieces, as well as the orchestral excerpts that she wanted to perfect.

By the end of the day she'd made good progress. She arrived home early, in an upbeat mood, with plenty of time to shower and wash her hair. She redid her toenails in a pretty mauve shade, and chose a little grey-and-white polka dot dress with shoestring straps and a white leather belt. Her white strappy sandals matched nicely. It was fun to be 'going out'.

Promptly at a quarter to six, Alice pulled up outside the cottage, and Flora was ready.

'Hey, cute dress,' Alice told her as she climbed into the ute.

Flora gave her a grateful smile. Alice had the kind of auburn-haired, pale-skinned beauty that could make a potato sack look glamorous, so her compliment carried weight.

'What have you got there?' Alice added, noticing the Tupperware box Flora had brought with her.

Flora still couldn't believe she'd ended up copying her mum's behaviour, but heck, she was back in a country town. It felt wrong to go somewhere empty-handed. 'Little caramel pies,' she confessed.

'Wow, you're a lifesaver!' Alice looked ecstatic. 'I've been a bit frantic about dessert. Seth was so casual and he told me not to worry, but I still have to do the salads when I get home. How thoughtful of you!'

Flora grinned and mentally thanked her mum. 'The recipe's dead easy. You just melt ready-bought gingernut biscuits into patty-tin shapes in the oven and then fill them with tinned caramel. A dollop of cream on top and hey presto!'

Alice grinned. 'Sounds brilliant. Practical but yummy. I'm still getting the hang of being a country woman.'

'Well, you've got your hands full with your business, plus Seth and Charlie.'

'I have, haven't I?' Alice was still smiling as she took off down the street.

'And I'm guessing you love it,' Flora said.

This brought an even wider grin. 'To be honest, I've never been happier.'

Flora smiled, too, genuinely pleased for her brother and this lovely girl. Then, without warning, she thought of Oliver and was hit by a whack of despair, which she quickly lassoed, tied up tightly and shoved into a bottomless crevice. Oliver was past tense.

A new life beckoned.

Alice drove them out of town over gently hilly, rolling downs country, softened by early evening shadows. These paddocks had been high with corn the last time Flora was home. Now they were freshly ploughed and the deep, chocolatey-red earth was striped with straight furrows of pale, finely chopped stalks.

She watched a tractor riding the rim of a hill, outlined against the western sky, like a child's drawing.

'I'm looking forward to seeing Tammy tonight,' she said, fingering a sweeping fringe of her hair. 'Actually, I'm going to need a hair trim soon.'

'We all love Tammy,' Alice said. 'She's a great hairdresser, and she's such a hoot. The stories she tells in her salon will keep you glued to her chair. And her boyfriend Ben's a born storyteller, too. They both have that knack. They're great company. I reckon they'll be the perfect distraction for Mitch.'

Mitch?

Kaboom.

'Is Mitch coming?' To Flora's dismay the question came out squeaking. What was the matter with her?

'Yes, this evening's as much for Mitch as it is for us.'

'Oh.'

Fortunately, Alice didn't seem to notice anything weird about Flora's reaction. 'We're trying to keep the poor guy busy when he's off-duty,' she said. 'It's not good for him to mope around at home.'

'No,' Flora agreed, and she berated herself for caring that Mitch had spurned both of her offers of hospitality.

So what? It made perfect sense that her brother was the person most likely to give Mitch the support he needed. Mitch had always looked up to Seth. And Mitch had, after all, chosen Seth as his best man.

'In a way, finding those bones has been useful,' Alice went on. 'They've at least given Mitch plenty of other things to think about apart from Angie.'

Flora nodded, and did her best to ignore the weird sensation that talking about Mitch seemed to cause. 'I wonder if they'll find out who the bones belong to?'

'I hope so,' said Alice. 'I don't like a mystery hanging over our heads.'

They were turning in at the gates to Kooringal now. Through the trees, the lights of the homestead flickered. A dog barked a greeting.

Alice parked her car on the driveway. Flora climbed out and collected her wine and her Tupperware box. The sweet smell of freshly mown grass lingered in the air and Seth's dog, Ralph, came forward eagerly, capering in ecstatic circles.

'Hello, Ralph, yes, I love you, too,' Flora told him. 'I'll give you a good scratch when I get rid of these things.' In Melbourne, she'd missed having a dog.

From inside the house came the sound of Charlie's happy squeals.

Alice grinned. 'Charlie loves visitors.'

The little boy met them at the top of the stairs. His T-shirt had green stains, as if he'd been rolling on the lawn. He smelled of grass and peanut butter as he submitted to their kisses and hugs.

'You haven't had your bath yet,' Alice told him.

'I can look after that,' Flora volunteered.

Alice beamed at her. 'That would be fabulous, thanks. I need to get started on the salads.'

In the kitchen, Seth had a tea towel slung over his shoulder as he sliced onions. He stopped and blinked watery onion eyes as he leaned over to kiss them both.

'You made good time,' he said as Alice set down a couple of grocery bags bulging with lettuce, tomatoes and herbs.

Flora looked around her. She really liked this new place. Alice had decorated the kitchen with some of her second-hand pieces, a scrubbed pine table, an old dresser painted in a distressed pastel green, and open shelving that was home to her collection of pretty glassware and crockery. But despite the care she'd taken, the kitchen benches were happily cluttered with toys and groceries along with a spanner and a small pile of nuts and screws.

Flora smiled. Nothing much had changed. Her mum had always grumbled at her dad for leaving bits and pieces from the tool shed lying about the house.

It all felt very familiar. For Flora, Seth and Alice's home had a welcoming atmosphere like a warm hug.

She felt herself relax. In a distant paddock a cow bellowed. It was almost like coming home.

Charlie tugged at the hem of her skirt. 'Auntie Floss.'

He was looking up at her with a sweet cheeky grin and she felt her heart melt.

'Okay, Charlie boy,' she said, taking his small grubby hand. 'Let's get you into the bath.'

After a great deal of splashing and suds-making and squeaking of rubber ducks, Flora emerged again, with Charlie scrubbed clean, towelled dry and glowing, dressed in his pyjamas, his damp hair neatly combed. She quite enjoyed doing the aunty thing.

By now, Tammy and Ben had arrived. Tammy was thin and tanned, with short, spiky blonde hair artistically streaked with pink and aqua. She also wore a row of little silver earrings in one ear, which no doubt appeared incredibly cool and trendy to the conservative folk of Burralea.

Tammy's boyfriend Ben had long tawny hair tied back into a ponytail. He also had a crushing handshake.

'If you haven't tried Ben's pies yet,' Alice told Flora, 'do yourself a favour. They're divine.'

Flora grinned. 'I can definitely see a pie for lunch in my immediate future.'

The evening was getting under way. Seth had gone onto the verandah to start up the gas barbecue. 'I'm cooking a sausage for you, Charlie,' he called. 'Won't be long.'

Ben was expertly chopping herbs, while Tammy made the salad dressings, measuring the ingredients so conscientiously, she might have been mixing hair dye. Alice had filled two salad bowls with delicious ingredients and now she was buttering a sourdough bread stick, which had come from Ben's bakery. Wine had been opened and poured.

'Mitch has been held up,' Alice said as she handed Flora a glass of chilled sav blanc. 'There's been a new development. Something to do with the bones.'

Flora thought of the story Edith had told her about Hattie and Joe, the chap who'd owned Kooringal until he sold it to Seth, and who had also, no doubt, broken Hattie's heart. She wondered if the bones had brought Hattie back to Burralea and she hoped this 'new development' didn't involve any more sadness for her.

'Let's go onto the verandah,' Alice suggested as soon as Ben's chopped herbs were sprinkled onto the salads, and they all helped with carrying food and plates and cutlery. Charlie, wanting to be part of the action, carried a packet of brightly coloured paper napkins, which he proudly offered for the barbecue table.

Tammy was impressed. 'You're very grown-up, Charlie. Alice, you're so good with him now. It's hard to remember you haven't been looking after him right from the start.'

Alice's complexion turned a pleasant shade of pink. 'Charlie's such a good-natured little guy,' she said. 'He makes looking after him easy.'

Seth was watching from his post at the barbecue. When his gaze met Alice's, they shared a special, secretive smile, the smile of lovers – knowing and intimate and absurdly happy. Flora stifled a pang of envy. She knew her day would come. She would find the right guy. First you had to kiss your share of toads . . .

Seth had held off cooking the steak and onions. 'Reckon we should give Mitch a little longer,' he said.

Everyone agreed. Alice cut up a sausage with some tomato and carrot and snow peas, and set them in a plastic bowl for Charlie. While he tucked into his dinner, the adults topped up their wine glasses. Seth moved the cooked sausages away from the heat and sent a text to Mitch, checking how long he might be.

The sun sank from view and in the surrounding trees, frogs and insects set up an evening chorus. Listening, Flora decided that

this evening ritual was almost like an orchestral performance. First
a buzz from the trees along the river, then a higher hum from the
crickets in the lilli pilli, until finally, on the very edge of dusk, the
piercing shrill of a single cicada that was quickly followed by the full
choir.

'Oh, God,' Alice cried as the noise became deafening. 'We should
have stayed inside until the cicadas were finished.'

Charlie looked delighted and stuck his fingers in his ears.

At least night fell quickly in the tropics, and it wasn't too long
before peace was restored. Alice lit fat outdoor candles as well as
mosquito coils. One by one, the stars came out, and Ben told a fishing story that shouldn't have been especially funny, but somehow
succeeded in making everyone laugh.

He definitely had the knack.

'I think I'd better throw these steaks on,' Seth said. 'Mitch must
be really caught up. He's not answering my text.'

And so, the wine flowed and the vibes around the verandah
table were convivial and relaxed. Ben told another funny story, and
Tammy spilled some 'safe' gossip about one or two of her custom-
ers. Alice was right. They were entertaining company, but Flora
wished she wasn't so aware of Mitch's absence.

'Poor Mitch,' Tammy said suddenly. 'You can't begin to imagine
how hard this week must have been for him, can you?'

Around the table, people watched each other, judging reactions.
Mitch's misery was, of course, the elephant in the room, the original
reason for this gathering.

'I mean, the whole town's talking,' Tammy said. 'I can't shut
them up in the salon. They're saying some pretty grim things about
Angie. Wow!' She shook her colourful head. 'You wouldn't believe
the venom. I bet that girl won't show her face around here again in
a hurry.'

The others nodded, looked a bit awkward.

'Between the non-wedding and the bones, it's been quite a week,' suggested Alice.

Charlie started to look tired and Flora offered to read him a bedtime story. 'I want to make the most of him while I'm here,' she explained.

Seth grinned. 'That's great. Thanks. Would you mind cleaning his teeth as well?'

'No probs.'

Reading by lamplight, snuggled together on Charlie's little bed, Flora was halfway through *The Very Hungry Caterpillar* when she heard the sound of a vehicle coming down the track.

Charlie had been sleepy and relaxed, but now he sat up, his bright blue eyes round with delight. 'Ooh,' he said. 'Car!'

Flora knew it was probably Mitch, and she couldn't quite suppress her own confusing reaction, but she was pretty sure Alice and Seth wouldn't want the little boy stirred up. So she merely nodded and kept on reading, pointing to the pictures, asking questions.

'Where's the caterpillar now, Charlie? What do you think he will eat next?'

Luckily, her ploy worked. Charlie was sufficiently distracted, and by the time she finished the book, he was happy to nestle down under the bedclothes.

Flora kissed him. 'Night night, don't let the bed bugs bite.'

The little boy giggled, shut his eyes, and she sat for a bit, waiting for him to settle as she listened to the sounds of the adults' voices drifting from the verandah, too muffled to properly distinguish.

It wasn't long before Charlie was perfectly still and quiet. She stood and was about to leave when Seth appeared in the doorway.

'All good?' he whispered.

Flora nodded and stood aside as Seth went to the bed and dropped a light kiss on Charlie's cheek. The little boy didn't stir.

'Good job,' Seth said with a grin, and they went outside into the hallway. Seth closed Charlie's door. 'Floss,' he said quietly.

She'd been about to head outside to the others, but now she turned back. 'Yes?'

'I thought I should let you know. I had a phone call from your boyfriend.'

CHAPTER FIFTEEN

Flora felt her blood drain to her knees, to her toes, through the floorboards. She couldn't speak.

They were standing in the hallway, however, and Seth was waiting.

'Oliver?' she managed.

Seth smiled. 'How many boyfriends do you have?'

'None. I broke it off with him. I thought you knew.' She'd never been sure how much info about Oliver her mum had passed on to Seth. Obviously very little, which was probably fair enough. Life had been rather hectic for the Drummonds while they were selling off Ruthven Downs, and her mum had never really guessed how truly freaked Flora was.

Meanwhile, Seth had been caught up with buying his farm, settling in here with Alice.

'Why would Oliver ring *you*, Seth?'

'I think he must have read about me – because of the bones – in one of the papers down south.'

'What did he want? What did you tell him?'

'He was kind of vague, but it was pretty clear he was fishing to know where you were.'

Flora's heart thudded. 'What did you tell him?' She knew she sounded panicked. She couldn't help it.

'I didn't tell him anything.' Seth was frowning now. 'I thought it was pretty strange that he needed to ring me. I mean, if you'd wanted him to know where you were, you would have told him. Right?'

'Yes. Exactly.' Flora tried to calm down. She knew she could trust Seth to be sensible, of course she could. But her fear ran deep. 'You're certain you didn't mention I was here?'

'No, Floss. I made sure I gave him no clue.'

'But what *did* you tell him?'

Seth was frowning deeply now. 'I simply said that the next time I spoke to you I'd mention that he'd called. He wasn't especially happy.' He studied her intently, his gaze narrowed, worried. 'You've really got the wind up, haven't you? What's this bastard done to you?'

Flora swallowed. 'He's the reason I resigned from my Melbourne job. I don't want to see him ever again.'

'Bloody hell, Floss. What happened?'

She didn't answer.

'He – he wasn't – he didn't hurt you, did he? He didn't hit you or anything?'

After a beat, she nodded. 'A bit, yes.'

The instant shock and worry in her brother's face brought tears to her eyes. Seth swore softly, then pulled her into his arms. His shoulders were huge, his arms warm and strong. It was a good place to be.

Shaking, she buried her face against his chest.

'You poor kid. I'm so sorry, Floss. I wish I'd known.'

Flora wished she could assure Seth there was no need to worry.

When he released her, she swiped at her eyes. 'Sorry. I'm probably overreacting. It should be fine, as long as I can lie low. I was actually hoping Oliver might have moved on – you know, found someone else, a new girlfriend.'

'I wish I'd given him an earful.'

She shook her head. 'No need. Water off a drake's back.' She sighed. 'Don't tell the others, will you?'

'Not if you don't want me to, although I think Mitch should be in the loop.'

Flora was about to protest. She didn't really want Mitch to know she'd made such a bad error of judgement in her choice of a boyfriend, but before she could say anything, footsteps sounded in the hall.

'Oh, there you are.' Alice smiled at them. 'I thought Charlie must have been playing up. You know Mitch is here?'

'Yeah,' said Seth. 'We're coming.'

Alice looked more closely at the two of them. 'Is everything all right?'

'Yes,' they both said together.

Mitch was tucking into his steak and salad when they returned to the verandah. Tammy was grilling him about the case.

She turned to Seth and Flora with an eager grin. 'We've just been hearing about the bullet Mitch found at the bones site this morning. He's quite the detective, isn't he? It's all very exciting.'

Seth merely nodded as if he already knew about the bullet. 'Have you been able to identify it?' he asked Mitch.

'Yeah, I managed to fast-track it down to Brisbane and we heard back an hour ago. It's a 30-calibre M1 Carbine round.'

'A Carbine?' Seth frowned. 'That doesn't sound like anything a farmer would use. You'd expect a 303 or a 22 on a farm around here. Or perhaps a 308, but they're more modern. Didn't you say those bones were old?'

'According to the experts, this bullet was US military issue from World War II.'

'US?' Seth looked shocked. 'Not the Aussies?'

Mitch shook his head. 'I thought it was strange, so I double-checked, but the Aussies didn't have the M1s that used those particular bullets.'

'And you reckon it's from World War II?' asked Ben.

Mitch nodded and everyone stared at him in puzzlement. Flora knew they were all thinking the same thing. How could a US military bullet end up on this part of the Tablelands? The American forces had been based on the coast, all eyes on the Coral Sea.

'Any Yanks in these parts were over at the Mareeba airstrip,' Seth said. 'It was the Aussies who were in this area in their thousands. They did their jungle training here before they went to New Guinea. I remember my grandmother telling me that, but I'm sure there weren't any Americans.'

'I know,' Mitch agreed. 'It's all quite a mystery.'

'Does that mean you might never find out the truth?' asked Alice.

Mitch shrugged. 'We can only keep plugging away. Actually, we've had a new development in a totally different direction this afternoon. The McCoys from over at Chillagoe marched into the office and claimed the bones belong to one of their great-uncles. They're pointing the finger at your neighbour the Murphys, Seth.'

Seth rolled his eyes, but then he seemed to have second thoughts. 'Well, it's true the McCoys and the Murphys have been at each other's throats for years, probably decades. It's all over cattle duffing. Both those families are prone to helping themselves on moonless nights to other people's poddy calves and even prime beef. Everyone knows that. It almost stopped me from buying this place.'

'Well, they're not admitting to anything like that, of course,' Mitch said. 'But the McCoys have certainly got themselves worked up. They've even been on talkback radio.'

Seth rolled his eyes. 'That will have the district buzzing.'

'But it's hardly likely that either the Murphys or the McCoys would have been using American bullets,' suggested Flora.

'Exactly.' Mitch acknowledged her logic with a smile.

Yesterday, a smile like that from Mitch would have made her blush. Tonight, after the news about Oliver, she simply felt numb.

* * *

After Flora left, driving Tammy and Ben home in Ben's truck, Alice retired, leaving Mitch and Seth on the verandah alone, finishing the night with a single malt.

Mitch helped himself to another of Flora's caramel tarts. 'These are more-ish,' he said, almost demolishing the dainty tart in one heady gulp.

Seth grinned. 'My little sister has hidden talents.'

'And she has the brains to stay under the limit,' Mitch added. 'I was worried for a while there. I didn't want to have to stop Tammy and Ben. Thank God Flora offered to drive them home.'

'Yeah, she's pretty sensible.' Seth studied his whisky glass, tracing the cut glass edge with his fingertips. 'I'm worried about her, though.'

Mitch caught the flash of genuine concern in his friend's eyes. 'Why's that?'

'Looks like she might have a problem with the guy she used to live with in Melbourne.'

A block of ice seemed to lodge in Mitch's chest. Flora in trouble? 'Really?'

'Maybe.' Seth grimaced unhappily. 'I thought he was just a nuisance. But it seems like Floss dumped him, and yet he's trying to track her down. She's obviously scared.'

Abandoning his relaxed pose, Mitch leaned forward, his gaze

narrowed and intent. 'Shit, Seth. Are we talking violence here?'

'I think so. I reckon that's why Flora got out of there.'

'Do you know if she took out an intervention order?'

Seth shook his head. 'I doubt it. I reckon she would have mentioned it if she had.' He tightened his fist around the glass. 'I'm kicking myself now that I haven't paid more attention.'

'Yeah, me too.' Mitch felt sick at the possibility that Flora might be in danger. Here. Right under his nose. While he was busy feeling sorry for himself. 'So what's happened?' he demanded.

'Well, nothing, really, at this point. I certainly didn't let on to this Oliver prick that Flora was in Burralea. But I suppose he might keep prying.' Seth worried the glass again, pushing it along the table like it was a chess piece, like he was trying to plot a strategy. 'You know much about violent types?'

'Well, obviously it's a huge issue for all coppers these days. And justly so.'

'So it really is as big a problem as they make out in the press? All those deaths?'

'Sure. It's always been a problem, of course, but these days, since more women have spoken up, it seems like it's a bloody epidemic.'

Seth nodded unhappily.

'I won't go into details,' Mitch added. 'But country towns aren't immune. We've got problems up here.'

'So what about Flora? What can she do?'

'She could apply for an intervention order. It would have to go through the courts. Kate Woods could see to that.'

Seth shook his head. 'Kate and Brad have just taken off for overseas. They're joining Mum and Dad for Christmas over there.'

'Damn. Oh, well, there are other ways and means, of course. And to be honest, if the guy's determined, those pieces of paper are about as useful as tits on a bull.' Mitch sighed. 'Flora's already made a good decision by lying low here. And I'll certainly keep an eye on her.'

'She's hoping to get a job in Brisbane,' Seth said. 'You reckon she'll be okay down there?'

Mitch frowned. 'I've got a few contacts in Brisbane. I'll have a talk to them. It wouldn't hurt to do a little forward planning.'

'Thanks,' said Seth. 'That would be a load off.'

'The main thing is, Flora's okay for the moment. So we take this one step at a time. Okay?'

* * *

Flora walked home across town, after dropping Tammy and Ben off. The night was cool, a complete contrast to the heat and storms of the previous night. A soft white veil of mist hung over the streets, and the lights coming from the houses and lampposts and the occasional vehicle glowed fuzzily golden.

Keeping to the footpath, Flora found the mist rather romantic and only slightly eerie. Normally, she would have enjoyed it, but tonight she was stressed to the eyeballs about Oliver. How dare he ring Seth.

He couldn't track her down here, could he?

Memories she'd been trying to suppress forced their way back, and she half-expected Oliver to suddenly appear, a spectre emerging from the white cloud. Tall, barrel chested, with a shock of thick blonde hair. She shivered and her mind raced in circles of panic.

Even if Oliver did discover that she was living here, would he really bother to travel three thousand kilometres just to annoy her? It was hard to imagine. And yet . . .

She felt she had to do something, take some kind of action.

Stopping under a streetlight, she pulled out her phone and sent a quick text to Ellen, her closest friend in Melbourne.

Oliver rang my brother. I'm freaking. If he asks you where I am, try to put him off the scent. Please remind him I'm at the Gold

Coast and about to head to Hong Kong.

Hope all's well. F xx

She walked on. The scent of night jasmine drifted towards her and she felt a little calmer, told herself she was overreacting. It was silly to get into a stew after such a nice evening out with family and friends. She'd really enjoyed everyone's company and it was great to see how happy Seth and Alice were together.

She'd been young when she'd left home, and she hadn't properly got to know her brother as an adult, so it was good to be back in the north, to have this chance to see more of him.

Mitch had obviously benefited from Seth's company as well. He'd seemed a lot more relaxed this evening and Flora was glad she'd been free of the silly flusters that had plagued her lately in his presence. Her fright about Oliver had wiped out such nonsense. She was back to reality, instead of acting like a schoolgirl who still had a stupid crush on her big brother's mate.

She was turning a mist-shrouded corner when her phone pinged. Quickly she checked to find a return message from Ellen.

Will do. Don't worry, am keeping a close eye on O. He's missed out on any of the major roles in The Ring Cycle. Not a happy chappy. Take care. E xx

Flora shuddered. Oliver would be furious at missing out on a decent singing role in such an important production as Wagner's *Ring Cycle*. This would feed into his darkness and self-hate and, almost certainly, he would want to find someone to blame for this failure.

Like the girlfriend who'd so recently deserted him?

Flora's chest tightened, and she thanked God that Seth had the brains to get rid of Oliver without passing on any info about her. And now Seth was probably telling Mitch about Oliver, for which she was also grateful. It was time to stop worrying about what Mitch might think of her. A policeman who understood her situation was a very good thing.

Maybe it was time to get an intervention order. Flora had been reluctant to do this before. It had felt too dramatic, too public, turning a small problem with her boyfriend into something huge. But it was reassuring to know the option was available. As a last resort.

Walking on, almost home, Flora passed the church where she practised, then next to it, the Burralea Lodge. The front door of the guesthouse was open, flooding its front garden with light and showing off the attractive tree ferns and bromeliads and clumps of ginger. People were leaving.

Flora recognised Hattie, the woman who'd sat in on her Tchaikovsky rehearsal. She was framed in the doorway, tall, silver-haired and elegant in a soft green dress, and she was saying goodnight to an elderly man, who was also tall and silver-haired.

'Goodnight,' Flora heard him call. 'I'll see you in the morning.'

Flora decided, as he walked down the path, that he had the lean, honed body of a man of the land. She wondered if he was Joe Matthews, the man who'd apparently let Hattie down very badly, many years ago.

Goodness. Despite her preoccupation with Oliver, Flora's curiosity was instantly piqued. It was an interesting coincidence that Hattie had arrived in Burralea so soon after the bones were discovered. But how on earth was Hattie's unhappy romance with Joe Matthews connected to the unsettling discovery on Kooringal?

CHAPTER SIXTEEN

'Oh, Hattie, you've beaten me to it.' April managed to look quite forlorn. 'I was just going to dash upstairs to see if you'd like help with your luggage.'

'That's a kind thought, but there was no need.' Hattie smiled as she set her room key on the counter. 'I've managed. It's only a small carry-on bag. I still had a hand free to use the stair rail.'

'Yes, you've managed very well. So you'd like to check out, would you?'

'Yes, please.'

Turning to her computer, April spoke over her shoulder. 'It's a pity you have to leave so soon. You haven't been able to see much of the district.'

'Another time, perhaps. I didn't really come here to see the sights.'

'No' April said with significant emphasis, and the glance she shot to Hattie, over the top of her reading glasses, was shimmering with blatant curiosity.

Hattie knew April was dying to ask her about Joe's unexpected visit to the guesthouse last night. April had been waiting on guests in the dining room, and almost certainly, she'd noticed how shocked Hattie had been when Joe first appeared in the doorway.

'Well, here's your receipt,' she said now, as the paper emerged from the printer on her desk. 'I hope you've enjoyed your stay.'

'I have, very much, thank you. The room was very comfortable and I felt as if I had that lovely jacaranda tree all to myself.' Hattie folded the receipt and slipped it into her shoulder bag.

'That tree's a beauty, isn't it? So – is there anything else we can do to help? Do you need a lift to the bus stop?'

Hattie flashed her a warm smile. 'Thanks, but someone's coming to pick me up. It's all organised.'

Hattie was pleased that she managed to sound calm as she said this. With a final goodbye, she went through to the foyer and set her small suitcase by an armchair. She was too restless to sit, however, and she stepped outside into the fresh mountain morning. She would take a little stroll in the garden while she waited for Joe, and she would once again think through what they needed to tell the police.

It had been such a huge surprise to see him last night.

The dining room had not been busy. Apart from Hattie, there was only one other party, a group of six young people who'd come to the Tablelands to traverse the famous mountain-bike tracks. Their table was set at the far end of the room and they'd chatted happily and with a great deal of laughter, while Hattie sat alone, used to her own company and quite comfortable.

She had just finished her dessert, a very tasty citrus tart, and she'd been deliberating over whether she would finish her meal with a cup of coffee, when her attention was caught by the sight of a tall, silver-haired figure in the doorway.

A now familiar figure.

The very man who'd invaded her thoughts all day, even though she'd tried, quite desperately, not to dwell on the past. Most especially she hadn't wanted to relive the pain of the heartbreak he'd caused. She'd thought she'd dealt with that and buried it years ago.

Added to that, Joe's current behaviour had been almost as upsetting. Hattie found his refusal to talk to the police about the bones very frustrating. It left her in a difficult position, now trying to decide whether she would act alone.

She was beginning to think she'd made a terrible mistake by coming back to Burralea.

And yet, infuriatingly, the sight of Joe, when she'd least expected it, had set a flurry of wings beating in her chest. Of course, she was desperately curious to know why he'd come.

As she might have expected, he didn't march straight into the dining room, but waited politely in the doorway. His expression was serious as his gaze met Hattie's and he gave her a nod, and she fancied she saw a faint smile as well.

Annoyingly, her legs were shaky as she got to her feet, and she had to grip the edge of the table to steady herself.

Luckily, April hurried forward, all smiles. 'Good evening, sir. How can I help you?'

Joe nodded again in Hattie's direction. 'I'd like a quick word with one of your guests, if I may.'

April's eyes were huge and the smile she directed towards Hattie was dazzling. 'Of course, sir. You wanted to see Mrs Macquarie?'

Joe probably didn't know Hattie's married name, but he nodded towards her.

'Over here,' said April. 'Please take a seat.'

With a polite bow of his head, Joe crossed the room to Hattie, who was still standing, clutching the edge of the table.

'Good evening, Hattie,' he said quietly.

'Hello, Joe.'

'I hope I haven't interrupted your meal.'

'No, no, I've just finished.'

'I felt I needed to speak to you. Something's come up.'

'Oh?' She waited a beat, but when Joe didn't elaborate, she said, 'Well, I'm happy to listen. Please, sit down.' She couldn't help feeling flustered. She *was* flustered. Terribly. What on earth had 'come up'?

'It might be better if we speak outside,' Joe said. 'Do you mind? I won't keep you for long.'

'No, I don't mind.'

To Hattie's relief, her legs had stopped shaking and she was able to cross the polished timber floorboards without mishap as she accompanied Joe out of the room.

In the small foyer, a padded cane chair faced a two-seater sofa over a coffee table that was scattered with tourist brochures extolling the sights of the Tablelands.

'Perhaps we could sit here?' Joe asked.

'Thank you.' Hattie took the two-seater and Joe sat opposite her. He was wearing pale moleskins and a finely checked blue shirt, and his tan boots looked freshly polished. 'So,' she asked impatiently. 'What's happened, Joe? What's come up?'

'There was a story on the news this evening. A family from Chillagoe, the McCoys, have been to the police claiming that the bones on Kooringal are almost certainly their great-uncle's. They said he went missing about thirty years ago.'

'But that's —' Hattie was about to say it was impossible but she checked herself. 'That's highly unlikely, isn't it?'

'Yes,' he said, and then he went on, without beating around the bush, 'I should speak to the police, Hattie.'

'Yes.'

'You're right,' he added with a wry smile. 'We can't let them waste their time on a red herring like the Murphys and the McCoys.

It's not fair to the people who are copping the blame.'

The relief, the sense of a weight lifting from Hattie's shoulders, was immediate and sweet.

'I'm glad that's how you feel. But what about your sister? Have you spoken to her?'

'Yes. I found myself telling her everything. She was upset, having all those memories stirred, but she wants the record set straight.'

'Good.' Hattie refrained from adding that she'd been certain this was what Margaret would want.

'I'll speak to Sergeant Cavello first thing in the morning,' Joe said.

She found that she could smile. 'I'm so pleased.'

Joe nodded. 'You should probably come, too. You're another witness and I'm sure the police will want to speak to you as well. They'll need you to corroborate my story.'

'Yes, I suppose so.'

'Would you mind?'

'No, not at all. As you know, I wasn't happy about keeping quiet. My only problem is, I have a return flight to Brisbane booked for three tomorrow afternoon.'

Joe frowned. 'You might need to change that. The police will probably want us to go out to Kooringal, to check our story with what they've found. It might take some time.'

'Yes.' Hattie realised she'd cut it rather fine, only allowing herself two days in the north. 'I should be able to ring the airline and change the flight,' she said. 'But I don't know about accommodation. I might be able to stay on here for a few extra nights.' She got to her feet again. I may as well check with April straight away.'

April, however, looked dismayed when Hattie queried her. 'I'm so sorry,' she said. 'It's market weekend. The Burralea markets are quite a tourist attraction these days and accommodation fills up quickly. I'm fully booked out. You could try the pub.'

Returning to Joe, Hattie gave a shake of her head. 'No luck here, I'm afraid. I suppose I'd better see if there's room at the pub.'

She didn't fancy the pub though, especially on a weekend. The bar would be full of noisy drinkers and there'd probably be a band playing, electric guitars twanging.

'I'd be happy to offer you my spare room.'

Joe's suggestion was so unexpected, Hattie needed a moment to digest it. Surely staying with Joe would be even less desirable than staying at the pub?

Perhaps her distress showed on her face.

He said, 'We're old friends, Hattie. I won't talk about – the *other* – not if it upsets you. But as an old friend, let me offer you a room for a night or two, until we get this matter cleared.'

He sounded like the Joe of old, the sensible, levelheaded school-boy she'd so admired.

I won't talk about – the other.

Hattie wished she could think of a hasty alternative. Perhaps she should ring around first. There might be a B&B somewhere. But when she remembered Joe's comfortable, book-filled cottage and his lovely dog, Marlowe, she asked herself why she should rush to reject his offer.

This was her chance to show him that she was quite recovered from the decades-old hurt he'd caused her – the 'other' he'd so deli-cately referred to. Besides, she prided herself on being open-minded.

'This is a small town,' she felt compelled to remind Joe. 'Tongues would wag.'

'I can cope with that, if you can,' he said calmly.

Hattie knew she was long past the age of minding what peo-ple said. And anyway, in a few more days she would be gone and it would Joe who was left to deal with the sidelong glances and nosy questions from locals. All things considered, she decided it would be silly, even prudish, to refuse him.

'Thank you, Joe,' she said graciously. 'That would be very helpful.'

His face had broken into a slow smile and by the time he'd left, they'd set a tentative plan in place.

Last night the plan had seemed eminently sensible. This morning, however, as Joe's silver-grey Subaru pulled up in front of the guesthouse, Hattie felt as if her life was turning in a new, totally uncharted direction.

* * *

Mitch tried not to look too surprised when Joe Matthews walked into the station with a woman he'd never seen before.

Joe introduced his companion as Hattie Macquarie. 'Hattie lived at Kooringal many years ago,' Joe said. 'When we were both school kids.'

Indeed? Mitch felt fine hairs lifting on the back of his neck. He knew this conversation was going to be significant. 'How do you do, Ms Macquar—'

'Hattie,' the woman said, and she smiled as she held out her hand. 'Call me Hattie.'

'Pleased to meet you, Hattie.' She was probably as old as Joe, nearing the end of her seventies, but her handshake was firm and her blue eyes sparkled with intelligence. Mitch guessed that she must have been a looker in her youth. 'How can I help you both?' he asked.

Joe seemed to visibly square his shoulders as if he was bracing himself for a difficult task. 'We've come to tell you about something that happened on Kooringal, way back in 1942. We think it might be relevant to the mystery of those bones Seth Drummond found.'

Aware of a hitch in his breathing, Mitch kept his demeanour deliberately calm. 'That's great. Thanks for coming,' he said, as he gestured towards the small interview room. 'We can talk in here.'

CHAPTER SEVENTEEN

Kooringal, 1942

Crouched in their hiding place near the caged finch, Joe and Hattie's ears were still ringing with the sound of gunshots when a truck roared out of the scrub and into the clearing in front of them.

'I think it's the Yanks,' Joe whispered.

'How do you know?' Hattie whispered back. 'They might be *our* soldiers.'

'There's a white star on the side of the truck. I've seen it in newspapers. It's the American Army's insignia.'

Joe knew all kinds of facts from books and newspapers. And now, as Hattie peered out through their screen of bottlebrush branches, two soldiers climbed out of the truck. They were dressed in khaki uniforms with heavy black boots, and they wore cloth caps rather than the slouch hats of the Aussie soldiers. Black armbands on their khaki sleeves showed the letters MP in solid white. Joe was probably right – they were almost certainly American soldiers – but their skin was pale, not dark and glossy like Gabriel's.

One of the soldiers carried a heavy-looking gun and the other man pulled a shovel from the back of the truck.

At the sight of the shovel fear ripped through Hattie. She

remembered soldiers with guns in Shanghai. Dead bodies lined on the edge of the road. Men with shovels.

'We have to get out of here,' she whispered.

'Yeah, I reckon.'

Thoroughly scared now, she reached for Joe's hand. At first, he didn't move, he simply gripped her hand hard, lacing his long fingers with hers while he stared ahead through the leaves. Then he gave her hand a squeeze.

'Okay. Let's go. Be very quiet.'

Together they stealthily crept away, leaving the little cage with the finch still sitting out in the open, plain to see. Hattie hoped the bird didn't start calling right now, not till they were well out of sight.

As they reached the cover of denser bush, they heard the soldier's shovel slicing into the earth, but they couldn't look back to see what was happening and Hattie didn't dare to wonder why he might be digging.

It was only when they were safely out of sight and out of earshot that they turned and ran. For their lives. To the homestead.

Joe's father was at the house, which was unusual. Normally, Mr Matthews worked outside from dawn till dusk, tending to his cattle, mending fences or fixing a water pump, tinkering with his tractor's motor or ploughing fields to grow lucerne for hay. There was always some chore to keep him busy outside, but today he was in the kitchen with Joe's mother, and the adults were so deep in conversation they seemed unaware of the children clattering up the back stairs.

Mrs Matthews was sitting at the kitchen table and her face looked blotchy, as if she'd been crying. She had a sodden handkerchief bunched in one hand. Mr Matthews was standing opposite her, leaning towards her with his hands on the table's scrubbed pine surface, bracing his weight. His face was flushed, his mouth trembling and he seemed to be pleading with his wife.

'Dad!' Joe cried and both his parents jumped.

Their faces fell when they saw Hattie and Joe.

'Where have you two been?' Joe's father demanded.

'Trapping finches,' said Joe. 'Down near the river.'

'We saw soldiers,' Hattie couldn't help adding importantly.

Mrs Matthews let out a cry and quickly covered her mouth with her crumpled handkerchief.

'We think they're Americans,' said Joe.

His parents exchanged desperate glances.

'We heard gunshots, too. What's going on, Dad?'

It felt like an age before Mr Matthews answered. It was so quiet and tense in the kitchen Hattie could hear the clock ticking on the wall and the slow drip coming from the tap over the sink.

Drip . . . tick . . . drip . . . tock . . .

Eventually, Mr Matthews drew a deep breath, making his chest expand, and he hooked his thumbs under his braces. He was a tall, spare man with wide shoulders and short brown hair flecked with grey – a bigger, grown-up version of Joe.

'Listen kids,' he said, pulling a long face. 'You know this is wartime. There's things that happen during a war that have to be kept a secret.' He set his solemn gaze on Joe. 'Your mum and I aren't allowed to tell anyone about this, or there'll be real problems. You mustn't say anything either.'

'What about *my* mother?' Hattie couldn't help asking. 'Can I tell her?'

Mr Matthews shook his head. 'Best not, Hattie. Joan and I will talk to Rose.' He cocked his head to one side, his eyes thoughtfully narrowed. 'You've seen what it was like in Shanghai. You must have known how dangerous the war was over there in China. Now the war's reaching us here, and there are some things you just can't talk about. It's not safe. Do you understand?'

Remembering Shanghai, Hattie nodded. She'd been told not to talk to her playmates about her Uncle Rudi.

Her mum used to tell her, 'You have to be quiet for Rudi's sake, Hattie. We mustn't say anything that might put him in danger.'

Memories of the secrecy surrounding her uncle prompted Hattie to ask, 'Where's Gabriel?'

At this, Joe's father looked extra pained, while his mother chewed on her lip and her eyes glistened with the threat of fresh tears.

'Gabriel's gone away,' Mr Matthews said.

'Gone?' Hattie stared at him in puzzled dismay. This didn't make sense. Why would Gabriel go away on the very day his fellow countrymen turned up at Kooringal? She sent a quick glance to Joe and saw her own doubts and questions mirrored in his eyes.

Then Joe spoke up. 'Why, Dad? Why'd Gabriel go away?'

Mr Matthews gritted his teeth, as if he was fast losing his patience. 'I've told you to drop the questions. He's gone back to the American Army and I don't want to hear any more about this.'

'But what about the shots?' Joe persisted. 'Was it the soldiers shooting?'

This brought another exasperated sigh from his father. 'For crying out loud, son. You'll just have to accept it's none of our flaming business. It's part of the bloody war.'

This still didn't make sense to Hattie and she was sure it didn't to Joe either. She felt sick, certain that the adults were hiding something awful. Something about Gabriel.

She thought about Joe's sister, Margaret, who worked as a typist in Burralea's stock and station agency. Poor Margaret wouldn't be home till after five and she would be heartbroken to learn that Gabriel had vanished without even saying goodbye.

Hattie thought about the day they'd seen Margaret and Gabriel kissing, and she was so caught up in these memories she didn't notice Joe's father crossing the room until he was standing in front of them.

'Joe,' Mr Matthews said, fixing his solemn gaze on his son. 'I want you to stand up straight, like a soldier, and I want you to promise you'll say nothing about any of this. Not to anyone.'

* * *

Burralea, 2015

Mitch sat quietly, his pen and notepad untouched, while he listened to Joe Matthews's story. At first, when he'd seen Joe striding into the station, Mitch had thought he was about to hear a gruesome confession.

Now he couldn't help feeling relieved that Joe and Hattie's story was one of childhood innocence and a wartime mystery. Chances were, though, that after so many years, they might never solve the entire mystery.

'If I took you out to Kooringal, could you identify the place where this happened?' Mitch asked.

Both Joe and Hattie nodded.

'I can show you the exact spot,' Joe said.

'That would certainly be helpful. The detective in charge of this case will want to talk to you as well, of course, so I hope you'll be available?'

'Yes,' they said together.

Detective Vince Cobram was currently deep in discussions with the Murphys and the McCoys. Mitch wondered how he'd react to this new lead. 'So you've given me details of what you both saw.' He looked directly at Joe. 'Did your father ever shed more light on this?'

Joe nodded. 'Eventually. But it was years later. The war was well and truly over. I was probably in my late teens by then.'

'And?'

The elderly man took a moment to compose himself. 'My father explained that Gabriel was a runaway from the American Army.'

'Right.' Mitch had suspected this and was pleased to have it confirmed.

'Back in 1942,' Joe went on, 'there was some kind of problem in Townsville between the black Americans and the white officers. Really bad racial discrimination, from what I can make out. Quite a skirmish. Dad seemed to think that some men were killed, but Gabriel managed to escape. A couple of Australian soldiers in a truck picked him up. They were on their way up here to the Tablelands for jungle training and they knew Gabriel would be in deep trouble if they turned him over. They were worried he might have been shot.'

Joe seemed to visibly relax now that this was off his chest.

'So how did Gabriel end up at your place?' Mitch asked.

'One of the Australians had worked on our property, and he knew my father had fought in World War I. I guess it was a long shot, but he took a punt that Dad would be sympathetic to Gabriel's plight. Turned out Dad had seen the Brits shoot young shell-shocked soldiers in France, and he was deadset against any army shooting their own men. So, he took Gabriel in – just until things settled down.'

Joe glanced sideways to his companion, and Hattie gave him a warm smile and a small encouraging nod.

Mitch couldn't help wondering about this pair's childhood friendship. He was trying to picture the white-haired, elderly couple as curious kids trapping finches in the bush.

'So I'm guessing these US soldiers that turned up at Kooringal were on the hunt for Gabriel,' Mitch said.

Joe nodded. 'They were Military Police. I'm not sure how they got the tip-off, but they'd heard about Gabriel and they'd come to collect him.'

'But are you suggesting,' Mitch asked carefully, 'that they shot him and buried him right there on your property?'

'My father believed the shooting was an accident. The MPs certainly collected Gabriel and bundled him into the truck. They said they were going to court-martial him back in Townsville, but it seems that Gabriel didn't believe them. He must have panicked and tried to escape – jumped out the back of the truck. One of the soldiers fired at him, to stop him. Dad reckoned he fired low, as if he only wanted to slow him down.'

Joe was sitting forward now, elbows propped on his knees. He dropped his gaze to his loosely linked hands, then looked up again. 'Unfortunately, the bullet hit an artery. The MPs were upset and they tried to save him. They applied pressure and everything, but Gabriel bled to death quite quickly.'

Mitch let out a low whistle. The forensics had reported finding a bullet hole in one of the thigh bones. It looked like Joe's story stood up.

'My parents were devastated,' said Joe.

'But your parents never spoke up?'

Joe shook his head. 'Those Yanks put the frighteners up them. Told them that if word got out, they'd be in trouble for harbouring a war criminal. They reckoned Gabriel was part of a mutiny, and they could have Dad locked up for the rest of the war. He could lose his property.'

'And the body?' Mitch asked.

'The MPs said they would take care of it.' Joe sighed. 'I went back the next day to collect the finch, and I could see a longish mound of dirt where they'd been digging. Looked to me like it could have been a grave, but Dad didn't want to know about it.'

'What about after the war?' Mitch asked. 'Your parents still didn't speak up?'

'No. They figured it was too late to change anything, and I suppose they were worried they might still end up in some kind of trouble. I don't think Dad could accept that Gabriel was buried on our property. He just wanted the problem to go away.'

CHAPTER EIGHTEEN

On the footpath outside the police station, the air was hot, the sun blazing, but the gruelling morning was behind them. Sergeant Cavello had taken Joe and Hattie to Kooringal and they'd confirmed that the place where they'd seen the US Army truck was indeed the same spot where the bones were found.

Detective Cobram had also taken them through a similar line of questioning to the sergeant's. There would probably be follow-up questions, but for now Hattie and Joe were free to go.

'You've done well,' Hattie told Joe. 'How do you feel now you've got that off your chest?'

'Worn out,' he said with a rueful smile.

'You should probably go home and rest.' The police had hinted at this, too.

Joe shook his head. 'I don't think I'd be able to rest.'

'But you must be relieved that you've spoken up about Gabriel?'

'Well, yes. It's a great weight off my mind.' He offered Hattie a cautious smile. 'Thanks for giving me the nudge.'

'In the end, I didn't really have to nudge.' Joe had come to the decision by himself.

Now he stood with his hands resting loosely on his lean hips and looked towards his car and then down the street to the row of little cottages beyond the police station. An elderly woman, who must have been about their own age, was standing on the front step of one of the cottages. Hattie recognised her house as the same one that she and Rose had lived in all those years ago.

Hattie had walked past it again yesterday, and she'd been interested to note changes. The weatherboard walls were now painted cream, but they were looking a bit cracked and cobwebby in places. A frangipani tree had grown enormous and was now covered in gorgeously scented apricot flowers that also spread in a carpet beneath. There was a new picket fence, painted white, and a neat, if unimaginative, garden with agapanthus and spider lilies planted in straight lines.

The cottage's current occupant was dressed in a floral apron and, despite the hot day, fluffy winter slippers. Hovering on the front step, she raised a hand to shade her eyes, and she stared at Hattie and Joe with unabashed curiosity.

'I feel like getting out of town,' Joe said, turning his back on their observer. 'How about I take you somewhere nice for lunch?'

Hattie was surprised by how strongly this suggestion appealed.

'Thank you, Joe. I'd like that.'

'What about the Teahouse at Lake Barrine?'

'Goodness, I'd forgotten about that place, but it was always lovely.'

'It hasn't really changed very much over the years, and the lake's as picturesque as ever.'

'I'm sure it is. What a good idea.'

'And you'll trust my driving?' His mouth tilted in the beginnings of a smile. 'I'm told I'm still competent.'

Hattie couldn't help smiling in return. 'Yes, I'm game.'

'Let's go then.'

Joe opened the car door for her, then hurried around to his side. The car was boiling after sitting in the sun all morning and he turned on the air conditioning with the fan on full blast, waited a bit for the interior to cool down, before adjusting the fan and driving off.

As they left Burralea along a road that crossed lush green hills dotted with dairy cows, Hattie experienced a moment of disbelief. Somehow the impossible had happened. She and Joe were together again, behaving almost as if they hadn't parted in such deep despair all those years ago, as if they hadn't spent several decades living completely separate lives with absolutely no contact.

She'd known other old friends who could pick up again as if no time had elapsed, but she'd never dreamed it could happen for her and Joe. Surely this was wrong? This man had left her desperately angry and hurt, and she was sure at some deeply subconscious level she'd never really forgiven him.

This should *feel* wrong, shouldn't it? And yet, to Hattie, spending more time with Joe and accepting his hospitality felt, perplexingly, right.

The road continued on through thick rainforest that crowded close to the edge of the bitumen. Lake Barrine, the site of the Teahouse, was a crater lake set right in the heart of the forest.

Joe turned in to the parking area that had been created on one level of the terraced gardens where mauve and pink bougainvillea sprawled over rock walls. Again, he behaved like an old-fashioned gentleman, coming to help Hattie out of the car and to keep a steadying hand at her elbow as they went down a crazy-paved path, past gardens filled with brunfelsias, hibiscus, rambling roses and impressive clumps of ground orchids.

The Teahouse stood below them on the bottom terrace, fringed by palms and tree ferns and lush, shaded tropical gardens. The building was a nostalgic 1920s design with white timber walls and a green gabled roof. It would have been pretty anywhere, but set against the backdrop of a sunlit, sparkling blue lake and ringed by dense green rainforest, the venue was stunning.

'Oh, it's beautiful, Joe. I'd forgotten. It's just lovely, isn't it? Timeless, really.'

He looked pleased.

They'd reached a flight of broad stone steps that led to the Teahouse's entrance, and although Hattie's knee was quite strong now, she still preferred to use the handrail. She noticed that Joe managed the steps without such assistance. She supposed all those years of working on the land had kept him fitter than most.

Inside, they found a table for two on a shaded balcony that offered a view of the lake. Hattie ordered quiche and salad, while Joe chose a hamburger with the works.

'What would you like to drink?' he asked. 'Do you fancy a glass of wine?'

Hattie laughed. It had been years since she'd drunk wine in the middle of the day. 'I'm afraid it would send me to sleep. I'd be happy with water and maybe a coffee later.'

'Okay. I feel like a ginger beer.'

'Oh!' Hattie couldn't remember the last time she'd drunk ginger beer, but suddenly her tastebuds were tingling. 'Actually, I'd like to change my mind and have ginger beer as well.'

'We can share a bottle if you like.'

'Perfect.'

While they waited for their meals, they sipped their refreshing drinks and looked out at the lake. In its centre, the water reflected the clear, hot blue of the sky, but merged into aqua and a deeper green closer to shore, beneath the shelter of the overhanging rainforest.

A small ferry boat carried tourists, taking them on a tour of the lake, nearing the shore at times for a close-up view of the huge trunks of centuries-old trees draped with tangled vines and lianas and home to a wonderful collection of tropical birds, or the occasional amethystine python. In the reeds close to where Joe and Hattie sat, a family of wood ducks paddled and dived.

Watching them, Hattie said, 'So, tell me about your family, Joe.'

He looked only mildly surprised and he responded readily enough. 'I have two daughters. Janelle is married to a fellow from over near Mareeba. He has orchards – lychees and avocados and mangoes. I think he has macadamias, too, and he seems to do very well. They have three sons, but they're grown-up now, of course.'

Hattie nodded and found herself momentarily caught up, thinking of the years and years of living they'd both been through since they'd last seen each other, the joys and sorrows, the moments of deep satisfaction or nerve-jangling worry. Janelle would have been the baby that had necessitated Joe's shotgun wedding. These days, of course, no one turned a hair about a baby born out of wedlock.

'One of Janelle's boys is a star footballer,' Joe said, cutting into her thoughts.

'A footballer? What's his name?'

'Fergus Grant.'

'Oh, really?' Hattie stared at him in surprise. 'I don't follow football, but I've certainly heard of Fergus Grant, and I've seen his photo in the papers. He's something of a household name, isn't he?'

Joe smiled. 'He's certainly well known in North Queensland.'

'That must be exciting for the family.'

'Yes, I suppose we all enjoy a little reflected glory.'

Hattie finished her drink. 'You said you had *two* daughters?'

'Yes, there's also Emma.'

Hattie wasn't sure if she imagined it, but she fancied Joe's voice had softened as he said Emma's name.

'Emma's a doctor in Brisbane,' he said. 'A heart specialist. She's married to a male nurse.'

She gave a light laugh. 'That's handy.'

'Yes, it is, I guess. I think I've had every health check known to man.'

'And are you in good shape?'

'Good enough, apparently. I've been lucky with my health.'

'That's reassuring for you. Do Emma and her husband have children?'

'Just the one – a little girl, Ivy. She turned three last month.'

'Three?' Hattie wondered if she'd heard correctly.

'Emma's only just turned forty. She's a lot younger than Janelle. She wasn't born until after I came back from Vietnam.'

This last piece of information was a shock. Hattie stared at him. 'You weren't involved in the Vietnam War, were you?'

'Yes, I was.'

Good heavens. Hattie couldn't hide her surprise. She knew Joe would have been too old to be conscripted. 'Did you volunteer?' *Surely not?*

Joe nodded. 'I don't know if you remember my mate Cliff Barnes.'

'Yes, I think so. Dark hair, wiry, good at sport?'

'That's the one. Cliff and I were both in the CMF – it was a fore-runner to the Army Reserve – and it involved a session once a week in the drill hall, and a camp a couple of times a year. So I'd had enough basic training to offer up my services.'

'How amazing. I don't think I would ever have picked you as someone who'd volunteer to be a soldier.' But then, Hattie reluc-tantly remembered, she also wouldn't have picked Joe Matthews as a man who would cheat on the girl he'd proposed to marry.

Joe picked up his glass, but all that was left were ice cubes, and he set it down again. 'I'm not proud of my real reasons for going to that war.'

Hattie braced herself. Was she about to hear another unpalat-able confession?

'I wanted a break,' Joe said. 'I needed to get away.'

'Away? From Kooringal?'

He kept his gaze lowered. 'It wasn't a happy marriage,' he said quietly.

Hattie sat very still, hardly daring to breathe, waiting for Joe to elaborate, but he didn't. He simply left it at that.

It wasn't a happy marriage. She thought of his bride, Gloria, a pretty girl with the very latest fashions in clothes and elaborately styled blonde hair that had spent a great deal of time in rollers under a headscarf. Gloria's family had owned the local hotel, and she'd always seemed to have her sights set on bigger and brighter places than Burralea. Instead, she'd ended up somewhere even quieter. Kooringal. With Joe.

And they hadn't been happy.

Hattie tried to remain unaffected, but to her dismay, her throat and eyes were stinging and she might have made an embarrassing scene if their lunches hadn't arrived at that moment. She was able to turn her attention to unrolling the paper napkin wrapped around her cutlery and to cutting and tasting a careful corner of her asparagus and feta quiche, which proved to be quite delicious.

For the next little while, they both paid attention to their meals until Joe asked politely, 'How's the quiche?'

'Very good,' Hattie assured him. 'And your burger?'

'Perfect. Just what I needed.'

After a bit, she felt calm enough to give voice to the thoughts going round and round in her head. 'I must say I can't really picture you as a soldier, Joe. You always seemed more – I don't know —' She gave a nervous laugh as she struggled to explain herself.

She hadn't pictured Joe as a pacifist exactly, but he was certainly a thinker, and she found his decision to volunteer for the army quite puzzling. How unhappy did a marriage need to be to send a man to war? To that very unpopular war in Vietnam?

'Cliff was dead keen to join up,' Joe said. 'I just wanted to get away. I was happy with working in catering or logistics, but Cliff wanted to be in the thick of things. He reckoned if you weren't in the infantry you were simply cutting oranges for the footie team. He ended up as a forward scout, of all things.'

'That sounds dangerous. Did he survive?'

'No.' Joe's mouth quivered, and he stared hard at something on the far side of the lake. 'Anyway,' he said. 'I managed to get into logistics, so my job was to keep the army supplied with munitions, food, with everything it needed, basically. I was never in the front line.'

'I – I see.'

'As I said, I'm not proud of running away, but I think Gloria was relieved to see me go. I put a manager in at Kooringal and Gloria took Janelle down to Brisbane. They lived there with relatives of Gloria's while I was deployed.' Joe let out his breath in a small huff. 'I think it gave us both a bit of a break.'

Hattie couldn't think of an appropriate comment. 'And then Emma was born after the war?' she asked.

'Yes.' Joe picked up his half-eaten burger and took a bite, and Hattie refrained from plying him with more questions.

Their coffees arrived – a long black for Joe, and for Hattie, her usual cappuccino. While Joe stirred in sugar, she took a sip, pleased to find that her coffee was strong and hot.

Then Joe asked, 'What about you, Hattie? You mentioned a second husband, so I presume there was at least a first.'

'Yes, a first, but not a third. Two were enough.' She had hoped to make him smile, but if he did, she missed it.

'And you lived in England?'

She nodded. 'At first I lived with my grandmother – my mother's mother. She lived in Devon.'

'That's supposed to be a beautiful part of the world.'

'Oh, it is, and my grandmother's house was a typically quaint

English country cottage perched on a sea cliff. You know, with fabulous views of the grey English sea, a thatched roof, and that deliberate kind of shabbiness that comes with grand old faded curtains and dog-haired sofas and drinking sherry in front of the fire.'

Now Joe smiled. 'It sounds rather appealing. Did you like it there?'

'Unfortunately, no, I didn't. I found it far too stuffy and old-fashioned. I was young, remember. And it was the very end of the fifties.' Hattie didn't add that she had also been struggling to recover from several bitter blows – Joe's defection and Rose's death, plus the shock of discovering the awful truth about her parents.

It hadn't helped that her grandmother wasn't especially sympathetic. Hattie had been quite rebellious at the time.

'It wasn't long before I headed for London,' she said. 'I found a girl to share a flat with, and I managed to get a job with a publisher, as a typist. Some years later, I became an editor.'

'An editor?'

'A very junior editor to begin with.'

Joe's eyes shone with genuine delight. 'What sort of books?'

'Fiction, mostly aimed at women.'

'That's wonderful.'

'Yes, I really enjoyed my work.'

Joe looked unexpectedly happy as he took another deep sip of his coffee. Relaxed seconds ticked by, before he returned to his questions. 'And what about your husbands?' This sounded casual enough, but Hattie saw the new intensity in his face.

'Oh, yes, my husbands,' she said slowly, sensing a small moment of power. 'My first husband was a journalist. He was also a wild child of the sixties.'

'Sex, drugs and rock'n'roll?'

'Yes, the whole cliché, more or less. Although in Roger's case it was whisky and cigarettes and endless partying. Our marriage didn't last very long at all. We got divorced and then my boss asked me to marry him.'

'That sounds —' Joe looked both concerned and uncomfortable. 'It sounds almost – predatory.'

'I suppose it might sound that way,' Hattie said. 'But it wasn't like that. Ian was a good man. Apparently, he'd been waiting patiently for me to come to my senses.' She shot Joe a very direct look. 'Believe me, I would never have been able to come back here, I – I wouldn't have found the courage to face you again, if it hadn't been for Ian. He restored my faith in men. In myself.'

Joe's face was solemn as he digested this.

'Anyway,' Hattie hurried on, 'Ian got a promotion and we moved to America, to New York. We were there for a long time. He died six years ago of a heart attack.'

She looked away, suddenly unable to meet Joe's eyes, and took a deep breath. 'Our son, Mark, still lives in Manhattan. He does something very clever in IT that I don't really understand, and he makes ridiculous amounts of money.'

'Are there grandchildren?'

'No. Mark's gay and he and his partner have no plans for a family.'

To her relief Joe accepted this without comment.

'So that's me,' she said with a small smile.

'Except you haven't told me why you came back to Australia.'

'Ah, yes.' Hattie chanced another smile. 'I came back with an Australian friend, a businessman, who wanted to retire on the Sunshine Coast. It sounded idyllic but I soon realised he intended spending his days on the golf course or with a fishing line in his hand. I'm not really a beach sort of person. But I did enjoy being in Australia again, so I found myself an apartment in Brisbane.'

With her story told, Hattie felt a fresh sense of relief.

There. They'd done it. She and Joe had shared potted histories of their last fifty years and it hadn't been too painful after all.

And they'd also finished their coffees.

Joe looked at his watch. 'I guess we should get home,' he said. 'I haven't taken Marlowe for his walk today.'

Hattie rose more stiffly than she would have liked, and she used the stair rail again on the way back to the car. They didn't talk much on the drive to his place. She was too absorbed in thinking over everything Joe had told her.

She thought about Ian. He'd been such a good husband – kind, conservative, intelligent. Loving. She'd been lucky.

If she'd had a vindictive streak, she might have enjoyed knowing that Joe's marriage wasn't a happy one, but she couldn't bring herself to take pleasure in his pain.

He showed her to a bedroom at the back of his house, a surprisingly feminine room decorated in white and palest lemon with a view through lace-curtained windows to a private, shaded garden.

'These were Emma's things,' Joe said, indicating the bed with wrought-iron ends and the pretty Baltic pine chest of drawers.

'It's a lovely room.' Hattie eyed a small bookcase loaded with some of her favourite authors.

'You might like to put your feet up for a bit,' Joe suggested.

'Will you have a rest?' she asked, not wanting to be treated as 'elderly' by a man who was actually older than her. 'I thought you were going to take Marlowe for a walk.'

'I'll leave that until later, when it's cooler,' he said.

'All right. I wouldn't mind a little toes up.'

Joe departed for his room. Hattie slipped off her shoes, then went barefoot across the cool, polished timber floor to the bookcase. She reached for *The Enchanted April* by Elizabeth von Arnim. She knew the story well. It was such an utterly lovely book with just the right balance of gentle humour, she could easily dive it into again. A comfort read was just what she needed after the emotional seesaw of the past couple of days.

'Hattie.'

Blinking, she woke to a room now striped with shadows. Joe was standing in the doorway. Gosh, how long had she slept?

He smiled. 'Would you like a cuppa?'

She was parched, could think of nothing better. 'I'd love one, thanks.' She sat up, saw *The Enchanted April* on the bedside table with an airline boarding pass from her flight north now used as a bookmark. She'd been so tired, she could scarcely remember putting it there before she'd dozed off.

After splashing water on her face and fingering her hair into a semblance of tidiness, she joined Joe in the kitchen and watched as he poured tea into mugs.

'You still use a teapot,' she commented.

He shrugged. 'Old habits, I guess. Do you use bags?'

'Yes.' She laughed. 'I've been a bag lady for years now.'

Joe grinned.

Hattie saw the way his eyes sparkled, the way his face creased with laughter lines. It was like catching a glimpse of the Joe she'd known all those years ago, and she felt her heart give a strange little thud.

'Do you and Marlowe have a set route for your walk?' she asked, needing to direct her thoughts elsewhere.

'We usually take the track along Burra Creek. It's shady and there are always plenty of possum and bandicoot scents for Marlowe to explore.'

A walk along a tree-shaded creek sounded very pleasant. 'Can I join you?'

'Of course.'

Hattie felt a little guilty as she sipped her tea. Surely it shouldn't have been so easy to slip back into such comfortable companionship with the man who'd broken her heart.

CHAPTER NINETEEN

The afternoon of the first children's concert rehearsal was excessively hot. Flora made it to the church hall in good time, only to find a dozen or so mothers and restless children hanging about in the sun, obviously waiting for her with dwindling patience.

'Sorry.' She flashed a smile, which she hoped looked confident. 'I didn't think I was late.'

'Mrs Fletcher is always here by twenty to four,' remarked a frazzled-looking woman with a grizzling baby balanced on her hip.

'Right.' Flora wished Peg had remembered to tell her this helpful detail, but she was determined not to be rattled.

'Are you the new teacher?' asked another mother, looking askance at the shorts and singlet top that Flora had chosen in deference to the heat. 'You're so young!'

Flora straightened her shoulders and lifted her chin. 'But I've had tons of experience.' She flashed another smile and decided this was not the moment to explain that her experience was restricted to playing in orchestras rather than conducting them.

A couple of other mothers asked kindly after Peg, and they actually gave Flora encouraging smiles, but she sensed that they, too, secretly doubted her competence.

Reaching into her shorts pocket, she found the key and opened the church hall and wished she'd asked Peg whether the parents usually hung around to watch these rehearsals. She fervently prayed that they didn't.

In this regard, at least, Flora's prayers were answered, but by the time the various mothers had driven off and she'd opened up the hall's windows, she was left with a pack of children who eyed her with an unsettling mixture of mistrust and smirking amusement.

'Right,' Flora said to them in her best teacherly tone. 'Why don't you put your instruments on that trestle table over there while we set up the chairs?'

'Billy and Simon are supposed to do the chairs this week,' announced a tall, blonde girl with braces on her teeth and a gleaming challenge in her bright blue eyes.

Flora swallowed. 'Well, obviously things are different this week, now that poor Mrs Fletcher's had her accident.'

'When will she be back?' demanded a skinny, freckle-faced boy with big ears.

'Not . . . for a while,' Flora said vaguely.

'So are you taking us for every rehearsal till the concert?' asked another boy.

'Yes,' said Flora.

'How old are you?' shouted another.

Flora bit back a groan. By now, two boys were shaping up for a boxing duel, and a trio of girls were whispering and laughing hilariously. At any minute she would lose them completely.

'Chairs everyone, please!' she called in her bossiest voice.

Only a couple of quiet, biddable children obeyed her, but she decided to just get on with setting the chairs in place with their help, otherwise they would never get started.

It was, however, as nightmarish as Flora had feared. By the time the chairs were set up, the two naughtiest boys had disappeared outside to swing from a tree branch, and a group of girls were sitting cross-legged on the floor and gossiping like office workers at Friday night drinks, paying absolutely no attention to Flora.

'Come on!' she called desperately. 'Everyone, get your instruments and take your places please.' She went to the door. 'You boys. Inside. Now.'

They happily ignored her and Flora felt a terrible, desperate desire to simply walk out. She hadn't wanted to do this. She'd known from the start she would be hopeless. She'd told Peg she had no experience and the way things were going, the orchestra wouldn't have played a single note by the time the parents came back to collect them.

It was a total fucking disaster.

Sick to the stomach, she wondered if she should just start with the few obedient children who were sitting in their places and tuning their instruments. But she couldn't leave those wretched boys outside. What if they ran onto the road and got themselves run over?

Flora was about to yell at the boys again, at the same time wondering if a threat to report their behaviour to their parents would have any effect, when she remembered something Edith had said on the night she'd come to dinner.

All you need to do is play a bit from one of your fancy pieces and the children will be stunned into silence . . .

Would it work?

Was it worth a try? Or would it only result in more chaos as kids ran amok?

Flora decided she had little choice. With a hollow stomach, she quickly unpacked her violin, tightened the strings, did a super-quick tuning check, then struck the first chords of 'Hoedown'. Loud and clear.

The reaction was instantaneous. Every child in the hall stopped and turned to stare at her.

She played a little more of the stirring, super-impressive, fast dance music.

'Wow!' said a small voice. 'You're really good.'

Flora knew she had their attention now, so she kept playing, and she actually felt so stirred, she knew she was playing at her best. Then she finished with a showy flourish, her bow high in the air.

By now, the boys had left their tree and were coming up the steps into the hall. The giggling girls were silent.

'Can you play "Star Wars"?' the skinny red-headed boy called.

Flora played the familiar fanfare and was rewarded by grins and cries of 'Wow!'

By the time she'd finished, the gossiping girls were in their seats with their instruments unpacked.

Flora let out the scared breath. Slowly and with enormous dignity, she walked to the front of the assembled chairs and stood waiting in silence as the last of the children, including the two deserters from outside, took their places.

No more talk or fidgeting. All eyes were on her.

'Right,' she said quietly and with a shaky sense of gratitude. 'Now, let's get started.'

'Will you play for us again?' asked the tall blonde girl.

'No,' Flora told her. 'It's your turn to show me what you can do now.'

* * *

Mitch stepped up to a window in the little church hall, hands on hips, listening intently. It was a sweltering afternoon – all the windows had been pushed wide open – and he was unashamedly eavesdropping on a children's orchestra rehearsal.

Father Jonno had mentioned that Flora would be helping with the Christmas concert, and now that Mitch knew about her unsavoury ex, thanks to his conversation with Seth, he was worried. He felt bad that he'd been selfishly holding Flora at bay, too wrapped up in his own hurt pride to accept her offers of a friendly meal.

It had never occurred to him that the poor girl might be in need of company, or more importantly, that she might need someone to watch out for her. Now, despite his increased workload, Mitch felt a nagging need to keep a careful eye on Seth's kid sister.

He only hoped he could do so discreetly, without pissing her off.

'Cellos, can you move forward a bit?' he heard her say. 'We need a bit more room for the brass.'

Chair legs scraped on wooden floorboards.

'Okay, nice and quiet now.'

To his surprise, Flora's request was obeyed.

'Here's your A,' she said next. 'Listen everyone. Eric's going to play your A.'

This was followed by the sound of a violin bow being drawn smoothly and competently over one string. Then there was a burst of sounds that could not be called music, as children on various instruments tried to echo their leader.

Now Flora's voice sounded again, raised above the chaos. 'Put your hand up if you need help with the tuning.'

More squeaks and trills erupted from the little orchestra.

A voice called, 'Miss Flora, our music stand's wobbling.'

'Okay, I'll tighten the screw. There, you should be right now. No plucking, violins. Nice and quiet, everyone.'

Intrigued, Mitch inched a little closer and caught the view through a window. Flora, dressed in shorts, a yellow sleeveless top and sandals, looked impossibly young as she stood in front of a motley group of youthful musicians in various school uniforms or sporting gear.

She didn't look worried or nervous, though, and apart from a couple of boys who were whispering and giggling up the back of the woodwind section, the kids seemed to be watching her, waiting and listening.

'Okay, everybody, we're playing "Silent Night" first.'

There was a rustle of pages being turned.

'Watching me?' Flora called. 'I'll give you two bars lead-in. Watch my beat. One, two, three, one, two, three —'

'Miss Flora,' called a boy in a smart-arsey voice. 'Why's a police-man outside the window?'

'A policeman?'

'Yeah, he's watching us.'

Shit. Mitch could hardly duck away. Flora was bound to see him and there was a wide expanse of lawn between him and the road.

He offered a casual smile as Flora appeared at the window.

'Mitch?' She looked, understandably, surprised.

'Hi.' He kept his smile in place, despite Flora's frown. 'Just doing my afternoon rounds. Making sure everything's okay in this neck of the woods.'

He hoped she wouldn't grin and make him feel like one of those fumbling, foolish cops in a TV comedy.

Fortunately, Flora actually looked grateful. 'Well, thanks,' she said. 'That's awfully good of you.'

Mitch felt his ears go red, which was damned annoying. 'Everything okay?' he asked quickly.

'Yes, perfectly, thanks.'

'Great. I'll be off then.'

Good as his word, he began to back away, while Flora returned to her students who were starting to chatter and giggle.

'It's just Sergeant Cavello doing his afternoon rounds,' he heard her tell them. 'Now, where were we? Let's start again and let's remember we want *pianissimo*. In the concert you'll be playing an introduction and then the choir will join in.'

* * *

Phew, it was over.

Flora waited till all the children had been collected before she closed up the hall. In the end, the rehearsal hadn't gone too badly. By the time an hour and a half had passed, the various sections were coming together and the children were sounding quite good. She should have known Peg Fletcher would have them well trained.

Inevitably, there was one child whose mother was running late. Today that particular child was one of the flute players, nine-year-old Molly Harper, a serious little girl with mousey curls and big grey eyes. She helped Flora to close the windows and to stack the leftover chairs.

'I'm sorry Mum's late,' she said, looking a tad worried. 'She was going to do some shopping while I was at rehearsal, but my baby brother's teething. He's probably yelled the supermarket down.'

'That's okay. Don't worry,' Flora assured her. 'When I was in the youth orchestra, my mum was often a bit late. She was always getting caught up in town, or doing CWA business.'

Molly looked at Flora with round-eyed surprise, as if this possibility had never occurred to her. 'You didn't play in this orchestra, did you?'

'Yes, until I went away to boarding school.'

'But you're so *good*.'

'Well, thanks. But that comes with lots of practice.'

After Flora had locked the hall's door and pocketed the key, they sat together outside on the shady front step to wait. Molly was painfully shy, and she sat with her skinny, freckled arms wrapped around her legs and her chin resting on her drawn-up knees.

Burralea was very quiet now. The only sounds in the village were the lazy, late afternoon bird calls. Somewhere down the street a dog was barking. A trio of schoolboys on bicycles whizzed past. Gently, Flora managed to coax Molly to chat about how long she'd been learning the flute and what school she went to, and what her favourite pieces were.

'Mum says I don't do enough practice,' the little girl confessed.

'I suppose you'd rather be outside playing with your friends,' Flora suggested.

Molly shrugged. 'I dunno. Maybe.'

'And I guess it depends how important the flute playing is to you.'

'I do love it.' Molly said this with such unexpected sincerity and such serious big eyes Flora wanted to hug her.

'Well, in that case,' she said, 'if you really love your music, and you want to be good at it, practice can make a huge difference.'

'Is that what happened for you?'

'It took me a while to work it out,' Flora admitted. 'Most people think being good at music is all about talent, but talent is overrated really.'

'Really?'

'Sure. Anyway, Molly, you already have enough talent, or Mrs Fletcher wouldn't have invited you to play in the orchestra.'

'You think?'

Flora smiled. 'I know it. And if you love playing the flute and you want to get even better, then it makes sense to put in the work. You'd be surprised. Even if you only did ten minutes' practice every day, it could make a huge difference, especially if you really concentrated for that ten minutes.'

'Ten minutes?' The little girl looked impressed.

'Each day, you could pick one thing that you wanted to work on,' Flora suggested and she watched Molly's lovely grey eyes widen even further as if this idea was sinking in.

'Like those high notes in "Silent Night"?' the little girl asked. 'The "sleep in heavenly peace" bit? Or those tricky fast bits in "Joy to the World"?'

'Yes, that's it exactly,' said Flora. 'You've got the idea. Chances are, if you practise those tricky bits, you'll get more and more interested in all of the music and you'll want to practise for longer, without anyone pushing you.'

To her delight, the little girl's face split into an excited grin. 'I'm going to do that. I really am.'

'Yay!' Flora held up her hand for a high five. They slapped their hands together and Molly giggled.

At that same moment, a car zoomed around the corner and came to a noisy halt. The thin, frazzled-looking woman, who'd been so annoyed with Flora's lateness, now jumped out and a series of lusty yells burst from the car.

'I'm so sorry,' the woman called.

Flora waved to her and began to walk with Molly towards the car. She offered Molly's mother her most reassuring smile. 'It's okay. No hassle. Honestly.'

The woman's mouth tilted in a sheepish smile. The fat, red-faced baby strapped in the back of the car stopped crying and stuck his toe in his mouth. The woman looked from Flora to her daughter, and her anxious frown softened by several degrees. 'Well, you look happy,' she told Molly.

'I am, Mum, and guess what?'

'What?'

'Flora's given me some tips and I'm going to practise my flute every day.'

'Good grief.' Half-smiling, the woman rolled her eyes as her daughter climbed into the car. 'I'll believe that when I see it,' she said over her shoulder to Flora.

Through the car window, Molly sent Flora a wink. Flora gave her a thumbs up and they were both grinning as the car drove away.

Well, that wasn't so bad after all, Flora thought and she set off home to the cottage.

* * *

Hattie was glad to be wearing sunglasses as she and Joe emerged from the green shade of trees into the blaze of late afternoon sunlight. She had thoroughly enjoyed accompanying Joe along the track beside the creek, while Marlowe, nose down, tail madly wagging, sniffed at tree trunks or mysterious clumps of grass, or dashed off to investigate enticing smells behind rocks.

On a deep bend of the lazy creek, they'd even caught sight of a platypus hurrying busily through the thick reeds along the bank, nudging here and there with its bill, rather like a frantic shopper darting through a 7-Eleven to grab last-minute ingredients for an evening meal.

Hattie had spent so many years living in big metropolitan cities that she'd rather lost touch with the simple pleasures of nature – the joy of birdsong, the beauty of dappled sunlight streaming through overhead leaves, the gently meandering course of a country creek as opposed to the practical straight lines of city streets.

Now, ahead of them, she saw the young woman, Flora, walking with her back to them. Flora's head was down as if she was deep in thought, her dark hair swinging forward, exposing her pale slender neck, while her violin case hung from a strap slung over her shoulder.

'I've met that girl,' Hattie told Joe. 'Her name's Flora. I heard her playing Tchaikovsky's violin concerto in the church hall. She was practising for some kind of important audition.'

'A concerto?' Joe said. 'That's highfalutin for little ol' Burralea. She must be good.'

'Yes, she is. I thought she was very good indeed. And listening to her brought back so many memories of when I was a child in Shanghai. I used to listen to a White Russian man playing Tchaikovsky.'

'A White Russian in Shanghai?' Joe's eyebrows hiked high. 'Who was he?'

'His name was Rudi Vastinov.' The very act of saying his name brought unexpected tears to Hattie's eyes. She could never think of him without being swamped by a rush of conflicting emotions. Loss and longing, fondness and pride. 'I always believed my father was an Englishman.'

Joe frowned. 'He was, wasn't he? His name was Bellamy and he was a merchant seaman. Wasn't his ship sunk by the Japanese?'

'Well, yes, that's what I was told. It's what I always believed.'

CHAPTER TWENTY

Shanghai, 1937

Rose wasn't a witness on the first occasion Lily asked for her parents' permission to marry Rudi Vastinov. She only heard about the unfortunate meeting later, when Lily stormed into her apartment in tears, desperate to tell her the whole sorry story.

Rudi had been dressed in his best suit. He'd looked wonderfully handsome. No man could have been more presentable, but their parents had given him the coldest possible reception, barely allowing the poor man to step over their threshold.

Rudi had been polite, a complete gentleman, which was more than Lily could say about her father. But absolutely, under no circumstances, would Roger Challinor allow his daughter, who had only just turned twenty, to marry a White Russian refugee.

It didn't matter that Rudi was well educated or that his family had been upper middle class and very well off when they'd lived in St Petersburg. It didn't matter that Rudi now had a steady job in an orchestra. Until she came of age, Lily wasn't, under any circumstances, permitted to tie herself in marriage to a man who belonged to a destitute and marginalised group, living on the very fringes of Shanghai's society.

Rose felt terribly sorry for Lily, but she was also mildly surprised by her sister's dogged devotion to her White Russian. Rose had expected Lily to revel in the vast choices offered by Shanghai's exciting social scene.

With the ever-increasing arrival of international military forces, as well as the ever-present bankers, brokers and young diplomats, there was a preponderance of young men. Girls had every opportunity to cram their social calendars with invitations to receptions, dinners and balls.

For most young people and even the not-so-young, life in this Far Eastern city was a giddy whirlwind, and Lily had such a fun-loving, outgoing personality, she should have been in high demand. Like most of the girls in their social circle, she should have been falling in and out of love at the drop of a hat.

So it was a surprise for Rose to realise that her exceptionally pretty, feisty little sister was rather like herself – not naturally inclined to play the field. Lily's situation was made so much harder, though, by the fact that she'd fallen head over heels for a man who was deemed completely unsuitable.

Rose could well understand Rudi Vastinov's appeal. The handsome Russian wasn't merely good looking. He was also charming, musically gifted and quite well educated. There was nothing to dislike about him, really, and she could see that Lily was completely infatuated, so despite her initial fears, she'd given up trying to influence her sister to forget about him.

Now, Rose realised, too late, that she should have tried harder to dissuade Lily from lavishing her affections on the dark-eyed, dashing Rudi. Like all the White Russians in Shanghai, he had arrived without a passport or visa and was rendered stateless, a citizen of nowhere.

Of course, their parents remained stubbornly stuck-up about every aspect of this situation, carrying on as if Rudi were a lowly pariah and they were some sort of privileged overlords of the East. Apparently, their mother had been downright rude to the man. Lily was incensed and there'd been an unholy row in the dignified three-storey house on rue Cardinal.

'I can't possibly stay there,' Lily declared now, as she flung herself into one of Rose's armchairs.

'But what will you do?' Rose was trying to imagine how Stephen would react if her little sister wanted to move in with them.

'I can have a room at Zara's,' Lily said next, as if she'd sensed Rose's concern.

'Zara Pemberton?'

'Yes.'

'But doesn't she live with that Chinese fellow?'

'Rose!' Lily cried, sending her sister a look of blistering scorn. 'Now you're sounding like *them*.'

Rose winced. She didn't want to be like their parents. She wanted to be more broad-minded, but the only Chinese she knew were servants and that was very different from mixing with them as equals.

'Chu Yuan is a scholar and a gentleman, as you jolly well know,' said Lily. 'He looks after Zara beautifully. He's even arranged to have her book published *and* he's as rich as Croesus. He's told me I'm welcome to stay in his house for as long as I like.'

'Well, then . . .' Rose wasn't sure what to say.

'But I want to be with Rudi.' Lily buried her face in a cushion to hide the sudden rush of tears.

The second time Lily tried to broach the prospect of her marriage with their parents, she came to their house on her own.

It happened three or four months after she'd moved out, and she turned up at rue Cardinal late on a Sunday afternoon, when the Challinors traditionally served high tea. Unless there were more pressing invitations, Sunday evenings were usually spent quietly at home, with just the family.

Since Lily's departure, Rose and Stephen had been the only extras. But on this evening, much to everyone's surprise, Lily came sailing through the tall wrought-iron gates and up the stone path that crossed the carefully manicured lawn.

It was midsummer, the evening was hot and humid, and all the timber shutters had been pushed wide open in an effort to catch any hint of a breeze. With the arrival of summer, the ceiling fans had been uncovered, straw rugs laid down and cotton covers placed over the brocaded furniture.

This evening, the dining table was set for tea with a starched white tablecloth edged in dainty crochet, rosebud china, and a tiered cake-stand holding cucumber sandwiches, delicate éclairs and napoleons.

Lily was dressed for the heat in a short-sleeved cotton frock and a glamorous white straw hat. She looked a little paler than usual, but there was a noticeable battle light in her eyes as she marched into the house bearing a box from Bianchi's.

Her parents managed to hide their surprise and made a commendable effort to look pleased.

'How lovely to see you, darling.' Adele's voice and manner were tense, but she kissed Lily's cheek.

'Are you well?' asked Roger, making no attempt to come closer, but eyeing his daughter carefully, almost as if he expected to find her harmed in some way.

'I'm perfectly well,' Lily assured him. 'Couldn't be better. Bursting with good health. Hello, Rose, darling. Hello, Stephen.' She kissed them both and gave Rose an extra hug. 'Rudi sends his love. He's busy playing in an orchestral concert at the Lyceum this evening.'

At this last comment, Rose and Lily, who had seen each other regularly during the intervening weeks, exchanged covert smiles, but a small chill fell over their parents until Lily handed her mother the cardboard box.

'I've come bearing gifts, an iced cake from Bianchi's. It's your favourite, Mother, ginger cake iced with lemon.'

Now there were tears glittering in their mother's eyes, and Rose knew the sudden emotion was not caused by the arrival of a cake. It was clear Adele had hated being estranged from her daughter. 'Thank you, Lily. How – how thoughtful.'

Lily smiled a little sadly and made no further comment as she removed her hat and gloves. The family sat down to tea and a Chinese boy came in, bearing a silver teapot, his feet in soft cloth slippers, soundless on the marble floor.

He set a place for Lily, then took her cake back to the kitchen and returned with it on a serving plate and with a silver-handled knife for cutting. Starched napkins were spread on laps, tea was poured and selections of dainty pastries made. The family's conversation turned to safe topics – the recent Race Day at the British Country Club, Stephen's latest voyage and the increasing number of bombings from Japanese planes, which were, thankfully, still falling outside the International Concessions.

Their father reported that some of the international community were having their nation's flags painted on the roofs of their vehicles to avoid possible strafing from low-flying Japanese planes. They all agreed that this seemed a trifle ridiculous.

Lily had very little to say, Rose noticed, but she attributed her sister's unusual quietness to the strain of her parent's continued snubbing of Rudi.

It wasn't until they were nearing the end of the meal, when Lily had helped herself to a small bunch of grapes, that she said, out of the blue, and with forced brightness, 'By the way, everyone, I have some lovely news. I'm going to have a baby.'

*

In the shocked silence that followed, everyone around the table stared at Lily, who chewed at a single grape with her shoulders braced and her chin high, as if she knew she was about to face the battle of her life.

Rose was not only shocked. She was also hit by a stab of painful envy. She'd been hoping to be the first Challinor daughter to make the happy announcement of a baby on the way. After all, she was the one who was properly married, but so far, there was no sign of a pregnancy for her. Lily, on the other hand, had not only beaten her in the motherhood stakes, but in doing so had brought shame on them all.

Rose was aware that Stephen was watching her and frowning ever so slightly, but she avoided meeting his eye.

'So, of course,' Lily said with a tight, fixed smile, 'I'm hoping that you will finally give Rudi and me permission to be married.'

Unhelpfully, their mother burst into tears. Their father, sitting opposite her, turned red in the face and placed his hands, firmly clenched, on the tabletop, as if he was ready to punch someone.

They all knew that someone must be Rudi.

Lily looked tense and pale. 'I'm actually happy about the baby,' she said. 'I love Rudi very much.'

'Oh, you foolish girl!' Adele cried. 'How can you possibly be happy? This is shameful. An absolute disaster. Surely you must know you're ruined?'

With a dreadful wail, their mother leaped from her chair and rushed out of the room, sobbing ostentatiously.

Rose met Lily's gaze and her sister rolled her eyes to the ceiling, then let out an exasperated, noisy sigh. 'I should have known she'd carry on like a wailing banshee.'

Their father exploded. 'Lily! How dare you!'

'How dare I, Father?' Lily gave an incredulous shake of her head.

'Mother's the one making a scene. What on earth do you mean?'

He thumped the table, as he'd been clearly longing to do from the outset. Rose had never seen their father looking so angry. He glared at Lily, his eyes bulging. 'How dare you bring such shame on your family.'

Lily looked shaken, but still defiant. 'For once in your life, why don't you and Mother stop worrying about your*selves* and your bloody reputations?'

Rose thought her father might explode. His face was as red as a ripe tomato, and his normally mild brown eyes glowed like fiercely burning coals. He breathed in and out deeply, desperately, struggling for control.

Rose wished she could think of something helpful to say. Something soothing. Diplomatic. She looked to Stephen, but her dear husband was wisely keeping out of this battle.

Her gaze drifted to the row of invitations on the mantelpiece behind her father, the evidence of the social prestige that was so frightfully important to her parents. The nearest one read:

> *Colonel and Mrs De Witt Peck*
> *request the pleasure of the company of*
> *Mr and Mrs Roger Challinor*
> *at dinner on Thursday August 12th*
> *at 8.30 pm*
> *Alan M*

Eventually, their father was calm enough to speak, albeit he spoke through gritted teeth. 'That attack is very rich coming from you, my girl. You've only ever thought of yourself and what *you* want. It's because of your selfishness, chasing after that Russian, that you've landed yourself and your family in this ghastly predicament. Now it's too late to think about the consequences.'

'The consequences are a sweet little innocent baby.' Lily made no attempt to hide her exasperation. 'And there'd be no problem for anyone if you would only allow me to marry.'

'That's not going to happen.'

'How can you be so cruel?'

'How can you be so foolish?'

Rose resisted her urge to jump from her seat to give Lily a hug. It would only make her father even angrier and it would probably make Lily cry.

But Rose was overwhelmed with sadness for her sister. It was true that Lily had been foolish, but being madly in love could send even the sanest people a little crazy.

Now, Lily said, 'I have no choice but to wait then. I'll marry Rudi next year when I'm twenty-one. The months will fly by and then everything will be all right.'

'Don't be so naïve!'

Lily opened her mouth to protest, but Roger raised a stiff hand, silencing her.

'Think of others for once, Lily. Even if you were to marry Vastinov – which I can't allow – think what such a marriage would mean for your child.'

'How could it harm my child?'

'Think, girl. Imagine what it will mean for your child to be born here in the Far East, a child of mixed blood. Forever an outsider. A pariah.'

'That's exactly right, Lily.'

Suddenly their mother, who'd obviously been listening through the wall, reappeared in the dining room doorway, her face blotchy, her eyes pink from crying.

'Think about your child,' she said. 'What would life be like for her or – or him? You'd have no hope of getting him into a decent school. And who would want to be friends with him?'

'He certainly won't need snobby British friends. He or *she* can have lovely Russian friends,' Lily responded stubbornly.

'Really?' Their father's voice dripped with sarcasm.

Lily's jaw remained tight. 'Yes, really.'

'And what kind of friends will these be? Children of the White Russian men pulling rickshaws? The offspring of the desperate women who sell themselves to sailors in back alleys?'

Now it was Lily who was red-faced and glaring. 'You're overlooking the many talented White Russians who've lifted Shanghai's cultural life by two hundred percent. All the writers and musicians and teachers and dancers.'

Their father ignored this. 'And what if there's a war?' he asked next.

For the first time, a chink showed in Lily's armour. 'A war?'

'Yes. Surely you must have heard about the growing tensions in Europe. You've seen the Jewish refugees pouring in from Germany. As you know very well, we have the Japanese bombing on our doorstep. It's not just their planes. There are many more Jap warships just offshore.' He flashed a sharp glance across the table. 'Aren't there, Stephen?'

Poor Stephen looked uncomfortable as he nodded, and Rose was sure her husband would have given anything to escape this family argument.

'If these troubles keep mounting, there could be a full-scale war. We might need to evacuate the women and children,' her father said next. 'But the Russians are stateless.' He gave the table another thump. 'Your husband, your child's *father*, has *no* passport. For all you know, your child might not be allowed to have a passport either.'

'But that's ridiculous.' Lily was trying to sound brave, but she looked frightened now. Her eyes were huge, almost pleading. Eventually, she said, in a much smaller voice, 'Is there really much likelihood of war?'

Everyone looked to Stephen, which wasn't really fair as he was a merchant seaman, not part of the Royal Navy.

'It's hard to say,' he said. 'But military numbers in the region are certainly building up and we've all heard the shelling and seen the smouldering ruins just on the other side of Soochow Creek. There's talk of a curfew. Things are definitely getting more serious.'

Rose knew this was true. The French Concession was something of an oasis, but they could hear the rattle of machine guns day and night. And lately Chinese refugees had been pouring into the city from nearby regions, bringing all their worldly possessions in cardboard boxes loaded onto bicycles.

'There's no sign of the Japanese backing away,' Stephen said. And then he added, almost unwillingly, 'I would certainly want to send Rose away from here if things got much worse.'

Lily sat very still as she took this in. 'I suppose it's not a very good time to be having a baby, is it?'

'Certainly not a bastard with questionable citizenship,' her father said darkly.

Lily's slender throat rippled as she swallowed. 'What should I do?'

It was only then that Rose wondered if this was the true reason Lily had come here tonight – not so much to throw her pregnancy at her family in an act of defiance, but to ask for help. Could her bravado be nothing more than bluff? Lily must have been aware of the problems she faced.

She must have known that even marriage to Rudi might not be enough security, but perhaps she was too proud to admit this? The poor girl probably felt terribly alone and really needed their help.

But how could their parents help her? Their father was a banker, not a diplomat. There was little they could do, apart from offering family solidarity, and so far that had seemed too huge a hurdle for their parents to clear.

The Chinese boy appeared and gave a small bow. 'I clear table?'

'Not yet.' Their mother waved him away. 'Actually, wait, Li Chen. I could do with more tea and we'll need fresh lemon.'

'Yes, Missy.' He left with the teapot.

'Well, I don't need tea. I need whisky.' Roger jumped to his feet. 'What about you, Stephen? I'm sure you could do with a dram.'

Stephen nodded his thanks, and there was silence around the table as Roger crossed the room to the crystal decanter on the sideboard, pulled the stopper and poured hefty slugs into two glasses. With small silver tongs, he took ice from a silver bucket, then brought the tinkling glasses back to the table.

Rose caught the whisky's peaty aroma as a glass was passed to her husband. She was feeling rather shaken and considered asking for a glass of sherry, but a last-minute request might only annoy her father, and his mood was already too fragile.

The fresh teapot arrived with a small dish of lemon sliced into slim wedges. Cups were replenished and Rose was conscious that no one had answered her sister's question.

'Tell me what you're thinking,' Lily demanded at last. 'What do you expect me to do? Find a Chinese herbalist and have an abortion?'

Rose gasped. 'Lily, don't say such things!'

'Perhaps you'd prefer me to leave the baby on the steps of a church?' her sister went on in a brittle voice, as if she was deliberately trying to upset them.

'You're talking about our flesh and blood,' protested Adele.

'Exactly!' cried Lily. 'I thought you hadn't noticed.'

'Now you're being ridiculous,' said their father. 'Pull yourself together, girl.'

Lily let out a huff of annoyance, but she held her tongue as she delicately squeezed lemon into her tea.

'The child must be part of our family,' their mother said firmly.

At last, a ray of hope. Rose realised she'd been sitting on the very edge of her chair. Now, she eased back, hoping against hope that their parents were reconciled, that they could discuss this like a normal, civilised family.

CHAPTER TWENTY-ONE

'There's really only one solution, Lily.'

Adele announced this with a glass of brandy in her hand. She had declared the drink necessary for her nerves, so, as the men prepared to down another whisky, she and Rose and Lily were given tots of brandy in shining balloon-style glasses.

By this stage the mood had mellowed a little, which was probably just as well. With her copper bangles tinkling and her lacquered fingernails gleaming dark red in the light of a chandelier, Adele held her brandy glass high as she declared, loftily, 'You should give your baby to Rose.'

Lily gasped. 'Rose?'

Rose's heart slammed against the wall of her chest. Surely her mother couldn't be serious? Lily couldn't give up her baby.

But her mother was deadly serious. By now, her tears were a thing of the past and she outlined her proposal simply and coolly, without emotion, making it sound logical, the only sensible option, really, if they wanted to secure the child's future.

Before the pregnancy became obvious, Lily and Rose should both go to Hong Kong. When the child was born, Rose and Stephen, who were both British citizens, would be registered as its parents.

The child would be British. *Safely* British. There would be absolutely no barriers to its acceptance into society. The child would have smooth entrée into the best schools, the pony clubs, the wonderful children's parties at the hotels on The Bund. He or she would enjoy all the benefits of the comfortable and gracious lifestyle that this city offered.

Their father joined his wife then, telling them all in his most serious tones that if the threat of war became worse, as many feared it must, the child would be easily evacuated as a British citizen, to Hong Kong or even home to England.

Rose knew it was this last argument about the baby's safety that swung Lily. While her sister bristled at the small-mindedness of British snobbery, she was anxious to protect her baby, even though it was probably, at this stage, hardly bigger than one of the grapes on her plate.

Just the same, silver tears shone in Lily's eyes and she pressed her lips together, trying to still the way they trembled.

Eventually, she turned to Rose. 'What do you think about this, Rose? How do you and Stephen feel about instant parenthood?'

Poor Rose's head was swimming. She'd never been assaulted by such a deluge of emotions. She felt an overwhelming, deep sadness for Lily and Rudi – she couldn't imagine how painful it would be to give up their precious child, a tiny, living expression of their love.

She was also conscious, however, of the practicality of her mother's suggestion. And she couldn't snuff out the little flame of joy, the kernel of warmth that glowed in her chest at the thought of a baby to love and to care for.

It was the most bizarre situation. The proposal felt both terribly wrong and wonderfully right, simultaneously.

Rose turned to Stephen, who was sitting quietly beside her, and she saw her own internal dilemma mirrored in his gentle eyes.

'Perhaps we need a little time to take this all in?' he suggested.

'Yes,' Rose readily agreed. 'And I'm sure you do, too, Lily. You'll need to talk to Rudi.'

Lily nodded unhappily. 'Rudi won't like it, of course.'

'If he's any kind of a *man*, he will put his child's needs before his own,' Roger responded stoutly.

Lily gave her father a long, hard stare and Rose held her breath, hoping her headstrong sister wasn't about to launch into a heated tirade about paternal support and consideration. Fortunately, Lily held her tongue.

They finished their drinks in silence. Lily looked very despondent and their father sat with his brow creased by a thoughtful frown while he stared at a spot in the distance.

At last he said, 'We could offer a sort of compromise, Lily.'

Lily made no attempt to hide her disbelief.

'What sort of compromise?' Rose felt compelled to ask, somewhat fearfully.

Her father addressed his answer to her sister. 'If you agree to this plan to hand your baby into Rose and Stephen's care, your mother and I will accept Vastinov into our home.'

'Oh.' Overwhelmed, poor Lily's face crumpled. She'd been brave for too long. Suddenly, she was weeping and Rose was out of her chair, kneeling beside her, hugging her close.

As both the girls wept, clinging tight, Rose knew what her decision must be and she was already making silent promises. Lily and Rudi would see their baby as often as they wanted to. They would be its loving aunt and uncle. Rose and Stephen would make sure they remained a close-knit family. No matter what. The closest unit possible.

*

It was time to depart and the ever-diplomatic Stephen called for their driver. 'We can give you a lift home,' he told Lily.

'Thanks,' she said quietly.

The sisters kissed their parents goodnight, and they went out into the hot Shanghai evening where the distant machine guns destroyed the peace of the night. The air pressed close and hot and damp. There was a small pond with a little fountain in their parents' garden, but not even the sight of the sprinkling water could relieve the oppressive, humid stillness.

'We need a thunderstorm,' Stephen said. 'At least it would give us a break from all this heat.'

'A thunderstorm?' Lily responded lightly. 'Haven't we just had one?'

The looks they exchanged were almost smiling as they climbed into the car.

CHAPTER TWENTY-TWO

Flora had plenty to think about on her walk home from the children's rehearsal. She wanted to plan the areas that most needed her attention at the next rehearsal, and she also thought through her practice strategies for her coming audition, which was still her top priority.

Inevitably, she also thought about Oliver, who'd been preying on her mind ever since she heard about his phone call to Seth. She didn't want to think about her ex, but he always managed to creep in.

Bloody Oliver. In her head, Flora had christened him B.O. and the acronym seemed fitting. She found it hard to remember now how she'd ever been so attracted to the guy. How could she have missed the clues to his viciousness? Perhaps there was something wrong with her relationship receptors?

Of course, if she was honest, when she'd met Oliver, she hadn't been nearly as experienced with men as she'd liked to think she was. Apart from a few semi-serious boyfriends, including Ethan who'd later become Eve, there'd been odd patches of casual dating that hadn't lasted long at all. Then, soon after she'd arrived at her new job in Melbourne, she'd met Oliver, handsome, talented and piling on the charm . . .

Lost in these troubled thoughts, Flora didn't notice Mitch until she was walking right past the police station. He was leaning against his vehicle with his arms folded over his chest, and he looked relaxed enough, although it was pretty obvious that he'd been waiting for her.

'Are you still on duty, Sergeant?'

'Just clocking off, actually, Ms Drummond.' Mitch abandoned his relaxed slouch. 'I hope you didn't mind me snooping around that rehearsal.'

Flora shook her head. 'It was good for the children to see first-hand that their local policeman is their friend.'

She smiled as she said this and Mitch smiled too. They stood, rather like awkward teenagers, smiling shyly.

Flora wished she could explain to Mitch that she'd found his presence reassuring. Incredibly comforting, actually. But Mitch had been so edgy since the wedding she didn't like to tell him anything too personal.

'How's it going with those bones?' she asked. 'Are you getting any closer to finding out what happened?'

'We're still checking out the World War II lead.'

He didn't seem too keen to expand on this, which was fair enough. Once again, Flora felt awkward and uncertain. She fiddled with the strap of her violin case. Mitch's gaze flicked to the ground and then back again.

He said, 'Seth's told me about this ex-boyfriend of yours.'

'Yes, I thought he might have.'

Now Mitch's coffee-dark gaze locked with hers, and she was sure he could see the fear that lurked inside her, even though she'd told herself a thousand times that worrying about Oliver was an overreaction.

'I – ah – also wanted to thank you for your invitations, Floss,' Mitch said quickly, as if this was something he needed to get out before he lost his nerve. 'I know you were just trying to help, but I'm afraid my head was in the wrong space for a few days there. You're right, though. It's not healthy to mope at home on my own.'

'I'm sure I didn't say that.'

'Well, no, you were far too polite and sensitive, but the truth is, I could do with a little company.'

Mitch smiled as he said this, and Flora had to blink as she tried to concentrate on what he was saying. He had the kind of smile that could dazzle a girl.

And now, she suspected he was angling for another invitation, and unfortunately, she was struggling to remember what she'd planned for dinner. 'I um —'

'I was going to throw a couple of chops on the barbie,' Mitch said. 'Thought you might like to come over.'

Flora blinked again. 'To your place?'

He shrugged. 'I'm no *MasterChef*, but I don't usually burn too much food.'

'Sorry. I wasn't implying that you can't cook.' She couldn't believe she was so flustered. Mitch was simply making the same offer she'd made to him. It was a gesture of friendship. Almost certainly, Seth had asked Mitch to help keep an eye on his little sister.

'Well, how about it then?'

'Sounds great.' Flora kept her response deliberately casual. 'Thanks. Can you give me a sec while I stow this violin away?'

'Sure.'

The temperature would almost certainly cool down after sunset, so Flora changed into slacks and a T-shirt. She did this quickly, added only the barest hint of lip gloss. She was excited to be seeing Mitch's home. He'd built it after she left the district, and although she'd heard rave reports from Seth, she'd never seen it.

In no time, they were heading off, out of town, whizzing through quiet countryside tinted with the muted violet and gold tones of dusk, before turning onto a much narrower road, little more than a single lane, that rode the top of a ridge.

Now, on either side of them, velvety slopes dropped steeply.

Mitch had to slow down as they rounded a bend and met a mob of black-and-white dairy cows, herded by an Akubra-hatted farmer riding a quad bike with his dog perched beside him. They grinned and waved as they crawled past. The farmer waved back.

'Hans Bloom,' said Mitch.

'I suppose you know everyone's names?' Flora said.

He shrugged. 'Most.'

Another turn and they were heading down a curving track lined with remnant rainforest. When the track climbed once again and took a final turn, they emerged out of the forest into a grassy field where a shed-style house was set into the side of a hill and gorgeous views reached all the way to the indigo ranges in the west.

'Wow, what a great spot.' They climbed out of Mitch's ute and Flora took in the expanse of smooth hills and valleys, dotted with cattle and patterned with twilight shadows. She caught a flash of sunlit water from a narrow finger of lake, and looked down into a steep valley edged with lacy tree ferns, which might have been a scene from *Jurassic Park*. 'How on earth did you find this place?'

Mitch grinned. 'Stroke of luck. I heard on the grapevine that Ted Jeffries was subdividing his old farm and selling off pieces. I nabbed this for the views and the tractor shed.'

Two beautiful border collies raced up, distracting him. 'Hey, you two.' Mitch knelt to fondle their silky ears. 'You been behaving yourselves? Of course you have.'

Satisfied with his greeting, they hurried to sniff at Flora's feet.

'Hello,' she said, delighted. She loved border collies. They were so quiet and intelligent and beautiful to look at. 'What are your names?'

'Maggie and Midnight,' supplied Mitch.

Flora grinned. 'How perfect. Hello, Midnight. Hello, Maggie.'

The dogs, having made their inspection, retreated politely at a signal from Mitch.

Flora looked towards the shed. 'So you turned a tractor shed into your home?' she asked.

'I did, yeah.'

She was instantly intrigued. Already she could see that Mitch had retained most of the shed's original corrugated iron, but he'd cut holes into the walls and used recycled windows and doors to turn a basic farm building into his home.

A solid front door was painted green, and bright nasturtiums sprawled in gardens on either side of the doorstep. At the side of the house there was a sizeable veggie garden, fenced off from the hens that roamed free to peck at insects and green shoots in the lawn.

She saw an outdoor table and chairs set on a small stone terrace that made the most of the beautiful view. A fire pit held the charred remains of a burnt log and she imagined sitting out there on a clear night, warmed by the fire and watching the stars. And enjoying Mitch's company.

For the umpteenth time, she wondered what on earth Angie had been thinking when she walked out on this man.

She followed Mitch inside where everything was decidedly rustic, but to Flora, just as appealing as the outside. Mitch had left the huge timber supporting beams exposed and he'd lined the walls with a combination of corrugated iron and timber boards. The kitchen benches were thick slabs of polished timber with open shelving for storage above and below. The floor had been left as plain concrete, which Mitch had polished and then softened with a scattering of variously patterned rugs.

There was no ceiling, which left plenty of airy space above the internal walls, and a bank of timber-framed bi-fold doors opened almost all of the north-facing wall to a view of rolling farmland that was as spectacular as the view to the west. The house felt airy and open to the natural surroundings, but cosy and welcoming as well.

'I love this, Mitch,' she said as she walked from the kitchen to the dining area where unmatched chairs were painted different bright colours and grouped around an old scrubbed pine table. Then on to the sitting area where faded sofas were covered with cream cotton throws and firewood was stacked in a huge copper pot beside a fireplace with a fat stainless-steel chimney.

'This is so awesome,' she gushed as she looked across the open-plan rooms to the views. 'Did you really do all this by yourself?'

'Yeah. Pretty much. It was a fun project.'

'You're so clever.'

Mitch looked pleased, but he merely waggled his eyebrows and shrugged.

'Did Alice help you to find the second-hand furniture?' Flora asked, remembering Seth's partner's keen interest in collecting old things.

'I got a few pieces from her. They're in the bedrooms. I'd already collected most of this other stuff before Alice opened her shop.'

'And what did Angie think of it?'

Flora couldn't believe she'd asked this out loud. She'd told herself that Angie shouldn't, *wouldn't*, be mentioned this evening, but she couldn't stop thinking about the girl who was supposed to have shared this home with Mitch.

'Sorry,' she said quickly, feeling her face go red. 'Scratch that question.'

Mitch gave a tight-mouthed nod, then looked sharply back towards the kitchen, staring hard. 'What can I offer you to drink? Beer? Wine?'

'I'd prefer wine if you've got it,' she said, grateful for the change of subject. 'Do you have any white?'

'Think so. I'll check the fridge.'

He found a nicely chilled sav blanc and poured it into a glass, flipped the top off a beer for himself.

Flora clinked her glass against his bottle. 'Cheers,' she said.

'Yeah, cheers.' Mitch glanced outside to the terrace that was bathed in the last of the sunlight. 'It's still hot outside. We might wait ten minutes before we go out there. Everything cools down quickly as soon as the sun sets.'

So they sat in the deep, slightly sagging sofas, while the sun, looking like an enormous orange dinner plate, slid slowly behind the distant hills.

Flora wondered what she should talk about if she was supposed to be cheering Mitch up.

'Those kids seemed to be enjoying their rehearsal,' he said.

'Yes, I think we actually made quite decent progress.'

'Sounded like you had them under control.'

Flora smiled. 'I was terrified at the start. Honestly, it was hopeless. Kids were running riot, but once we got over that, they were actually very sweet. And they tried hard with their music.'

'They probably wanted to impress you.'

'They did impress me. They were great.'

'Don't stress about it, though,' Mitch suggested. 'It wouldn't matter if they weren't great. No one expects a children's orchestra to be the Berlin Philharmonic.'

'I know. My main aim is to keep Peg Fletcher happy. She used to be my music teacher yonks ago.'

Mitch nodded. 'Peg's certainly a pillar of the Burralea community. I hope she gets over that fall without any hiccups. The place needs her.'

'She seems to be doing well.' Flora took another appreciative sip of her wine. 'I was actually pleased to see you there, today, Mitch. Truly. I don't mind if you want to patrol around the rehearsals.'

He eyed her steadily. 'Has that ex of yours got you nervous?'

'I suppose he has, a bit.' She gave a deliberate shrug. 'It's silly, of course. He's in Melbourne, so I shouldn't really worry.'

'Does he know you're here?' Mitch looked serious as he asked this.

Flora shivered. 'No, I don't think so. I've covered my tracks and Seth certainly didn't let on.'

Mitch nodded. 'I'll have a word with Finn Latimer, the editor of the *Burralea Bugle*. I'll make sure he doesn't mention your name in any coverage of the Christmas concert. It's worth taking precautions. Even the smaller regional papers are on the web these days.'

'Thanks. That's a good idea.' Flora took another, deeper, sip of her wine.

They looked out at the view. The sun was only a shimmering line along the tops of the hills and the light was fading fast.

'I'll put the chops on the barbie,' Mitch said. 'And you might like to check out the veggie patch and pick a few salad things.'

'Yeah, I'd love that.'

Already, it was pleasantly cooler out on the terrace. Mitch snipped a sprig of rosemary from a pot near the door and sprinkled the rubbed leaves over the lamb chops. In the veggie garden Flora found a variety of lettuce leaves and rocket, some beautifully ripe cherry tomatoes, a bunch of shallots and a few sprigs of parsley, chives and basil.

She caught the aromatic scent of the fresh herbs on the evening air, felt a soft breeze brush the back of her neck. She smelled the lamb cooking on the barbecue, and she saw Mitch, changed into jeans and a faded plaid shirt, throwing handfuls of grain into the chook pen and shutting his hens in safely for the night. Beyond him stretched the dark hills and valleys that formed the spectacular backdrop.

She realised how much she'd missed this – the simple pleasures of country living. For the first time in a long time, perhaps ever, she wondered if she was meant to be a big-city musician. It was so good to be here, reconnected to the outdoors, to the earth and the sky.

She'd grown up on a cattle property. Maybe a link to the land was somehow embedded in her DNA?

As she went back to the kitchen to rinse the veggies and find a salad bowl, she wondered if she should be considering a life like Peg's, living in a small rural community and helping generations of children to enjoy music. Wouldn't she like to become a 'pillar' of some small country community?

The prospect had definite appeal, but Flora's thoughts took a sharp about-turn as soon as she remembered her beloved violin. When she considered the thrill of playing the dazzling Tchaikovsky concerto in a beautiful city concert hall, she was pulled in a completely different direction.

Her father claimed that her musical streak stemmed from the same source that had inspired her Aunt Deborah to become a successful artist living at the Daintree. Whatever had given birth to her passion, the pull was strong.

'You're frowning,' Mitch said, coming into the kitchen. 'You must need a top-up.' He fetched the wine bottle from the fridge.

'Thanks,' she said, as he splashed wine into her glass.

'You're not still worrying about that ex, are you?' he asked.

'No, I was thinking about the whole country–city thing, actually. It's strange being back. When I'm in the city, I love everything about my life there, and then I come home to all the beauty up here and I realise how much I've missed it. I think I could be happy here, too, maybe teaching.'

'But you have an amazing talent. You'd be wasted in the bush.'

'Not necessarily.' She gave a smiling shrug. 'I don't suppose you've ever considered working in the city?'

'I have, actually.'

Flora had been tearing basil leaves into a bowl of lettuce, but now she looked up. 'Really? I thought you were totally focused on becoming Burralea's favourite country cop.'

Mitch pulled a face. 'I do love it here. I've enjoyed making this place my home and I have good friends, but there *was* a time when I dreamed of becoming a big-city detective.'

'What stopped you?'

Standing in the middle of his kitchen, Mitch looked at her for what felt like ages. Flora swallowed and felt her cheeks grow hot, which was damned annoying. What was he thinking? Why should his answer be difficult?

'I'm not sure,' he said at last. 'Maybe I just took the easy road.'

Disconcerted, Flora reached for a chopping board and began to attack the parsley.

'I think the chops are ready,' Mitch said. 'I'll grab the plates and cutlery. Can you bring that salad?'

'Sure. Do you want a dressing for it?'

'There's a jar in the fridge – a mix of olive oil and balsamic and we can add a dash of lime. I've found it works quite well.'

'Sounds great.'

They carried everything to the table outside. It was dark now and the first stars were showing. A late-flying nightjar swooped low, on the lookout for its last chance for dinner.

Mitch lit fat candles in attractive metal lanterns. The chops were crispy, just the way Flora loved them, the salad ultra fresh, with the squeezed lime adding a perfect tang.

'Yummo,' she said, tucking in. 'Sometimes I think about becoming a vegetarian and then I remember lamb chops and I know it'll never happen.'

Mitch laughed. 'And what about bacon? How could you go through life without ever tasting another slice of bacon?'

'I know, I know. Mind you, I do have a thing for mushrooms – and a gorgeous salad like this, straight from the garden. It's amazing.'

They talked about food for a bit, about their favourite meals now, as adults, but also when they were kids. They talked about cooking triumphs and disasters, and Flora told Mitch about Melbourne's huge variety of cafés and restaurants. Mitch filled her in about some of the great new produce that local farmers were experimenting with.

It was easy to talk to Mitch. Easy and pleasant – maybe way too pleasant. She felt happy and bubbly, almost as if she still had a crush on the guy, which of course she didn't. That had just been a silly, childish thing, something she hoped he'd forgotten.

He poured her another glass of wine.

'What about you?' she asked. 'Are you having another beer?'

'Better not. I'm driving you home.'

'Oh, yes, that's right.'

Flora twisted the stem of her glass, not sure that she wanted to drink alone.

'Unless you wouldn't mind sleeping over,' Mitch said, sending her a look from beneath lowered lids that was both cautious and challenging.

The look caused a ridiculous zap, as if she'd touched a live wire. 'On the couch?'

'Well, it doesn't have to be the couch. There's a spare bed.'

'Right.' It was silly to feel coy. 'Then why don't I stay over so you can relax and enjoy another beer?'

CHAPTER TWENTY-THREE

'The crazy thing was that I didn't see it coming.'

It was nearly midnight. Mitch and Flora had moved inside again and Flora was drinking hot chocolate. Conversation had been flowing easily all night, touching on a wide range of topics – favourite dogs, dream travel destinations, a deep psychoanalysis of their mutual friends – the kind of talk that can only happen late at night, after a drink or three.

Mitch had deftly avoided talking about Angie, though, and Flora had been equally careful to avoid that touchy topic. She hadn't seemed keen to talk about her ex either. So Mitch was stunned to find himself suddenly spilling his guts about the shock of his no-show wedding day.

'I can't imagine how hard that must have been for you,' Flora said gently. 'But I hear you about not seeing it coming.' She gave a small sigh. 'I was the same about Oliver. I thought he was lovely until . . . he wasn't . . .'

They were sitting opposite each other on sofas now and they shared sorry smiles.

'So what does that make us both?' Mitch asked. 'Naïve, gullible dickheads?'

'Maybe.' Flora's smile faded. Her expression turned serious again. 'I suppose, when you're in a relationship, you can be blinkered. You just see what you want to see. Maybe it's the whole rose-coloured glasses thing. Or maybe the clues are easy to miss.'

'Or maybe some people are just plain dishonest,' Mitch suggested, darkly.

'Well, yes . . . that's true. They can be downright devious, can't they? Saying one thing to your face and thinking something else entirely.'

'Yeah.' Mitch knew exactly what Flora meant. He still couldn't believe that Angie had never once mentioned Kevin, and yet she'd probably been pining for her old boyfriend the whole time.

As he thought about Kevin now, however, he realised that he could do so tonight without the terrible gut ache that made him want to punch someone. The pain wasn't nearly as bad as it had been all week.

Chilling out with Flora had obviously been good for him. He was relaxed around her these days. She'd grown up a lot in the past couple of years. Now they seemed to be able to tune into each other, and there was no bullshit, no trying to show off or flirt – the kind of stuff that usually happened in mixed company.

He and Flora had both been burned, of course, and no doubt that had helped. His enjoyment of Flora's company had nothing to do with the pretty picture she made, curled on his couch, her dark hair gleaming in the lamplight, her eyes brimming with warmth, her slender, expressive hands hugging a blue pottery mug.

Now, she drained her mug and let out a yawn.

'We should call it a night,' Mitch said.

'Yeah, I guess so. It's been a lovely evening, though. Thanks, Mitch.'

'And thanks to you, too. I'll show you to your room. The bed's already made up.'

It was a double bed covered by a bright cotton rug made in India that Mitch had found at a market in Cairns. The lamps in the room were covered by shades that made the space look more glamorous than it really was.

Flora was still exclaiming over how lovely the room was as Mitch said goodnight. She didn't need his help to find the little guest bathroom, and he was suddenly aware that being with her in close proximity to a bed was still as bad an idea as it had been six years ago.

By the time Mitch had showered and got into bed, the house was quiet, apart from the hum of the dishwasher. He supposed Flora was already asleep. He only hoped he could fall asleep quickly as well. Problem was, he couldn't help wondering if she was also thinking about that night. The night neither of them mentioned. Ever.

It wasn't a memory he wanted to dwell on, and yet, as he lay alone, knowing Flora was just down the hallway, it wouldn't leave him. He could see the shed at Ruthven Downs, the cattle property that had belonged to Flora's father, Hugh Drummond. The shed was a simple one – even the push-out windows were made of corrugated iron – and it was used to house stockmen who were employed there from time to time to help with mustering or fencing.

It had been Mitch's home for the twelve months that he'd lived with the Drummonds, and it had suited his needs just fine. With the windows pushed wide, he could lie in bed and watch the Southern Cross climbing the night sky.

He'd been so grateful to the Drummonds for taking him in. He'd arrived at their place an angry kid with a huge chip on both shoulders, but they'd welcomed him to join the family for meals, which was a whole new experience, and Hugh Drummond had kept him busy with interesting and challenging tasks during the day.

Mitch had huge respect for Hugh, who treated him with kindness and encouragement, almost like he was another son.

The whole family – Hugh, Jackie, Seth and Flora – had accepted him wholeheartedly, each of them in his or her own way gently peeling back the tough outer shell, the sulky moodiness that Mitch had worn through his teen years as protective armour. He'd begun to feel valued, normal, as if he'd stepped out of a shadow into sunlight.

Then the thing with Flora had happened, coming as a total shock.

Mitch had been walking back to his shed after a night out in town with Seth. It was a full moon and the tin shed shone bright silver. When he opened the door, the whole room was filled with moonlight, so he saw her at once.

Flora.

Lying in his bed, with the sheet pulled up to her chin and her long dark hair spread over the pillow. On the chair nearby, her clothes were neatly folded, with her pink sneakers lined precisely on the floor beneath.

Sweat broke out all over Mitch. *Fuck*.

He'd known Flora was sweet on him. He'd seen her watching him, and he'd been aware of the flirtatious, girly smiles, the lowered lashes and the blushes. And he couldn't deny he thought she was damn cute with her long legs and her silky dark hair and flashing eyes. But no way was he going to make the serious mistake of hitting on her.

She was his boss's daughter. Just seventeen. Her parents had taken him in out of the goodness of their hearts. They trusted him.

To find their daughter in his bed was a total disaster.

Mitch stood stock-still in the centre of the room staring at Flora. 'What are you doing here?'

'What does it look like?' She sounded brave, but her eyes looked scared.

'But, Flora, you can't. This is wrong.'

'No one will know.'

'You can't guarantee that. And anyway, that's not the point.'

'I'm not a little kid. I'm old enough to know what I'm doing.'

As she said this, she slid the sheet down to reveal her youthful body. Her beautiful, perfect body. Her pale, soft skin, and pink-tipped breasts, her slim, girlish hips and the dark curls at the junction of her thighs.

She was temptation at its sweetest and purest. The most dangerous kind of entrapment.

Mitch was engulfed by a desire unlike anything he'd ever known before. He choked back a groan. 'Flora.' He knew he sounded shaken, but he couldn't help it. 'This can't happen. It mustn't.'

'Don't you like me?'

'It's not that. Of course I like you, but this is wrong. You must know it is.'

She continued to lie there, uncovered, and anger joined the riot of emotions storming through Mitch. Stepping forward, he grabbed the sheet and pulled it roughly over her.

Then he whirled away, with his back to her. 'I'm not going to stuff things up with your family after what they've done for me.' The words were a tight snarl fired over his shoulder. 'Get dressed.'

No sound came from the bed, but Mitch stood his ground and waited, trembling. It felt like an age before he heard movements. He continued to stand with his back to Flora, glaring grimly ahead at the door, not daring to look back to catch another glimpse of her. And he prayed that no one up at the homestead had noticed she was missing.

Eventually the soft sounds of dressing stopped and Flora came to stand beside him, fully clothed. She didn't speak, and when Mitch saw her white face and the glitter of tears in her eyes, he suspected that she wasn't capable of saying anything.

He bit back the impulse to tell her he was sorry. It was far better to be tough on her, to make sure that this was never repeated.

'Goodnight, Flora.' He opened the door and watched her walk off in moonlight so bright he could see her all the way to the house.

Remembering that night, Mitch swallowed, hoping to ease the sharp pain, the knot of emotion that felt like a bone stuck in his throat. The pain didn't make sense. The tensions with Flora were all in the past.

Neither he nor Flora had ever mentioned that night again, but there'd always been an awkwardness, a hesitation between them. He was glad it was gone now, that their tension was resolved, and they'd both moved on. It was good to know they'd finally reached this new place where they could enjoy a comfortable, uncomplicated friendship.

So it made no sense that he still couldn't sleep.

* * *

'You look happy today,' Tammy announced as Flora settled herself in a swivel chair in front of a mirror.

Flora looked up to meet the hairdresser's smiling reflection. 'You sound surprised. Don't I usually look happy?'

Tammy shook her head. 'The other night at Seth's you seemed like you had the weight of the world on your shoulders.'

'Oh, yes. I was a bit worried the other night.' It was tempting to tell Tammy about Seth's phone call from Oliver.

Tammy was warm and friendly and her small, old-fashioned salon had a welcoming, cosy vibe, with cream-painted tongue and groove timber walls and a sweet bay window with blue sills. In a corner, there were deeply cushioned cane chairs and a glass-topped table with the latest magazines. On the counter a huge bowl of pink and cream roses from Burralea Gardens sat beside a pottery dish of gorgeous-smelling handmade soaps.

Flora had felt relaxed as soon as she'd walked inside, and she was tempted to tell Tammy the whole story about Oliver. She knew Tammy would be all ears, lapping up every detail, and brimming with empathy and good advice.

Just in time, Flora remembered that it wouldn't be wise to say more about her ex, given that she didn't really know Tammy very well. After all, Mitch was going to the trouble of keeping her name out of the local newspaper, and it was still important for her to lie low. She would be foolish to risk the possibility of gossip.

'I'm feeling much better today,' she said instead, as Tammy draped a cape around her shoulders.

'Yes, I can see that.' Tammy smiled, then looked more thoughtful as she combed Flora's hair, studying its texture and shape. 'So, are we keeping this asymmetrical look?'

'Yes, I'm happy with it.' Under the cape, Flora crossed her fingers. She wasn't ready for a dramatic change in hairstyle, certainly not with a hairdresser she hadn't used before.

'And what about the colour?' Tammy asked. 'Are you going to keep these purple streaks?'

Briefly, Flora considered the looming orchestra audition, but of course, she would be performing behind a screen. The music was what mattered, not the performers' age or gender, or hair colour. *What the heck?*

'Why not?' she said. 'Let's stick with the purple.'

Tammy grinned and gave her a cheerful thumbs up. 'I'll put your colour on first and then cut afterwards, okay?'

'Okay.'

Tammy crossed to behind the counter to mix the colour.

'I think Mitch is starting to feel a bit better, too,' Flora said, knowing that Tammy liked nothing better than to chat.

'That's great.' Tammy looked up from her task and her eyes held a knowing twinkle. 'I thought I saw him dropping you back home this morning.'

Flora's heart thumped. *Oh, God.* Had Tammy jumped to the wrong conclusions? 'Mitch has been a friend of our family's for years,' she said. 'He needs company at the moment and we're all trying to keep an eye on him.'

'Of course.'

Flora found herself nervously studying Tammy's face. 'It's purely a friendship thing. You know that, don't you?'

And I'm making this worse by overreacting.

'Good grief, yes,' the girl said in her most soothing tone. 'God knows, it's going to take Mitch ages to get over Angie.'

'Yes.' Annoyingly, this comment didn't comfort Flora nearly as much as it should have.

CHAPTER TWENTY-FOUR

When Hattie woke and found herself in Joe's house, she lay for a few minutes, readjusting to her surroundings. She listened to the busy chatter of birds in the grevillea outside her window and let her mind work through all that had happened in recent days. Her arrival in Burralea, coming here to Joe's house for that first meeting, then the visit to the police station and lunch at Lake Barrine.

Last night after dinner, she and Joe had spent a very sedate but surprisingly pleasant evening reading in comfortable lounge chairs, while Marlowe slept on the carpet between them and ABC Classic FM played Mendelssohn and Brahms quietly in the background. Now, another morning had dawned, and Hattie found herself accepting, once again, the astonishing fact that she had moved in, under the same roof as Joe Matthews. Sleeping with the enemy, so to speak.

She thought about the anger and hurt Joe had caused her all those years ago when he'd married Gloria. She still found it hard to accept that Joe had broken his word to her, that he'd been unfaithful and had consequently been trapped in an unhappy marriage. The recklessness of that long-ago birthday party seemed so out of character with both the man she'd known then, and the man she'd met again now.

Perhaps she'd always expected too much of Joe. Even the strongest people had human frailties.

There was a knock at the door. Joe's voice. 'Hattie?'

'Yes,' she called. 'I'm awake.'

'Would you like a cup of tea in bed?'

She wasn't ready for him to see her in her nightie. It seemed too . . . intimate. 'No, thanks. I'll get up.'

Out of bed, she washed her face, then dressed and applied tinted moisturiser, which made her skin look a little smoother without being obviously made-up. Despite her advancing years and the inevitable lines, she was still a little vain about her complexion.

The table in the kitchen was set for two and there was a teapot under a cosy. Hattie smelled toast and heard a familiar voice on the radio reading the ABC news. Joe, in a white T-shirt over blue striped pyjama bottoms, was standing at the stove, stirring something in a pot.

From outside came the sound of a car door slamming. 'Is it my imagination or is there more traffic this morning?' Hattie asked.

'Cars everywhere,' said Joe. 'It's market morning. They start early.'

'Oh, yes.' She'd forgotten about the markets. There'd been nothing like that when she'd lived here.

'You might like to take a look later, if the cops don't hold us up for too long.'

'I'd like that. If the markets are so popular, they must be worth seeing.'

Marlowe had been snoozing on the back porch, but now he nosed the flyscreen door open and came into the kitchen to greet Hattie.

'Hello, old boy.'

'I'm doing scrambled eggs,' Joe said. 'How does that sound?'

Hattie normally had a small bowl of muesli for breakfast, but she nodded and smiled. 'Lovely, thanks.'

'Good morning, by the way.' He smiled at her. He hadn't shaved yet and there was soft white fuzz on his jaw, which should have made him look even older and less attractive, but didn't. 'How did you sleep?' he asked.

'Brilliantly. It must be the mountain air.'

Joe nodded. 'Help yourself to the teapot.'

She pulled out a chair at the table and poured herself a good strong cuppa and sat, sipping tea and listening to the stock market report on the radio, letting the figures roll over her, without paying any real attention. Joe turned the radio off, then piled the eggs onto toast on two plates and brought them to the table. They took it in turns to use the pepper grinder.

'You certainly know how to scramble eggs,' Hattie told him after her first mouthful and she was amazed by how normal this felt, as if this wasn't the first time they'd woken in the same house and had breakfast together, almost as if her married life with Ian had existed in a separate world, a parallel universe, perhaps.

She thought about the loneliness of the past six years, and she had the strangest feeling that Ian wouldn't mind too much about this.

'I've had a text message from Mitch Cavello,' Joe said. 'The detective from Brisbane will be in the station at ten and he wants to see us.'

Hattie nodded. 'Right.'

'I daresay it'll be a matter of going through the same story as yesterday.'

'I guess so.'

'And I suppose —'

The front doorbell rang. 'Yoohoo!' a woman's voice called. 'Are you there, Dad?'

Joe's eyes widened with surprise. 'That sounds like Janelle.'

'Your daughter?'

'Yes.' He didn't look particularly thrilled as he got to his feet.

Hattie remembered that his daughter lived at Mareeba. She must be an early riser to have driven over here at this hour. She sat, listening to Joe's footsteps as he went down the hall, heard the front door open. Heard voices.

'Janelle, I thought it must be you.'

'Hi, Dad. I had to come over this way and thought I'd pop in.'

'How lovely.'

'Sorry, I should have called to let you know I was coming. It was a bit spur of the moment.'

'That's okay. You'd better come in.'

'Thanks. I could hardly find a parking spot with all the cars here for the markets.'

Their footsteps approached and Hattie swallowed a piece of toast a little too quickly. Marlowe left the kitchen and went back to his spot in the sun on the back porch. Hattie set her knife and fork carefully on the plate, and she was dabbing at her mouth with her napkin as Joe and his daughter came into the kitchen.

Janelle came to an abrupt halt when she saw Hattie. She was a rather large woman, in her fifties, with plump freckled arms, an untidy mass of curly grey hair and a belligerent glint in her eyes. She was dressed in a shapeless olive-green cotton garment that hung loosely to her ankles and her feet were encased in pink raffia sandals.

'Oh,' she said, looking at Hattie with a decided lack of warmth.

'This is Hattie,' Joe told her. 'She's a very old friend. She lived in Burralea back before you were born. Hattie, this is my daughter Janelle.'

'Hello, Janelle.' Hattie offered a warm smile as she held out her hand.

'Hello.' Janelle took her hand limply, almost unwillingly. Then she hitched the strap of a huge vinyl bag higher on her shoulder and addressed her father. 'I heard on the news about that awful business on Kooringal. The reporter said the police were talking to you.'

'That's right,' Joe said smoothly. Then he pulled out a chair. 'Won't you sit down? Hattie and I haven't quite finished our breakfast, and our eggs are getting cold. Would you like a cup of tea?'

'No, thanks. I had Macca's and takeaway coffee in the car.' Janelle sat heavily and watched impatiently as Joe resumed his place at the table. Then she shot a glance to Hattie. 'So you're staying here with my father?' It was a definite challenge.

'Yes.' Hattie smiled again and felt obliged to explain. 'The town's booked out for the market weekend and Joe kindly offered me a —' Under this daughter's unsmiling scrutiny, the word 'bed' seemed to stick in Hattie's throat. 'Accommodation.'

Janelle turned to her father, who had resumed eating. She frowned as she let her gaze travel over him in an unspoken but obvious criticism of his attire and his unshaven jaw. 'You'll have the neighbours talking, Dad. Entertaining strange women in your pyjamas.'

'Hattie's not a stranger,' Joe responded tranquilly. 'I told you that. In fact, she lived on Kooringal for a while, when we were children. That's why she's here.'

'Because of Kooringal? And those bones that Seth Drummond found?'

'Yes.'

'So what's the story with that?' Janelle looked worried now.

'It's nothing to worry about, Janelle. I would have let you know if there was a problem. It was something that happened back during the war. The US Army was involved.' Joe gave her an abbreviated version of what they knew about Gabriel.

'Right. Okay.' For the first time since she'd arrived, Janelle smiled at her father. 'Well, it doesn't sound like you'll be carted off to gaol, so that's a relief.'

Joe smiled too.

'I have to admit I was worried – a scandal in the family could be bad publicity for Fergus.'

'We certainly wouldn't want to upset his career,' said Joe. 'I don't think there'll be a scandal. More importantly, how are Antonio and the boys?'

As Janelle filled her father in with her family's latest news, which seemed to involve football, macadamia harvests and unsuitable girlfriends, Hattie couldn't help thinking how very unlike Joe his daughter was. She could see no similarities in their physical features. Janelle was round and plump and curly-haired, whereas Joe had always been tall and lean, with tough, straight hair and light hazel eyes as opposed to his daughter's dark brown ones. And their personalities seemed to be poles apart.

Hattie supposed Janelle took after her mother's family.

Janelle suddenly turned to Hattie. 'How long will you be staying here?'

'Oh, not long at all,' Hattie quickly reassured her. 'As soon as the police are satisfied, I'll be heading back to Brisbane.'

She chanced a glance in Joe's direction and something about the look in his eyes made her feel ridiculously warm-cheeked and shy. She realised Janelle was watching her with a narrowed gaze. A suspicious gaze.

Hattie found the woman annoying. For heaven's sake, she and Joe were almost octogenarians. They didn't need vigilante daughters watching their every move and telling them how to behave.

She was rather relieved when Janelle got to her feet. 'I'll say goodbye then. I may as well check out the markets while I'm here.'

'It's been lovely meeting you,' Hattie lied.

'You, too,' Janelle said with a noticeable lack of sincerity.

Joe accompanied his daughter to the door and they talked on the front step for a few minutes. Hattie didn't try to listen in, but she sensed that Janelle was offering her father rather strong advice, which he seemed to be fielding with his usual equanimity.

Hattie rose and began to clear the table. Joe didn't have a dishwasher, which was a pity. He'd told her last night that a woman came once a week to do the general cleaning, but Hattie didn't like to think of an old widower living alone, having to bother with doing the dishes three times a day. She supposed he probably left them to pile in the sink when he didn't have visitors.

Perhaps she should make it her mission, while she was here, to persuade Joe to have a dishwasher installed. She could see exactly the right spot for one of those neat, drawer-style appliances.

Having cleared the table and stacked the dishes ready to be washed, she was just coming back from the garden, where she'd tipped the leaves from the teapot, when Joe returned.

'Thanks for getting this started,' he said. 'I'll wash up.'

'All right. I'll dry.'

'So now you've met Janelle,' he said as he filled the sink with hot water.

'Yes.' Hattie searched for something positive to say. 'It must be nice to have family living reasonably close.'

Joe merely nodded and began to wash plates.

'I miss my son,' she said. 'But he lives at a very hectic pace and, somehow, I couldn't face the idea of growing old in New York. Or London, for that matter. I'd always had the idea that I would eventually come back to Australia.'

'Has your son been to visit you in Brisbane?'

'Oh, yes. He comes at least twice a year.'

Joe made no comment to this, but he looked thoughtful as he attacked a saucepan with a scourer.

Hattie said, 'I'm glad you won't be going to gaol and causing a scandal that could somehow ruin your grandson's football career.'

At this, his mouth tilted in a wry smile. 'Now Janelle only has to worry about my respectability.'

'Is your respectability in danger because I'm staying here? Do you think it really bothers her?'

'Janelle loves drama,' Joe said. 'She likes to beat everything up until it's a thousand times better or worse than it really is.' He gave a rueful smile. 'She should have been a journalist.'

'Does she have a career?' Hattie asked.

'No, that's half the trouble. She's a farmer's wife and the life is far too dull for her.'

Hattie imagined that many farmers' wives led very fulfilling lives, throwing themselves into the family business and becoming involved in the community. Clearly, those roles had no appeal for Janelle. 'She must be very proud of her son, though,' she said. 'The footballer.'

'Oh, *yes*. No doubt about that. Fergus's career is the best thing that's ever happened to Janelle.' Joe sighed. 'But she gives her other boys a hard time.'

He put the final knife in the dish drainer and began to wipe down the sink, and Hattie couldn't help saying the thing that had been preying on her mind.

'Janelle's not at all like you, Joe. I was struggling to find any resemblance.'

Joe stopped wiping. Over his shoulder, he said, 'There's a reason for that.'

Hattie, in the process of hanging tea mugs on hooks, turned and stared at him. 'What do you mean?'

He was suddenly very still and he said quietly, 'I'm not her real father.'

'Joe.' Hattie gripped the edge of the bench for support.

In a shocked flash, she was reliving the dreadful night, the worst night of her life, when Joe had come to her, white faced, fighting tears, to confess that he'd made Gloria Walker pregnant and that he was going to have to marry her.

Now, Hattie's knees almost gave way, and she reached for the back of a chair, which offered more support than the narrow edge of the bench. 'What on earth are you saying?' Her voice was little more than a whisper.

Joe looked pained. 'I'm sorry. I didn't mean to upset you. I shouldn't have said anything.'

'No, tell me. I want to know.'

He swallowed. 'Another man fathered Janelle.'

Hattie's heartbeats drummed wildly. She clung to the chair.

'I didn't know until well after Emma, my second daughter, was born,' Joe said. 'She must have been about seven or eight and I made a comment one day to Gloria about how different our two girls were. Gloria was in a terrible mood. We'd been arguing a lot – well, no more than usual, I suppose – but that was the way things were with us. Anyway, Gloria suddenly let it all out. I suppose she told me because she wanted to hurt me.'

Joe was still holding the dishcloth that he'd been using to wipe the benches. He took it back to the sink and dropped it in. 'Gloria had a fling with someone who'd been staying at the pub. By the time she realised she was pregnant, the fellow was long gone and she had no way of tracking him down. She didn't want to, really.'

'But she needed to produce a father for her baby?' Hattie guessed.

'Yes, that's the long and the short of it.'

'And then you were there at the pub, having a rowdy birthday party.'

'A rather drunken party, yes.' Joe didn't make eye contact, but Hattie could see the downward turn of his mouth and the way his

Adam's apple jerked as he swallowed again. 'I suppose I was an easy mark.'

'Oh, Joe.'

'I'm not trying to make excuses. It was still unforgivable of me.'

Perhaps. But all Hattie could think about was the huge price Joe had paid for that one mistake. She'd given up feeling sorry for herself years and years ago. With Ian, she'd lived a fulfilled and happy life.

How terrible for Joe, though, to have suffered years of unhappiness and then to have learned the truth far too late. She hated the fact that his marriage had been so wretched that he'd gone to the Vietnam War to escape, only to discover years later that he'd been well and truly conned. But despite all of this, he'd stayed with his wife, no doubt for the girls' sake, or perhaps to punish himself, and he'd nursed Gloria through her long illness.

'Does Janelle know about this?' she asked.

'Good God, no. I couldn't do that to her. I have no idea who her real father is, so there wouldn't be any point.'

'Joe.' Grief and outrage welled in Hattie's throat. 'You poor man.'

He'd spent a lifetime paying for the mistake he'd made that night.

At the sink, he turned on the tap to rinse the dish cloth, and as Hattie watched him perform this simple task, she was so overcome she couldn't help herself. Almost blinded by tears, she crossed the room to him. He hadn't moved from the sink and she slipped her arms around his waist and hugged him close.

'Hattie.' His voice was choked.

'Ssh.' She held him tight, with her arms wrapped around him, the side of her face pressed against his back, listening to his heartbeats.

'I'm sorry,' he said again.

'So am I, Joe, but I'm sorry for you, not for me.'

CHAPTER TWENTY-FIVE

It was late in the day when Hattie answered a phone call from Oliver Edmonds.

By then, she and Joe had dealt with the second round of police interviews, and once again, they'd told the detectives everything they could remember. After they'd been dismissed, they'd walked over to the markets, which was quite an undertaking, given the sudden massive increase in Burralea's population.

People and cars had seemed to be everywhere and, with no pedestrian crossings, getting over the main road had been rather daunting for an elderly couple. A kind-hearted driver had stopped for them, however, and Joe had taken Hattie firmly in hand and steered her safely across. Then they'd spent an absorbing hour wandering through lanes of colourful, busy stalls.

'You need a hat,' Joe had told her. It was certainly hot and he'd sensibly worn his Akubra, slightly battered but appropriately rural.

They'd found Hattie an attractive, wide-brimmed sunhat made of a woven fabric that was easy to pack in her suitcase, then they'd continued to explore the astonishing variety of local produce. All manner of vegetables were available, along with sweet red pawpaws and ladyfinger bananas, spidery mushrooms and little chickens in cages.

Hattie hadn't minded jostling with the crowds. She'd quite enjoyed the mingled clamour of voices and music, the host of smells from cooking and animals, the overloaded trestle tables groaning with handicrafts, pots of chutney and second-hand books. The bustle reminded her of Shanghai and of walking with her amah. All her life, she'd felt quite at home and peaceful in a crowd.

Joe had bought three punnets of vegetable seedlings, and Hattie had chosen handmade lavender soap. From an Italian food stall, they'd selected a little box of cannoli filled with vanilla custard to take back to Joe's place as a treat.

In the cool of the afternoon, after a decent rest, Marlowe took them for another leisurely and nosy walk along the creek.

Now, Joe was in his back garden staking his tomato plants and Hattie was in the kitchen. She was slicing vegetables for a stir-fry when Joe's phone rang.

The phone was mounted on the opposite wall, and by the time she'd wiped her hands and crossed the room, it had almost rung out. The caller ID showed 'unknown' and she considered leaving it. It was probably someone from Mumbai trying to sell Joe solar panels.

At the last minute she relented. 'Hello?'

'Good evening,' said a man's voice. 'Is that Joe Matthews's place? Do I have the right number?'

He was very well spoken, his voice rich and sonorous.

'Yes,' Hattie said cautiously.

'That's wonderful. I'm so pleased.'

'Joe's in the back garden. I'll just have to call him.'

'No, don't do that,' came the quick response. 'I don't want to trouble him. I understand that Joe has had contact with the Drummond family, but you might be able to help me too. I'm a music agent, and I'm ringing from Melbourne. I'm actually trying to make contact with Flora Drummond. I don't suppose you know her?'

'Well, yes.' Hattie was smiling now with delight. 'I've met Flora. I've heard her play. She's a very talented violinist.'

'Isn't she just? What a lucky coincidence that you've met her. I have some good news for her about her career.'

'Oh, I see.' This sounded terribly exciting, but Hattie wondered why the man had rung Joe. It seemed rather odd. 'What did you say your name was?'

'Oliver Edmonds,' he replied, without hesitation. 'My problem is that my phone's been stolen and I've lost a host of important contacts. It's incredibly annoying. I really need to make contact with Flora. It's one of those urgent matters that has to be sorted quite soon. I've tried her brother's homestead, but I could only leave a message on the answering machine.'

'Oh.' Hattie felt a little helpless and still rather confused about why this man was ringing Joe.

'I don't want to sound too desperate,' Oliver Edmonds said next, as if he'd sensed her concern. 'All I need, really, is to confirm that Flora is still in Burralea. If she's already moved on to the Gold Coast, that's fine. I can use my contacts there. Otherwise, I'll just wait till her brother gets back to me.'

'I see.' His explanation was beginning to make sense now, and Hattie supposed she was silly to worry. 'I can tell you that Flora is most definitely still in Burralea,' she said, and then, because she liked to be helpful, she passed on a little extra detail that Mitch Cavello had mentioned when they were at the police station. 'I heard just today that Flora's helping to put on a children's Christmas concert here, so I imagine she'll be in Burralea for some time yet.'

'Ah . . . thank you,' said Oliver warmly. 'That's excellent news. I'm so relieved.'

'It's bad luck about your phone,' Hattie said in sudden sympathy.

'Yes, it's been a real nuisance, but you've been very helpful. Thank you.'

'My pleasure. I hope Flora gets her good news soon.'

'Oh. I'm sure she will. Once again, I thank you.'

Hattie was smiling as she hung up. Behind her, she heard Joe at the back door. He had taken off his boots and came into the kitchen in his socks.

'Who was that?' he asked.

'It was actually someone looking for Flora Drummond.'

Joe frowned. 'Seth Drummond's sister?'

'Yes, the girl I pointed out in the street the other day, the violinist. Her agent was ringing from Melbourne. He told me his name – Oliver someone – and said he was trying to track Flora down.'

'But why was he ringing here?'

'I'm not sure exactly.' Oliver had made everything sound perfectly logical, but now that she'd hung up, Hattie was feeling confused again. 'He gave me some story about his phone being stolen and losing his contacts. And Seth Drummond wasn't home, so he could only leave a message.'

'So he rang here?' Joe was still frowning.

'It does seem a bit strange, doesn't it? I wonder why he chose you. He did seem to know that you had some connection with the Drummonds. Maybe he read your name in a news story.'

'Yes, that's probably what happened.' Joe was nodding now. 'Mitch Cavello said he'd been inundated with journalists wanting the story on the bones, especially now with the connection to the US and the war. I suppose my name and Seth's were both mentioned.'

'Yes, and by now the story could be in the southern papers and maybe even on the TV news.' Hattie gave a small shrug. 'Anyway, all I told this Oliver chap was that Flora is still in town. He said he had good news for her, so I thought it was okay.'

Joe still looked serious.

'It was all right to tell him that, wasn't it?'

'Yes, I'm sure it was,' he said soothingly.

'Should I let Flora know? I don't have her phone number, but she's staying in that pretty pink cottage down near the creek.'

'I certainly don't think you need to rush over there now. This fellow's down in Melbourne, isn't he?'

'That's what he said.'

'And he's left a message with Seth Drummond, so Seth will pass it on.'

'Yes, of course he will.'

'I'd leave it to Seth, if I were you.'

Reassured, Hattie went back to the stove. She turned on the gas. 'I'll get on with this stir-fry then?'

'Yes, please.' Joe smiled at her. 'And I'll pour us both a glass of wine.'

At bedtime, Hattie showered and changed into a long nightgown of pale blue cotton dotted with tiny white flowers. Then she sat in front of the dressing-table mirror, rubbed moisturiser into her face and neck, and combed her hair.

'You'll do,' she told her reflection, before she rose and walked out of the bedroom and down the hall, her slippers making soft pats on the polished floorboards.

She stopped in the doorway to Joe's room, a pleasant, simply furnished room with a long padded seat set into a bay window. There were curtains in a cream and gold fabric, a tallboy with an oval mirror and, beside it, a matching chest of drawers. Joe was in bed, reading by lamplight.

He looked up, obviously surprised to see Hattie. They'd already said goodnight.

'Hattie.'

She smiled bravely. 'I wondered if you might like a little company?'

He didn't answer immediately. No doubt he was taken aback and Hattie couldn't blame him. She had the advantage that she'd been thinking about this all day.

Most especially, she'd been thinking about the years of unhappiness Joe had endured, the potential loneliness during his marriage and all the years since.

Even so, she might have backed away now if he hadn't smiled.

'I'd love *your* company,' he said and he took off his glasses and set them on top of his book on the small table beside him. 'Come here.'

By the time Hattie crossed the floor to the bed, Joe had pulled back the covers. She kicked off her slippers and climbed in beside him. The sheets were clean and smooth, the pillow pleasantly plump.

'I don't know about you, but I get a little lonely at night,' she said.

'I do, too.'

'But I'm not asking you to make love to me, Joe,' she quickly added, in case he was worried about her expectations. 'I just thought it was silly for two lonely old people to be lying at opposite ends of the house.'

'It is,' Joe said. 'It's ridiculous.'

They smiled at each other. In the bright lamplight, his face was wreathed in wrinkles. She supposed her face was too. She didn't care.

'Should I turn out the light?' he asked.

'Only if you're ready to. I don't mind.'

He did so and the darkness felt friendly. He reached for her hand. Her fingers were knobbly with arthritis, but then so were his, and his skin was a little rough, but she found the texture rather comforting. They lay for a bit, holding hands.

She was aware of the warmth of his body right next to hers, of the fine skin on their inner arms touching. He rubbed his thumb over hers in the friendliest of caresses.

'Thank you,' he said. 'Thank you for coming back into my life.'

'I'm so glad I did.' Apart from the pleasure of seeing Joe again, if she hadn't come back, she might never have learned the truth. Now, the old wounds that she'd kept buried deep inside her could heal.

'Do you want to talk?' he asked.

'Not necessarily.' They'd spent a lot of time talking over the past few days. 'Just being close is nice.'

He kissed her forehead, and his lips were warm and soft. She nestled closer, letting her head snuggle into his shoulder. As she closed her eyes, she caught the scent of soap on his skin.

'We never did make love,' he said. 'Not "all the way" as we used to call it.'

'I know. I was such a prude.'

'You were never a prude, Hattie. Just cautious.'

'I had so many lectures from Rose about "saving myself" until I was married.'

'I know.' She could hear the smile in his voice. 'I remember, but it was what most mothers taught their daughters back then.'

Hattie refrained from stating the obvious – that Joe might never have been tempted by Gloria if she, Hattie, had been more forthcoming.

Joe said, 'You were always a fabulous kisser.'

She smiled, remembering, and now, in the darkness, it was easy to picture Joe as a young man. *Her* young man. Tall and lean, with thick dark hair and warm hazel eyes, and a quiet smile that made everything in her world feel safe and right.

As for his kisses . . . she could remember the way he'd stirred her, making her wild with a longing so strong she was almost bursting out of her skin. If he kissed her now, she would be that young girl again, eager and curious and more than a little desperate.

'Hattie,' Joe whispered against her cheek, and that was all it took before their lips met, before he gathered her closer and their kiss became real.

Emotion flooded her, filled her with joy. This was her Joe. Again, at last. Warm, alive and loving, no longer a figure of regret from her complicated past.

CHAPTER TWENTY-SIX

Hong Kong, 1937

Lily seemed to sail through her pregnancy. At times Rose wondered if she'd forgotten about it completely, but Lily had agreed to hand the baby over to Rose and Stephen as soon as it was born, so the subject was a touchy one to raise.

'Don't fuss,' Lily would say, if Rose suggested that she shouldn't rush about quite so much, visiting people, or shopping, or entertaining new-found friends in their tiny flat in Hong Kong. 'Don't be a pudding, Rose.'

This hurt. Pudding was the name Lily reserved for stuffy, boring people.

Their Chinese landlady was on Rose's side, however. She told Lily that she wasn't resting enough and that she was eating too much fruit, but of course Lily pooh-poohed this.

'I'll only *drink* fruit then,' she joked. 'Rose, darling, fetch me a half bottle of champagne.'

But no matter how much Rose worried and fussed during the latter months of Lily's pregnancy, nothing prepared her for the anxious hours of pacing the hospital corridors, waiting for news of the birth.

Those hours, to Rose's horror, stretched into days. The baby was overdue at this point, but Lily's labour pains kept starting then petering out. Lily and Rose paced the corridors together, because Lily was told that walking would help. Her contractions would start up again, and she would be carted off into another room, while Rose waited and fretted, only to be told an hour later that everything had stopped.

Secretly, Rose wondered if Lily wasn't really trying, but then, she knew very little about giving birth.

She felt terribly alone and she missed Stephen dreadfully. Lily missed Rudi too, of course, but she at least had a team of English and Chinese hospital staff fussing over her night and day.

'I'm obviously not meant for motherhood,' Lily said on one of her long tramps with Rose past trolleys with bedpans. 'It's just as well you'll be doing the honours when it actually comes to caring for this child, Rose.' But she looked so rueful as she said this, Rose knew she didn't mean it.

On three separate nights, Rose was sent home to get some sleep. Their little flat was halfway up The Peak and there never seemed to be taxis available, so getting home involved a bouncing bus ride along winding, potholed roads. Then, even though Rose was exhausted by the time she fell into bed, she couldn't sleep. She was sure something must be wrong – with Lily's insides, with the baby.

On the fourth night she refused to leave, which was just as well, because the doctors suddenly decided they had no choice but to operate. Rose told herself this was a good thing. If Lily had been in England the operation would probably have been performed days ago.

Now, Lily was going to have a spinal something-or-other, so that she would remain awake, able to watch the whole procedure, while feeling no pain whatsoever. It would all be over quite quickly, and Rose could wait close by. She would be kept informed.

After so many days of fruitless waiting, Rose found it hard to believe this operation would be quick, so she was shocked when she suddenly heard a baby's cry coming from the other side of the closed door. At first the sound was little more than an indignant yowl, and she wondered if she'd imagined it. But then she heard it again, louder and stronger.

And again.

Standing stock-still in the corridor outside, eyes wide, with a hand clasped over her mouth, Rose hoped and wondered. And prayed.

At last a nurse appeared, an English girl, all smiles. 'It's a girl,' she told Rose.

A girl. A tiny baby girl.

Then another, more senior, nurse came to the doorway and beckoned. 'You can come in now. Your sister wants you to meet the baby.'

Rose could scarcely feel her feet moving as she went forward. As she passed a glass window, she caught a glimpse of Lily lying on a trolley and covered by a sheet from the neck down. Two doctors were leaning over her, still apparently busy.

'Has my sister seen the baby?' she asked the nurse.

The woman nodded. 'Yes, she's very happy, of course.'

By now, Rose was standing next to a crib that had been lined with blue cotton sheeting. She knew next to nothing about newborn babies, but this one looked awfully small.

'Is she all right?' She felt terrible for asking.

'Yes,' she was assured. 'A healthy baby.'

'But she's too tiny?'

'No, not at all. Quite a good size.'

Now, feeling a little calmer, Rose looked again. The baby had a cap of fine dark hair and bright wide eyes that stared and blinked. She poked her tongue out. It was tiny and pink and perfect, like a rose petal.

'Hello,' Rose whispered and she waited to feel the wave of motherly love that she understood most women felt instantaneously. But she was too overawed to feel anything. She really was quite numb. 'What about my sister?' she remembered to ask. 'Is she all right, too?'

'Yes. She just needs a little more attention from the doctors. You'll be able to speak to her when they're finished.'

The doctors, Rose discovered later, had removed a fibrous mass that had impeded the baby's birth. It meant that Lily was in pain for quite a few days after the caesarian. The nurses expected her to breastfeed the baby, but Lily was reluctant. After three days, just as the milk started to come in properly, she said she'd had enough.

'There's no point,' she confided to Rose. 'Besides, I hate feeling like a dairy cow and it will be easier for you if we get her started on a bottle now, while we're in hospital. Anyway, my tummy aches so much, it hurts to hold her.'

Rose suspected that these excuses were a kind of self-defence mechanism, but Lily seemed a lot happier and generally stronger after she'd emerged victorious from the feeding battle. She was keen to talk about the baby, though. In fact, once she started, she was hard to stop.

'She's looking prettier every day now, isn't she? Not so squashed looking as she was at first. I think she looks a bit like Rudi, don't you, Rose? But I don't think she's going to be dark like him. I want to call her Anya. It's Rudi's grandmother's name.'

'It's a pretty name,' Rose said, 'but it's very —'

'Very Russian, I know.' Lily smiled. 'So her second name should be Harriet after *our* grandmother. Rudi and I have talked about it and he's agreed. And I think we should call her Hattie. Hattie Bellamy is a perfectly acceptable English name.'

Rose had also been dreaming of potential names for the baby.

She rather liked Elizabeth or Marjorie, but she couldn't deny Lily this motherly right. 'Yes, Hattie's a sweet name,' she said. 'Hattie she is, then.'

Lily's smile slowly faded. 'Oh, heavens, I miss Rudi.' Now her eyes glistened with a silver sheen. 'Loving him was never a mistake, Rose. Never.'

'No,' Rose agreed, but her poor sister had paid the highest price for that love.

'If only I could get better quickly,' Lily said next. 'I can't wait to get home.'

Hattie was a month old when they travelled back to Shanghai. Rudi and Stephen were both waiting on the hot and crowded docks to greet them. As the women left the ship, Rose carried Hattie, wrapped in a lacy shawl, while Lily raced ahead, ducking and weaving through the crowds, and then launching herself into Rudi's arms, almost knocking the poor man off his feet.

'My darling!'

They were so busy re-enacting Heathcliff and Cathy, it was Stephen who saw the baby first.

'She's very sweet,' he said, and then he kissed Rose's cheek and smiled his special smile just for her. 'A baby suits you,' he murmured. 'The two of you look perfect together.'

The four adults, plus baby Hattie and their mountain of luggage, piled into the waiting car and they drove back to Rose and Stephen's apartment. Once there, Rose took Lily and Rudi through to the main bedroom, where she left them alone with their little Hattie.

Closing the shuttered doors on the trio, she came back into the sitting room. She didn't have to explain anything to Stephen. The dear man understood that Rudi and Lily needed this time alone with their baby daughter.

Stephen had organised for a pot of tea and when the boy brought it, he and Rose sat, drinking tea and talking quietly.

'I'm getting used to her,' Rose told her husband. 'I was terrified about bathing her at first, but I think I'm getting the hang of it. The worst thing is getting up in the middle of the night to heat bottles.'

Stephen nodded sympathetically. 'I wish I wasn't going to be away for such long stretches,' he said. 'But I've found an English-trained amah to help you with bathing and formulas and doing the baby's washing, and anything else you might want help with. She only needs one afternoon a week off and a full day each month, and she can start as soon as you like.'

'Bless you, Stephen. Thank you, that's brilliant.'

Rose leaped from her chair and promptly sat in her husband's lap so she could kiss him properly. He really was the loveliest man.

More months passed before Lily turned twenty-one and she and Rudi were finally able to marry. By then, Hattie was a placid and sweet-natured little cherub with big blue eyes and honey-coloured curls. She could say 'Mumma' and 'Dada' and she was quite a good crawler. And Rose's maternal instincts were well and truly established. She loved Hattie fiercely.

As for the situation all around them in Shanghai, the war between China and Japan was more intense than ever. The numbers of Chinese refugees in the city had increased fourfold. Wounded Chinese found themselves recovering in nightclubs temporarily transformed into emergency hospitals.

The position of the stateless White Russians was also more precarious. The Japanese had discovered a lucrative business in kidnapping wealthy White Russians. If the families couldn't pay, the victims were killed and the corpses left on the family's doorstep.

With so much danger and darkness all around them, Rose felt

there was no question of giving Hattie back to Lily and Rudi. To her relief, as the wedding plans went ahead, the suggestion was never made.

The ceremony was held in St Nicholas's Russian Orthodox church, an ornate white building tucked away on rue Corneille, a quiet tree-lined street in the French Concession.

To Rose's and Lily's dismay, their mother and father refused to attend, even though they had kept their earlier promise to accept Rudi into their home. Of course, this snubbing hurt Lily dreadfully. After all, she'd acceded to their wishes by giving up her precious child. But she was damned if she would also give up Rudi.

To make matters worse, Stephen was unavoidably delayed at sea. So, on the day of the wedding, Rose was a solitary and lonely figure in pale lavender georgette, sitting in the front pew, with her back straight and a brave smile held carefully in place. Zara Pemberton, Lily's former chaperone and mentor, splendid in feathers and silk, big bold jewellery and a veiled pillbox hat, sat in the pew behind Rose, along with a handful of Lily's arty friends. An exuberant band of Rudi's friends and relations filled the other side of the church's central aisle.

In an act of defiant independence, Lily had insisted that Zara Pemberton's Chinese lover give her away. Chu Yuan was, in fact, one of the most influential men in Shanghai, much further up the social ladder than their father, and he looked exceedingly dapper in a grey morning coat and striped trousers.

Rose was filled with admiration for Lily. Such a brave and beautiful bride she was, looking utterly radiant as she came down the aisle, carrying a sheath of the elegant white flowers that were her namesake. Lily only had eyes for her waiting bridegroom, who stood proudly, handsome as a prince, with his wide shoulders, dark wavy hair and shining chocolate-brown eyes.

As Lily came to a standstill beside him, Rose watched the ceremony through a veil of mostly happy tears.

The reception was held in the flat that Lily and Rudi had found in Avenue Joffre. The flat was on the ground floor, opening onto a small courtyard, which at least caught a breeze, but the rooms were long and narrow and rather shabby.

Lily, however, had bought yards of burlap from the Ewo Cotton Mills, where cotton sacks were made, and to Rose's admiring amazement, her sister had dyed the coarse fabric a henna colour and made surprisingly attractive curtains and cushion covers.

From the Chinese markets, Lily had bought brightly coloured rugs, crockery and second-hand bookshelves. Rudi's contribution was a solid timber wardrobe and bed, as well as a studio couch that gave their sitting room quite a sense of style. Together, they'd found a man called Chin Lien to cook for them, and as a wedding gift, he'd given them a bowl of goldfish.

Zara Pemberton was very impressed. 'How clever of Lily to lure Mr Chin away from the Harrington-Smythes.'

Lily and Rudi were blissfully happy, and the wedding party that night was lively and joyful, with plenty of Russian music and singing and dancing. Even though neither her parents nor Stephen were there, Rose thoroughly enjoyed the evening.

Two days later, she received the news that Stephen's ship had been bombed by the Japanese.

CHAPTER TWENTY-SEVEN

Shanghai, 1941

'Mary Duffield found Japs in her kitchen yesterday.' Rose's mother was in high dudgeon when she joined her daughter for afternoon tea. 'The cheeky blighters told her they were sightseeing. Can you believe it? And there were more Japs out on her lawn taking photographs of the house and the garden.'

'It's just another very clear sign that we should leave,' Rose said. 'It's why I was so anxious that you come to tea, Mother. We need to make plans. We've been acting like ostriches for far too long.'

Rose was no longer the easily persuaded daughter she'd once been. Toughened by the twin fires of widowhood and motherhood, she'd learned to stand on her own two feet, to make her own decisions.

After Stephen's death, her parents had wanted her and Hattie to move in with them. However, despite her overwhelming grief, Rose had resisted.

Of course, the news of Stephen's death had been a devastating blow. Rose had been desolate. Flattened. Sunk in a deep despair she feared she might never survive.

Now, looking back, she knew that the one thing that had given her strength was her commitment to Hattie. She was still a mother and her child needed her.

And in those dark days, Rose had drawn a measure of comfort from remaining in her own home, in being surrounded by all the things that she and Stephen had chosen together. She had reminisced about the happy, carefree days of their early marriage when they'd shopped for their furniture, their pot plants, their silver and chinaware.

Just the same, Rose had lived in fear of hearing those dreaded words from Lily – *I'll have to take her back*. It would have been easy for Lily to insist that Rose couldn't possibly care for Hattie now.

Lily's silence in this regard had won Rose's eternal gratitude, and the fact that the rest of their close-knit community accepted that Hattie was her and Stephen's child had also helped.

Stephen's death, however, had made Rose much more attune to the terrible tragedy that was about to overtake their part of the world. The Japanese had blatantly bombed a British ship, and the British had reacted with outrage, but little else. Meanwhile, the Japanese response was just what they'd come to expect.

So sorry. A terrible mistake.

So disingenuous, yet so dangerously effective.

It was naïve to suggest that the Japs weren't intent on taking over the entire International Concession. And now, time was running out, she was certain.

Curfews were in place. Everyone had to be home before ten o'clock, and the French Concession was surrounded by a barbed wire fence with the Japanese guards checking anyone who went in or out.

It was all very depressing. The old, glamorous Shanghai, the exciting international playground that had once been known as the Paris of the East, had been stripped and crushed. The international residents were surrounded by devastation. Blackened fields and wrecked buildings stretched all the way to The Bund, and the distant skyscrapers glinted like an eerie mirage.

Rose's mother looked pained as she selected a dainty éclair. 'I hate to give in to *them* and I'm dreading the thought of Hong Kong.'

They'd both heard stories about overcrowding and poor treatment in the Hong Kong refugee camps. There were also rumours that cholera was raging and that the people who weren't in camps were paying ridiculous amounts of money for a quarter of a room. Some of their British friends who'd evacuated when the bombings first started had actually come back to Shanghai.

With a wistful smile, Rose's mother said, 'I heard an amusing story from Sylvia Devenish the other day. Poor Christopher's had to put up with the most dreadful rows every morning on his way to work, because his Chinese driver was refusing to take his cap off to the Japanese sentry on guard. The sentry would retaliate by sticking his bayonet through the open car window.'

'Goodness,' said Rose politely.

'Of course, Christopher simply pushed the bayonet to one side and told his boy to drive on. But Sylvia was worried things would get out of hand, so she came up with the perfect solution. She confiscated the driver's cap.' Rose's mother chuckled. 'And that was the end of it.'

'But I'm sure it's not the end of it,' said Rose. 'That's the problem, isn't it? Things can only keep getting worse.'

Her mother sighed. 'You do know how to spoil a good story, Rose.'

Rose didn't apologise. She was tired of pretending.

Then her mother relented. 'But of course, you're right, darling.'

'It doesn't have to be Hong Kong,' Rose said.

'Well, I don't think England's an option. Our poor homeland's being blitzed by Hitler's bombs. They're worse off than anywhere at the moment. It's all so terrifying.'

'There's always Manila. The Jessops have gone there.'

This brought a shudder from Rose's mother.

Rose said, 'And I've been thinking about Australia.'

'Australia?' Her mother looked horrified. 'But we don't know anyone in Australia.'

'I know, but it's well out of the war zone. And I quite liked what I saw when I went there for my honeymoon.'

Rose had been thinking about Australia quite a bit lately, and the more she thought about it, the more she liked the idea of escaping there with Hattie. She had fond memories of the trip she and Stephen had taken up into the mountains.

There'd been a lovely hotel and a pristine lake encircled by lush green forest. She was sure she could also remember a tiny township, and she rather liked the idea of taking Hattie somewhere quiet and pretty and, most importantly, peaceful and safe.

'I've been making enquiries,' she said. 'There's a ship taking Jewish refugees to North Queensland quite soon, and there'd be room for us.'

'But Australia's so far away, Rose. At least we would be surrounded by people we know in Hong Kong. We'd have friends. And connections.'

Rose shook her head. She didn't want to take Hattie to crowded, vulnerable Hong Kong when there was a far safer option in Australia. She wasn't keen to see their family separated, but Lily was determined to stay in Shanghai with Rudi, and if her parents were equally stubborn, Rose would be stubborn too.

Before she left Shanghai for good, Rose took Hattie to spend a whole day and a night with Lily and Rudi. They were very sombre the next morning when it was time to collect the little girl.

Hattie, on the other hand, was all starry-eyed and excited. 'Aunt

Lily read me lots of stories, Mummy. *Winnie the Pooh* and *Milly Molly Mandy*. And Uncle Rudi played his violin and we danced. And I had three kinds of jelly with ice-cream and peaches for my supper.'

'Goodness.' Rose struggled to speak, her throat was so choked. 'What a lucky little girl.'

Rose and Lily had agreed that they wouldn't try to explain to Hattie that she was going away to another country for what would probably be a very long time. Ah Lan took Hattie outside to look at the goldfish in the little sunken pond, while the sisters said farewell.

Tears glittered in Lily's eyes and her mouth was trembling. 'Write to me, won't you, Rose?'

'Yes, of course.'

'And send me photos if you can.'

'Yes, darling.'

'Rudi and I are so happy that she'll be safe in Australia.'

'You stay safe, too, Lily. You both have to be very careful now.'

'We'll be sensible, don't worry.'

'As soon as this is over —' Rose stopped, unable to go on, unwilling to make impossible promises.

'Yes,' said Lily, throwing her thin arms around Rose and hugging her tight. 'When this bloody war's over, everything will be all right . . . I know, darling, I know.'

CHAPTER TWENTY-EIGHT

Flora was nearing the end of a long rehearsal session when she forced herself to take another look at the Mozart concerto. Even though she knew this music inside out, it could never be over-practised.

The challenge was to avoid making the familiar music sound perfunctory and pedestrian. She needed to really concentrate and not think about what she was going to have for dinner. Mozart was deceptive, of course. His music sounded simple and light, but it had a secret liveliness, a confident playfulness, and a high skill level was needed to bring these qualities to life.

Lifting her bow, she pictured herself at the Brisbane audition, playing the piece perfectly and sending the judges' eyebrows shooting up to their hairlines.

She grinned. Okay. One more try.

This time, as she started again, she could hear Dr Fielding, her old teacher from the Conservatorium, calling to her, 'Dance, Flora, dance, dance, dance!' It had been his way of reminding her to keep the music light and moving.

'Flora.'

A sudden voice coming from behind her broke into her concentration. Flora turned to see the elderly woman, Hattie, the one who'd listened to the Tchaikovsky rehearsal. Today, Hattie came into the church hall tentatively, and she looked rather worried.

'Hello,' Flora said, with an appropriately polite smile.

'I'm so sorry, Flora, I didn't mean to disturb you. I actually thought you'd finished, but then you started up again just as I —' Hattie trailed off and looked apologetic.

'It's okay. I was getting obsessive. To be honest, this music is too tricky for the end of a practice session.' Flora sensed that Hattie hadn't come to listen again. 'I should probably call it a day,' she said. 'Were you wanting something, Hattie?'

'I wanted to check to see if your agent got through to you.'

'My agent?' Flora frowned. She didn't have an agent. 'I don't understand. Who do you mean?'

'The fellow from Melbourne. I forget his last name, but I'm sure his first name was Oliver.'

The blood in Flora's veins turned to ice-water.

'He told me he had some very good news for you,' said Hattie. 'He couldn't get through to your brother, so —'

'Oh, God.' Flora felt so suddenly sick, she almost let her violin slip from her fingers to crash to the floor.

'What is it?' Hattie cried. 'What's the matter?'

Just in time, Flora tightened her grasp on the neck of her precious instrument. Then she set it, with her bow, on a chair for safe-keeping and willed herself to calm down.

It was only a phone call and she didn't want to alarm the poor woman.

'Why did Oliver phone *you*, Hattie?' she asked.

'That's the puzzling bit,' Hattie admitted. 'He actually rang Joe Matthews's phone. I'm staying at Joe's place now. I was in the kitchen and so I answered. We can only assume that this agent –

Oliver – chose Joe because his name has been linked with your brother's over the business with the bones. And Oliver couldn't get through to Seth. But he said he needed to get in touch with you because he had some very good news.'

'Really?'

'I thought it was some kind of marvellous job offer.' Hattie's eyes were wide, her eyebrows high in her wrinkled forehead. 'So you haven't heard from him?'

'No.' Flora dropped her gaze so Hattie couldn't see how frightened she was.

'And your brother hasn't been in touch with a message?'

Flora shook her head. 'Not about a message from Oliver, no.'

'That's very strange.'

Yes, it was strange, but Flora knew that this devious behaviour was very typical of Oliver. He liked nothing better than to bother and upset her, to keep her guessing and on edge.

'When did you get this call?' she asked.

'A couple of evenings ago.' Hattie made an anxious, hand-wringing gesture. 'I knew I should have gone straight to you then.'

Hating to see the elderly woman's distress, Flora dredged up a smile. 'No,' she reassured her. 'There was no need for you to be involved at all. Thanks for telling me now, though, Hattie. I'll – ah – I'll check with Oliver and see what it's all about.'

'Right.' Hattie's shoulders relaxed, as if a great weight had been lifted. She smiled. 'I hope he was right about the wonderful news.'

Somehow, Flora managed an answering smile. 'That would be nice, wouldn't it?' As casually as she could, she asked, 'Was there anything else? Was Oliver asking questions about me?'

'Not really. He just wanted to make certain that you were still here in Burralea and not at the Gold Coast. So I assured him you were definitely here and I told him about the Christmas concert with the children.'

Oh, fuck. So now Oliver knew everything.

Flora pictured Oliver turning up here in Burralea, pestering her, threatening her, hanging about, still trying to control her. Hurt her.

She felt dizzy and sick. It was all too easy to imagine him as a menacing figure, lurking in the background while she tried to manage a hall filled with children. Thinking of the children, Flora felt a hot flash of panic, and she was sure she should sit down before her legs gave way.

But she didn't want Hattie to see her distress, so she turned to her sheet music, folded it quickly and set it on the chair with her violin, then she proceeded to collapse the music stand.

'He sounded so nice on the phone,' Hattie said, but then she must have noticed Flora's tension. 'Was it a mistake to tell him that you're here?'

Flora didn't want to upset her any more than was necessary, but she saw no point in pretending that everything was hunky-dory when it clearly wasn't.

'I should explain the situation in case he tries to bother you again,' she said. 'Oliver's not my agent, he's a former boyfriend. We parted rather acrimoniously, and I've been trying to lie low for a bit. Hoping to avoid any kind of contact.'

'Oh, goodness no, and now I've blown your cover.'

'But you weren't to know,' Flora added kindly. 'And – and thanks for telling me now, so at least I can work something out – I can be prepared.'

'Oh, dear. I hope this won't cause too much trouble for you.'

'No, no, Hattie, please don't worry.'

When Hattie continued to look quite worried, Flora reached out and patted her arm. 'How long will you be staying in Burralea?' she asked, hoping to divert the woman.

At this, Hattie gave a shy little laugh. 'I'm actually thinking now that I might stay on. It's not long till Christmas.'

'How lovely.' Flora walked with her to the door. 'Perhaps you'll come to the Christmas concert then?'

'Oh, definitely. I wouldn't miss it.'

'Wonderful.'

'And perhaps *you* should speak to that nice Sergeant Cavello,' said Hattie. 'Just as a precaution.'

'I will,' Flora assured her. 'He's actually a friend of the family, so he's already in the loop.'

'Ah . . . that's handy.'

Hattie was almost smiling as she left. Flora noticed that Joe Matthews and his rather handsome dog were waiting for her on the footpath. Flora waved to Hattie and Joe and there were smiles all round, then she went back inside, to pack away her violin, carefully covering the delicate instrument with an old silk scarf as she settled it into its velvet-lined case. She loosened the bow and stowed it next to the spare, safely inside the lid.

She tried not to panic about Oliver.

Okay, so he'd found out where she was, but that was bound to happen some time. She couldn't hide from him forever, especially if she scored a position in another major orchestra. And the fact that he'd tracked her down didn't mean he was going to jump on a plane and travel all the way up to Far North Queensland.

He wouldn't go that far, would he?

No, of course not.

By panicking, she was blowing up her own self-importance.

Just the same, Flora decided, as she closed the windows and checked that she'd left nothing behind in the hall, she would ring Seth and Mitch as soon as she got back to the cottage. She would feel better if they both knew about Oliver's phone call.

With that decided, she made a deliberate effort to turn her thoughts away from B.O. Instead, she wondered about Hattie

and Joe Matthews. Edith, her neighbour, had claimed that Joe had
broken Hattie's heart many years ago. Clearly there'd been a recon-
ciliation. And now Hattie was staying till Christmas!

Flora wondered if Edith knew about this, and as she slung her
violin case over her shoulder and locked the hall's front door, she
allowed herself a smug smile. It wasn't often that she had a little
Burralea gossip up her sleeve.

Mitch wasn't at the station when Flora called in on her way home.

His offsider wasn't forthcoming with details of Sergeant Cavello's
whereabouts either, although he did confirm that Mitch was on duty.
At least Mitch had given Flora his phone number, so she left him
a message and then she rang Seth. The phone rang and rang.

'Hi, Floss,' Seth said at the last minute.

'You busy?'

'In the middle of pregnancy-testing cows.'

'Ouch. Bad timing.' Flora knew this task involved inserting
a gloved arm up a cow's backside, which no doubt explained why
Seth had taken ages to answer. 'I'll call you later, then.'

'No, I'm here now. Tell me.'

His impatience reminded her of the bossy big brother she remembered from her teens. She told her news as quickly and concisely
as she could.

'Shit, Flora.' Seth was clearly worried now. 'What do you want
to do? You'd better come and stay here.'

'That's very kind, Seth.'

'Well, it's sensible. I don't like to think of you in town on your
own.'

His offer had instant appeal for Flora. She would feel very safe
out at Kooringal with Seth's little family, and it would be great to
have more time with Charlie.

'But it wouldn't be very practical,' she suggested with some reluctance. 'I don't have a car and I'd send you all bonkers if I was practising for hours every day.'

There was a noticeable pause. Seth had never shared Flora's love of classical music. Back in his teens, he'd teased her mercilessly, and he'd gone around the homestead wearing industrial earmuffs, even when she wasn't practising.

'Just in case you start up when I'm not prepared,' he used to tell her.

Okay, Seth had grown out of his teasing teenage habits, but Flora knew he must have misgivings now.

'We have Alice's ute as well as mine,' he said, nevertheless standing by his offer. 'We should be able to figure out a way to share the vehicles, so you can still get into town. Then at least you'd be here in the evenings.'

Flora was touched and grateful that her brother was so willing to help. 'The problem is, I also have the children's orchestra and the choir rehearsals. They go quite late, and next week there'll be an extra rehearsal with the kids in the nativity play,' she said. 'The cottage is so handy, Seth. And honestly, I can't imagine Oliver would actually bother to come all the way up here.'

'You can't be sure of that, though, can you?'

'I'm fairly sure.' Unfortunately, this didn't come out quite as confidently as Flora would have liked.

Seth sighed. After a bit, he said, 'Have you spoken to Mitch?'

'Not yet. He's busy, but I've left a message.'

'He might have some better ideas. Have a talk to him and then let me know. We can make a decision then.'

'All right, thanks, Seth.'

'No probs.' After a beat, 'Hey, Floss?'

'Yeah?'

'I love you, kiddo.'

This was somehow unexpected and she was suddenly blinking. 'Thanks.' Damn it, and now her voice was choked. 'Love you, too.'

It was almost nine when Mitch finally called. He'd been caught up with an accident at the top of the Gillies Range.

'I got your message. Are you all right?'

'Yes, I didn't want to alarm you, but I thought you should know.'

'Of course,' Mitch said. 'Glad you called. I'll come over to your place now.'

'But it's late. You must be tired.'

'Already on my way.'

She knew that her sudden flush of happiness and relief was OTT, but she couldn't help it. Mitch was coming.

Hastily, she tidied the few things she'd left scattered about the kitchen, and she was just stepping out of the shower when the doorbell rang. She had to answer it wrapped in a towelling bathrobe. 'Gosh, you were quick.'

Mitch nodded. He had changed into civvies – jeans and a grey T-shirt that stretched tight over his muscly chest – and his hair was damp. He must have showered before he'd made the call.

Flora was about to invite him inside when a porch light flashed on next door, flooding the garden. She saw Edith hovering on her front step.

Grrreat. No doubt her neighbour would jump to all sorts of conclusions about why Flora was greeting Mitch Cavello in her bathrobe.

'Just looking for Geraldine,' Edith called.

Mitch muttered out of the side of his mouth to Flora, 'Who's Geraldine?'

'Her new kitten.'

He lifted a hand to wave. 'Hope you find her. Goodnight, Edith.'

The old woman responded with an eager wave and undisguised curiosity. 'Goodnight, Sergeant.'

Mitch came inside quickly, and as Flora shut the door she noticed that he looked tired and more than a little subdued.

'Was the accident very bad?' she asked.

He nodded. 'One fatality – and two injured had to be rushed down to Cairns hospital.' His mouth tightened, pulled out of shape. 'The fatality was a local – Brad Murray from over near Tolga.'

'Oh, no, Mitch.' Flora knew the Murray family. She'd gone to school with Brad's sister Louise.

Mitch's duties probably involved going to the family to give them the bad news. How awful. Flora couldn't begin to imagine the impact of dealing with a tragedy like that. Being a cop, even a cop in a small country town, involved so much more than picking locks for little old ladies.

In the face of this sobering reminder of the dark realities of a policeman's life, her niggling concern about Oliver suddenly felt more like a whine than a real problem.

'Have you had dinner?' she asked as Mitch followed her down the hallway to the kitchen.

'Yeah,' he said after the slightest of hesitations.

Flora eyed him shrewdly. 'You *haven't* eaten, have you?'

'I wanted to come straight over here. I knew you were worried. Seth's worried too.'

'Well, come on through to the kitchen. I have leftovers. You can nuke them in the microwave while I get into something more respectable.'

Stupidly, she blushed as she said this. Was she never going to forget that crazy mistake from her teens? The last thing she'd intended was to draw attention to her state of undress.

In the kitchen, she was businesslike as she pulled a covered dish from the fridge.

Mitch eyed it warily. 'What is it?'

'Lamb korma and rice.' She couldn't resist having a dig at him as she took off the lid so he could inspect it. 'You don't trust my cooking, do you? *That's* why you've declined all my invitations to dinner.'

'Not at all.' He must have known she wasn't serious, but he held out his hands, as if protesting his innocence. 'I've had firsthand evidence that you're a brilliant cook.'

'Really?'

Now, at last, Mitch's dark eyes flashed with amusement. 'Those little caramel tarts you took to Seth's place.'

'Oh, yeah.' Flora had forgotten about them.

'And I'd love to eat your lamb korma. My stomach's rumbling at the very thought.'

They were both smiling now – grinning, actually – and the air in the kitchen seemed to zap and sparkle. Flora was slightly breathless until she remembered again why Mitch had come to her house.

He was simply responding to her call for help, and he was here in the role of a conscientious policeman and family friend. None of which warranted the buzzing glow that seemed to fill her from the toes up.

'I'll be back in a jiffy.' She set the food to heat in the microwave and placed a dinner bowl and fork on the counter, then scurried off to her room to drag on more suitable clothing.

As Mitch concentrated hard on the container of food circling behind the glass door, he tried to clear his brain of the image of Flora in the white towelling robe.

It was crazy to be so distracted by a wing of wet hair tucked behind a neat ear, by a V of pale skin exposed by a bathrobe's neckline, by bare feet and purple nail polish. Mitch supposed he could attribute his tiredness and the rawness of his emotions to coming here so soon after the gruesome crash scene.

No doubt he'd be back to normal as soon as he had some food inside him.

The microwave pinged and he removed the container, lifted the lid and gave its contents a stir. The combined aromas of lamb and curry and rice smelled good. Extra good.

He tipped the steaming food into the bowl Flora had left, took a taste and smiled. Then he carried the bowl with him as he wandered about the cottage, checking window catches and screens, double-checking the front door lock, before he returned to the kitchen to check out the back door.

'What are you doing?'

Flora came into the room, changed into slacks and a floral shirt with all the buttons done up and with sleeves that skimmed her elbows. Her feet were encased in woven slip-ons. She was virtually covered from head to toe.

Mitch hoped to hell she hadn't caught him staring at her.

'I'm just checking the cottage's security,' he said.

'Oh.' She looked worried. 'You don't really think Oliver would try to break in, do you?'

Mitch shrugged. 'It pays to be safe. Plenty of women have made assumptions about their husbands or boyfriends and then been caught out.'

Flora frowned and seemed to chew the inside of her cheek. She went to a window, slid a flyscreen open and fiddled with a lock. Outside, in the dark foliage of a mango tree, a possum made a soft growl. 'So what's the verdict?' she said. 'Am I safe?'

'This house has been well maintained. All the doors and windows have decent locks, so that's a good start.'

'But I can't keep everything locked all the time. It would be too hot. And at the moment, Oliver's two states away.'

'Yeah, but it's good to know you can make this place safe if you need to.'

'I guess.' She turned back from the window. 'Seth was suggesting I should stay out at Kooringal, but I really need to be in top form for this audition and all the practising would drive them nuts, I know.'

Before Mitch could respond, she jumped in quickly, 'Honestly, Mitch, I really can't imagine that Oliver would turn up here. I'll admit the phone calls freaked me, but he probably knew that both Seth and Hattie would tell me he'd rung. He just wanted to keep me rattled and on tenterhooks. I'm sure he gets a kick out of knowing he can still upset me from a long distance.'

'Yeah, but he *is* hassling you, Flora, and combined with his previous behaviour, it amounts to emotional and psychological abuse.'

Flora's face fell and she stood very still as she took this in.

'Yes,' she said at last, very quietly. 'Yes, I suppose you're right.'

Folding her arms over her chest, she leaned back against a cupboard. With her head slightly bowed, she stared at a spot on the floor, lost in thought. Her hair swung forward, exposing her pale, slender neck, and she looked so sad and vulnerable Mitch had to fight a deep urge to cross the floor and take her in his arms.

To protect her.

No other reason.

Yeah, right.

'How's the lamb korma?' she asked.

He was grateful she dragged his thoughts back to the curry. 'Yeah, it's great,' he said. 'It's amazing. You should consider a new career as a chef.'

Flora's half-hearted smile had *as if* written all over it. 'Don't exaggerate, Mitch Cavello. I like to think of you as a totally bullshit-free zone.'

Mitch swallowed to clear the sudden constriction in his throat. 'Okay. Totally no-bullshitting, this curry is delicious.'

'Thank you.' With an almost regal gesture, she indicated the kitchen table and chairs. 'You've had a huge day. Why don't you sit down?'

'Yeah, I will, thanks.'

'And I'll put the kettle on, or would you prefer a cold beer?'

Mitch was hanging out for a beer, but he hadn't come here to kick back, and given the crazy thoughts he'd been having just now, relaxing could be downright dangerous. He needed his wits about him.

'I'll have tea, thanks.'

* * *

The vibe between them had changed. Flora sensed this as she set the kettle to boil and made the tea. The light-hearted friendship she and Mitch had enjoyed at his place the other evening had morphed into something else, something that was at once more serious and more personal.

It was almost as if they'd crossed an invisible line and couldn't go back.

Bloody Oliver. Was he going to infiltrate every corner of her life?

'So what's your advice?' she asked as she brought their mugs to the table and sat across from Mitch.

'Well, you could apply for an intervention order. I could organise the application for you.'

'If I put in the application, what would happen then?' she asked.

'There'd have to be a hearing with a magistrate. We'd lodge the application and then they'd set a date for the hearing. I'm sure we could try to fast-track it for you.'

'I see.'

'If you fill in the application, you should try to include as much information as you can, to make the court fully aware of your situation.'

'Really? Everything?'

'Yeah. When an event happened, where it happened. Who was there. Any injuries you've suffered. How you felt.'

Flora shuddered. She'd been trying to forget about Oliver, not recall every last horrid detail. What would she tell the court? That her boyfriend frightened her? That yes, he'd hit her, but he hadn't actually broken anything? Oliver's main danger was the way he messed with her head and sapped her confidence.

She supposed Mitch was right, though. Oliver's treatment of her was emotional abuse, but she felt very uncomfortable about going before a magistrate and publicly reporting on his behaviour. Even if it was at a private court hearing, it still felt like a huge step, the kind of action she'd only take if things really spiralled out of her control.

'I don't know,' she said. 'I'm not sure I'm ready to go that far. I mean, it would be different if Oliver was here in town and threatening me.'

Mitch nodded. 'I agree, it's a tricky situation.'

'And he would have to know I'd made the application, wouldn't he?'

'Yeah, of course. He'd have to be served with a summons, including a copy of your application.'

'Oh, God. And he'd be there in court, as well?'

'If he bothered to turn up.'

Flora groaned, covered her face with her hands. The last thing she wanted was to have to face Oliver again. She needed to keep him as far away as possible.

She could just imagine him in court, scoffing at her claims, turning on the charm and telling the magistrate in that rich, cultured voice of his that poor, confused Flora had exaggerated, that she'd misconstrued his good intentions.

'I don't want a hearing,' she said. 'I don't want him there. I don't want to see him.'

Concern was written all over Mitch's face. 'It's a damn pity Kate Wood's overseas.'

It was Kate who'd persuaded Flora to leave Oliver and had offered her this house.

'I just want to retreat, Mitch, to lie low, to look after the kids' concert and practise for my audition.'

He sat without comment, quietly watching her. What was he thinking? Did he see her as a coward? She let out a heavy sigh.

Then he reached across the table and covered her hand with his. His hand was big and square and warm.

'It's okay, Floss,' he said. 'The last thing I want is to push you into something you don't want.'

'I'm sorry if I've wasted your time.'

'Not at all. Seth rang me, as well, and I promised him I'd come over. And at least I know how you feel now. I just wish there was something more I could do.'

A hug would be nice.

No way would she ask for that.

'Actually,' she said. 'One thing that does bother me is the children's Christmas concert. Hattie told Oliver about it. I don't think he would turn up for something like that, but it would be just awful if he did.'

Mitch frowned. 'You think he could be a danger to the children?'

'No, not really. As far as I know, I'm the only person Oliver's ever been mean to. If he came, it would be to taunt me, or distract me, to try to fuck up the night for me. For the whole community.'

'Well, I'll certainly be there, keeping an eye out, and you'll have friends there as well.'

'You're right. I'm sure it'll be fine.'

'And if he bothers you in any way in the meantime, if you're worried or scared for any reason, maybe you should reconsider staying out at Seth's place.'

'Yes.' Flora noticed Mitch made no suggestion that she could spend another night at his place.

That was fair enough. Mitch would probably always be wary of her, and there was still the Angie factor. As Tammy had so rightly pointed out, Mitch would take ages to get over that blow.

'So, you're sure you're okay for now?' he asked.

Flora nodded. 'Thanks for coming, Mitch. It's good to know I can turn to you and Seth, if I need to.'

His hand was still lying over hers and now his dark eyes shimmered with an unreadable emotion that seemed to reach deep inside her.

Don't. Don't think about him that way. She forced herself to recall all the reasons why she mustn't.

'I should probably head home,' he said.

'Sure.'

They both stood and Flora walked with him down the hallway to the front door.

'Thanks for coming,' she said again.

'Let me know if you're worried about anything. Anything at all. Okay?'

'Okay.'

Before she opened the door, Mitch stepped closer. Keeping his hands firmly in the back pockets of his jeans, he kissed her cheek.

'Night, Floss.'

'Goodnight.' So silly to feel her skin catch fire at such a fleeting, brotherly brush of his lips.

'I'll be off then.'

Flora opened the door and a waft of cool, silky night air floated in. She took a deep breath and Mitch wasted no time in heading up the path and across the footpath to his vehicle. Then came the firing of his motor, the blaze of headlights and he was off.

Flora wished Edith could see how appropriately dressed she was now, but every light in the old woman's house was out.

CHAPTER TWENTY-NINE

Hattie feared she was too late as she knocked and waited on the front step of Flora's cottage, listening for sounds from inside. She had spent an anxious night after delivering Oliver's message to Flora. She couldn't stop thinking about the way the girl's face blanched at the news, and although Flora appeared to recover quite quickly, Hattie had sensed real distress.

This had shocked her, particularly as she knew Flora's anguish was caused by the same man who'd spoken so charmingly on the phone. Oliver's deviousness was unsettling in the extreme.

This morning, Hattie hoped to catch Flora before she set off for another rehearsal session. She wanted to reassure herself that the poor girl wasn't still too upset. Unfortunately, although the little pink and white cottage looked especially pretty in the morning sunlight, it remained disobligingly silent.

'Are you looking for Flora?' called a voice.

Hattie turned to see a woman of about her own age peeping over the side fence. She had a plain little face framed by lank grey hair, and her pale eyes gleamed with a watchdog wariness behind steel-rimmed glasses.

'Flora's already gone to practise her violin,' the woman said.

'Oh, I see. Thank you.' Hattie was disappointed. She had obviously lingered too long over breakfast with Joe and now she would just have to wait. She wasn't going to interrupt Flora's practice a third time. 'I'll have to try again later.'

As she stepped back onto the path she felt compelled to ask the woman, 'Have you spoken to Flora this morning?'

The neighbour nodded.

'Did she seem all right?'

'I should think she's fine. Sergeant Cavello seems to be keeping a very close eye on her.'

'Oh?' Hattie fancied she heard a note of criticism in the neighbour's voice, but she couldn't imagine why. Surely a policeman's attention was exactly what Flora needed.

'You're Hattie Bellamy, aren't you?'

The blunt question almost sounded like a challenge, but Hattie smiled, nevertheless. 'Yes,' she said and she crossed the short strip of grass to the fence. 'I'm Hattie Macquarie these days.'

She squinted a little as she studied the other woman's face, her mind trekking back through the years. There was something familiar lurking there, perhaps in the shape of her small, dimpled chin, the fall of her straight, limp hair, the alert, watchful expression in her eyes.

Then it came to Hattie – a scrap of memory from the playground at Burralea Primary – a gaggle of schoolgirls with a skipping rope and another girl looking on, a girl with a round, sober face and mousey plaits, and a patched and faded hand-me-down uniform.

'Edith!' she said, as the name came in a flash. 'You're Edith Little. I remember you.'

The woman stared at her.

'You are Edith, aren't you? Have I got the name right?'

'Yes, and I'm still Edith Little. Never married.' She allowed herself a wry little smile. 'I'm surprised you remember me.'

Hattie was surprised too. She often had trouble recalling people's names, even the names of people she knew quite well. And while she hadn't thought of Edith in decades, the name had come in an instant. Such a fluke, winging down through the years.

'Of course I remember you,' she said warmly, perhaps more warmly than she might have normally, for she was now remembering other things about Edith, including the way she'd never quite made it into the 'in crowd' at school, how she'd been shy and had always hung back. She'd lived quite a distance out of town on a rather run-down dairy farm. In high school, she'd been even more of a loner. She'd never gone to the dances or social nights.

Hattie wished she could remember extending the hand of friendship to Edith, but she couldn't really. She didn't like to think of herself as uncharitable, but she had a horrible suspicion that even though she'd been aware of Edith's loneliness back then, she'd reacted with the callous disregard so typical of young people. Teenagers could be very selfish.

'You were brilliant at maths,' Hattie said, astonished at the sluice of memories now and wanting to somehow make amends for the long-ago past. 'I remember you helped me with algebra, and Mr Halverson wanted you to go to university to study physics. I don't suppose you did.'

Edith gave a scoffing little laugh. 'Of course not. I got a job in the Commonwealth Bank.'

Hattie wasn't really surprised. Back in the fifties, it would have been unthinkable for a struggling dairy farmer in Far North Queensland to send his daughter all the way to Brisbane to study something as lofty and other-worldly as physics.

'You went to England,' Edith said.

'Yes. I've lived in England and America, but I came back to Australia after my husband died. I have an apartment in Brisbane.'

'And now I live in your old house,' Edith said.

'Yes. I wasn't sure if you knew that I used to live in that place.' She shot a curious glance to the curtained windows. 'Have you been there long?'

'About thirty years.'

'A very long time then.' Hattie smiled. 'I have fond memories of the house. Sad ones, too, of course, from when my mother was so ill.' She wondered if Edith might invite her in to see the house again. For old time's sake.

But Edith merely nodded and then frowned. 'I thought I saw you with Joe Matthews.'

Yes, Hattie thought. Half of Burralea had seen her with Joe and no doubt the gossip was rife.

'I came back here because of the bones that turned up on Kooringal,' she said.

'I thought so. I heard about that on the radio.'

Hattie nodded. She supposed Edith was one of the few people left in Burralea who also knew the highs and lows of her history with Joe.

'Listen,' she said on a sudden impulse that was, no doubt, fuelled by nostalgia for their shared past, plus a tinge of regret, 'I'm staying at Joe's place now, because all the accommodation filled up last weekend. Why don't you come around there for afternoon tea? It would be lovely to have a proper catch-up. So much better than talking over the fence.'

Edith looked so shocked Hattie thought she must have said something terribly wrong.

'It was just a thought,' she amended, wondering if she should retract the invitation. 'Only if you have time.'

'Oh, I have time, all right.' Edith's lower lip trembled. 'I just wasn't expecting . . .' Her mouth pulled out of shape and Hattie worried that she might actually cry.

'When would suit you?' Edith asked.

'What about tomorrow afternoon? Let's say half-past three?' Hattie mentally crossed her fingers, hoping Joe wouldn't mind that she'd invited someone into his home without consulting him first.

'Thank you,' Edith said with a wobbly smile. 'I'll bring some yeast buns. My mother's recipe. She used to win prizes at the Atherton Show.'

It was hard to tell if Joe minded, but he didn't look particularly thrilled when Hattie gave him the news.

'I'm sorry,' she said. 'I'm not normally so impulsive. I know I should have spoken to you first. It was high-handed of me to invite someone out of the blue, when I'm only a guest in your home.'

They were just finishing their lunch of asparagus soup and buttered bread rolls. Across the table Hattie sent Joe a searching glance. 'You don't mind, do you?'

'No, I don't mind,' he said, unconvincingly. 'I'm just surprised you chose to invite Edith Little.'

'Well, yes. I can imagine you might be. I think I surprised myself.'

'You weren't especially friendly with her, were you?'

'No, we weren't close. But when I thought about it, I couldn't remember anyone being close to Edith. She was always shy and a bit prickly.'

Joe smiled. 'You make her sound like an echidna.'

'Well, she was, Joe, don't you remember? And I think she might still be a bit that way. She's never married.'

He looked away, staring off into the distance, and a muscle in his cheek twitched, pulling the corner of his mouth into a lopsided smile that seemed rather sad. Hattie wondered what had suddenly absorbed him. In just a few short days, she and Joe had, miraculously, become incredibly close again, but there was so much she still didn't know about the man.

She dipped a corner of bread roll into her bowl, scooping up the last of her soup.

'Edith likes to send cards,' Joe said, quietly.

'Do you mean *play* cards – like canasta or bridge?'

'No, she sends them – greeting cards – she sent me a valentine once, when we were still in high school.'

'Goodness.' Hattie almost choked on her piece of bread. *She* had been Joe's high-school sweetheart. All their classmates had known that. She'd never really considered the possibility that another girl in their year might have fancied him.

'When I married Gloria —'

'Don't tell me Edith sent you a congratulations card,' pleaded Hattie.

'No, but she did send us Christmas cards every year,' he said. 'She never added any snippets of news and her message was always the same – "Happy Christmas and kind regards" – or something along those lines. She sent a sympathy card when Gloria died. But the strange thing is, I've hardly ever spoken to the woman except to say g'day.'

'Perhaps popping a card in the post is her way of reaching out,' Hattie suggested. 'You should have seen her this morning, Joe, peering over that fence. I got the feeling that she's still an outsider.'

'You're probably right. I certainly haven't seen her very often, even though she's lived in this district the whole time.'

'That's why I invited her to tea. It seemed so sad that Edith's lived here in Burralea for all these years, virtually on her own. I mean, most people in country towns are very outgoing and have all kinds of connections.'

'Edith could have joined any number of groups – the bowls club, or the bridge club, the CWA, one of the art societies.'

'I suppose she could, but some people aren't natural joiners. When I think about it, Edith never was, even at school. She was never in a sporting team or a choir or debating. Maths was her thing. She was brilliant.'

'Was she?'

Hattie smiled. Joe had been very good at maths too, but Edith had often beaten him in their exams. Obviously his male ego was well intact, and he'd erased that small detail from his memory.

'Anyway, she's bringing yeast buns,' Hattie said. 'Made from her mother's prize-winning recipe.'

Joe's eyes glowed warmly as he smiled at her across the table.

CHAPTER THIRTY

'If this is going to be a proper committee meeting, we should have someone taking notes,' announced Peg Fletcher. 'I'll volunteer to be secretary.'

'Thanks, Peg, that's very good of you.' Father Jonno offered her a suitably diplomatic smile. 'We won't need resolutions or minutes, or anything too formal, though. Just a record of who's doing what, so everything's clear.'

It was late in the afternoon and the Burralea Christmas Concert committee had gathered around a long table at one end of the church hall for a final, important meeting. Peg Fletcher, with her vast experience of running these concerts, was an essential member of the group. Appropriately, she was at the head of the table with her new wheelie walker beside her.

Flora was also there, as Peg's stand-in conductor, along with Father Jonno, who was taking care of the nativity play. The other committee members were Finn Latimer, the editor of the *Burralea Bugle*, who was going to write a story promoting the concert, and Linda Jones, the parents' representative, who was also a teacher at Burralea Primary. Flora hadn't expected to see Mitch, but he arrived at the last minute. Apparently, he'd been roped in to be Santa over the past couple of years.

'Okay,' said Father Jonno, adopting the role of unofficial chairperson, 'I suppose one of the first things we need to make sure is that all the children will have transport on the night. It mightn't be easy for some of them who have to come in from outlying farms.'

'Can't we rely on their parents to look after that?' asked Flora. She had clear memories of the car pools her mother had set up when she'd been involved with youth orchestra rehearsals.

'Well, yes, the parents are usually quite reliable,' agreed Peg. 'But you should send a note home and ask them to sign it, just to make sure every child definitely has transport. You don't want to turn up on the night and discover you don't have a trombone.'

'Right,' said Flora.

'I can have a note printed off at school if you like.' Linda, the teacher, was a very efficient-looking woman in her forties, with neat dark hair pulled into a simple ponytail. She was also the mother of one of the first violinists. 'I'll make sure that's done tomorrow, and I'll drop the notes over here to the hall in my lunch hour ready for the rehearsals. How many will you need?'

'You'd better do sixty to cover the choir, the orchestra and the nativity play,' said Father Jonno.

'No problem.'

'That would be wonderful, thanks.' Flora also sent her a grateful smile.

Father Jonno waited while Peg conscientiously jotted these details down. He was dressed casually in jeans and a plaid shirt. With his golden freckles and straight rusty hair that reached to his collar, Flora thought he looked more like an outback ringer, or even a stray member of a rock band, than a parish priest.

Not that she had strict ideas about how a priest should look. She'd had a few brief conversations with Jonno about this concert, and he was very down-to-earth and likeable, a man who gave off genuine 'good guy' vibes and won everyone's respect.

Peg finished her note-taking with a flourish of her pen, and Father Jonno continued. 'So, before we get onto the concert itself, we should probably discuss Santa Claus, and then Mitch can get back to his important policing duties.'

Peg jumped in. 'Mitch did a great job last year.'

'I was amazing,' Mitch agreed with a cheeky grin. 'But I'm afraid I need to bow out this time. I feel I need to be part of the crowd, keeping a general eye on things.'

'Oh?' Peg looked slightly put out.

Flora, on the other hand, felt her pulse pick up pace. She was pretty sure that the possibility of Oliver showing up was a major reason for Mitch's precautions. She saw a sideways glance pass between Mitch and Father Jonno, which undoubtedly meant they'd already discussed this.

'I agree with Mitch,' Jonno said. 'These days, it never hurts to have a policeman on the lookout at a public gathering. As for our Santa, I've actually been wondering if Burralea's illustrious newspaper editor might do the honours?'

Finn Latimer – lanky, mid to late thirties, with a brooding but handsome face and a lot of thick dark hair – had been slouched in his chair with his long legs stretched in front of him and crossed casually at the ankles. Flora suspected he'd been close to nodding off, but now he sat up abruptly. 'Me?'

Father Jonno grinned at him. 'You'd be a good sport and put your hand up for the Santa gig, wouldn't you, Finn?'

Finn scowled.

Peg chimed in. 'Where is the Father Christmas suit kept? We'd need to make sure that it fits Finn. He's a bit taller than Mitch.'

'I'm sure Diana, my secretary, has that in hand,' said Father Jonno. 'She has a cupboard at the back of the vestry that's full of

Christmas costumes.'

'And you don't have to worry about the suit fitting,' said Mitch. 'The costume's huge. I had to hitch it up with a belt last year. And there was still plenty of room for pillows.'

Father Jonno sent a smile down the table to Finn. 'So what do you reckon?'

The editor pulled a long face. 'Won't you need to do a paedophile and character check on me first?'

Mitch's smile was droll. 'You'll be posing for a few photos and saying, "Ho, ho, ho". Not bouncing kids on your knee.'

'And Mitch will be watching you,' said the priest.

'*And* you'll arrive in grand style in the rural fire brigade's truck,' added Peg, before shooting a sharp glance to the other end of the table. 'Have you teed up the fire brigade, Father?'

'Yes, yes,' he said. 'All sorted.'

Peg dutifully made more notes.

'I don't know.' Finn still looked uncomfortable. But there was also a shrewd gleam in his eyes. 'I wouldn't want to outshine Mary and Joseph.'

'No chance of that,' asserted Jonno. 'Sammy Henderson's playing Joseph and he's going to have a *real* beard.' Comically, Jonno widened his eyes and mimed a long beard with his hands. 'Sam has an uncle working out on the mines who's been growing a Ned Kelly beard for over a year now – and he's willing to sacrifice it for Sam's big role as Joseph. And Sam's mum's researching on the internet. She wants to make it look as authentic on the kid as possible.'

'Well, there you go,' said Mitch with a grin. 'I think Finn's just run out of excuses.'

'All right. All right.' Finn managed to look both put out and amused.

'Wonderful.' Father Jonno sent a glance around the table, then made a small throat-clearing sound. 'While we're discussing Joseph and the nativity play, there is one thing I should mention that's slightly contentious. Jeremy Harper wants to bring a donkey.'

'A proper live one?' asked Linda.

'Yes. A foal. The boy has his heart set on it.'

Peg looked as if she might burst a blood vessel or three. 'I hope you told him it's out of the question.'

'Well, no, not yet. Jeremy's brought me photos and I have to admit, the animal is *impossibly* cute. I told him I'd give it some thought.'

'Good grief, Father,' Peg cried. 'You know what they say about children and animals on the stage. You already have sixty children. They'll be a big enough challenge. You're only asking for trouble if you have a donkey, as well. It'll be a total disaster.'

'I know it's risky, but the boy's so keen and if it worked —'

'Father Jonno will handle it,' Mitch said smoothly. 'After all, he wrestled bulls when he was a rodeo clown.'

Peg gasped. 'He was a *what*?'

'A rodeo clown. You know those guys who —'

Peg cut him off. 'I know about rodeo clowns, but you've never done that kind of thing – I can't believe – you haven't, have you, Father?'

Father Jonno shrugged and smiled. ''Fraid so.'

Peg let out her breath rather noisily. For a long moment she stared into space, clearly in a huff. Eventually, she said, 'Then I daresay we should leave the decision about the donkey to you.'

'Thank you, Peg.'

She made a point of writing this down in her notes. Then, in a most businesslike, but slightly offended, tone, she went on. 'All right, let's see what I can tick off here. Are the sets all in order?'

'Yes,' said Jonno. 'All in hand. We have a manger and Jock Holmes is providing the hay bales. We don't need many props.

There'll be so many kids, with the orchestra and choir as well, we're keeping the set very simple.'

'Costumes?' asked Peg.

Father Jonno nodded. 'It's mainly a matter of sheets, tea towels and angels' wings.'

'And the wise men's crowns and gifts?'

'Diana has all the props and costumes from previous years carefully stored in her cupboard.'

Peggy turned her attention to Flora. 'And you have enough chairs and music stands for the orchestra?'

Flora nodded. 'A-huh. All good.'

'The concert's outdoors under a marquee, of course. It might be windy, so you'd better remind the children to bring pegs for their music.'

'Yes, I've already mentioned that,' Flora said. 'But perhaps you could add it to the note that's going home, Linda?'

'Will do.'

'And I'll bring extras just in case,' Flora said. 'Along with spare strings and a clarinet reed or two.'

'Good girl,' Peg said approvingly. 'Now, what else?' She surveyed her list. 'There's the supper afterwards, but the CWA ladies have that in hand.'

'I've made up a run sheet for the night,' said Father Jonno. 'There's a copy here for each of you. And Finn, you're welcome to include it in the paper with your story.'

Finn nodded.

'As for anything else,' said Father Jonno. 'The rest of you will just have to trust Flora and me.' He sent Flora a smiling wink. 'We creative types need total artistic freedom, you know, so you lot simply have to turn up on the night and be stunned by our brilliance.' As he said this, he gave an exaggerated coy flick of his long hair.

Everyone chuckled, except Peg, but she did manage a smile.

'Now we just have to keep our fingers crossed that it doesn't rain on the night,' Peg said.

'Or we could always pray,' responded Father Jonno with another cheeky smile.

* * *

Joe's cleaning woman, Suze, proved to be an efficient and agreeable dynamo when she arrived, fortuitously, the next morning. She greeted Hattie warmly, and without raising her eyebrows, for which Hattie was grateful.

Even more impressively, when Suze heard that Hattie was baking a cake in readiness for a planned afternoon tea, she obligingly skirted the kitchen and attended to all the other rooms first, bustling about energetically with duster, vacuum cleaner, furniture polish and mop. The whole house was positively gleaming by the time she had finished.

Hattie wanted Edith to feel as comfortable as possible, so she planned to keep everything about the afternoon tea very casual. They would drink from mugs, rather than dainty cups and saucers, and she would use paper napkins. Her clothing would be a simple matter of white slacks and a loose silk top. This was summer in the tropics, after all.

Hattie picked flowers for the table, but although Joe's garden boasted a couple of gorgeous rose bushes, she chose more humble sunny-faced white and yellow daisies, and she put them in an old blue jug, rather than a fancy glass vase.

Pleased with the casual simplicity she'd achieved, she was rather taken aback when she greeted Edith on the front doorstep. Her dumpy guest was dressed to the nines in a tight-fitting lace suit, the kind of jacket and skirt women usually forced themselves into for weddings. The suit was in an unbecoming puce shade, and Edith had teamed it with sturdy black-and-white sneakers.

At least Edith's feet would be comfortable, Hattie thought, as her guest proudly held out her plate of yeast buns.

'Oh!' She beamed. 'They do look very professional, don't they? So plump. Thank you, Edith.'

Hattie removed the plastic film and set the plate on the table beside the lemon cake with passionfruit icing that she had made. Edith also carried a biscuit tin under one arm. The tin remained closed, however, and was stowed on a spare chair under Edith's voluminous yellow handbag.

Joe came into the room, shaved and smelling delicious, and looking rather smart in pale chinos and an aqua shirt with the sleeves rolled back.

'You know Edith, of course,' Hattie said.

'Of course. How are you, Edith?' He gave their guest one of his especially charming smiles.

The poor woman looked suddenly mortified. She kept her eyes lowered and didn't offer her hand, so Joe stepped forward and kissed her cheek.

Edith turned beetroot.

'Please, take a seat,' Hattie said quickly. 'What would you prefer to drink, Edith? Tea or coffee?'

Edith shrugged nervously. 'I don't mind. Whatever comes.'

Oh, dear.

'How about I make a pot of tea?' suggested Joe, launching to his feet again and looking, to Hattie, as if he were more than happy to escape.

'Thank you, Joe,' she said warmly. Then she turned to Edith, but the other woman was watching Joe, her eyes as round and faithful as a puppy's, as she followed his every step while he crossed the room and disappeared through a doorway.

Hattie was normally at ease in social situations, but she suddenly found herself struggling to come up with a simple opener.

'Isn't it getting hot?' she said, dismayed that she'd fallen back on the weather so soon.

Edith nodded. She did look rather flushed. Her lace suit was probably far too warm.

Hattie wondered if she should mention that she'd spoken to Flora, that the girl had reassured her she wasn't still stressing about Oliver Edmonds's phone call. But she didn't know how much Edith knew about Flora's situation, so she opted for a much safer topic.

'Your buns look lovely, Edith. I've never been very successful with yeast. Do you use a bread-making machine?'

'No, no.' Edith gave a vigorous shake of her head. 'It's all about keeping your ingredients at the right temperature. The dry ingredients need to be at room temperature and the liquids should be between 37.8 and 43.9 degrees Celsius.'

'Really? Well, there you go, that's my problem. I'm not nearly precise enough.'

'And the milk must be warm,' added Edith. 'But the eggs are best kept at room temperature.'

'Yes, I've heard that about eggs, but I never seem to remember to take them out of the fridge in time.'

'And free-range eggs are best.'

'Oh, definitely.' Hattie laughed. 'At least I get that one right. I always buy free-range.'

'Free-range eggs?' asked Joe, coming into the room with the teapot covered by a knitted cosy with pom poms.

'Yes,' said Hattie. 'Edith was telling me about her yeast buns.'

'Ah.' Joe bestowed another warm smile on Edith. 'I can't wait to try one of those.'

The poor woman turned bright red again.

After that, the conversation limped along painfully. Hattie and Joe did their best, but Edith was nowhere near as responsive as she'd been yesterday when she'd chatted over her fence. Hattie supposed it must be Joe's presence that was making her extra shy, or perhaps she was always tense in more formal social situations, just as she'd been in her school days.

Hattie tried to talk about their school days, mentioning the names of the few other girls in their class that she could remember. Edith seemed to know what had happened to most of them, but she supplied the information concisely, with very little elaboration.

In the end, Hattie decided to talk about Shanghai, knowing this was probably something way outside Edith's experience that she might find interesting.

Fortunately Edith was – very interested – so her face became quite animated and she asked eager questions. When Hattie mentioned Lily and Rudi, Edith jumped to her feet.

'Wait!' she exclaimed. 'I've got something important to show you.'

She went straight to the mysterious biscuit tin that she'd left on an armchair under her handbag. The tin was old and scratched and dented, with navy blue sides dotted with golden stars and a Christmas·scene on the lid. Hattie had taken little notice of it earlier, but now the tin was suddenly, shockingly, familiar.

'I remember *that*,' she said.

Edith nodded. 'Some of your furniture was still in the house you rented when I bought it from the Stapletons.'

'And the tin was still there? Where was it?'

'In an old Singer sewing machine. In the bottom drawer. I decided to sell the sewing machine. I'd brought a lot of things from my parents' place and there wasn't room for everything. I never liked sewing, anyway. But the bottom drawer was stuck – I don't think the Stapletons had ever bothered to open it – and when I finally got it open, I found this tin.'

Shyly, Edith held the tin out, and Hattie was awash with memories.

'It's full of cards,' Edith said. 'Postcards, birthday cards, Christmas cards. I never expected to see you again, but I couldn't throw them away.'

'Oh, I'm so glad you didn't. Thank you so much, Edith. I always wondered what happened to this tin. At the time, when I was packing up, it was all so hectic and I was so sad —'

'Your mother had just died,' said Edith.

'Yes.' Hattie didn't dare to look in Joe's direction. They didn't need a reminder of the other reason for her sadness at that time.

Not to mention the shock of her mother's revelation about Lily and Rudi. In those final weeks before she'd left Australia, Hattie had been flattened, numb, a barely functioning robot.

'It wasn't till I unpacked my trunk in England that I realised I'd left this behind. I was so disappointed. It was all I had from – from —'

'Your aunt and uncle,' Edith supplied.

'Yes.'

Now wasn't the time to explain her complicated family history. Hattie tried to lift the tin's lid. 'It seems to be stuck,' she said. 'Or perhaps my darned arthritis is the problem.'

'Here,' said Joe. 'Let me try.'

He freed the lid in a matter of moments, and there they were – yellowed envelopes with Chinese stamps, and some stamps from the Philippines, and America.

Hattie could remember her excitement as a child whenever one of these envelopes arrived in the mail. It had been such a thrill, knowing they'd come across oceans and all the way to her letterbox in Burralea. Each arrival had helped to keep alive enchanting, magical memories.

Lily, golden-haired and glamorous, always so much fun. Rudi, dark and dashing and so very talented. Even as a child, with the limits of a child's understanding, Hattie had sensed that her aunt and uncle were exotic and romantic and different from the rest of her family. More exciting and even, possibly, more loving.

She could remember the thrill of an envelope's arrival, rushing into the kitchen to carefully slit the paper open with a knife. Finding a card inside.

'Goodness,' she whispered now, as she saw a faded black-and-white postcard with a picture of Shanghai's Bund, and another of the horse racetrack.

She didn't open all the cards now, but she knew there would also be beautiful birthday cards with magical pictures of woodland animals and fairies, and Christmas cards with robin redbreasts and nostalgic snow scenes.

Inside or on the back, there would be messages in Lily's round, looping script, or in Rudi's handwriting, thick and dark.

Hattie could almost remember some of the shorter messages word for word.

To our dearest duckling, with much love from Aunt Lily and Uncle Rudi.

Or perhaps a plea. *It's ages since we've seen a photo of you, Hattie. Please remind your mummy that we need another one.*

Your ever-loving aunt and uncle.

Edith was looking exceedingly pleased now. 'I thought you might like to see these again. I've always liked to collect cards myself.' She gave a shy little shrug. 'They always have such lovely verses. I could never think of words like that.' She flicked a shy, awkward glance to Joe, then looked away quickly, eyes downcast. 'The cards can mount up, though.'

'These cards are very special,' Hattie assured her. 'They bring back so many memories.'

With another shy smile, which carefully avoided Joe, Edith picked up her handbag. 'Right, well, thanks for the afternoon tea. I'll leave those last two buns with you, but I'd better get home.

Geraldine will be missing me.'

'Geraldine?' Hattie had to ask.

'My new kitten.'

* * *

It was quite late when Joe came into the bedroom, and Hattie was sitting on the bed in her nightdress with the cards scattered around her, lost in bittersweet memories. She'd read every one of them, sometimes smiling, at other times shedding a tear.

Joe came to stand beside her. They were still sharing his room – there'd never been any question of her returning to the guest room. The arrangement was quite settled. Hattie would stay in Burralea until the week before Christmas, and then she and Joe would both fly to Brisbane. She would return to her apartment, while Joe spent Christmas with his daughter Emma and her husband and little Ivy.

'That's quite a collection,' he said, looking down at the spread.

'I know. I'm lucky that Edith has such a fondness for cards. Anyone else would have thrown them out years ago.' Hattie picked up a postcard of New York's Empire State Building and thought of her son. 'I wonder if Mark would ever want these.' She dropped the card back on the pile. 'I don't suppose so. He's not one for clutter. His apartment is super modern and minimalist. All glass and stainless steel.'

'You should ask him, though,' said Joe. 'He probably has plenty of storage space hidden behind sliding doors.'

'Oh, yes, I'm sure he has.'

She began to collect up the cards and put them back in the tin, and Joe went through to the bathroom. By the time she finished, he had reappeared, changed into pyjamas.

From outside came a roll of thunder. Another summer storm threatened.

Joe got into bed, slipping under the sheets, and Hattie set the tin aside and followed him. She turned out the bedside lamp, and they lay together listening to the claps of thunder and watching the flashes of lightning that shimmered at the edges of the curtains.

Again Hattie was reassured by a sense of cosy rightness about being here with Joe.

'What are you thinking about?' she asked him.

'About you. About how this has happened so quickly.'

'By *this*, I assume you mean us?'

'Yes.'

'I hope it hasn't happened too quickly for you?' Hattie was acutely conscious that she'd been the forward one who'd walked down the hall to this room.

'Not too quickly, no.' He reached for her hand. 'My only problem is, it feels almost too good to be true. Like a miracle.'

Hattie smiled. 'I know.'

They settled comfortably together, holding hands in the dark while the storm rumbled and rolled towards them.

'Tell me more about Lily and Rudi.' Joe knew by now that this couple were actually Hattie's parents, but he knew very few of the details.

'What would you like to know?'

'Whatever you're happy to tell me. What happened to them in Shanghai after you and Rose left? It was in the middle of the war, wasn't it?'

'Slap-bang in the middle, yes.' Lily and Rudi's story had been a huge mystery to Hattie for so many years, but by now it was very familiar. 'The war with the Japanese got even more intense after we left,' she said. 'The Japs rounded up most of the foreigners, especially the British and Americans, and herded them into internment camps.'

'Including Lily?'

'Yes, Lily was imprisoned. But not Rudi. That was the irony. The Japanese were actually quite tolerant of the White Russians. They weren't at war with them, you see. They even formed a bureau for the Russian émigrés and gave them identification papers for work and travel. But they made them choose between Soviet citizenship and remaining stateless.'

'I don't suppose Rudi wanted to join the Soviets.'

'Not on your life. So he had to wear a badge with the colours of the Czar. But he was able to visit Lily in the camp, and he took her food or medicine if she needed it, so they managed, poor things.'

'And they both survived?'

'Yes. Miraculously. But they had only just struggled through the Japanese occupation, when there was a new war, between the Chinese nationals and Mao Tse-tung's communists. That's when Lily and Rudi finally had to leave Shanghai. A refugee ship took them to the Philippines. And from there they went to America.'

As Hattie said this, the rain arrived outside Joe's cosy cottage, bringing first the smell of dampening earth and bitumen, then the sound of drumming on iron rooftops. A gust of wind set a curtain flapping, and Joe got up to close the windows.

'That'll be good for your garden.' Hattie raised her voice above the din.

He came back, settled down beside her, and she thought he might let the conversation drop now, but after a bit, Joe said, 'I'm pretty sure there were White Russians who came to North Queensland.'

'Yes, I've imagined how different things might have been for us all, if Rudi and Lily had come here. Apparently, they did consider it, but Rudi would have found it hard to get a job. He really only had the one skill, playing the violin, and there were no professional orchestras in North Queensland. New York was the sensible option. He already had contacts there.'

'And plenty of work for him, I should imagine.'

'Yes, of course.'

'But it must have been hard for Lily to move even further away from you.'

'Perhaps . . . although in some ways I think it was easier. It was too late to undo the arrangement with Rose, and she could start a whole new life in America.'

'Did she have more children?'

'No, there was some sort of complication when I was born. She needed extra surgery. I'm not sure of the details.'

'So when did you finally meet up with them again?'

Hattie swallowed, fighting the sudden tightness in her throat. 'Not for ages.'

CHAPTER THIRTY-ONE

1167A W 15TH STREET
NEW YORK
DECEMBER 3, 1958

Dearest Hattie,

I hope this letter reaches you before you leave Australia for England. I can't imagine how hard it must be for you to lose your dear mother and then to have to pack up your life and leave your home.

When I heard that Rose was desperately ill, I began to make plans to fly down there to see her, but then Mother phoned to warn me it was too late. I'm so sorry. I know you looked after Rose beautifully and we're all in your debt. You've been a wonderful daughter, but life can be so cruel, Hattie darling.

Dear Rose was a wise and loving sister, and I have the deepest gratitude for the many, many ways she has helped me over the years. I shall miss her so much.

Hattie, you will find your grandmother's house in Devon

*very peaceful, and I hope you will take as much time as you
need to recover from this dreadful ordeal. You are forever in
our thoughts and if there is any way we can help you, please
don't hesitate to ask.*

*Perhaps, when you are ready, you might come to visit
your Uncle Rudi and me in New York. We have quite a nice
little two-bedroom apartment in the West Village, and we
would adore to see you – but I'm sure it's too soon to speak
of such things.*

*I know your Uncle Rudi will want to write to you as
well, but he is incredibly busy at the moment with rehearsals
and endless concerts. He's in high demand these days and
it's quite wonderful to see his talents fully recognised at last.*

Take care, my sweetest girl, and travel safely.
With deepest sympathy and masses of love,
Your Aunt Lily and Uncle Rudi xxxx

WICKER COTTAGE
VICARY LANE, TORBAY
DEVON
FEBRUARY 10, 1959

Dear Lily and Rudi,
*I am now safely arrived in Devon and Grandmother
is taking good care of me. I miss Rose and a lot of things
about Australia, and I'm still slumped in a deep fog that
is taking a long time to lift. Each day I go for a long walk
along the sea cliffs, however, and I'm slowly starting to feel
a little clearer.*

*You will notice that I've addressed you as Lily and Rudi
without the aunt and uncle tags. Rose – I can no longer call*

*her Mother – told me everything before she died. I don't
think I need to elaborate.*

To say that I was shocked was an understatement.

*Right now, while I'm still in the midst of this dark and
suffocating fog, I can't begin to understand or accept the
decisions you made. It seems incomprehensible to me that
you could blithely hand your baby over to your sister,
because it was more convenient.*

*I certainly have no plans to come to New York in the
near future.*

*For as long as I can remember, I've always looked on
you and Rudi as very special people in my life, but to be
honest, I now feel cheated, not to mention angry and hurt.
And completely confused.*

Grandmother sends her regards,
Hattie

1167A W 15TH STREET
NEW YORK
MARCH 9, 1959

Dearest Hattie,

*I am surrounded by balls of crushed up paper from all
the letters I've tried to write and then abandoned. To be
honest, I have no idea where to begin, because I know that
anything I say will probably upset you. But I do understand
your anger. You must feel as if your life has been cruelly
ripped apart and turned completely upside-down.*

*I hope you will, however, accept my deepest apology
for causing you so much grief and confusion when you are
already coping with the huge sadness of losing Rose. I'm*

truly sorry that you had to receive this news at such a sad time, but, darling, I can't pretend to be sorry that you finally know the truth.

I will not try to make excuses for myself or to lay blame anywhere else, except to say that I was very young when I met Rudi, even younger than you are now, Hattie, and I was deeply and hopelessly in love with him. I hope you may also experience that blissful, glorious blossoming of love one day, but not under such difficult circumstances as ours.

However, I must admit that I was also very stubborn at the time, and I have paid an enormous price for my youthful impetuosity. You will learn, as you grow older, that our lives are mapped by a series of choices. Decisions that seem clear-cut and sensible at the time can result in a host of unimagined consequences.

Mistakenly, I thought the difficult decision I made all those years ago would only hurt me once, for a short time. I had no idea that it would go on and on, that would I suffer the pain of losing you over and over. Forever.

But perhaps this is not the time to talk about my own hurt. Darling Hattie, I only ask that eventually, when you feel ready, you might give your father and me the chance to apologise, to reach out, and to possibly atone.

Until then, stay safe, Hattie, and I hope you soon find ways to be happy.

You are forever in our hearts.

With my very deepest love,

Lily

CHAPTER THIRTY-TWO

Hattie dreamed of Lily and Rudi . . . a confusing dream, where Lily and Rudi were young again, but she, Hattie, was an adult and they were all in Shanghai together . . .

Ah Lan, her amah, was there as well, and they were walking down the narrow lanes of old Shanghai where electricity wires snaked over the exterior walls of rickety houses and washing was strung on poles. Bicycles whizzed and wove everywhere, everywhere – often with astonishing loads of huge cardboard cartons or bulging plastic bags.

A woman stood outside her home, making dumplings, while another was doing her washing by hand in a concrete tub. A man had a tank of live fish on his footpath, and he was cleaning fish on a timber slab. A stall was piled with smoked chicken feet and duck heads. A bucket by Hattie's feet was filled with a mysterious green stew, while a hawker bobbed in front of her, pleading with her to buy a watch.

Lily, dressed in a gold and glittering evening gown that clung to her slender body, was laughing. 'Isn't it wonderful to be back? To be home?'

Ah Lan held Hattie's hand. Perhaps she was a child again now . . . for she felt wonderfully safe, but excited, too . . . eager to see what lay around the next corner.

Before she could reach the corner, however, the dream began to recede, slipping away like mist.

Hattie woke, blinked. Bright sunshine shimmered at the edges of the bedroom curtains. Last night's storm was well and truly past, and Joe was still sound asleep. She lay for a bit, thinking about Joe, so steady and gentle and strong. Then she thought about her dream, lingering in that lazy, drowsy space between waking and actually getting out of bed, remembering that final corner . . .

She'd encountered a few unexpected corners in her life.

Was that what her dream had been about? The turmoil and confusion of her early years in England? The loneliness of the cliff-top house in Devon with just her cranky old grandmother for company. Escaping to London and meeting Phil, who'd proved so unsatisfactory in so many ways. And then, the momentous day when she'd finally met up with Lily and Rudi again.

Hattie drew a long deep breath, remembering herself at the ripe old age of twenty-five, already married and divorced.

She'd been in very low spirits, unlucky in love, and feeling very lost and alone in the world, when she'd passed on the news of her divorce in one of her perfunctory letters to Lily.

Heaven knew what silly decision she might have made next, if it hadn't been for the steadiness of her job at Crompton & Thistle, and Ian, her kind and intelligent boss. Ian took her to Covent Garden to hear the London Symphony and afterwards, to drink brandy alexanders in a trendy new bar.

Out of the blue, he'd confessed the impossible, that he was very much in love with her. So it was thanks to Ian, stepping into the role of her knight in shining armour, that she'd been in a more receptive mood when she'd received yet another letter from Lily.

It was little more than a brief note this time, written inside a card with a picture of the Angel of the Waters in New York's Central Park.

> *Darling Hattie,*
> *Rudi and I have made an executive decision. We're worried about you and we feel we have to see you, so we're coming to London. We'll be staying at the Tavistock Hotel in Bloomsbury and by the time you receive this letter, we'll probably be in the air. Expect a phone call very soon.*
> *Lily xxx*

Hattie had known she could no longer avoid this reunion with her parents and, in the end, it wasn't the melodramatic soap opera she'd feared. Lily and Rudi, although older and greyer, were as handsome as ever, but by the late 1960s, the rest of the world, especially swinging London, seemed to have caught up with them.

When Hattie shyly greeted them in the lovely Art Deco foyer of the Tavistock Hotel, the couple she'd always thought of as youthful and Bohemian and exotic were well into middle age and rather conservative in appearance. Hattie wasn't sure if they'd dressed super-carefully for this meeting with her, or whether two decades of living in America had tamed them. They'd certainly been very cautious about not upsetting Hattie and they'd taken their lead from her.

She'd walked with them to Russell Square, where the three of them had sat on a bench in the peaceful green park, watching pigeons and dog walkers while they talked about . . . everything . . . about Shanghai, about Rose, about Lily and Rudi's new life in Greenwich Village, about Hattie's mistake in impulsively marrying such a radical rocker as Phil.

Lily still spoke with a very British accent, but Hattie noticed that Rudi's deep Russian voice had acquired a slight American twang.

Eventually, she told them about Ian, and she bravely decided to organise a meeting between him and her parents. They all went to dinner at the Criterion where they had veal cordon bleu and beef stroganoff and sensational parfaits in long-stemmed glasses.

The evening was surprisingly relaxing. Lily entertained them with funny stories about some of the larger-than-life people she and Rudi knew in New York. Ian and Rudi talked about music and books, and they got on so well that by the end of the night, Hattie knew she could no longer put up a fight.

She'd been won around. Her parents were people she once again wanted in her life.

Before they returned to New York, Lily made a point of having a little time alone with Hattie.

'Darling, I know I can never expect you to understand why I chose Rudi at the expense of losing you. I know I make my love for him sound enormously romantic, like something out of a Victorian melodrama, but it really did feel like that. I don't think I'm wired to be calm and sensible and practical. Maybe I was reacting against the way I was brought up in a stuffy English family and an even stuffier boarding school. I know I was incredibly influenced by Shanghai as soon as I arrived. Suddenly there seemed to be so many alternative ways of looking at the world, and the old ways didn't make any sense to me.'

'And maybe Grandmother and Grandfather should have been more tolerant,' suggested Hattie, who had experienced her own share of her grandmother's sharp tongue and narrow-mindedness.

'I wasn't going to mention that, but yes. I suspect they were examples of British conservatism at its worst.' Lily's mouth twisted in a self-conscious little smile. 'I think we've all been punished enough for this. Can you forgive me, darling?'

And Hattie had found it surprisingly easy to say yes.

She and Lily had smiled and hugged each other, and their hug was the proper, unreserved sort, the kind of loving hug they'd shared years before, when Hattie was just a little girl and Lily was her glamorous aunt.

Even now, Hattie could still feel the healing warmth of that hug, and she was smiling and felt almost light-hearted as she got out of bed, tiptoeing, so as not to disturb Joe. She would make him a lovely, steaming cup of tea.

In slippers and a long white cotton dressing-gown, she went out to the kitchen where Marlowe greeted her with a vigorous wagging of his tail.

'Hello, old boy,' she whispered. 'I guess you'd like to go outside.'

She opened the back door and Marlowe went ahead of her, sniffing at the new day. His paw prints made green tracks in the dew-spangled grass as he headed across to his favourite spot in the garden beneath a bottlebrush tree.

Not wanting to get her slippers wet, Hattie stayed on the back step. The air carried a damp, earthy scent and hibiscus flowers, battered by the storm, spilled petals.

Nevertheless, the morning sparkled with a freshly washed brightness, and the birds sounded especially cheerful as they tweeted and whistled and chirped. It was a good day to be alive, Hattie thought, stretching her arms high as she took a long deep breath.

From inside the kitchen came the sound of the phone ringing.

Darn.

Hattie hurried inside. 'I'll get that,' she called, knowing that Joe would be stirring. She lifted the receiver from its cradle on the wall. 'Hello. This is Joe's place.'

'Oh,' a woman's voice said and she sounded distinctly disappointed. 'You're still there?'

Hattie was instantly tense. 'Is that Janelle?'

'Yes, can I speak to my father?'

'Yes, just a moment, and I'll get him.'

As she said this, Joe appeared in the kitchen doorway, his snowy hair ruffled from sleep, but his eyes alert, eyebrows raised.

'Ah, he's right here, Janelle.' Hattie injected an extra dollop of brightness into her voice, in a vain attempt to counter Joe's daughter's vinegary tone.

Joe looked resigned as he crossed the kitchen floor in bare feet. Hattie handed him the phone and went to fill the kettle.

Behind her, Joe said warmly, 'Hello, Janelle, love, how's tricks?' After a brief pause, 'Well, yes, Hattie will be here until I leave for Brisbane.'

Across the kitchen, Joe's glance met Hattie's and he rolled his eyes. 'No, I won't be staying with Hattie in Brisbane. I'll be with Emma and Nathan. You know I'm having Christmas with them and little Ivy.'

There was another longer pause, and Hattie decided against turning the kettle on. The noise of it coming to the boil would probably incense Janelle further. She collected mugs and set them quietly on the bench.

Marlowe appeared at the door. Hattie pointed to the mat that was his special spot. He knew he was to stay there until his paws dried.

'I'm not sure,' Joe was saying. 'I might.' A small silence followed. 'Yes, she might. We haven't really talked about next year yet.'

Hattie wondered if she should discreetly leave the room. If this conversation had occurred a week ago, she probably would have left, but she and Joe were completely comfortable together now. They'd talked at length about their lives and the long years they'd spent apart, about their families, their personal foibles, their regrets and triumphs.

They hadn't talked very much about the future, but she liked to think they'd reached an understanding. Now they'd found each other again, they were loath to spend their final years alone.

At any rate, if she was being discussed, she had a right to know at least half of what was being said.

'Janelle, I think I'm old enough to work these things out for myself,' Joe said. Then, with a dismayed huff, '*Too* old?'

Again, his gaze met Hattie's. He gave another eye-roll, another annoyed grimace. 'I'm sorry, Janny. I think you're being unreasonable. And it's too early in the morning to have an argument.'

With this, Joe lifted a hand in a gesture of frustrated helplessness. 'No, I don't want to discuss it now. I'd like you to calm down first. I think you should think hard about what you're saying. Perhaps we can talk again later when you're feeling more reasonable. Bye, darling.'

Joe hung up, and let out a long, weary sigh. 'I'm sure you got the gist of that.'

'Janelle's not my number-one fan?'

He smiled, pulled out a chair from the kitchen table and flopped down into it. Hattie switched the kettle and it hummed to life.

'I'm not sure why she has her nose so out of joint,' Joe said.

'I suppose she's been taken by surprise,' Hattie suggested. 'She's used to you living on your own. She probably has you pigeon-holed as her dear old dad, a lonely widower. I don't suppose it ever occurred to her that you might want company.'

'I'm sure you're right. Janelle never has had much imagination. She finds it hard to see anyone else's point of view.' Joe shook his head. 'I shouldn't have hung up on her, though.'

'As you said, it will give her time to think,' Hattie suggested gently.

'Or to stew.'

The kettle came to the boil. 'Are teabags okay?' Hattie asked.

'Yes, sure.'

She poured steaming water into mugs, added a little sugar and milk, dealt with the bags, and brought the mugs to the table where Joe was still frowning into space, apparently lost in troubled thought.

'Janelle seemed terribly worried that you might come back next year and be a permanent fixture,' he said, still staring bleakly ahead. 'She's friends with Suze, so I suppose she'll quiz her to find out if we're sleeping together.'

Hattie remembered the energetic cleaner, *The Enchanted April* and her reading glasses sitting on the bedside table in Joe's bedroom. *Too bad*, she thought.

She said, 'Don't forget your tea while it's nice and hot.'

'Right, thanks.' But Joe still looked distracted as he sipped.

Hattie found her own sense of annoyance stirring, growing hotter. Joe had given up so much for this daughter. He'd been a wonderful father for her, even after he'd found out the hurtful truth from Gloria. And he'd looked after Gloria all that time when she was ill, even though he'd known she'd more or less tricked him into their marriage.

The injustice of his situation still bothered Hattie and she couldn't resist speaking her mind. 'Janelle doesn't know how lucky she is to have you, Joe. You certainly don't deserve to be lectured like this.'

He nodded again, looked sad.

'Perhaps it's time she knew the truth.'

'No.'

'But Janelle has no idea how much she owes you, and yet she's treating you like —'

'No, Hattie. Just leave it.'

Silenced by the sudden certainty in his voice, Hattie sat, chastened. She sipped at her tea and thought, again, about her own painful reaction to the truth about her parents.

'I'm sorry,' she said. 'I should know better. You're right. You can't tell Janelle now.'

'No, I can't. Janelle loved her mother. They were very alike, peas in a pod. The truth would destroy her. And her mother's dead so Janelle wouldn't even have a chance to talk to her, to get Gloria's side of the story.'

'That's a very generous way of thinking.' Hattie had never really allowed herself to imagine Gloria's plight – but she did so now, picturing her former rival as a single girl in the 1950s, the daughter of the town's most successful businessman, finding herself pregnant, but abandoned by the baby's fly-by-night father.

'It doesn't change the fact that you don't deserve to be criticised now,' she said. 'I still feel upset for you. Defensive.'

Joe smiled, reached for her hand. 'I appreciate that. I really do.'

Hattie finished her tea, lost in thought, worrying. 'I suppose Janelle might see me as a threat to her inheritance prospects.'

'Possibly. Their farm does well enough, but she's never been emotionally secure. I've done my best to reach her, but most of the time she's been on another wavelength.'

'I wouldn't want to make things worse between the two of you.'

Now, for the first time, Joe lost his distracted air. He looked straight at Hattie. 'You've got that the wrong way round, Hattie. I'm not going to allow *Janelle* to make things worse between you and me.'

Across the table they smiled at each other. Two old people, still in their pyjamas, sitting at a simple kitchen table. So unglamorous. So right.

CHAPTER THIRTY-THREE

A conspiracy had started in Burralea, Flora was certain. A benevolent conspiracy. People seemed to be looking out for her, and in the days leading up to the Christmas concert, she hardly spent an evening alone.

First Hattie popped in – she'd been worried ever since she'd passed on the news of Oliver's phone call – and she brought a sizeable wedge of delicious lemon cake with passionfruit icing. Flora fed this to Mitch when he called by, and she convinced him to stay for another impromptu evening meal.

'Almost as good as your little caramel pies,' he pronounced as he demolished Hattie's cake, and his dark gaze remained locked with Flora's for a shade too long, creating all kinds of crazy chaos inside her.

At least he left before she said or did anything silly, and she supposed she had to be grateful for that.

Other Burralea folk were keeping an eye on her as well. Edith popped her head over the fence every other day, and then one evening Edith, shyly, invited Flora to tea. *Just shepherd's pie.*

Flora assured Edith that she adored shepherd's pie, and she took

the old lady a bunch of pink roses from the Burralea rose farm.
Edith was quite overcome.

'But why?' she sniffed, lifting her spectacles to swipe at her tears
with a crumpled handkerchief.

'Because you've invited me to tea and that's very kind of you.'

Edith shook her head and wiped her eyes again. 'No one's ever
bought me flowers before.'

Slightly shocked, Flora tried to make light of this sad fact. She
smiled. 'You know what they say. There's always a first time for
everything.' She wondered how often Edith had invited anyone
into her home.

Over dinner, Edith didn't once ask a question about Mitch, so
Flora decided to put her mind at rest about his extra vigilance by
explaining briefly about Oliver.

'What's he look like, this Oliver?' Edith demanded.

'He's rather big, actually. Tall, big shoulders and chest, and thick
blonde hair.'

'Right. I'll keep an eye out.'

'Oh, I don't really think he'll show up.'

'Just the same, an extra pair of eyes is always useful.'

They had ice-cream and tinned peaches for dessert, and afterwards, Edith and Flora played three games of Scrabble, while the
kitten Geraldine slept curled in Flora's lap. Edith beat Flora in every
game and was an absolute whiz at adding up the scores in her head.

'I do believe you're an undiscovered genius,' Flora told her.

Edith merely shrugged and looked at the roses that she'd put in
a glass jar at the end of the table, then sighed.

Twice, Alice called in to collect Flora for dinner at Kooringal and to
enjoy a little 'Charlie time', and on both occasions Alice and Seth
insisted that Flora stay the night.

'I can easily drop you back into town in the morning,' Alice told her.

Flora couldn't deny that she enjoyed all this company, and it was a relief to be distracted from thinking about B.O. She noticed that even Father Jonno was more inclined to pop into rehearsals for a quick hello, always with an encouraging word for her and a joke for the children, who all seemed to adore him.

On the afternoon of the final combined rehearsal, Flora borrowed Alice's ute to collect Peg and the wheelie walker that she was using now. Flora was rather nervous. No one else in Burralea would watch these performances with a more critical eye than Peg. The children were Peg's pet project after all, and she gave many of them private lessons as well as conducting the groups.

Fortunately, the kids were quite obedient these days, so there was no embarrassing misbehaviour as they assembled out on the lawn next to the church under a big marquee.

Flora was pretty relaxed about the choir. Only a couple of carols needed to be sung in parts, and most of the children had also sung these at school, so they were quite accomplished little singers.

The orchestra had been more of a hurdle, but meeting that challenge had proved far more rewarding than Flora had expected.

To Flora's relief, Peg was satisfied. More than satisfied, actually. Tears glittered in her eyes as she gripped Flora's hand tightly in both of hers.

'You've got it,' Peg told her in little more than a whisper. 'That was wonderful.'

'I was channelling you, Peg.'

Peg looked touched, but she shook her head. 'No,' she said. 'You have something extra. *And* you have a natural flair for working with children.'

'I'm afraid I didn't really think of them as children,' Flora confessed. 'Not after I got over my original nerves.'

'That's the secret, though. Treat them with respect and they'll
rise to the occasion every time. Those kids were wonderful, Flora.
Their parents are going to be bursting with pride. And so will I.'

'Thanks.'

'And what about little Molly Greeves?' said Peg. 'I see you've got
her leading the flutes. They were wonderful. Hasn't she come on?'

'Yes, she's so keen.'

'How did you do it?' Peg looked genuinely curious.

'We had a little chat about practice and now she's all fired up.'

'I think you'd better have that little chat with all of then, then.'

They both laughed and, to celebrate, Peg insisted on shouting
Flora to dinner at the Burralea pub, where the big, old-fashioned
dining room was already decorated for Christmas with tinsel and
fairy lights.

There were so many people Flora knew. Tammy and Ben were
at a table with another young couple. One of the children from the
choir was there with her parents and brothers and sisters and grandparents. It seemed to be a family celebration.

Finn Latimer was at a table in the corner on his own. If Flora
hadn't been Peg's guest, she might have considered inviting him to
join them, but he probably would have found the conversation too
focused on music. Besides, he had rather a lone wolf vibe and she
sensed that he might not welcome their company.

'I seem to know half the people here,' she told Peg.

Peg smiled. 'If that surprises you, you've obviously been in the
city too long.'

'Well, yes. That thought's occurred to me more than once.'

'I wasn't serious, Flora.' Peg was frowning now. 'You need the
city. You need the stimulation.'

'I guess.' Flora certainly still wanted the symphony orchestra job. It wasn't just a matter of personal satisfaction, she wanted to prove to Oliver that he no longer had a hold over her. And she needed to prove to herself that she could move on and be successful. Without a backwards glance.

And yet . . . she had to admit that the allure of living in the city wasn't nearly as bright and beckoning as it had been when she'd first left home to study at the Con.

If she managed to get the orchestra job, she supposed she would find an apartment in the inner city, and she would soon make new friends and they would go out to bars or dinners, or the theatre, or have occasional jam sessions in each other's homes.

It wouldn't take too long to get used to the busyness of the city again, the constant noise of traffic, the crowded shops. But she would miss this peaceful, pretty country town with streets wide enough for huge shade trees and parked cars in the middle, and footpaths lined with lampposts bearing gorgeous hanging baskets filled with tumbling flowers that conscientious residents took turns to water. She would certainly miss Seth and Alice and Charlie.

And Mitch.

Thud-*thud-thud*.

Yeah, Mitch was turning into something of a problem for Flora, a completely different kind of problem from Oliver.

Whenever Mitch was around she felt safe and deeply happy, as if the world had been in danger of spinning off kilter, but was now settled all around her and whispering in her ear: *This is right. This is okay. This is how it's meant to be.*

It was rubbish, of course.

She could only be truly happy with Mitch if the attraction was mutual.

***

On the day of the concert, Flora woke to sunshine and a quick check of the weather bureau's radar map showed absolutely no rain in sight. She smiled. Father Jonno's prayers had been answered.

She spent the morning practising her audition repertoire at the hall, then took herself home for lunch and a quiet, relaxing afternoon – a little cooking and housework, washing her hair and repainting her fingernails. She would wear one of her classy black Melbourne dresses for the concert, with glittery Christmassy earrings.

The concert started at six, and the children had been told to assemble at five-thirty. Flora would make sure she was there by five.

At four forty-five she checked that all the necessary music, pegs for music stands, spare strings and reeds were packed. She wouldn't eat until after the concert – a lasagne was ready in the fridge. It would be easy to reheat and she hoped Mitch might be free to join her.

Excitement fizzed as the time to leave ticked closer. It didn't matter that this was just a children's concert in a tiny country town and not a grand performance in Sydney's Opera House. Flora was eagerly looking forward to it. She knew the kids would do their very best, and their parents and friends were going to be proud and maybe a little emotional.

Tonight, the Burralea community would be abuzz with happy vibes and the concert would be a perfect launch for their Christmas season.

Flora was giving a final touch-up to her lipstick when the front doorbell rang. It was possibly Mitch, popping in for a last-minute check that all was well, and she was smiling as she hurried down the hallway and flung the door open.

Not Mitch.

A tall, blonde, barrel-chested figure loomed on her doorstep.

'Hello, Drumbeat.'

CHAPTER THIRTY-FOUR

The nickname that had once sounded so cute now sent dread, cold as death, sinking through Flora. She couldn't speak. In her head she was screaming.

She had to grip the doorknob for support.

Oliver's smile didn't quite reach his eyes. 'You're looking very well. You're looking great, actually.'

Go away! she wanted to scream. How on earth had he found her? He seemed horrifyingly huge. Standing on a step below her, he was still taller than she was. So broad and solid. There'd been a time when she'd found his hugeness attractive.

'You're all dressed up,' he said and this time he let his icy grey eyes travel deliberately over her, making it obvious that he was taking in every detail of her carefully styled hair, her festive earrings, her dress, her nail polish.

'It's good to know you haven't let your standards slip now that you're hiding away in the deep north.'

'You shouldn't be here,' she said.

'I wanted to see you.'

I don't want to see you. 'How did you find me?'

'The folk around here are very friendly and helpful, and I had to see you, Flora. You left without a proper goodbye. It really knocked me, the way you took off like that.'

She shook her head. This was bullshit. She could see the cold anger in his eyes. He wasn't 'knocked', he was furious that she'd had the audacity to leave him without his permission. But if she had tried to say goodbye to Oliver, he would have found a way to talk her out of it.

When it came to verbal sparring, she could never outwit him. Her only choice had been to pack her bags while he'd been at a late rehearsal and then hurry to the safety of Ellen's flat.

'Can I come in?' Oliver asked now, super smoothly.

Flora didn't answer him. She didn't budge either. Still gripping the door handle, she willed him to leave. Now. Fast.

Of course, he stayed put. 'Come on, Flora, be a good sport. We had so many happy months together. All that music, the parties, the blazing sex. You can spare me five minutes.'

A curtain flickered at Edith's window next door. Oliver saw it, shot a narrow-eyed scowl in Edith's direction, then looked back over his shoulder to the other houses in the street. 'I suppose there's a strong gossip network in a hokey little redneck town like this.'

Flora let out her breath in a noisy huff. 'I can't stand around chatting. I'm about to go out.'

'I'll take five minutes of your time, tops. You owe me five minutes.'

Despite the hammering of her heart, Flora stood her ground. She wasn't letting Oliver through the door. One sniff of victory and he would become all-powerful. Her limited confidence would be whittled away.

'What do you want?' she asked.

Oliver smiled. 'You must know what I want, my sweet girl. I want you.'

'That's not going to happen. *You* know why I left you.'

Flinging his arms open wide in the time-honoured gesture of innocence, he said softly, 'That's my point. That's why I'm here. I don't know why you left. You owe me a decent explanation.'

Flora swallowed nervously. She had no time to offer explanations now. And anyway, she knew it would be no use. Oliver would debate everything she said. He would twist her words, confuse her. 'I'm sorry,' she said. 'I really have to go now.'

'To the children's Christmas concert?'

Oh, God, don't let him show up at the concert. Flora's flashes of panic returned, sharper and hotter.

'I'll see you afterwards, then. After the concert,' Oliver said next. 'You owe me the chance to have a proper conversation.'

'I don't owe you anything.'

'I shared my life with you. My apartment. My bed. We had so much in common.'

You made my life miserable. You bullied me. You hit me.

There was no point in continuing this conversation. Flora knew how it would end. Oliver would keep up the relentless pressure, waiting for a chink, a tiny glimmer of weakness, and when he found it, he would pounce. She would be cornered, defenceless. Scared. He would have her exactly where he wanted her.

She swung the door shut.

Or at least she tried to, but with panther-like speed, Oliver shot a foot forward, blocking the door.

'Not so fast, sweetheart.'

'I have to go.'

'I'll let you go, if you promise to see me after the kids' show.'

'No.'

'Flora, be reasonable.'

Oh, help! If only she'd taken out that intervention order. How could she have been so naïve? She should have known Oliver would pursue this personal battle to the bitter end. His ego wouldn't allow failure. He was more relentless than the very worst high-pressure salesman.

She drew a deep breath. 'You have to accept that it's over between us.'

'Baby Drumbeat, I've come a very long way to ask you *very* nicely for a chance to discuss this, and *you* need to be reasonable. You can't walk out on me like this – I won't let it happen. You're not going to decide this.' His smile had vanished. His face was cold now. Granite-cold. Deathly cold.

Flora thought of the children, all so innocent and happy, arriving to perform for their parents. For their sakes, she almost said yes, just to appease Oliver. She had resolved never to give in to him again, but she was scared that her refusal might anger him and somehow put the concert in danger.

Then again, she was probably overreacting. The Burralea community wasn't Oliver's target, and Mitch would be at the concert, watching. There'd be plenty of other adults around.

'I'm sorry,' she said, mentally crossing her fingers as she made her decision. 'I don't want to have any more to do with you, Oliver. Now, please go away.'

'You're sorry?' Oliver stared at her with simmering menace. He leaned closer, hissing into her face, 'I'm very sure you *will* be sorry, you stupid little bitch.'

Before Flora could respond, he turned and departed, his long legs eating up the short front path with surprising speed.

Flora slammed the door shut and ran down the hall, her heart racing. Her fingers fumbled as she reached for her phone, deep in an inside pocket of her music bag, then searched for Mitch's number and pressed it.

Mitch answered on the second ring.

Thank you, God.

'Hey, Flora? All ready for the concert?'

'Oliver's here.' She couldn't help whispering.

'At your place? Now?' Mitch's voice was instantly alert, serious.

'No, he's just left, but he was here. He's probably still in this street.'

'Damn. I'm already at the church hall. Have you spoken to him?'

'Yes, but I wouldn't let him into the house. I told him I didn't want to talk to him. He was pissed off. And he more or less threatened me. I – I – Mitch – he knows about the concert.'

'Okay.' Mitch managed, with that one word, to sound calm and in control. 'Can you give me a description?'

'Tall. Big. Thick chested. Blonde hair.'

'And what's he wearing?'

'Ah – a white business shirt – black trousers – no tie.'

'Good girl. I'm on my way to collect you.'

'But perhaps you should stay at the hall with the children? I'll be okay to walk over there.'

'No, Flora, don't leave the house.'

'But the children —'

'The children are fine. If anyone's in danger, it's you, Floss, not these kids. Besides, there are adults galore here. Stay inside till I get to you.'

'Okay, thanks.'

Flora disconnected and stood, shaking. She was mad with herself for feeling so scared. Almost certainly, Oliver would wait till the concert was over before he tried to annoy her again. And by then, she would have Mitch's protection. Oliver was a singer, a performer. Deep down, she was confident he wouldn't try anything crazy at such a public event. He wasn't stupid.

But he sure as hell had the ability to spook her.

Deep breaths, come on. You'll be okay.

She checked her appearance in the hall mirror. She looked pale and stressed. Older. So different from the happy, excited girl who'd beamed at her reflection as she'd threaded in her festive earrings.

Bloody Oliver. She shouldn't let him wreck this evening. It was too special – a much anticipated highlight for Burralea. She mustn't let him rattle her. She pinched a little colour into her cheeks, forced a smile.

The doorbell rang and this time she peered through the stained-glass inset before opening the door. When she saw the blue of Mitch's uniform, she was hit by a sweet flood of relief. She flung the door wide and he opened his arms.

Oh, Mitch.

So good to sink into him, to feel his strong, capable arms around her, holding her safe. 'You're going to be okay,' he murmured, giving her a hug.

'I know.'

He kissed her forehead. 'I promise, Floss. I won't let the bastard near you again.'

She nodded, rested her head for a moment on his solid, comforting shoulder, and then stepped back, ever conscious of her need for restraint when she was with this guy.

'Right,' she said. 'I guess the children are waiting.'

Mitch's dark eyes shimmered with unexpected emotion, but he smiled. 'Yep, they're waiting. They're practically jumping put of their skins with excitement.'

She told herself this evening was going to be great. Fabulous.

'Floss . . .'

'Yes?'

'Thought you might like to know you look sensational.'

The shiny light in Mitch's eyes robbed her of breath.

*

The children were indeed waiting with eager impatience.

'Miss Flora!'

'She's here!'

'You look pretty, Miss Flora.'

Flora kept her smile carefully in place as she greeted the orchestra members and the choir kids who were dressed as shepherds and angels.

'Hello everyone,' she said brightly. 'How are you all? You look wonderful. Are you looking forward to this?'

Enthusiastic nodding ensued.

'Okay. Orchestra people can line up here,' Flora said, pointing. 'Strings first, then woodwind and brass. The stands are already set up. You know where you're supposed to sit. Do you all have your music? Is anyone missing?'

'Just Molly,' called one of the flute players.

'And Eddie's not here yet,' said someone else.

Molly was now their star flautist, and Eddie was to play the special trumpet fanfare that announced the arrival of the 'heavenly host'. Flora reminded herself to stay calm. Molly's mum was often running a bit late. She checked the time on her phone.

'Who was Eddie coming with?' she asked.

'I think his dad was supposed to be bringing him,' said Alistair, another of the trumpeters.

'No worries. We've got another few minutes before we need to start tuning.'

Flora looked out through the doorway to the stage area, which was set at one end of the big marquee. Bales of hay and a timber manger took centre place, with space at the back for the choir, and another area at the side set with the orchestra's chairs and music stands. Father Jonno had organised for one of the fathers to set up microphones, and the sound had worked well at the rehearsal. She could only hope it would reach all the rows of seats now filling with parents and siblings, grandparents and friends.

Flora looked to the other doorway at the back of the crowded
little hall. Father Jonno was just outside, talking to a couple of children in costume, presumably Mary and Joseph. She saw the flick of
a grey tail, a droopy ear. Goodness, with so much on her mind, she'd
almost forgotten about the donkey. Like Peg, she was rather concerned that an animal in this setting could spell disaster.

When did I become such a worrier?

The answer wasn't hard to guess.

Just in time, Molly arrived, running, flute case in hand, looking
flushed and apologetic.

'Mum said to say sorry. She was going to bring my baby brother,
but he's been teething again and he wouldn't stop crying, so we had
to take him out to Nan's place.'

'Poor little fellow,' said Flora. 'But you're here now, so that's
wonderful.' She showed the girl where to stow her music case and
where to line up.

Come on, Eddie.

The audience seats were filling fast. Soon there would be standing room only at the back. Peg, of course, had pride of place in the
front row, and there were many other familiar faces. By now, Flora
could recognise most of the parents, plus the woman from the post
office, the couple who ran the Burralea pharmacy, a family who
lived across the road from her cottage.

Hattie and Joe were there as well, and Alice, with little Charlie
on her lap. Seth hadn't been able to come – he was keeping watch
over a cow in labour.

Father Jonno appeared at her elbow. 'It's probably time for you
to get your orchestra set up,' he said. 'Are they all here?'

'All except one. The star trumpeter.'

Father Jonno's eyebrows shot high. 'Eddie? The boy who plays
the fanfare?'

'Yes.'

'Hmm. Do we have a contingency plan?'

'You could always send up a quick prayer,' Flora said with a cheeky smile.

'Oh, I will, don't worry, and I'm sure Eddie will turn up. But I might have to warn the angels, just in case, so they're prepared. We don't want them with their noses out of joint simply because they have to process without a fanfare.'

They both grinned. And Flora decided she was damned lucky to have guys like Mitch and Father Jonno on her side. Both men had the happy knack of calming her fears.

She signalled to her musicians to take up their positions. 'Okay, let's go.'

A burst of applause greeted them as she led the lines of excited children onto the stage.

The orchestra played 'O, Holy Night' and the donkey, without mishap, processed with Mary and Joseph down the hay-strewn aisle. The wonderfully bearded Joseph kept a firm hand on the animal's lead as he took his place beside the carefully swaddled baby doll in the manger.

Tea-towelled shepherds moved into place. The orchestra started up again and everyone, including the audience, sang 'While Shepherds Watched Their Flocks'.

All was going well. The angels, who were ready to process without their fanfare, almost squealed with excitement when Eddie arrived in the nick of time. He was a little out of breath from rushing, but he made a fair fist of his important fanfare, and the angels made their grand entry in gowns created from white sheets and wings of cardboard covered with cotton wool and silver stars.

Then it was time for Father Jonno's little sermon.

'Many of you kids are from farms,' he said. 'So I think it's probably easy for you to picture how tough it must have been for Mary and Joseph. Sure, they were in a completely different part of the world – but imagine if the Christmas story had happened here. We've been blessed with good weather tonight, but at this time of year, it could just as easily have been pouring with rain. There might have been a cyclone coming.

'Picture this – all the motels are full. Mary and Joseph are poor. They're refugees with nowhere to go and the only place available is down in Jimbo's milking shed. Mary has her baby in a pile of Rhodes grass hay.'

Kids were grinning. A few giggled. All were listening, entranced.

'And then,' Father Jonno continued, 'miraculously, the rain stops and it's all clear and the Southern Cross is high in the sky. Three princes turn up and announce —'

Flora didn't hear what came next. She glanced across the smiling audience and saw a tall blonde figure standing at the very back.

Wham!

She flinched. Oliver was there with his shoulders back, his arms crossed over his massive chest, watching her with a smile that was distinctly menacing.

She shot a frantic glance to Mitch who was also at the back of the audience, some distance from Oliver.

Mitch caught her eye and must have sensed her tension. He turned, surveying the crowd, and she knew the very instant he spotted Oliver. She saw the tightening of his jaw, the sudden caution in his gaze.

Father Jonno wound up his story with a message about loving one another.

It was time for Flora to conduct 'Silent Night'.

The children were waiting and watching her expectantly. The show had to continue, but she was acutely aware of Mitch moving quietly towards Oliver, weaving his way through the throng of people who were standing at the back. Somehow, she dragged her attention from the rear of the marquee and took her place in front of the orchestra, with her back to the audience.

As she did so, she saw, out of the corner of her eye, Mitch speaking to Oliver.

Please don't let him make a scene now.

In front of her, twenty children were poised, ready to play their favourite carol. To her left the nativity scene and the choir stood, expectant. Flora raised her arms and began to count them in. *One, two, three; one, two, three.*

The choir and the orchestra began beautifully on time and Flora willed herself to concentrate on the music. To her delight, the children remembered everything she'd taught them about intonation and timing, about volume and pitch. They performed the famous carol beautifully, and by the time they reached the end, she knew quite a few parents would be sniffling, surreptitiously wiping their eyes.

They were nearing the final phrase – 'sleep in heavenly peace' – when the kerfuffle broke out.

'Eeek!' screamed a frightened girl's voice.

This was followed by cries of, 'Oh, no!'

Flora desperately wanted to turn and look behind her, but the commotion wasn't coming from the back of the marquee. It seemed to be coming from the choir – from the angels.

'Miss Flora! The donkey's eating Tiffany's wing.'

Sure enough, a huge chunk had been bitten out of Tiffany Carmichael's left wing, and the donkey was merrily chewing the cardboard and preparing to take another big chomp.

By now, most of the children were either giggling or squealing – squealing with delight rather than fear – and there were titters coming from the audience. The final notes of 'Silent Night' were lost in all the fuss.

Fortunately, Father Jonno came to the rescue, stepping calmly forward and taking the donkey's lead from Joseph to shepherd the animal off stage.

With equal aplomb, the evening's narrator, a tall, red-headed Year Six boy, the son of a local vet, coolly stepped up to the mike and continued to tell the next instalment of the nativity story in a clear and steady voice.

The giggles settled down. The play continued. The Wise Men were about to arrive.

It was only as Flora resumed her seat that she allowed herself to check out the situation at the back of the audience, but by then, Oliver had disappeared.

'I warned him off,' Mitch said later.

Flora told herself there was no need to worry.

By now, the play was over and the children, Flora and Father Jonno had all taken their bows to enthusiastic applause. Peg had hobbled to her feet, with the aid of her wheelie walker, and had given a small speech of thanks, which had brought another round of applause.

Afterwards, happy, chattering families had lined up at the CWA's trestle tables where supper was being served: tea and scones with jam and cream, cans of lemonade and sarsaparilla, sausage rolls and slices of watermelon. Any minute now, Santa would arrive on the fire truck.

Meanwhile, Flora kept her eyes peeled, but so far she'd seen no further sign of Oliver.

'I suppose you recognised him from my description?' she said to Mitch.

'That, plus the fact that you went white as a sheet when you saw him.'

'Really? Was it that obvious?'

Mitch's smile was gentle. 'I was probably watching you more closely than most. I doubt anyone else noticed. Anyway, you didn't let Edmonds rattle you for more than a moment or two. You carried on like a trouper. That took courage, Floss. You were great.'

She was probably more warmed by Mitch's praise than was warranted. 'What did you say to him?' she asked.

'Asked him whether he was Oliver Edmonds.' Mitch shrugged. 'He reacted exactly the way those blokes always do. Got on his high horse and tried to lecture me about his rights.' Mitch's lip curled with distaste. 'He's so up himself. So sure he's cleverer than the rest of us.'

'But you obviously got rid of him. He took off.'

'Well, yeah . . . he started to bluster. Wanted to know if I was threatening him. I told him I wouldn't waste my breath on threats. If necessary, I made arrests.'

Flora's eyes widened.

'He badly wanted to call my bluff, but then he backed off. I suppose he wasn't expecting anyone to challenge him.'

'At least he didn't spoil the concert. I was imagining a brawl.'

'Well . . . to be honest, I wanted to sock it to the smug bastard.'

'I'm glad you didn't. Imagine the unholy row.' Flora's smile was fleeting. 'The only problem is, now Oliver must know that I've spoken to you, that I've dobbed on him.'

'Don't worry, it's all good, Flora. He thought he was safe, but he was caught out.'

Yes, but Flora couldn't help worrying. Oliver would want revenge for being caught out. 'I wonder where he is now,' she said.

'I saw him drive off. It looked like a hire car. I got the registration.'

At least that was something. But how far had Oliver gone? Would he come back during the night?

'Stop worrying,' Mitch told her, watching her face. 'I won't let him get near you.'

Flora wondered exactly how Mitch planned to protect her. When he didn't elaborate, she asked, bravely, 'Does that mean you'll stay at my place tonight?'

Mitch didn't miss a beat. 'Yeah, sure. All part of the service.'

Flora and Mitch were among the last to leave, having stayed back to help with stacking chairs and stowing props in the hall. At last all was in order, and they walked back to Flora's cottage under a night sky as clear and starry as a Christmas card.

Flora drew a deep breath. 'If I get the job in Brisbane, I'm going to miss this place and the fresh mountain air.'

'Nah,' said Mitch. 'You'll be too busy being a hot-shot muso. The last thing you'll want is peace and quiet.'

Flora wasn't so sure. This evening, despite Oliver's unnerving appearance, she'd felt embraced by the strong sense of community in Burralea. There'd been a massive feel-good factor to their humble little concert and it seemed to prove the old adage that the simple things in life really were the best.

She was wary, though, as she and Mitch turned into her street and saw the row of modest cottages, many already in darkness. She half-expected to see a car parked outside her cottage at the very end of the row. To her relief, the space was empty.

'Are you hungry?' she asked Mitch.

'Are you offering dinner?'

'I am, actually. I've made a lasagne.'

Mitch came to a dramatic halt in the middle of the road. 'Lasagne? Really?'

'I thought you might like it, being Italian and all.'

He shook his head. 'I don't simply *like* lasagne, Flora. I *lurve* lasagne. I adore lasagne.' He groaned theatrically. 'You know this means I might have to marry you.'

He was joking, of course, attempting banter to put her at ease, but as soon as the words left his mouth, Mitch looked as if he wished he could take them back. Flora could see his face clearly in the moonlight, and she knew he was reliving the pain of his disastrous wedding day.

Damn.

'I suggest you wait till you've tasted my version of lasagne before you make any rash promises,' she said lightly.

'Well, yeah, good advice.' Mitch resumed walking and tossed her a playful smile. 'Then again, if your lasagne's as good as your caramel —'

Now he stopped again, frowning, staring ahead.

Flora followed the direction of his gaze and her heart stilled. In the glow of a streetlight, she could see a huddled shape near her front steps. On the ground.

'Oh, God, Mitch.'

Already, he was racing ahead of her. Flora ran to catch up, and she was panting a little as she reached her gate. But she was breathless from horror as much as from the running. Poor Edith was there, on the grass, hunched and shivering.

Aghast, Flora dropped to her knees. 'Edith, what happened?'

Mitch was also kneeling beside the old lady, slipping an arm around her shaking shoulders.

Edith seemed dazed, and her face was stained with dirt and tears, but she was grateful as Mitch helped her into a more comfortable sitting position. 'Oh.' She winced. 'My shoulder.'

'Sorry,' Mitch said gently. 'Are you hurt anywhere else?'

'My leg,' Edith said. 'My bad knee. I think I twisted it.'

She looked up at them with round, frightened eyes. 'He pushed me. He was so rough. He pushed me out of his way, and he didn't care when I fell down. He didn't even try to help me.'

'Oh, I'm so sorry,' Flora said, taking her hand.

'He's not still here, is he?' asked Mitch.

Edith shook her head. 'He drove off.'

'Did you see the car?'

'Yes, it was white. A small sedan.'

'That's brilliant, Edith. You're a first-class witness.'

By now, Flora had found her key, and she pushed the door open and turned on the hall light. She wouldn't put it past Oliver to try to break in, but at least the house seemed to be just as she'd left it, so that was one good thing. Perhaps Edith had disturbed him before he could do any damage.

She grabbed cushions from a cane chair in the little front room and brought them back to Edith. 'Let's see if we can at least make you a bit more comfortable.'

'Thanks.'

They made a little seat for Edith on the bottom step, propped her against the railing, with a cushion beneath her knee and another at her back.

Once she was settled, Mitch asked, 'Did you manage to get a look at this fellow?'

'It was that blonde chap.' Edith frowned up at Flora. 'The big fellow. The same one who was here earlier. I heard a noise over here, you see. I knew you were at the children's concert, and I could see him snooping around, so I got my torch.' Her face collapsed and she was fighting tears. 'It was stupid of me, I suppose.'

'No, you were very brave.' Flora hugged her gently. She was so furious with Oliver she wanted to scream.

Mitch retrieved Edith's torch, which had rolled across the grass, then took out his phone. 'I'll call for an ambulance.'

The old woman looked worried. 'I don't need an ambulance.'

'You need a doctor to check you over,' Mitch told her. 'And I don't think we should try to shift you any more than we already have. Not when there's an ambulance ten minutes away.'

'What about a glass of water?' suggested Flora. 'Can I get you a drink, Edith?'

'I – yes, thanks.'

As Mitch spoke into his phone, giving instructions to the ambulance, Flora headed down the hall to the kitchen.

And that was when she screamed.

CHAPTER THIRTY-FIVE

Flora sagged against the kitchen door post, shaking, hardly daring to look.

Her beautiful violin was on the kitchen table. Smashed. Broken into countless pieces. Like a delicate bird crunched under car wheels.

She couldn't hold back her wretched scream of horror. This couldn't be true. It was a nightmare, surely? But when she closed her eyes and opened them again, her precious violin was still there, shattered, damaged beyond repair.

Oliver.

She slapped a hand to her mouth to cut off another agonised cry, but hot tears streamed down her cheeks.

Behind her, Mitch's footsteps pounded in the hall, then he came to a skidding halt beside her.

'Fuck.' He looked as stunned as Flora was. 'Sorry,' he said, 'but I don't really know what else to say.' He slipped an arm around her shoulders, drew her head against his bulky shoulder.

'I can't believe it,' she whispered.

Her violin was her most treasured possession. Only hours ago, she'd cleaned it carefully with a lint-free cloth, as she did after every practice, before wrapping it carefully in the silk shawl that had once been her grandmother's, then tucking it away in its case.

Now, the shawl lay in a green and silver puddle on the floor where Oliver had hurled it and the violin's delicate wooden body was demolished, the neck broken and hanging crookedly, the burst strings sticking up from the shattered bridge like bristles.

How could Oliver be so vindictive? So cruel?

Flora wanted to scream again. Scream with rage, with heartbreak.

Of course, Oliver knew exactly how important this violin was to her. An extension of herself. Her livelihood. Her life.

With a grim face, Mitch touched his fingertips to an exquisitely curved shard of varnished maple. 'I've spoken to Atherton and they're checking all the accommodation in the district.'

Even as he told her this, his phone rang. 'Right,' he said and he gave Flora the thumbs up. 'Thanks. I'll head straight over there.'

He disconnected. 'Edmonds is staying in a motel at Tolga. According to the manager, he's actually in the restaurant right now, stuffing his face.'

'You need to go.'

Mitch nodded. 'As soon as the ambulance arrives.'

Flora swiped at her tears. She'd been so scared Oliver might have come back to hurt her. Instead, his goal had been to ruin her audition dream, to make a mockery of her ambitions and the hours and hours of practice she'd put in over the past weeks.

Glass crunched under Mitch's shoes as he crossed the room, and she noticed that the window beside the back door was smashed.

'So that's how he got in,' Mitch said, fingering the broken glass with quiet contempt.

'He wants to ruin my career.'

'Don't let him,' Mitch said simply. His dark eyes flashed with concern. 'Is it crass to suggest you can get another violin? Was this one insured?'

It was almost like asking if her child was insured.

The year she'd been accepted into the Conservatorium, her parents had been through a bad season of prolonged drought. Their budget had been tight, but they'd taken out a loan to buy this violin for her. They'd even travelled to Brisbane with her while she made the all-important selection, testing dozens of instruments, both old and brand new, until she'd found the one that suited her perfectly. Her parents had wanted the best for her, or at least, the best they could afford at the time.

Flora didn't want a new violin now. It would take ages for her to get used to it, to be able to play at her best. She wanted this violin. She loved it. And Oliver knew that.

What a bastard. He'd found the very worst way to hurt her.

Mitch said, 'We should go back out to Edith.'

'Yes, of course. She'll be so worried.'

'The ambulance should be here soon. You should go to the hospital with her. That way you can keep each other company.'

Flora nodded. The last thing she wanted was to stay here alone. She grabbed a handful of tissues from a box on the counter and mopped at her face.

'I hate to abandon you,' said Mitch, 'but I'm dying to take this prick out of circulation.'

'Yes. Yes, do that.'

He slipped his arm around her shoulders again, gave her another reassuring squeeze, another kiss to her forehead.

Together, they went back down the hall to Edith.

* * *

Tolga was a tiny town just on the other side of Atherton, and driving there involved passing through a patch of dense rainforest that arched overhead, forming a tunnel.

As Mitch emerged from this and turned into the car park of the Flame Tree Motel, he could see the soft glow of the restaurant through plate-glass windows. Decades earlier, the owners had gone to quite a deal of trouble to give the place a touch of class with thick, dark carpet and maroon-and-silver striped wallpaper. Now the place was a little faded and dated, but discreet wall lights and candles in glass holders gave it an intimate ambience.

A scattering of diners chattered quietly, but Mitch recognised Edmonds straight away, sitting relaxed and alone at a table near the back wall. In front of him sat a half-eaten steak dinner, a bottle of red wine. Mitch watched him swilling a glass, holding it up to the light like a wine buff and taking an appreciative sniff.

Mitch's fists clenched. He itched to land a punch on that arrogant nose, but he kept his cool as he pushed the glass door open and headed inside.

Edmonds looked momentarily taken aback when he saw Mitch, but he quickly recovered. 'Sergeant,' he said coolly in his super-cultured voice. 'This is getting very close to harassment. I'm warning you not to overstep the mark.'

'*You're* warning *me*?' Mitch scoffed quietly. The guy's bluff and bluster were priceless.

'You fronted me at that children's concert, as if I was a criminal suspect.' Oliver spoke with his typical air of superiority, but his face had flushed bright red. 'I was simply watching my partner conduct her junior orchestra.'

Mitch shook his head. 'Flora Drummond had already told you she didn't want to see you.'

'Is that what she told you? A clever clogs like you must know there are two sides to every story, and I'm very familiar with Flora's habit of twisting the truth.'

'Is that so?'

'She's prone to excessive exaggeration.'

'Very interesting,' said Mitch. 'The only problem is, I've got a few straightforward facts – an old woman in hospital with several nasty injuries, and an obvious breaking and entering into Flora Drummond's house. Not to mention the destruction of a valuable violin.'

Edmonds stood abruptly, tossed his napkin aside and stepped forward, leaning menacingly closer till he was in Mitch's face. 'You can't link me to any of that. You can't touch me.'

'Oh, I can touch you, all right.' Mitch wasted no time grabbing Oliver's shoulder and spinning him round. 'And I'm arresting you,' he said, accompanying this statement with the clink of handcuffs.

Two middle-aged couples at a nearby table gaped at them, their jaws slack with obvious shock and curiosity.

Aware of the audience, Oliver thrust his chin high.

Mitch whispered fiercely in his ear, 'I suggest you come quietly.' And he kept a firm grip on his shoulder.

'This is outrageous,' Edmonds protested for the benefit of those watching. 'I demand a lawyer.'

'Of course you can have a lawyer.' Mitch steered him out, past the hovering motel manager, who was trying not to look too excited, through the doorway and into the parking lot.

'You'll also have your fingerprints taken,' he said. 'And you might be surprised by how quickly we can match them to prints at Flora Drummond's home. We'll take your mug shot, too. I daresay the injured pensioner who's now in hospital will be able to identify that pretty quickly, but don't worry, mate, we'll try to get your good side.'

Their footsteps crunched on gravel. At the car Mitch opened the back door. 'Get in.'

'Where are you taking me?'

'You'll spend tonight behind bars and tomorrow you'll meet our local magistrate. Believe me, she's very efficient.'

It was only then that Mitch realised the guy was shaking.

***

Edith was asleep by the time Mitch got back to the hospital. The doctor had been to see her, had examined her injured shoulder and her twisted knee, had tested her for concussion and listened to her heart.

The good news was that nothing was broken, but she was bruised and sore, and badly shocked. Given her age and elevated blood pressure and the fact that she lived alone, the doctor wanted her to stay in hospital overnight and possibly for another day or so.

Flora rather suspected that Edith was quite happy about this. After a lifetime of managing for herself, she would probably enjoy a little pampering.

When Mitch arrived, Flora was desperate to hear about Oliver.

'He's safely locked up,' was all he said when she asked where Oliver was now, and she couldn't bear to ask more.

'I rang Father Jonno,' Mitch said next. 'He's organised one of his parishioners to nail a sheet of plywood over your broken kitchen window.'

'Oh, that's wonderful, thanks. Wow, you've covered everything, Mitch.' Flora almost told him he was a hero, but she knew he would hate it. Instead, she said, 'I haven't told Seth about any of this yet.'

'Tomorrow's soon enough. He would only have a sleepless night.'

'Yes, that's what I decided.'

They left the hospital through heavy glass doors. The car park was empty now, the night air delightfully cool, and the moon was riding high as they climbed into the car.

'How about we go back to my place rather than yours?' Mitch said, as he fired the ignition.

Oh, yes, Flora thought, and she was filled with a deep sense of gratitude. She hadn't been looking forward to returning to the cottage tonight and confronting again the brutal evidence of Oliver's hatred.

'That would be perfect,' she told Mitch. 'But you'd miss out on the lasagne.'

'I grabbed a burger earlier and now I reckon I've passed the hungry stage.'

'Yeah, me too.' At the hospital she'd had tasteless coffee in a cardboard cup and a packet of potato crisps.

'And there's always tomorrow,' Mitch said.

Flora heard the smile in his voice and found that she was smiling too. Her world felt shattered. Invaded. Her dreams were in pieces, but the thought of spending more time with Mitch tomorrow could still make her smile. She settled into the passenger seat, let her head sink back and closed her eyes.

It had been a tumultuous, exhausting evening. First, Oliver's appearance on her doorstep, then the concert and the distressing discovery at the cottage, followed by hours of waiting at the hospital. During those hours, however, she'd had plenty of time to think.

She'd witnessed nurses and doctors rushing to an emergency behind a drawn curtain, she'd seen patients wreathed in bandages or being trundled out of surgery on trolleys, and she'd been able to view her own situation with a little more perspective.

A broken violin did not equate to a broken life. It was a distressing offence, the violent destruction of a beloved possession, but she should not view it as a personal tragedy.

She would get over this. She would. She must.

And now, driving through the night, knowing that she and Mitch were going back to his tractor-shed house, Flora felt a little more of the horror and sadness slip away.

She thought again about the concert. Joseph with his marvellous black beard. The donkey crunching a hole in the angel's wing. 'Silent Night'. . . the orchestra had played it so well . . .

And yet, the night had come within an inch of disaster. She should never have come back to Burralea. She should have known Oliver would —

Mitch's voice reached her. 'I hope you don't blame yourself for any of this.'

Flora opened her eyes. 'Oliver wouldn't have come here if I wasn't —'

'No, Floss, don't think that way. If you start blaming yourself, he still wins.'

'Yeah,' she said quietly. 'You're right.'

Flora looked out the car's side window, saw a small creature, possibly a bandicoot, scurrying out of the glare of the headlights and into the safety of long grass on the side of the road.

Then Mitch's voice again – quiet but steady. 'I know what it's like to blame yourself. I've been feeling like a prize idiot, believing in this wonderful vision of how life was going to be with Angie. It seemed like a perfect plan. A country cop and a country school teacher.'

'Two or three kids?' said Flora. 'Living in a place where everyone knew you?'

'Exactly.'

'With dogs, chickens and a veggie patch?'

Mitch nodded, let out a sigh.

Flora could imagine the huge appeal, especially for a guy like Mitch who'd never known normal family life. She wondered if he'd been more in love with the dream than the girl. It wasn't a question she could ask, of course.

'I still think Angie needs her head read,' she said gently. 'I can't believe she's got a better deal with Kevin.'

'Yeah, well . . .' Mitch turned to her, and in the lights from the dashboard she could see his wry smile. 'As they say . . . there's no accounting for taste.'

He turned off the main road onto the narrower strip that skimmed the ridge, and deep slopes fell away on either side of them.

'I know I was attracted to Oliver because he seemed so wonderfully confident,' Flora said, deciding it was only fair that she should reveal a little of her mistakes too. 'And then we had our music in common. That was a big deal, or at least it seemed important at first. And he certainly knew how to turn on the charm. I didn't realise his confidence was all a bluff, that underneath he was deeply insecure.'

Now, thinking about the wretched results of Oliver's insecurity, she felt her anger rise again. 'I still can't believe he could smash my violin like that. He's a singer, for God's sake. He works with musicians. He knows how we feel about our instruments.'

She screwed her face tight to stop a fresh rush of tears. Took a deep breath.

Mitch shot her a searching glance. 'You okay?'

'Yeah. Just bloody furious. He couldn't have cared less about my violin. He couldn't give a shit for its beauty or its history. None of that meant anything to him. He's a fucking fraud.'

'That's what makes those blokes so dangerous,' Mitch said quietly. And then, after a bit, 'I guess we've both learned a thing or two.'

'I guess.'

And yet . . . Flora was uncomfortably aware that where Mitch was concerned, she'd learned very little. Nothing, really. She was still as smitten as she'd been in her teens, still thought he was the hottest thing on two legs.

Luckily, he had no idea about her unhealthy obsession, but *cringe* – she was crazy to have agreed to come back to his house again.

They both fell silent as Mitch followed the track that led through the little patch of rainforest and then climbed the final hill to his house. Now, as he pulled up on the terrace, the moonlight spilled in a silvery flow over the tumbling hillsides. Somewhere in the distance a curlew let out its long, mournful cry.

The dogs hurried forward to greet Mitch. 'Hello, you pair.' He bent to scratch behind their ears. 'You're up late.'

When they were satisfied with the greeting and attention from their master, they turned to Flora, quietly inquisitive, their tails waving like plumes.

'You remember me, don't you, you beautiful things?' she stroked their silky black-and-white fur.

Mitch opened the back door and reached inside to turn on a light. Flora followed him into the house, and the dogs returned to their baskets by the back door.

She watched as Mitch fed them biscuits.

'Are you sure you're not hungry?' he asked her. 'Grilled cheese on toast and a glass of vino?'

As he asked this, he removed the belt that carried his gun holster and loosened a button at the top of his shirt. His dark hair glowed black as a crow's wing.

Flora wasn't hungry. She was feeling unexpectedly fragile, and what she really wanted was to have Mitch's arms around her again, his lips brushing her cheek. Well, actually, she would have liked his lips elsewhere, but even brotherly kisses from Mitch were better than nothing.

She had to remember to be sensible, though. Making a move on this guy once in her teens had been forgivable. Now, restraint was not only sensible, but compulsory.

She gave a slow shake of her head. 'I'm fine, thanks.'

Watching her, Mitch came a little closer. 'I'm really sorry about . . . tonight . . . about your violin.'

'Yeah . . . it was a horrible shock, but you're right. It's insured and I can always get another one.' Easier said than done, of course, but by now she'd almost convinced herself.

'Brave girl.' As Mitch said this, the look in his eyes was no longer gentle or brotherly.

A new awareness whispered over Flora's skin. Something had happened. Changed. Mitch's habitual wariness was gone. Now, unmistakable heat shimmered in his dark-brown Italian eyes. When a corner of his mouth tilted in another smile, she felt as if he'd reached inside her and plucked a string, sending vibrations deep and low.

Surely she was dreaming again.

Mitch wouldn't.

Even as she told herself this, he took an almost imperceptible step closer, and a hopeful demon whispered in Flora's ear that this was, quite possibly, the night when . . .

He *might.*

She found herself locked in his dark, gorgeous gaze, and she couldn't speak. The air in the kitchen crackled with so much tension – hers and his – she forgot to breathe.

Mitch.

She wanted to lean closer, but she didn't have to move. By now he was close enough to touch and every inch of her skin flamed with longing. Her thoughts raced ahead, willing him to lower his lips to hers, teasing her, tempting her —

Yes, please. She wanted his lips – seeking – taking everything, anything . . .

A beat passed, and just when she thought she might faint with wanting, Mitch slipped his arms around her waist, and she felt the heat of him through the fabric of her dress.

'Floss,' he whispered, and without the slightest hesitation or caution, he kissed her.

And all the fantasies Flora had ever entertained about being kissed by Mitch Cavello were suddenly eclipsed by the stunning reality. His kiss was sensational, astonishingly good, making her feel as if she'd never been kissed before, as if the two of them had just invented this brand-new fabulousness, starting slow and dreamy, and building in intimacy until she thought she might melt into a puddle in his arms.

It was only when they bumped against a wall that she realised they'd left the kitchen and were on their way to the bedroom. Now, Mitch stopped and drew her hard against him, his hands hot on her skin as they kissed and kissed.

When he slid her dress's zipper down, the ache of longing low inside her tightened and curled. She pulled his shirt free, undoing the buttons with an almost desperate urgency, sliding her hands over his smooth, hard chest.

At last.

She glided her palms over his wide shoulders that she'd admired for so long, nibble-kissed the line of his collarbone, pressed another kiss to the base of his neck. And when she looked into his eyes, she caught the hint of a smile, mingled with fire.

It seemed he wasn't going to send her away this time. Not at all. With an arm around her shoulders, Mitch led her to his bedroom, where starlight streamed through a high window, and he helped her out of her dress.

'Flora.' His face was in shadow, but she felt the trembling in his hands as he touched her, tracing the lacy edge of her knickers.

'I'm sorry,' she blurted suddenly, the unplanned apology bursting from her in a panicky rush. 'I'm sorry about that other time. I was so, so stupid. Too young. It was the craziest thing I've ever done and I cringe whenever I —'

'Ssh.' Mitch silenced her with a finger against her lips, and he followed this with an even more silencing kiss, a deep and skilful kiss. A thoroughly grown-up kiss of unmistakable possession. He was, most definitely, staking a claim, and there was no sign of a tremble this time when he touched her.

Restraint was a thing of the past. Flora gave herself up to splendour.

CHAPTER THIRTY-SIX

Out of habit Mitch woke at first light, while Flora slept on beside him, breathing softly. His bedroom was on the eastern side of the house where sunrise and dawn's birdsong woke him, rather than the annoying buzz of the alarm or his mobile phone. Now, the pale shimmer of morning gleamed through a high window, exposing the tangle of bedsheets, the smoothness of Flora's bare white shoulders and arms, the satiny spill of her dark hair.

He wanted to stare at her, to cherish each unique detail. The straight line of her nose, the pretty swell of her mouth, the sweet roundness of her soft, pink-tipped breasts. And he wanted to remember *everything* about this past night, to relive each amazing moment of making love with her.

The sweetness of Flora's warm, eager mouth, her lovely body, now familiar territory that he'd touched, caressed and kissed.

Incredibly, the memories brought tears. How crazy was that? Mitch had never felt so emotional about sex, so over-the-top happy and yet so rocked to the core.

How could he have guessed that making love with Flora would be so much hotter and sweeter, so much deeper and more meaningful than anything he'd ever known before?

Talk about chemistry.

But it wasn't just a matter of chemistry. What had happened here last night was beyond mere fireworks. Making love with Flora was dangerous, as dizzying as a high-speed car chase, and yet it was so much more than a mere meeting of flesh.

Mitch wasn't normally poetic, but last night he'd sensed a true mingling of kindred spirits, the sort of experience that changed a guy forever.

This morning the wonder lingered. He was stunned. Smitten. Addicted.

But now, in the clear light of dawn, he had to ask himself what the hell he'd been thinking. Hadn't he promised himself this would never happen? Hadn't he sworn on that night at Ruthven Downs, when he'd found Flora lying so temptingly naked in his bed, that she was out of bounds? Always?

Her destiny lay elsewhere. He'd known it then. And he knew it still. Starting something with her was crazy, and yet last night he'd lost it. She'd looked so sweet and sad and vulnerable, he'd wanted to give her his usual brotherly hug. Until he'd seen that look in her eyes, an invitation he'd no longer been able to resist.

Hell. Mitch got out of bed, slipped on a pair of boxers and strode to the far end of the room where a window offered a view of valleys filled with white mist.

Last night he'd found something that he'd been searching for all his life. Was it love? Perhaps, he wasn't sure. But the lonely boy who'd lost a mother too young, who'd lived with an emotionally distanced father, who'd become a man who'd habitually chosen women for all the wrong reasons, had finally experienced the special closeness that had always eluded him.

But it was also a closeness he wasn't entitled to. He'd crossed a forbidden line.

Hadn't he sensed, years ago, that it would be like this with Flora? Hadn't that secret knowledge been the true reason he'd kept his distance all these years? Even when he'd told himself that he'd been trying to protect her, or that he'd wanted to respect her family, even though he'd been dreaming about Flora for most of his adult life, hadn't he known it was futile?

She was a brilliant musician. Her destiny lay elsewhere.

Now it was time to cut through the romantic crap in his head and to face the sad truth that he'd given in to a highly dangerous temptation. Without considering the consequences. And, for fuck's sake, the timing couldn't have been worse. Flora was in a mess, in shock after her abusive ex had done his wretched best to wreck her career. And he, Mitch, had been dumped at the altar only a few weeks ago. He should have known better.

'You're worrying, aren't you?'

Flora's voice cut into his storming thoughts. She was still lying in bed, had barely moved, but her eyes were wide open, watching him.

She looked so beautiful lying there. Mitch swallowed and tried for nonchalance as he came back to stand by the bed. 'Why would I worry?' He smiled at her.

Flora smiled too, rolled onto her side and lay looking up at him. 'I wish I could read your mind.'

Not a good idea. Mitch lowered himself to sit on the edge of the mattress. 'I should warn you it's R-rated.'

This brought another smile, swiftly followed by a small frown. 'No, honestly, Mitch, I really wish I knew what you thought about – about this – about us.'

He swallowed uneasily. With other girls, pretty compliments tripped off his tongue quite effortlessly, but he didn't want to be glib with Flora, to skim over the layers of his emotions with an easy, one-size-fits-all response.

Problem was, if he tried to explain his complicated feelings, the words were bound to come out wrong. He'd send the wrong message. He needed time to get his head sorted.

'Seems to me, you're the one who's worrying,' he said, knowing it was a cop-out.

Flora didn't try to argue. 'Perhaps,' she said softly. 'But I'm trying to work out what happened to us. It wasn't just stress-relief sex, was it?'

'No.' He reached for her hand. 'No, Flora, it wasn't that. Last night was —' He swallowed. 'Is amazing the right word?'

'It'll do.' With a soft sigh, she rolled away and lay on her back, staring up at the ceiling, or perhaps at the window filled with daylight and the dancing branch of a rose gum.

'For me,' she said, 'it seemed like our bodies were telling each other all the things that we haven't dared to put into words.'

'You might be right,' Mitch said, knowing full well that she was dead right.

A small silence fell.

'Don't worry.' Flora reached for his hand, linked her fingers with his in a comforting, companionable kind of way. 'I'm not going to demand a postmortem.'

Shit. Now he'd just fallen another thousand miles deeper for her.

'Probably just as well,' he said as casually as he could. 'It's going to be full on today with the court hearing and everything.'

'Oh, God, yes.' Now Flora looked scared again.

Mitch's heart rocked. Reaching for her, he gathered her in, kissed her forehead, her nose, her eyelids. 'Don't worry, Floss. You don't have to be there.'

'No.'

She rubbed her cheek against his. Then she leaned back and smiled, although her pretty grey eyes were glistening a little too brightly as she traced her fingers over the rough beard on his jaw.

'Yeah, I know.' Mitch grimaced. 'I need a shave. A shave and coffee.'

'And breakfast?' she said hopefully. 'I'm starving.'

CHAPTER THIRTY-SEVEN

Edith's hospital room was crowded with both flowers and people when Hattie and Joe arrived. Joe had heard the news that the poor woman had been assaulted when he'd gone to the newsagent's first thing in the morning to pick up *The Australian* for Hattie.

'And apparently Flora Drummond's house was broken into as well,' Joe had reported. 'Some fellow from Victoria.'

'Oh, dear God.' Hattie was instantly plagued by guilt. 'Do you think it was that Oliver fellow? You know, the one who rang here pretending to be Flora's agent?'

Joe frowned. 'Perhaps. No one mentioned his name and I didn't think to ask.'

'I should go to see Flora. She's bound to be upset.'

'I doubt she'll be home,' Joe said. 'Word is, Ted Jensen patched up her broken kitchen window last night, but she wasn't staying at the cottage.'

'That's probably just as well. Oh, heavens, the poor girl. And poor Edith.'

To Hattie's relief, Joe put up no argument when she declared that she must visit Edith in hospital. On the way to Atherton, they called in at the Burralea rose farm and together they chose a cheerful bouquet in shades of red, pink, yellow and apricot.

They found Edith with her arm in a sling, but she looked rather flushed and excited as she sat up in bed, a crocheted bed jacket in a becoming shade of pink draped around her shoulders, supported by a bank of pillows and surrounded by flowers.

'I feel like a celebrity,' she said, looking overawed as she thanked them for their posy.

Father Jonno was there and he immediately offered his chair to Hattie. Flora was also among Edith's well-wishers, as well as the editor of the Burralea paper, who was introduced to Hattie as Finn Latimer. Another elderly woman, Gail, whom Hattie hadn't previously met, occupied the only other chair and was apparently a neighbour of Edith's.

Edith seemed quite overcome by all the fuss, especially when Finn Latimer announced that he wanted to take photos of her.

'Don't be ridiculous. You don't want a photo of me.'

'But that's why I'm here. You're a Local Hero,' Finn told her.

Edith went bright red. 'Hardly a hero.'

'You are. You did your level best to stop a criminal. It was an incredible feat. A little old lady standing up to Goliath.'

'He was big, but not that big.' As always, Edith was a stickler for accuracy.

'Oliver's nearly twice your size, Edith,' interposed Flora, who was looking rather pale and subdued.

'And as far as the *Burralea Bugle*'s concerned, that qualifies you for Local Hero status.' Finn Latimer had the kind of dark and brooding good looks that were totally transformed when he smiled, and now he bestowed a grin on Edith that sent her blushing to the roots of her straggly grey hair.

But her face quickly fell into her usual negative lines. 'I couldn't stop him from smashing Flora's violin.'

Hattie gasped, turned in horror to Flora. 'No, that can't be true.'

'I'm afraid so,' said Flora quietly.

'Not your violin. How could he?' Hattie was appalled. Flora's violin was beautiful. In Flora's gifted hands it was magical.

She couldn't bear to imagine that delicate wood smashed. The thought that someone could wilfully break it was sickening.

'It's okay,' Flora said, obviously sensing Hattie's distress. 'It was insured, so I'll be able to get another one.'

The girl didn't look very happy as she said this, and Hattie wasn't convinced. She, more than most, understood the almost mystical bond between musicians and their instruments. She knew how deeply her own father had loved his violin. Rudi had gone to great lengths to bring it with him when he'd fled from Russia to China and then later to New York. His violin had always seemed to be part of him, almost like a second soul.

Lily used to joke that Rudi's violin was like a mistress who would sulk if he didn't pay her enough attention. Joking aside, the instrument had always been regarded as a member of their family.

Hattie kept these thoughts to herself, of course. She didn't want to add to Flora's distress. Instead, she offered to fix Edith's hair for the photo.

'It will be hard for you with your arm in a sling.'

Edith thanked her shyly, and when Finn snapped a photo of her, with her hair combed off her face and Hattie's bunch of roses in her arms, she was smiling. No, she was beaming.

'It's a ripper of a photograph,' Finn told her.

And Edith, transformed by her rare but genuinely attractive smile, no longer looked plain.

* * *

'Now, are you sure you're okay?' Father Jonno asked Flora when he dropped her back at the cottage.

'Yes, I'm fine, thanks.' She felt she had to say this, even though she actually felt rather miserable. She couldn't stop thinking about Oliver's court hearing, which was being held in Atherton that morning. She felt quite sick about it, but Father Jonno had been wonderful about getting her broken window sorted, and she knew he had far more important responsibilities than trying to cheer her up. She wasn't even a churchgoer.

'You have my phone number,' he said. 'So, if there's anything at all, even if you just feel a bit down, give me a call.'

'Thank you.'

As Flora waved him off, she automatically looked towards Edith's front window, almost expecting to see the flicker of a curtain. There was no movement, of course.

She walked up the path, set the key in the cottage's front door lock and took a deep breath, bracing herself for what she would find inside. As she pushed the door open, she saw the hallway with its glowing, honey-toned timber floor, the white-painted stand with a mirror above it and the green glass bowl in which she'd floated scented white frangipani.

Everything looked the same, but Flora knew it was a false perception. Nothing was the same. Oliver was in court, her violin was shattered beyond repair, and she'd slept with Mitch.

In just a few short hours, her life had spun one-eighty degrees. She felt lost, disoriented, with no idea how to move forward.

One step at a time, perhaps?

In an anxious daze, she went down the hall to the kitchen where her dismembered violin still lay in a sorry mess on the table. She forced herself to pick up the pieces quickly, without tears, and to stow them in the velvet-lined case. *Like a coffin.* And she told herself, sensibly, that at least her bow hadn't been harmed.

A good-quality bow was almost as important as a good violin. As soon as Flora had been able to afford to do so, she'd invested in a gold-mounted Hill & Sons bow. So that was something to be glad about.

I'm a regular Pollyanna. This brought a rueful smile, and she went through to the kitchen, swept up the remaining pieces of broken glass and put them, wrapped in newspaper, into the dustbin.

With these two steps taken, she felt a little calmer. Next, she needed a shower. She went through to the bathroom, stripped off the black dress and turned on the taps. Standing under the steaming shower, she felt the tight muscles in her shoulders begin to relax. She lifted her face to the bracing pinpoint needles, relishing the heat of the water, the cleansing force of it.

Reaching for a shampoo bottle, she squeezed out a hefty dollop of scented gel and lathered up. Just like the old song, she would wash 'that man' right out of her hair . . .

Her phone rang while she was towelling herself dry. Clutching the towel around her, she ran to answer it.

Mitch's name showed in the caller ID. He'd been at the court hearing all morning, and now, her heart banged in her chest. 'Hello.'

'It's all over,' Mitch said. 'Edmonds pleaded guilty.'

Flora couldn't think of anything to say. She felt numb and sick as she slumped into a lounge chair. 'I – I guess that's good news then?'

'Yes, it's a good result, Flora.'

'How – how was Oliver?' It was ridiculous to feel guilty. She was the victim, not the perpetrator. In her head, she knew this, but she had been Oliver's girlfriend, and it was hard to shake off the feeling that she was somehow responsible for his destructive behaviour.

Baby Drumbeat, I've come a very long way to ask you very nicely for a chance to discuss this.

She squashed the unsettling memory. 'What happened?'

Patiently, Mitch explained that Oliver had engaged a lawyer,

Delicia Kingston from Cairns, who'd sensibly talked him out of a not-guilty plea. There was too much evidence stacked against him. His threats to Flora amounted to assault, and the charges were supported by Edith's description of him, not to mention the fact that his fingerprints were all over the kitchen and the violin case.

The lawyer had spoken for Oliver, reminding the court that he had a clean record and also claiming that he was extremely remorseful and under a lot of pressure after losing his contract as a high-profile opera singer, while also suffering the breakdown of his relationship.

'Don't take that bit to heart,' Mitch warned Flora as he reported this detail. 'His type always tries to blame the victim.'

Flora was grateful for the reminder.

'The magistrate gave him a tongue lashing about his vicious, uncaring behaviour,' Mitch said next. 'And the charges held – assault, breaking and entering, and wilful destruction of private property.'

She sat very still, her wet hair dripping onto her shoulders, as she clutched the phone in one hand and her towel with the other. 'Right. I – I see. So what happens now?'

'Edmonds copped a stiff fine, and he's been ordered to pay damages and to have no further contact with you.'

'But he won't go to jail?'

'No,' Mitch said carefully. 'Not for a first offence.'

So. Flora let out her breath, but the hoped-for relief didn't come. She still felt flat, downhearted.

'He looked pretty downbeat,' Mitch said, as if he sensed her reservations.

But would that be enough? She couldn't imagine Oliver meekly walking away and leaving her now. He would still want revenge for this humiliation, surely?

Flora had a sickening feeling that the court hearing was little more than applying a fresh coat of paint over graffiti, while she was left to spend the rest of her days looking over her shoulder, scared.

She shuddered. She had hoped to feel unburdened once the hearing was over, but now her future still seemed very bleak. Apart from worrying about Oliver, the prospect of finding a new violin and getting it ready for the audition on time loomed as daunting as climbing Mt Everest.

She wondered if she still had the heart for it.

It didn't help that Mitch was quite matter-of-fact and perfunctory, sounding like a policeman and not at all like the blissfully passionate lover she'd known last night.

'I'll ring Seth?' Mitch said next.

'Thanks. You might be able to calm him down. He was ready to commit murder when I rang him earlier this morning.'

'Yeah, I don't doubt it.' After a bit, Mitch asked, 'Are you okay, Floss?'

'Yes.'

'You don't sound okay.'

She rolled her eyes to the ceiling. How was she supposed to sound? 'I'll try harder, then.'

'Listen,' Mitch said more gently. 'There are things here I have to see to, but I should be able to get off early tonight. We're still on for that lasagne, aren't we?'

She'd forgotten about the lasagne. It was sitting in the fridge, covered in cling wrap. 'We are,' she said. 'Reheated lasagne and salad and a nice bottle of red.' It was something to look forward to. She remembered the way Mitch had joked about lasagne and marriage.

Had that light-hearted conversation really happened less than twenty-four hours ago? 'And can I expect your marriage proposal in return?'

After a beat that took, to Flora's ears, a shade too long, Mitch said, 'Sure.'

* * *

It was dusk when Mitch arrived at the cottage, having first detoured home to feed Midnight and Maggie, to shut the chickens away and to change into a T-shirt and jeans.

A welcoming scented candle burned in a pottery bowl on Flora's front step. The front door was open and he could hear jazz music playing inside, slow and bluesy. Then Flora came down the hallway, looking gorgeous in a sleeveless floral dress that hugged her slender curves.

She greeted him with a kiss, winding her arms around his neck and pressing close. He caught her scent, as fresh as a flower garden, just like her name, and it took all of his self-control to resist steering her to the couch and performing an encore of the previous night. But damn it, he had to be more sensible this evening, had to remember the realities of their situation.

'I know, I know,' Flora said, releasing him with a self-conscious smile. 'Lasagne comes first.'

Linking her hand with his, she led him to the kitchen where the table was set with a red-and-white checked cloth. Where had she found that? And the air was aromatic with the scents of tomatoes, oregano and basil. Mitch grinned and rubbed his stomach.

'It's an authentic Italian recipe,' she said. 'I found this fantastic blog on the internet written by an American chef who's living in Rome.'

'Lucky guy.'

'Yes, isn't he just? Have you been to Rome?'

'Not yet. I'd love to go.'

'Mmm. I'm actually nervous now, hoping this meal will live up to your expectations.'

'There's no such thing as a bad lasagne.'

'I hope you're right. Would you like a little wine first?'

'Will you join me?'

'Absolutely. I could really do with a drink tonight.'

Now that their greeting was over, Mitch thought Flora looked uncharacteristically pale and tense as she set wine glasses on the bench and unscrewed the cap from a bottle of shiraz.

'Flora,' he said quietly. 'It really is over. Edmonds is on his way back to Victoria.'

She looked up from the task of pouring the wine, her gaze sharp, unsmiling. 'But there are no guarantees that he'll stay there.'

'I guess not,' he admitted reluctantly and then he looked away, silently cursing, hating the limits of the law, the feeling of helplessness when he wanted so desperately to keep her safe. 'You could still take out an intervention order.'

Flora gave this a mere moment's consideration before she shook her head. 'That would mean taking Oliver to court again, and I reckon it would only make him angrier. A red rag to a bull.'

Unfortunately, Mitch knew from his own experience, that she was almost certainly right. Those orders had limitations.

'I suppose I can only hope that he might give up on me,' Flora said quietly as she handed Mitch a glass.

He nodded. 'And you should take all the usual precautions – change your phone number again, your passwords, go anonymous on Facebook.'

'Right.' She was kind enough not to remind him that those measures had already been in place and failed. With a solemn little smile, she held up her glass. 'Here's cheers, anyway.'

'Cheers.'

'And thanks for all – your help, Mitch.' She sat at the table and he took the chair opposite her.

The ruby-red wine was rich and subtle.

'Ah . . . that's perfect.' Mitch gave a appreciative sigh.

Flora's smile, however, remained a pale shadow of her usual sunny one, and Mitch feared that Oliver and the pressure to find a new violin weren't the only matters troubling her. He had an uneasy feeling it went deeper than that. Almost certainly last night was involved.

'I suppose you'll have to head south to find the right violin,' he said.

Flora nodded and looked pensive as she sipped her wine. 'Unfortunately, it's not just a simple matter of finding an instrument. Even when I find one I like, I'll still have to work damn hard to get used to the feel of it, to break it in.'

A tall order, he realised, especially with Christmas just around the corner.

'I thought I might be able to borrow Peg Fletcher's violin. I rang her not long after I spoke to you and she said she was happy to hand it over, if I was really stuck. But she swore that it wasn't good enough.' Flora twisted the stem of her wineglass. 'It was around lunchtime when we had that conversation, and then the weirdest thing happened this afternoon. I had a visit from Hattie – you, know, Hattie Macquarie.'

'Joe Matthews's friend? Sure.'

'I think she's actually moved in with Joe. I suspect it's all rather romantic.' Flora studiously kept her gaze lowered as she said this. 'Anyway, Hattie wanted to offer me a violin. It was her father's and it hasn't been played for a while, although her son played it after her father died, apparently. Her son's in America and he was studying music quite seriously for a while, but then he decided that IT was really his thing and he gave music away.'

'But Hattie brought the violin with her to Australia?'

'Yes.'

'It was very kind of her to think of you,' Mitch said.

'Yes, I know. I was so surprised.'

The world beyond the kitchen window was quite dark now.

'We should eat.' Flora got up, took a pair of padded oven mitts from a hook on the wall by the stove, and lifted the lasagne dish out of the oven. She set it on a tablemat, all golden-brown topping and oozing sauce beneath – and it looked and smelled sensational.

'Anything I can do?' Mitch asked.

'You're welcome to cut this up for me.' She slid a drawer open and made a selection. 'Here's a sharp knife.' She also handed him an egg slice for lifting out the pieces.

'The salad's ready,' she said, going to the fridge. 'I just need to add a little dressing.'

It was all very domesticated and pleasant. As the twilight deepened outside, Mitch managed to lift the mouth-watering layers of meat, cheese and pasta without any mishap, then he refilled their glasses. Flora lit a candle for the table. The background music pulsed warm, lazy jazz.

They sat opposite each other again and Flora helped herself to salad, but Mitch was too impatient. He had to taste the lasagne. Her eyes were wide as she sat with her fork poised, waiting for his verdict.

'Mmmmm. Oh, my God.'

'Is that oh, my God, good?'

'Oh, my God, the *best*. Honest, I'm not just saying that. The flavours, the texture. I reckon it's perfect.' Mitch grinned at her. '*Perfetto*.'

She smiled, revealing her enchanting dimple. 'I used Italian sausage meat and three kinds of cheese for the sauce.'

'Amazing. Well done.' Mitch half-expected Flora to add another joke about the expected marriage proposal, and he was guiltily relieved when she didn't. Right now, his feelings for her were as complicated as the Middle East.

He had a scary suspicion that he had, despite his best intentions,

fallen deeply in love with Flora. For weeks now, he hadn't stopped
thinking about her. He'd been ready to throw himself in the path of
Oliver Edmonds, to kill the bastard with his bare hands if necessary.
Now, he still wanted to protect Flora. And, after last night, he could
scarcely breathe for wanting her again.

Nevertheless, taking things further with Flora Drummond was
almost as irresponsible now as it had been when she was seventeen.
She was an amazingly talented musician and he was a country cop
who'd never realised his higher ambitions. Their futures lay in different directions, and he had no right to stand in the way of Flora's
goals.

'Do you think Hattie's violin is likely to be any good?' he asked
as he helped himself to the salad.

'At this point, I don't really know.' Flora gave a small shrug. 'But
there's a chance it could be quite amazing. Hattie said that her father
brought it out of Russia during the communist revolution back in
1917. He took it to China, to Shanghai, and then later to New York
where he played in the New York Philharmonic.'

'Wow.'

'I know. It's like, triple wow. He must have been a fantastic violinist.' She sounded excited enough about this amazing possibility,
but the excitement didn't quite show in her eyes.

'The violin's Italian,' she added. 'Not a Stradivarius or anything
outrageously famous and valuable, but it's probably quite lovely.'

'So you'll give it a go?' Mitch prompted.

'Well, yes, I think I should. As you said, it's very kind of Hattie
to offer something that means such a great deal to her.'

'I don't suppose she has it with her up here?'

'No, it's safely stowed away in her apartment in Brisbane. She
and Joe are going down there soon, for Christmas, so I should
probably go, too. I'm running out of time to get organised for this
audition, and even if the violin's in really good shape, it'll probably

need a few adjustments from a professional luthier before I could play it.'

'A luthier?'

'A person who crafts and repairs stringed instruments.'

'Right.'

They ate for a minute or two in silence. An inexplicably tense silence that took the edge off Mitch's enjoyment of the carefully prepared, delicious food.

Suddenly, Flora set down her knife and fork quite deliberately. 'Mitch?'

He frowned, sensing a change in her. 'Yes?'

'I don't have to go to Brisbane.'

'Of course you do.' His response was automatic, but when he looked up, he saw pain and disappointment, stark and unmistakable, clouding her lovely grey eyes.

'Is that what you want?' she asked in a small, tight voice. 'You want me to go away?'

Mitch swallowed to relieve the sudden constriction in his throat. 'Flora, I know you're probably scared still —'

She shook her head. 'I'm not talking about Oliver now. Forget about him for a moment. Take him out of the equation.'

'Right.' So this question was about *them*. Their relationship. Again, Mitch swallowed. 'Isn't – isn't the job in Brisbane exactly what you want? Another position in a good orchestra?'

Flora's mouth pulled out of shape as her attempted smile turned sad. 'I've been thinking that maybe the music isn't so important. Not if you —' Her lower lip quivered and she looked away, clearly unable to finish the sentence.

Oh, Flora. Mitch was struggling with his own emotions now. 'I can't ask you to give up your career.'

'Why not?'

A huge challenge lay in those two small words. Mitch almost

faltered, but he was sure it was important to hold firm, to stick to the path he knew was right. 'It's too much to ask of you. You're too talented.'

'There are plenty of talented people in the world. They're not all happy.'

She threw this at Mitch like a slap in the face and, for a moment, he could only sit, stunned. Was she right? By encouraging her to follow her God-given talent, was he condemning her to a lifetime of unhappiness? He knew that without her, his own chances of happiness would be slim, but how could he live with himself if he held her back?

'I could get a job like Peg's,' Flora said, driving her point home. 'I could teach. Peg says I have a knack for working with kids.'

'I'm sure you have.' The temptation to keep her by his side was huge, but Mitch was sure he had to hold firm to his plan. 'I don't think you've thought this through properly, Flora. So much has happened in such a short time. You're probably still in some kind of shock.'

'I'm in love, not shock.'

He almost lost it then, especially when he saw the bright sheen in her eyes. He almost leaped from his chair, hauled her into his arms. 'Floss.'

'Don't call me that. Not if you're going to send me away.'

'I'm not sending you away,' he said carefully. 'I'm letting you go. There's a subtle, but very important, difference.'

Silenced, Flora sat very still, blinking.

'You have an exceptional talent.' Mitch spoke with quiet, necessary determination. 'I don't need Peg Fletcher to tell me that, although she has, quite pointedly.'

'Has she?'

'On several occasions. She seemed to have it in her head that we might —' He stopped before he made things worse. Tried again. 'I've always known, ever since you were a kid, that you belonged in the stratosphere, way out of my league.'

To his dismay, Flora rose from her chair, slender and lovely in her flowery dress, her dark, purple-streaked hair gleaming. Rounding the table, she came to him, leaned down and kissed him.

'Poor Mitch.' Settling seductively onto his lap, she linked her arms around his neck, and kissed him again. Fragrant and sexy and as tempting as Eve.

'Flora.'

She rubbed her soft cheek against his day-old beard. 'What if I don't want to be in the stratosphere? What if your league feels like the perfect fit for me?'

Blood pounded in Mitch's loins, thundered in his ears. An inner voice screamed at him to give up the fight. How could he be so damn sure he was right?

He was drowning. Any minute now, he'd go under.

But he knew there were important questions to ask. Points to be made. Could he ever forgive himself if he kept Flora from exploring the true depth of her talent? Would she forgive him in six months' time, in a year's time, when she came to her senses and realised just how much she'd sacrificed?

'You've got to go.' His voice sounded alien, rough with emotion, but he forced himself to continue. 'If you give up now, it will look like a win for Oliver Edmonds. And Hattie's offering you an amazing opportunity and – I don't know – it almost feels as if destiny or Fate is at work here. Something bigger than us.'

She sat very still, her eyes huge and sad as she stared at him, but he could see that she recognised the truth in what he'd said.

She let out a heavy sigh. 'You're talking sense. I hate it, but I know you're right.'

Mitch kissed her very lightly on the lips. Or at least that was the intention, but somehow the kiss took a little longer than he'd planned.

When they finally pulled apart, Flora said, 'I'm in love with you, you know that, don't you?' And her eyes were too shiny again.

He wanted to tell her that he loved her too, that he had probably always loved her, that he always would love her. But she needed words that would set her free. His task now was to research the best way to keep her safe when she moved back south.

For the longest time, they sat, intimately close, not moving. Outside, it began to rain, pattering softly against the window.

'Make love to me, Mitch.' Flora trailed teasing kisses along his jaw.

Fuck. How was a guy supposed to resist? Every cell in him wanted to take her now. Sex, hot and hard, right here in the kitchen.

But there were a thousand reasons why they shouldn't. 'You know that's a very bad idea.'

'I don't care.' Flora rested her head on his shoulder, whispered close to his ear. 'Just do it anyway. I'll go to Brisbane. I won't fight you on that, but I need one last time with you.'

She was soft and sweet and alluring. She was Flora. Loyal, loving, clever Flora.

Mitch gave up the battle between his head and his heart. Scooping her into his arms, he carried her to the bedroom where a shaded lamp was lit, as if in readiness, and the double bed was freed of its crisp white quilt, which was neatly folded on a chair.

Little minx, he thought fondly. Flora had schemed for this. She'd always been as determined as she was sweet and sexy, and now, while evening settled into dark, silent night, Mitch made love to her. Slowly and tenderly, on cool, lavender-scented sheets. Kissing and caressing, drawing soft, needy sounds and moans from her, making each exquisite moment last and last. And when she clung to him, winding her legs around him, cleaving close and then closer, she climbed with him to the highest dizzying peak.

'Thank you,' she whispered afterwards, and he thought she

might cry, but she was bravely dry-eyed, and she made no protest as he dressed again, his heart quietly breaking.

He kissed her goodnight and she remained in the bed, alone, as he let himself out of the cottage and drove away, through the tiny town and out along dark, narrow country roads.

CHAPTER THIRTY-EIGHT

Hattie was secretly amazed by how easily she had settled into living with Joe. She wondered if Joe had gone out of his way to please her, although she thought it more likely that by their age, they'd both learned there was little point in squabbling over minor differences.

Joe had seemed to accept that she wasn't the same girl he'd known decades ago, that she was now more confident and opinionated. She knew they'd both made mental adjustments, and it helped that they really did have very similar tastes.

Lingering over breakfast had become a pleasant ritual. After rising early for a cuppa and a little gardening before the sun grew too hot, Hattie would come indoors to set the table and get everything ready, while Joe walked to the corner store to collect the paper.

After their muesli or eggs, they enjoyed toast and marmalade and a second cup of tea while they read the papers, sharing pages, sometimes reading interesting snippets of news aloud, musing over Hattie's favourite puzzle page.

On the day Edith's photo was featured on the front page of the *Burralea Bugle*, they forewent the gardening in lieu of packing for their departure to Brisbane on the following morning.

Joe came back with two copies of the *Bugle*. 'Just in case Edith misses it for some reason,' he told Hattie.

Hattie was pleased. 'That's very thoughtful of you. Although I think Edith's days of remaining a recluse might be behind her. That Edmonds fellow has dragged her into the limelight.'

'You never know, she could revert,' Joe said. 'Old habits die hard.'

Hattie moved to stand behind him, looking over his shoulder at the large photo of Edith under the heading 'Local Hero'. 'Oh, look at her. What a wonderful grin. I don't think I've ever seen her looking so happy.'

'Nor have I. Finn Latimer did a good job with that story.' Joe frowned, however, as he stabbed his finger at another story on the front page. 'I'm not so impressed with his efforts here.'

Hattie squinted. Without her reading glasses, she could just make out the headline: 'Kooringal Bones Mystery Solved'. Her heart gave an uncomfortable thump. 'What does it say? What's Finn done?'

'It's more what he hasn't done. You'd think he'd have the decency to tell us he was about to publish the coroner's findings. We were involved in the investigation, for heaven's sake. And the paper's a weekly. Even if he didn't want to mention it at the hospital the other day, he's had plenty of time for a phone call.'

'But is that worth getting in a stew about? I don't suppose editors make a habit of telling everyone about the stories they plan to print, even if they run a small paper in a country town.'

Joe scowled at her and continued to scowl at the paper as she went to the kettle that had come to the boil. She filled the teapot – teapots being a new habit she'd adopted, as a concession to Joe – and she brought the pot back to the table. 'So, what does the story say?'

'It says a bloody lot, that's what it does. The findings are all here on the front page and there's more inside. Finn's run extra material from the historians at the university in Townsville about what happened down there during the war.'

'That doesn't sound too bad.'

Joe shrugged. 'It's not bad, exactly.'

'But you're still upset?'

He sighed as he accepted the mug she handed him. 'The thing is, it all came flooding back, as soon as I saw those headlines. Gabriel. Margaret. My father. Sometimes I wish the bones had stayed buried.'

'But they were Gabriel's bones, Joe.'

'Yes, I know I'm being irrational.' Joe helped himself to a spoonful of sugar. 'And I know I was only a kid at the time, and I couldn't have done anything to stop what happened, but I've always felt sort of responsible. It's hard to explain.'

'You loved Gabriel. We both did.'

'Yes.'

'You loved your father and Margaret, too. And you hated not knowing what really happened.'

Across the table, Joe's troubled gaze met hers. 'I suppose a shrink would tell me I have some kind of suppressed guilt. I mean, you were dragged into it, too, and you weren't even family. You were there because of me. And now —' He gave the paper a shake. 'I just don't enjoy seeing it splashed all over these pages.'

'I do understand,' Hattie said. 'But I, for one, am very grateful the bones were found. Now, Gabriel can be properly laid to rest.' Hattie waited a beat before she added, 'And it brought us together again.'

At this, Joe stopped frowning. His face softened and a slow smile warmed his features. 'Touché. Good point.'

'So, can you pass me one of the papers so I can read the story?'

'Of course. Here.'

Hattie buttered a piece of toast and added locally made cumquat marmalade. Slipping her glasses on, she began to read, skimming the opening paragraphs that repeated what she already knew until she got to the crux of the matter.

> The coroner has ruled that the death was caused by a person or persons unknown, and the fatal injury was almost certainly a gunshot wound that severed the femoral artery.
>
> After the discovery of his dog tags at the grave site and assistance from US military records, the victim was identified as Gabriel Wright, a private in the United States Army, who had been stationed in Townsville. Previously, he had been recorded as a deserter, whereabouts unknown after May 22, 1942.
>
> The coroner made special mention of the important evidence provided by Mr Joe Matthews and Mrs Hattie Macquarie and the excellent groundwork undertaken in the local community by Sergeant Mitch Cavello. The coroner said the sergeant's response and follow-up to the discovery of the bones greatly assisted the crime-scene detectives in providing him with detailed information in a very timely manner.
>
> The coroner was unable to identify any individual who should be further investigated and the likelihood of charges being laid were 'remote in the extreme', especially as the death occurred over seventy years ago.

Hattie stopped reading, took off her glasses, and looked across the table to Joe.

'So, no one's being held responsible?'

Joe frowned. 'Have you read the reference to the American soldiers?'

'No, not yet.'

'It's on the next page. I've got it here. I'll read it out if you like.'

'All right.'

'"There is compelling evidence to suggest that the fatal gunshot was accidental. Forensics found traces of a wound dressing with the body, indicating that attempts were made to stop the bleeding. This was consistent with anecdotal reports that shots were fired by members of an American squad, most likely military police, who had somehow located Private Gabriel Wright on the property.

'"The coroner noted that Private Wright was a member of a segregated company of African-American army engineers engaged in building Kelso Airfield on the outskirts of Townsville during World War II."'

Joe looked up. 'This next bit is interesting. It explains a lot.'

'"Recent professional historical research strongly supports the view that African-American soldiers in this particular battalion staged an armed mutiny at Kelso Airfield in May 1942 over alleged repressive and racist treatment by white officers, and that shots were fired. Some records indicate that the US military had issued orders to shoot deserters."'

Again, Joe looked up from the page. 'Gabriel must have been terrified when the MPs turned up.'

'He thought he was going to be shot? That's why he ran away?'

'Sounds like it.' Joe continued reading. '"In this situation, it is likely that Private Gabriel Wright feared severe punishment by American military authorities. It's possible that through an encounter with Australian troops and a series of events on which I am not prepared to speculate, he ended up on the Tablelands property Kooringal, where he found sanctuary with the Matthews family."'

'Poor Gabriel.' Hattie sat very still, remembering. 'I wonder why the Americans buried him on Kooringal?'

'Good question. The Coroner says the MPs committed a serious breach of both civil and US military law.' He read from the paper again. '"By burying the body in a shallow grave and not reporting the shooting to their superiors, or facing up to the consequences of their involvement in Private Wright's death, these persons showed a callous disregard for life. This is a matter for further enquiries by United States authorities."'

'Well . . . at least there's been closure, if not justice,' Hattie said quietly.

'Yes.' Joe looked grim. 'The US Embassy in Canberra are giving their full cooperation. Gabriel's being treated as a casualty of World War II, and his remains are being repatriated to his family in Chicago with full military honours.'

'Oh, that's very good news,' said Hattie. 'Imagine how his family must feel. I suppose they must be Gabriel's brother's family. Remember how he used to tell us about his clever little brother, Robert?'

'Of course.'

'I wonder if Robert grew up to be as amazing as Gabriel hoped.'

'There's a bit more about the family inside,' Joe said. 'Under the editor's by-line. Seems the Embassy tracked down a niece.'

'Robert's daughter?' Hattie felt a little shiver. She was remembering the stories Gabriel used to tell them, sitting on the front steps at Kooringal. The way his eyes would shine in his big dark face as he told them about Chicago and Bronzeville, and about Robert.

'Just imagine how that poor family must have felt,' she said. 'Gabriel just disappeared during the war, labelled a deserter, and there was nothing in the army records to give them any comfort.' She blinked as tears filled her eyes, smiled a very wobbly smile. 'I'm so glad he's going home at last.'

Joe nodded and smiled bleakly.

'It's all because you remembered and you spoke up, Joe.'

He looked down at the paper, gave a small huff of surprise. 'I hadn't read this last bit. It seems Finn's been in email contact with this niece in Chicago, and she's planning to come over here to visit. She wants to see the place where Gabriel found sanctuary for a while.'

'Oh, that's perfect. Good for Finn. How can you be mad at him, Joe?'

'I hadn't read that before.' Now Joe's mouth worked and he looked close to tears too. 'You and I are probably the only people still alive who met Gabriel. We're certainly the only ones who can talk about how proud he was of this woman's father.'

'You will talk to her, won't you?'

Joe nodded. 'I will, yes.' He tapped at the paper with a shaky finger. 'Remember how damn nice Gabriel was? With that big smile, those jazzy dance steps?' He stopped, looked away, blinking. 'So full of life.' Joe's voice broke as he said this, and he tried for a smile, but instead, a tear slipped down his cheek.

Hattie hurried to hug him and for a moment they clung together. Remembering Gabriel. Smiling in spite of their tears.

When they released each other, Joe let out a little huff of breath, a small sigh, perhaps of relief. 'I hope I don't start blubbering, if we do meet,' he said.

'Of course you will, Joe. We'll all be crying, but they'll be good tears. Healing tears.'

* * *

It was evening. Hattie's and Joe's bags were packed, except for last-minute items like toothpaste, make-up and shaving gear, ready for the flight to Brisbane the next morning. It had been a busy few days, dealing with all the small things Hattie needed to attend to, but now the last was completed, all items crossed off.

During the day they had visited Edith, who already had a copy of the paper but was grateful that they'd thought of her.

'I'll cut out one picture for my scrapbook and keep the other intact,' Edith told them with a delighted smile. 'I still can't quite believe I've been in the paper. And on the front page.'

Edith was so entranced by her sudden fame, she hadn't read the bones story yet, which was a good thing. Hattie knew Joe wouldn't want to discuss it.

Edith's Christmas plans were also in place. She was going to spend the day with her neighbour Gail, so that was another worry Hattie could cross off her list.

Flora had also been in touch and in two days' time she would be flying to Brisbane as well, where Hattie would show her Rudi's violin. Meanwhile, Joe had driven to Mareeba to visit Janelle and to deliver Christmas presents to her family, and the subject of Hattie had been carefully avoided.

Now, as they settled in the lounge room with their books and their mugs of cocoa, Hattie on the sofa and Joe in his favourite armchair, Hattie looked forward to relaxing for an hour or two before bed.

Yesterday, she'd been quite engrossed in her novel, *When We Were Orphans*, which was mostly set in Shanghai. A scene set in this city's busy streets had brought back long-suppressed memories, and she'd found herself readily picturing the market tables loaded with vegetables, fish and meat. The mountains of artichokes, cabbage and bamboo shoots. The baskets of brown eggs. The poultry in bamboo cages and tanks of seawater with fresh seafood.

Last night those scenes had all seemed so vivid. She could picture the confusion of colours, hear the sounds, smell the mingling aromas of spice and earth and sweat. This evening, however, her attention wavered. She was conscious of a new vibe, a kind of restless excitement. No doubt it was caused by the prospect of their imminent journey, and the fact that once they arrived in Brisbane, she and Joe would go their separate ways – she to her apartment and he to his daughter Emma's, although Hattie had been invited to Emma's for Christmas Day.

Perhaps Joe was experiencing the same restlessness. Instead of becoming absorbed in his own book, he set it down with his mug and came to sit on the sofa beside Hattie.

'Can I interrupt you for a moment?' he asked.

'You're not interrupting,' she said. 'I hadn't got started. I don't think I'm in the mood for reading.'

'Good, then perhaps we can talk.'

'Of course. What about?'

Joe smiled. 'I thought we might talk about us. About our future.'

The thump in Hattie's chest was possibly her heart overreacting. 'All right,' she said cautiously.

'We probably should have talked about it before this.'

She nodded. She'd been waiting for Joe to bring this up. It hadn't been easy to wait, but Hattie had been determined to hold her tongue. After all, she was the one who'd invaded Joe's life. She knew he'd been pleased to have her company, but in terms of the future, she'd wanted to leave any next step to him.

Now she was nervous. How would she react if he asked her to stay in Brisbane? Not come back?

'Okay, I'm raising the subject now,' Joe said equably and then he gave another charming smile. 'And, without beating around the bush, I was hoping you might marry me.'

'Marry?' Hattie echoed faintly.

'Yes.'

She couldn't think of a response. She was too stunned.

'I know I don't really have the right to ask you a second time.' Joe reached for her hand, and she let him take it. The back of his hand was sun-tanned, covered in age spots and a smattering of white hair, but the shape of it was just as she remembered from when they were young. A long palm and even longer fingers. Gentle hands, despite the work-worn calluses. Gentle fingers.

The fluttering of a thousand wings filled her chest. Silly perhaps, but in the various scenarios she'd envisaged when she'd considered a future with Joe, she'd never entertained the possibility of marriage.

'You have a perfect right to ask,' she said shakily. 'But —' She stopped, searching for the right words.

'And I know it's a bit soon to be jumping in with a proposal,' he said. 'But at our age each day is precious, and I thought we've been very happy together these past few weeks. I certainly have been.'

'I've been happy, too. It's been wonderful.'

'I was hoping we might continue.'

'Yes, so was I.' Hattie flashed him a smile, but it felt rather strained. 'It's just – I'm not sure about marriage, Joe.'

'No?'

'I've already been married twice. A third time seems – unnecessary.'

'You're not worried about – what did they call it when we were young? Living in sin?'

'Not in the least. It's not the 1950s any more. And I think living together makes perfect sense at our age. We're too old to worry about what other people think.'

'Even our families?'

Perhaps she should have been more sensitive. 'Is that the issue, Joe? You don't want to upset Janelle?'

'It's not why I asked you to marry me.'

'I know my son Mark wouldn't mind who I lived with, as long as I was happy.'

'I'm sure that's how my Emma would feel too, and I wouldn't marry you just to please Janelle.' Joe looked down at their linked hands. 'I'm being entirely selfish.'

'I see.' Hattie looked at their hands too. So wrinkled and knobbly. She thought of the many times they'd held hands in the past – as children, when Joe helped her over stepping stones in the creek, as shy teenagers at their first high-school dance, as lovers engaged to be married.

'I love you, Hattie,' Joe said softly. 'I've always loved you. Finding you again has been a miracle I never dared to dream of. I don't deserve such happiness.'

Hattie leaned close and kissed him. 'Thank you,' she said. 'I'm immensely happy too. But wouldn't you like to just go on like this? Just being happy together?'

'Yes, we could. I just thought —' Joe stopped, heaved a deep, shuddering breath. 'The worst day of my life was the day I told you I couldn't marry you. I was so ashamed and heartbroken, and I know I hurt you, too. I've never forgiven myself, but I've hoped that you might forgive me.'

'I have, Joe.' She was glad she could assure him of this. That hurt had completely and finally healed when she'd learned how Joe had been duped into his marriage with Gloria. 'Of course I've forgiven you.'

He nodded and blinked hard. Gave a soft, shy little laugh. 'Maybe I'm a conservative old fogey, but it would mean so much to me if I could still marry you. Make vows in a church, keep the initial promise I made when I first proposed to you.'

Hattie pictured Burralea's little white wooden church, the site of her greatest youthful heartbreak. She remembered Joe standing so stiffly beside his frothy bride. The day had been as dreadful for him as it had been for her, and he'd paid a terrible price.

Really, there could only be one answer. Nestling close, with her head on his shoulder, she said. 'I'd love to marry you, Joe. Thank you.'

As soon as she told him this, she wondered why she'd ever hesitated.

CHAPTER THIRTY-NINE

When it was Flora's turn to travel to Brisbane, Alice drove her to Cairns airport. The journey took a bit over an hour, driving across the Tablelands through Tolga, on past coffee and avocado plantations to Mareeba, and then to Kuranda at the top of the range, before finally following a winding road down the rainforest-covered mountain to Cairns.

'It's no problem to take you,' Alice assured Flora. 'I need to go to Cairns anyhow for shopping.'

'Shopping for antiques?' Flora asked.

'Not today. I'm really looking forward to browsing in dress shops. It's ages since I've indulged in any clothes shopping. I'd love to find something new for Christmas, and I still have all the usual Christmas shopping to face.'

Christmas. Flora realised, somewhat guiltily, that she hadn't given any thought to shopping. There were some lovely gift shops on the Tablelands, but she'd left her run too late. Now she would have to try to find time for shopping while she was in Brisbane. She needed gifts for Alice and Seth and Charlie, but it would also be nice to bring back a little something for Edith and Peg, and Hattie of course. And she really needed to find a special gift for Kate and Brad Woods, who'd so kindly lent her their holiday cottage.

Then there was Mitch.

An unhappy little *clunk* in her chest sent her staring miserably at coffee trees flashing past, and she found herself remembering again the look in Mitch's eyes on that last night when he'd said goodbye.

'So what's the story with you and Mitch?' Alice asked, as if she could read Flora's mind.

Caught out, Flora pulled a face in a vain attempt to suggest she had no idea why Alice would ask such a question. 'There is no story.'

'Oh, come on, Flora. You two were so pally for a while there. It was lovely to watch you. There was practically steam coming off you the other night at the children's concert.'

Really? That obvious?

'And now Mitch is all withdrawn again, just like he was a few weeks back, and you're touchy.'

'I'm not touchy.'

Alice smiled a knowing *as if* look. 'I know you've had the awful business with Oliver to deal with, but it's more than that, isn't it?'

'Not really.' Flora liked Alice very much, but she couldn't bear to go into details about her relationship with Mitch. She would almost certainly get weepy. When Alice slid her a quick, searching glance, she was glad she was wearing sunglasses.

'I'm not going to pry,' Alice said more gently. 'But you remind me of myself a few months back. Not long after I first met Seth, we broke up and I was a mess. I was sure it was all over. I couldn't imagine us ever getting back together.'

Flora couldn't deny she was curious about the history of her brother's relationship with this lovely girl, but she didn't want to ask Alice about it. Any problems that Alice might have had with Seth could never be as huge as Flora's own problems with Mitch.

Besides, the unspoken rules of girl-to-girl confidences would require Flora to talk about her own issues in return for Alice's story, and sharing about Mitch was impossible. Flora's pain was too raw and confusing to bring out into the open.

To her relief, Alice didn't push the matter, but Flora could imagine her reporting back to Seth later.

I tried, Seth, honestly, but your sister was as tight-lipped as a razor clam.

For the rest of the trip they mostly talked about Charlie – the latest mischief he'd been up to, what he wanted for Christmas, the difficulty of timing Skype sessions with his mother in England – always in the evening when he was tired and not at his best – and how cute and excited he was going to be on Christmas Day.

Hattie had suggested that Flora should stay with her in her apartment in Brisbane. Naturally, Flora had been uncertain, not wanting to impose, but Hattie was so very warm and friendly, insisting that she would enjoy Flora's company, especially as Joe would be at his daughter's place. And in the end, Flora had gratefully accepted. She knew she would appreciate having company, too. So much better than a hotel room and being on her own, staring, unseeing, at a TV screen, while morbidly brooding over Mitch.

If all went well, she would only need to impose on Hattie for a night or two. It all depended on finding the right violin quickly – either Hattie's or one from a private store – and then, slight alterations might be required. Perhaps the fingerboard would need to be shaved a bit, or the soundpost adjusted. If she settled on an older violin, such as the one Hattie had so kindly offered, it would probably need a good, professional clean and polish, a new bridge and a new set of strings.

*

A two-hour flight and a short taxi ride from the airport through the city found Flora standing outside Hattie's apartment block. An intercom system was set in the wall beside huge glass sliding front doors. Hattie had warned Flora that she would need to punch in the apartment's number.

Flora did so, and immediately she heard Hattie's cheerful voice.

'Hello? Is that you, Flora?'

'Yes, just downstairs.'

'Wonderful, I'll let you in. Take the lift up to Level Seven.'

A buzzer sounded and the big glass doors slid open, admitting Flora to a spacious, grey-tiled foyer. Hitching her violin case over her shoulder, she wheeled her overnight bag, and found the lift, sped upwards and was greeted, a scant minute later, by a smiling Hattie.

'Hello, there.' Hattie gave her a kiss and a hug. 'I hope you had a good journey.'

'I did, thanks.' Flora looked back to the lift's polished stainless steel doors as they slid soundlessly shut once more. She grinned. 'This is all so high tech and urban, Hattie. It's hard to believe I was in a country town with not even a traffic light this morning.'

'I know. The contrast hit me, too.' Hattie led Flora down a hall-way to an open door. 'So here we are. This is my little place. My city pad, I suppose I should call it now. So, what about a cuppa?'

'I'd adore a cup of tea, thanks.'

'And something to eat? Or did you have lunch on the plane?'

'I did, actually. A rather soggy sandwich.'

'Yes, I'm afraid aeroplane food's not what it used to be. I can offer you soup, or a slice of shortbread. Or both?'

'Aren't you wonderful? Tea and shortbread would be perfect.'

Hattie's apartment was lovely, which didn't really surprise Flora – the elderly woman was always very smartly dressed – but it was also very modern, which she hadn't expected, with loads of glass and marvellous views over the Brisbane River to Southbank, where Flora's audition would be held, as well as views to the mountains in the west.

'How awesome for you to be in the heart of the city and still see a river and mountains,' Flora commented as they carried their mugs to a glass-topped outdoor table on the balcony.

'I chose this apartment because of the view of the hills. I've been lucky enough to enjoy some marvellous sunsets.'

Flora's thoughts flashed to Mitch's tractor shed with its similarly gorgeous views, and she felt a stab of loss so sharp and painful she almost groaned aloud. She couldn't bear to think of him alone on that hill each evening, with only his dogs and his chickens for company.

Stop it.

But she couldn't help it. She knew now that she was deeply, irrevocably, in love with the man. She had always been in love with him, and a few days ago she'd come within a hair's-breadth of insisting that she couldn't leave him. Ever.

I'm not sending you away. I'm letting you go. There's a subtle, but very important, difference.

Mitch had felt morally compelled to do the right thing, to push her towards the path he believed was best for her. Unfortunately, it was hard to argue with someone so quietly noble and brimming with common sense. Her desire to give everything up and to stay with him had seemed childish and impetuous by comparison, and she hated to feel that way around Mitch, as if she was still as foolish now as she'd been at seventeen.

So. The decision was made and here she was. Now she just had to forget romance and concentrate on her music. After all, music had always been her passion, and she knew that a lot of people, especially her parents, would be very disappointed if she abandoned it after so many years of hard work.

Also, she couldn't ignore the Oliver factor. Mitch was right about that as well. Oliver would be triumphant if he heard on the grapevine that she'd given up the violin. It was bad enough having the spectre of him still haunting her, scaring her. She couldn't let him enjoy that victory as well.

Flora realised, suddenly, that Hattie was speaking to her. 'I'm sorry,' she said. 'I was a bit sidetracked there. Very rude of me.'

'Not at all. You've had a lot on your plate over the last couple of days. So – would you like to see the violin now? Or would you like a rest first?'

Flora smiled at the notion of taking a rest in the middle of the day, but then she remembered her hostess's increasing years. 'What about you, Hattie? Would you like a rest?'

'Not really. I'm keen to see what you think of this instrument.'

'Right.' Flora smiled again, politely this time, to cover her sudden nervousness.

'Remember, though, there's no burden of expectation,' Hattie added, as they left the balcony and returned inside, shutting the doors to seal in the air conditioning. 'I totally understand that my father's elderly violin may not suit a modern young woman.'

'It's wonderful to have the chance to try it.'

Hattie went off to a small room that she used as an office. Flora stacked their mugs in the sink and then unpacked her bow, which she was tightening in readiness for playing when Hattie reappeared carrying a violin case.

'The case is fairly new, of course,' she said, placing it gently on the dining table and undoing the clips.

Flora held her breath, overcome by the significance of this moment. Hattie's violin had so much history, had been loved for at least a hundred years, probably much longer.

The lid was lifted and there it lay on a bed of moss-green velvet.

'Ohhh.' Flora couldn't hold back her excited gasp. The violin was beautiful. The golden brown of burnt sugar, old certainly, and with its original varnish, but at first glance, still in a very good state of preservation.

'Feel free to pick it up,' said Hattie.

Flora lifted it gently. 'I can't quite read the name of the maker.'

'I checked. It's Scarampella,' said Hattie. 'Have you heard of him?'

'Oh, my God, yes. His violins are incredibly valuable.'

'I have some paperwork about him along with the valuation papers.'

Overawed, Flora schooled herself to calm down as she studied the instrument carefully. It seemed to be in wonderfully good condition. Apart from a scratch in the varnish on the upper back, it was pretty much unblemished. There were no cracks or visible signs of repairs. No chips on the scroll, or the edges. Even the strings looked fine – fairly new in fact.

'It's beautiful,' she told Hattie. 'I'm a bit gobsmacked, to be honest.'

Hattie smiled. 'I can't wait to hear how it sounds.'

'Yes.' Everything depended on the sound.

Flora drew a deep breath, let it out slowly, then tucked the violin under her chin. First, she plucked the strings, testing the tuning. Adjustments were needed, and the pegs were a little stiff when she tried to turn them, but after a little bit of effort, she was satisfied. At last, she lifted the bow.

Fine hairs lifted on her arms as she touched it to the strings. *Oh, my!* She played open strings at first, then a little melody, a touch of Bach.

She knew. Straight away. She loved it. *Adored* it.

She played a series of arpeggios, exploring the various positions and string crossings, moving from major to minor tonalities to see and hear what it felt like under her fingers.

Then she tried the start of the Mozart concerto that she'd prepared so fastidiously.

The violin sounded fantastic, every bit as inspiring to play as it was to look at. The sound was very rich and clean – warm and enveloping, but with plenty of sparkle in the upper registers. The high reaches of the E were clear, sweet and musical – and everything in between was well-balanced. No weak points or wolfy notes.

Flora stopped playing and Hattie looked at her expectantly. Flora smiled.

'What do you think?' Hattie asked cautiously.

'It's absolutely brilliant, Hattie. Just so beautiful.'

'Oh, I'm so pleased.' A huge smile lit up her face. 'It sounded amazing to me. Does it – feel comfortable?'

'It feels a little different from what I'm used to, but not too much.' Flora tried a few bars from the Tchaikovsky concerto.

When she finished, she discovered that Hattie had lowered herself to a chair and was sitting with a hand pressed to her chest, her eyes sparkling with tears. 'It was almost as if he was still here,' she said softly.

'Your father?'

'Yes.'

'What was his name?'

'Rudi. Rudi Vastinov.'

As Flora set the violin back in its case, she thought of the story Hattie had told, of Rudi Vastinov escaping the Russian Revolution. Such a glamorous history, such a beautiful instrument – surely far too glamorous and illustrious for an ordinary girl from the North Queensland bush.

'Do you think you would like to use it?' Hattie asked.

'It would be an honour to play it,' Flora responded carefully. 'But are you sure, Hattie? I know it must be very valuable.'

'I had it valued in New York,' Hattie said quietly. 'But Flora, there's not much point in having a lovely instrument like that sitting around in a case when it could be making beautiful music. If you could make use of it, I'd be very happy.'

It was one of those occasions when words – any words – were completely inadequate. Flora went to Hattie and hugged her. They shared teary smiles and then they hugged again. Flora knew she was going to have to practise like crazy, but having such a beautiful instrument was the impetus she needed to refocus on the audition. On her career.

CHAPTER FORTY

Mitch was at the police station, up to his elbows in paperwork, when Seth rang.

'Sorry, mate,' Seth said. 'I should have rung earlier. Just wanted to check that you can join us for Christmas Day.'

Mitch grimaced. 'I've been rostered on for Christmas Day.'

'You're joking.'

'Someone's got to do it, Seth. I had Christmas off last year, if you remember.' Mitch had been lucky enough to spend the previous Christmas and several other Christmases before that with the Drummond family out at Ruthven Downs. Jackie Drummond had always put on a fantastic spread – turkey and ham, pudding and mince pies and all the trimmings.

Those feasts had been an eye-opener for Mitch, who'd been brought up on his father's rather spartan Christmas fare of tinned ham and KFC – before Mitch had taught himself how to cook.

'I'm afraid I can't swing it this year,' he told Seth.

'But you're the senior officer,' Seth protested.

'Yeah, but Jack, the constable, has three little kids. He really should be home for Christmas Day.'

Seth didn't try to argue with this. 'That's tough, mate.' He sounded genuinely disappointed. 'Could you at least make it out to Kooringal for lunch? It's going to be a quiet one this year with Mum and Dad still away overseas.'

Mitch didn't rush to answer. His social life was more complicated now that he'd stuffed things up with Seth's sister. Flora would be at Kooringal for Christmas, of course, and sitting across the lunch table from her wouldn't be exactly jolly ho, ho, ho.

'Flora's coming out on Christmas Eve and staying overnight,' Seth said as if he guessed the reason for Mitch's hesitation.

'Right.' Mitch hoped he sounded nonchalant. He knew Flora had already returned from Brisbane with a new violin. He'd seen her walking up to the hall to rehearse, and they'd waved to each other, but they'd made no attempt at closer contact. Which seemed prudent, although Mitch knew they couldn't avoid each other forever.

In actual fact, Christmas lunch with her family could provide a plausible 'safe' situation to interact with her again.

'Look, I'm sure I could manage lunch,' he said. 'Unless there's an emergency. Thanks for the invitation.'

'Good,' said Seth. 'That's great. We'll set a place for you and see you any time after twelve.'

'I'll certainly try to be there. Thank you.' Mitch hung up, took a deep breath and told himself he had this covered.

* * *

The days leading in to Christmas were sweltering. A monsoonal low settled over the Gulf of Carpentaria, and the whole of the far north suffered, desperate for relief from cooling rains. Cattle, dogs and chickens found whatever shade they could and were loath to move. Farmers pumped more and more water from Tinaroo Dam to keep their crops alive, and the water level sank dangerously low.

Even the normally lush rainforests of the Tablelands showed signs of heat stress, with tree ferns wilting, trailing their long, blackened fronds like widows' veils. The folk in Burralea who had birdbaths in their gardens woke to the noisy squabbling of currawongs, peewees and Torres Strait pigeons, all vying for the chance to bathe and to drink precious water.

Everyone complained about the heat. In Ben's bakery, at the post office, at the tiny supermarket, the weather was the main topic of conversation.

'But it's even worse down on the coast,' Tablelanders would tell each other, taking some consolation from this comparison. Everyone agreed that even a wet Christmas would be preferable to the prolonged heat and humidity.

Flora, doggedly practising in the church hall, had pushed all the windows and doors wide open and arranged two pedestal fans focused on her, but she still sweated, and she worried about the effects of the heat and humidity on Hattie's violin. She was beginning to wish that she'd rented out a studio apartment in Brisbane and holed up in there until the audition.

On the second intensely hot afternoon, Father Jonno popped his head around the door and instantly took pity on her.

'You need air conditioning,' he said as Flora mopped at her face, her neck and hands.

'The cottage doesn't have any,' she told him. Very few people in the mountains had air conditioning. The climate was normally so pleasant, it wasn't needed.

'Look, there's a little room attached to my office,' said Jonno. 'I think you should use it. It's a bit crowded with parish paraphernalia, but there'd be room for you and your music stand, and more to the point, it has AC.'

This sounded like heaven. 'But,' Flora felt obliged to protest, 'you won't want a violinist practising right next to you all day long.'

Jonno waved this aside. 'I'm not in the office all day long. I'm pretty busy with house calls and charity work at this time of year, and Diana's on leave. Anyway,' he smiled one of his charming, freckle-faced smiles, 'I like hearing you play. You never know, you might inspire me to lift the tone of my Christmas sermon.'

Flora didn't need much persuasion. 'Thanks so much, Jonno.'

'My pleasure.'

* * *

The rain finally arrived late on Christmas Eve, dumping a tropical downpour that went on through the night and into the next morning.

'Be careful what you wish for,' Mitch thought as he drove to work through grey sheets of driving rain with his windscreen wipers thrashing. Already the creeks were rising and culverts on the edges of the roads were half-filled with muddy water. When he reached town, the decorations on the plastic Christmas tree outside the pub drooped and dangled forlornly, and the gutters were awash.

Mitch's first task was to contact Counter Disaster to find out if there'd been any landslips or bridges that had already gone under. Roads might need to be closed. They didn't want a tragedy.

He was pulling up outside the police station, about to dash from his vehicle into the office, when he saw a pink umbrella bobbing about in Edith's front yard. What was she up to? Frowning, Mitch zipped up his rain jacket and headed down the footpath. 'Morning, Edith,' he called. 'Merry Christmas.'

Despite the umbrella and cumbersome, duck-yellow rubber clogs, Edith was quite drenched and bedraggled. She still had one arm in a sling and she was trying to search through shrubbery while she held the umbrella in her good hand.

'Oh, Sergeant Cavello.' She looked and sounded desperate.

'I can't find Geraldine.'

Terrific. A little old lady with a kitten lost in the rain. Christmas was getting better by the minute.

'How long's she been missing?' Mitch asked, dubiously scanning the dripping shrubbery in Edith's front garden and glancing up into the branches of the frangipani.

'No more than ten minutes. I opened the front door to check the weather and out she dashed. So foolish of me. I should have known better.'

Mitch looked back to her house. The front door was now shut. 'I hope you remembered to bring your door key with you.'

'Oh.' Edith's face fell. 'I was so worried about Geraldine, I forgot, and I forgot to use your door stopper, too.'

Rain was running under Mitch's collar. 'Edith, tell me your back door's open.'

'Why would I leave the back door open in all this rain?'

Why indeed? A wry chuckle escaped Mitch. He gave her garden another cursory glance. 'Listen, I'll pick your lock before we worry too much about the cat. You never know, she may come back by then. And anyway, you shouldn't be outside in this rain, Edith. This path is slippery. You don't want to risk another fall.'

She seemed to recognise the common sense of this. Rubber clogs squelching, she plodded back to the steps to watch him deal with her lock. As Mitch pushed the door open, he was greeted with a small meow.

Edith gasped. The kitten sat demurely on the mat in her hallway, as if baby mice wouldn't melt in her mouth.

'How did she get inside?'

'Must have ducked back when you weren't looking.' Before the rascally bundle of fur could dash away again, Mitch scooped her up in one hand. Then he took Edith by the elbow and guided her up the stairs. He closed the front door, wiped his feet on a coir mat just inside the door and took Edith's umbrella, closed it and waited patiently while she freed herself of her clogs.

He handed her the kitten. 'Where would you like me to hang this?' he asked, indicating the umbrella.

'Would you mind putting it on the back porch?'

'No problem.'

He went down the hall to the back of the small house, which was looking rather festive, mostly due to all the colourful Christmas cards arranged on the coffee table, on the TV cabinet, on the sideboard, pegged onto a string across a mirror, tucked into picture frames. Edith might not mix in Burralea social circles, but she was obviously a great Christmas correspondent.

'No more gadding about in the rain,' Mitch told her when he returned.

'I'm going over to Gail's later for lunch.'

'Lovely. Make sure you take your damn key.'

'Yes, Sergeant.' She gave him a sheepish smile.

'And I'd better get to work.'

'Work? On Christmas Day?'

'Yes, I'm on duty. That's why I'm here.'

'Does that mean you won't be seeing Flora for Christmas?'

Mitch did his best to ignore the sudden slug of regret. 'Flora's spending Christmas with her brother at Kooringal. I might duck over there for a half-hour or so. Depends on how many call-outs I get.'

'Hmm.' Edith was clearly unimpressed, and she eyed him steadily, her gaze accusing. 'What did you do to upset Flora?'

'I didn't upset her.' Justifiably outraged, Mitch glared back at the woman. 'It was that other fellow, Edmonds, if you remember.'

'I remember him all right, but there's more than one way to upset a young woman. Flora didn't care for that other chap the way she cares for you.'

Mitch gritted his teeth. The last thing he needed was an elderly spinster trying to tell him how to run his love life.

'Merry Christmas, Edith,' he said grimly, and he turned to leave.

'Merry Christmas, Sergeant, and thanks for your help.' Edith clutched the kitten to her chest, as he opened the door again. 'And be careful.'

'I will be.'

'Careful about Flora, I mean.'

'Edith, I don't think —'

She stopped him, raising her fat, wrinkled hand like a traffic cop. 'Just remember, all it takes is one silly mistake when you're young, and you can be left to live a long, lonely life with regrets.'

***

For Flora, Christmas Day was the slowest ever and it was no one's fault but her own. She told herself she was twitchy because she couldn't rehearse. On other days, the music would distract her, and she'd be driven by a strong sense of purpose. Today, she told herself to concentrate on others – that was what Christmas was about, after all – and those others should not include Mitch Cavello.

Despite the rain, there was plenty to enjoy. Seth and Alice were lively company, and Charlie's delightful excitement over unwrapping his gifts certainly provided plenty of entertainment. Tammy and Ben arrived mid-morning, laden with gifts and delectable goodies, and they reported that a couple of the lower-lying bridges on side roads were already under.

'I doubt we'll see Mitch,' said Ben. 'We caught up with him at Stoney Creek, and he reckons he's going to be too busy monitoring creek levels, putting up road signs and redirecting traffic.'

'Oh, poor Mitch.' Alice looked straight to Flora as she said this.

Flora sang a line from a song about a 'policeman's lot' in a flippant attempt to cover her deep disappointment.

'That's a bit callous.' Seth scowled at her.

'It was meant to be a joke.'

'Why joke about Mitch when he's out there in the rain, saving motorists?'

Flora drew a sharp breath of annoyance. She and Seth had always been able to needle each other, but she'd thought they'd grown out of it.

'Seth,' Alice intervened in a warning tone, sending him an admonishing scowl to match.

Fortunately, Charlie's squeals of excitement over the bright yellow cement mixer Tammy had brought managed to break the tension. After that, Flora forced a cheerful smile and accepted another glass of champagne. The rain didn't let up and their Christmas Day rolled slowly on. Minus Mitch.

Flora's girlfriend Ellen rang from Melbourne.

'Merry Christmas, Flora. I heard on the news that you're having a really wet one.'

'Yes,' Flora said. 'It's teeming here.'

'I think I can actually hear the rain all the way from Melbourne. Is that even possible?'

'Probably. It's making quite a racket on the tin roof.'

'Wow.'

'Anyway, we're fine,' Flora said. 'Safe and dry inside. Not like the poor cattle. Happy Christmas, Ells. Lovely to hear from you. Are you having a good day?'

'Lovely, thanks. It's bedlam here at Mum and Dad's, of course. My brother and sister are here with their families, so we've got kids running everywhere. My uncle's already two-thirds cut and Gran's in the corner, quietly slipping in a sly sherry when she thinks no one's watching.'

Flora grinned, imagining it all. 'Did you make it to any

pre-Christmas parties with our old gang?'

'Oh, sure. Actually, I wanted to tell you about last night. We went to Eau De Vie and it was great. Everyone was there and we really missed you, Flora.'

'What about Oliver? Did he turn up?' Flora had to ask. By now Ellen knew all about what had happened.

'He did. I couldn't believe it. I wanted to scratch his eyes out. Actually, Beth and I were so disgusted with him. He must have known we knew all about your violin and everything, but he carried on as if nothing had happened. Beth and I walked out, actually, and so did Dave. We were so mad, but apparently Amy hung around, and she rang me later and gave me all the latest goss. You'll love this, Flora —'

'What?'

'Oliver's scored a job.'

'Really?' A little flame of hope flared in Flora. 'A singing role?' If Oliver had a job, he might be distracted enough to ease off on stalking her.

'Yeah,' said Ellen excitedly. 'And you'll never guess where.'

Flora tried to guess but she was too simultaneously hopeful and scared she'd be disappointed that she couldn't think straight. Please, don't let it be in Brisbane. 'I haven't a clue,' she said. 'Just tell me.'

'He's got a gig on a cruise ship.'

Holy shit. 'You're joking.'

'No, I'm deadly serious. Amy swore it's definite. Oliver's resigned from his day job and he showed her the contract and the schedule. He's leaving on New Year's Eve. Sailing to the UK.'

'Oh, my God.'

'I know. It's incredible, isn't it?'

'Is he happy about it?' Flora had to ask. The job was, after all, something of a come-down for Oliver after singing with the Australian Opera.

'According to Amy, he's over the moon,' Ellen said. 'Putting a very positive spin on it. Sees himself as the star of the show, singing in the ship's ballroom every night.'

'Crooning,' Flora corrected.

'Well yeah, exactly. But no point in crushing his over-inflated ego.'

'Of course. He'll love being a star.' And no doubt the old ladies would all love him, too, Flora thought. Oliver could be very charming when it suited him. 'How long will the cruise last, I wonder?'

'Oh, don't worry. He won't be rushing back to Australia. He must have given them a great sales pitch or found a good agent. He's already lining up gigs in the UK, and cruises in the Mediterranean and the Caribbean.'

'Wow.' Flora hadn't realised she was shaking until now, but she was giddy with relief. This was the best possible news. Oliver would be gone. Out of the country.

She actually cried a little when she finished the phone call and shared the news with the others. Alice rushed to hug her and everyone else crowded round excitedly, cheering, patting her on the back, obviously thrilled for her.

'It's like a reversal of the old days,' Seth said with a wide grin. 'The Brits used to send their convicts out here and now we get to ship them back.'

Everyone laughed. Flora dried her eyes and accepted a restorative glass of wine. For the first time in weeks she felt a new lightness inside. If only she could have told Mitch.

It was late before they heard from him. By then, several neighbours had arrived to join the party, and Seth and Charlie had Skyped with Charlie's mother in England and talked about plans to visit her in March. A sleepy but protesting Charlie had been put into bed, and

Flora and Seth had spoken to their parents, who were now in New York City, spending an exciting white Christmas with Kate and Brad Woods and another Australian couple.

It was Seth who answered Mitch's call, and he reported back to the others. 'I'm afraid we won't be seeing Mitch tonight. There's been an accident on the road to Peeramon. Some young kid driving too fast in wet weather, completely missed a sharp turn and rolled his car. He's going to be okay, but he's totally stuffed up Mitch's Christmas.'

'That's such bad luck. The poor guy. Can't he still call in for a little supper and a Christmas nightcap?' Alice asked.

'Yeah, we'll soon cheer him up,' added Ben.

Seth shook his head. 'It's been a long day and he's knackered.'

Flora had a horrible feeling this was code for, *He wants to avoid any nonsense Flora might throw at him.*

The others made disappointed noises while she slipped away to Charlie's room to see if he'd settled to sleep. He hadn't, so she read him *The Very Hungry Caterpillar.*

Seth came in just as she was finishing the story for the second time. Charlie was almost asleep. Seth kissed the little boy, then he and Flora tiptoed out of the room.

'Thanks for that,' Seth said, after he'd closed Charlie's bedroom door.

'No probs. I love reading to him.'

Seth nodded, but he didn't move. He stood with his hands on his hips, watching Flora with his head to one side, his eyes narrowed.

'What?' she said. 'Why are you looking at me like that?'

'Because I know something's wrong.'

'Nothing's wrong. I'm fine.'

Seth gave a slow shake of his head. 'You're don't have to worry about that Oliver prick any more.'

'I know. It's wonderful.' She still had to pinch herself, but it was slowly sinking in.

'So maybe it's Mitch?'

Zap. Flora dropped her gaze lightning fast. She had to, even though it was a dead giveaway. She couldn't let Seth see how she really felt about Mitch.

From outside came a burst of laughter. Tammy was telling another of her funny stories.

'Floss, I know you used to be keen on Mitch when you were a kid.'

'So what?'

'So, if he's the one making you miserable —'

'It's not his fault, Seth. Butt out of it, please.'

Her brother continued to stare at her, like he was sizing her up.

Flora glared back at him. 'Don't you dare breathe a word to Mitch. This is none of your business.'

It felt like an age before Seth relented. 'Okay,' he said at last. 'But I don't like having to worry about you.'

'Then stop worrying. I'm fine. I'm going to Brisbane next week and with luck, after that, I'll be out of your hair.'

Seth let out a heavy sigh and Flora took pity on him. Stepping forward, she kissed his cheek.

'I'll be okay. Honestly. But thanks for caring.'

She was rewarded with a hug and a cautious smile.

On New Year's Eve, Flora received a text message from Mitch.

Where are you? I hope you enjoy tonight. Such good news that OE is shipping out of Oz. Happy New Year. XX

She felt immediately guilty. She'd deliberately chosen to leave Burralea on New Year's Eve, because she couldn't bear to spend another festive celebration miserably alone. She texted back:

Thanks. Off to Brisbane today. Audition on Tuesday. Happy New Year. X

Mitch rang her straight away, and Flora stared at his name on her phone's screen, torn between desperately needing to answer it and knowing she'd be a mess if she did. She pictured his face, his dark eyes, his square, grainy jaw. His sexy lips. At the last moment, she pressed to connect.

'Hey, Floss.' His voice was deep and husky, sending sweet shivers over her arms.

'Hi, Mitch.'

'Just ringing to wish you all the best for the audition.'

'Thanks.'

'So you're heading down to Cairns?'

'I'm already down here. Seth and Alice dropped me off. They're staying down here tonight for the fireworks.'

'Right.' Mitch sounded subdued. Cautious. 'Jonno tells me the new violin's sounding great.'

'It is. It's fantastic. I'm feeling so lucky.'

'I'm sure you'll do well. You'll ace the audition.'

'I'll do my best.' The only way Flora could cope with this conversation was to talk to Mitch like he was someone else – *anyone* else making a polite enquiry. 'I have a rehearsal with the orchestra's pianist on Monday.'

'All the best for that. What should I say? Break a leg?'

'Yep, that'll do just fine. Thanks, Mitch.'

'Will you be staying with Hattie?'

'Yes, she insisted. Joe's back in Burralea, but Hattie stayed on in Brisbane especially. She's been so good to me.'

'Good for her. It's great that you don't have to worry about Edmonds now, but I'm still glad you won't be on your own.'

Don't be nice to me, Mitch.

'What time on Tuesday?' he asked next.

'The audition? Ten-thirty.'

'I'll be thinking of you.' He said this softly. With too much feeling.

Oh, Mitch. Standing in the departure terminal, surrounded by happy travellers, Flora felt her face crumple. She couldn't do this. She didn't want to give him up.

'They're calling my flight,' she lied, her voice clogged and squeaky with emotion. 'I've got to go.'

'Okay. All the best, Flora.'

'Thanks.'

'Happy New Year.'

'You, too. I hope it's the best year ever for you.'

When she disconnected, she went straight to the Ladies, to hide in a cubicle while she mopped at her face. She was still red-eyed twenty minutes later when her flight was called.

CHAPTER FORTY-ONE

Hattie's apartment was wonderfully convenient, and on the day of the audition Flora was able to simply walk across the Goodwill Bridge to the Southbank studios next to the Queensland Conservatorium.

She was remarkably calm. Once or twice over the past few days, she'd worried that she wasn't hungry enough for this job, but then she'd told herself that her calmness was due to Hattie's steadying influence. Her hostess really was incredibly accommodating, and she hadn't minded in the least that Flora still wanted to practise.

'It doesn't bother me at all,' Hattie had said. 'I've listened to my father and my son practise for hours, so it takes me back. And don't worry about the neighbours. These apartments are quite sound-proof, especially when they're closed up with the air conditioning going. So just treat this place as if it's your own.'

Despite these reassurances, Flora had kept the practice to a minimum. She'd already put in many, many hours to work up the new violin. Now, in the final few days before the audition, she just wanted to keep in touch with her prepared pieces without wearying herself or boring herself to death.

Her nerves kicked in finally when she arrived at the studios and gave her name at the desk to a rather officious young blonde woman, who showed her to a long, empty room set aside as a warm-up space. At the far end of the room, another young woman, tall and thin and with flaming red hair, was already practising, impressively whizzing up and down the scales.

Flora's stomach tightened. This was it. It seemed she really was nervous, after all, and it was time to remember all her calming techniques. Deep, slow breathing. Visualising a perfect performance. And her favourite comforting thought – from a dinnertime conversation with her dad all those years ago . . .

So you wouldn't mind if I wanted to play in an orchestra?

Why would I mind, love? I'd be proud as punch.

The other girl stopped playing, turned to Flora and smiled. Beneath her glowing halo of hair, her smile was friendly and warm, yet endearingly shy. 'A fellow victim,' she called.

'Yes.'

They walked towards each other, met in the middle of the room. 'Hi,' the girl said. 'I'm Victoria.'

'I'm Flora. Hi.'

'How are you feeling?' Victoria asked.

'Not too bad. A little sick in the stomach.'

'I thought I was going to throw up before.'

'Oh, no. You'll be fine. You're sounding great. Would you like a glucose tablet? They can help to calm your stomach.'

'I would, actually. That'd be great, thanks.'

Flora fetched her handbag, snapped a tablet from a foil pack and dropped it into Victoria's slender hand.

'Thanks so much. I keep trying to tell myself this isn't life and death. There are always other jobs.'

'That's true.'

'And teaching's a good fallback.'

'Yes.' Flora had never seriously considered teaching until recently. She'd actually tried to sound out Peg Fletcher, wondering if she might be retiring soon – meanwhile, picturing an idyllic life for herself with Mitch in Burralea – but her old teacher had given her an earful about not burying herself in a country town when she had so much talent.

Yikes. She wasn't supposed to think about any of that now. Today she had to blank Mitch from her mind. 'Well, break a leg,' she told Victoria. 'I guess I'd better warm up.'

'Sure. Thanks for this.' Victoria popped the glucose tablet into her mouth, and almost like boxers in a ring, they returned to their corners.

Flora drew a deep breath and undid the violin case. She tightened her bow, checked the violin's strings, then carefully began to tune. She wouldn't play any of her pieces now. She would begin with arpeggios, using extra-slow bowing to control any shaking from adrenaline. Then scales, trying out different bowing.

And again she conjured her father's gentle, loving smile.

Why would I mind, love? I'd be proud as punch.

***

Hattie was taking a quiche from the oven when she heard the key turning in the apartment's front door lock, signalling that Flora was back.

It was silly to be nervous, but she couldn't help caring about Flora. The girl had been working so incredibly hard for weeks, and Hattie really wanted her to succeed.

Footsteps sounded in the hall, and Hattie set the quiche on a mat, took a deep, steadying breath, remembering times in the past when she'd waited for her son, Mark, to come home after he'd sat for important exams. Mark had always been easy to read, and

Hattie had usually known at first glance whether he was pleased or disappointed with his efforts.

The footsteps stopped. Flora had gone into her bedroom, probably to put the violin away before she came through to the kitchen. Was that a bad sign? If Flora was really pleased with herself, wouldn't she have come straight into the kitchen, flushed and triumphant? Or at the very least, relieved?

Hattie practised smiling. Whatever Flora's mood, they should have a glass of wine with lunch, a small celebration after all her hard work.

She was tossing the salad when Flora rounded the corner. 'Ah,' she said, holding onto her smile. 'So —'

'So you can relax, Hattie. It all went very smoothly.'

'Oh!' It was only then Hattie realised how very tense she'd been. 'That's wonderful. I'm so pleased.'

'Yes, it's good to have that behind me.'

'And you were happy with the violin?'

'It was fabulous. I was ridiculously happy with everything. As soon as I went in there, I felt uncannily calm and together.'

'It's because you practised so hard.'

'Perhaps, but I was surprised it went so well.' Flora almost looked guilty as she gave a small shrug. 'Even when it came to the Tchaikovsky, I played all the tricky bits just the way I wanted to.' She gave a puzzled little smile. 'Why wasn't I nervous?'

Hattie laughed. 'I'm sure it's better to be ultra calm than overly nervous.'

'You're probably right. I guess I'm just hard to please.' Flora turned her attention to the meal Hattie had prepared. 'Wow! Look at this. Is the quiche for our lunch?'

'Yes, it's mushroom and asparagus. I hope you like it. I thought you deserved wine as well. A small celebration.'

'Hattie, you're such a sweetheart.'

To Hattie's surprise, Flora opened her arms wide and gave her a lovely big hug.

It was rather hot on the balcony in the middle of the day, so they ate inside. Flora was a model guest and made rapturous noises about the quiche, but Hattie sensed, after a while, that the girl wasn't quite as happy as she'd first made out.

Perhaps she was just tense now about waiting to hear the results of the audition, which was perfectly understandable.

'When should you know if you've got the job?' she asked.

Flora shrugged. 'Not for a day or two. There are more auditions scheduled for tomorrow.'

'So I guess the trick is to find pleasant things to do in the meantime. Perhaps you'd like to catch up on a movie or two.'

'Yes, there are a couple of new releases I wouldn't mind seeing. But Hattie, I'll feel bad if you're hanging around here just to keep me company.'

'Oh, don't worry about it. Joe doesn't mind, if that's what you're thinking. I'm guessing it probably suits him to have a little time to himself.' In a more confiding tone, she added, 'He needs time to talk his daughter in Mareeba around to accepting me as part of the family.'

'Part of the family?' Flora's eyes widened. 'Does that mean —? Are you and Joe —?'

Hattie couldn't rein in her happy smile. 'We're going to be married next month. It'll be my third marriage, and it's rather late in the day, but why not?'

'How fantastic.' Flora raised her glass. 'That's so awesome, Hattie. I have to drink a toast to you and Joe.'

They clinked glasses and sipped the cool crisp wine, and Hattie couldn't help feeling pleased. It was gratifying to have their news so well received. Joe's daughter Emma had been similarly enthusiastic, and Mark had been mildly amused, but completely accepting.

'Where are you going to live?' Flora asked.

'Oh, in Burralea. I couldn't imagine Joe ever leaving the north, but I'll keep this place, too. We'll come down here every so often to visit Joe's daughter.' With a wink, she added, 'Maybe catch a symphony concert.'

Hattie was so pleased and relaxed now that she almost missed the sudden shadow that flitted over Flora's face. But there it was – just for a moment – a flash of unmistakable pain in Flora's eyes, and in the downward, sad tilt of her mouth.

'Flora.'

Flora swallowed, opened her eyes wide and set her mouth in a strange little smile, as if she were forcing herself, unsuccessfully, to look bright and upbeat.

'Flora, is everything all right?'

'Of course. Why?'

'I don't know,' Hattie said, which was true, and yet she'd sensed that Flora had been flat ever since her return from the audition. The girl had put on a cheerful enough face, but the only time she'd looked genuinely happy was when she'd heard about Hattie and Joe's impending marriage, and then the joy had only been fleeting. 'I just thought you seemed a bit —'

'I'm all right, Hattie.'

Hattie nodded. 'I suppose it would be normal to feel a sort of anticlimax now.'

'Yes, and I'm probably tired.'

'I'm sure you must be,' Hattie said cautiously. 'But if there *was* anything you wanted to talk about —'

Flora fiddled with the stem of her wineglass. 'Like how I almost hope I don't get this job?'

'Well, no, I didn't —' Hattie stopped and stared at her. 'You can't mean that, surely?'

Flora shrugged, looked away.

'Why wouldn't you want the position?' Hattie asked. 'After all those hours of practice?' But almost immediately she guessed the answer to her own question. 'Does this have anything to do with that rather toothsome young Sergeant Cavello?'

Flora rolled her eyes. 'I should have known you'd see through me.'

'Oh, dear.' With a soft sigh, Hattie excused herself and went to the fridge, collected the wine bottle and topped up Flora's wineglass. 'So, I'm guessing,' she said as she sat down once again, 'that you may have to choose between Sergeant Cavello at Burralea and the Queensland Symphony Orchestra.'

'In a nutshell.'

'Oh, Flora, you do have my sympathy.'

'Thanks.'

Hattie wished she felt wiser. 'At my advanced age, I suppose I should be able to offer you all sorts of good advice, but matters of the heart are so intensely personal. No one else can know how you feel.'

'I guess. But if you have any advice, I'm all ears.'

Hattie considered this. She wanted to help, and she was certainly well versed in the pain that love could bring, as well as the difficult, heart-rending decisions that often came with falling deeply in love. She watched Flora's earnest, troubled face and her heart went out to her.

She thought of Joe's terrible dilemma, and the choice he'd made between the girl he loved and the girl he'd believed he'd made pregnant. She thought of the distressing choice that Lily, her own mother, had been forced to make in war-torn Shanghai, between keeping her child and keeping the man she loved.

'Falling in love often requires very difficult choices, Flora. Although telling you that doesn't help you, I know.'

'The thing is,' Flora said, 'I haven't just fallen in love with Mitch recently. I've known him for years. I was seventeen when he first came to work for my father, and I had an instant crush on him then. I made a bit of a fool of myself, actually.'

'But then you went away to study music and to start your career.'

'Yes, and I dated other guys, and they weren't all as bad as Bloody Oliver.' Flora stopped, pressed her lips together tightly.

'But you believe Mitch really is The One,' suggested Hattie gently. 'And there are no symphony orchestras in Burralea.'

Flora nodded, then closed her eyes and screwed up her face, as if thinking about this was just too painful and difficult.

And of course it was, Hattie thought. Very difficult. Decision-making often came with a huge burden, and the task of making the right choice was especially hard for young people. Their lives stretched infinitely into the distance ahead of them, and there was no crystal ball to help them.

Unfortunately, not everyone got a second chance like Joe to make amends for a wrong decision.

'It's much better if you can make the right choice when you're young,' said Hattie. 'Then you don't have to live with regrets.' She thought again of Lily and Rudi. 'But for what's it's worth, even decisions that seem wrong at the time usually work out all right. Life can be more flexible than we imagine.'

Flora sat for a bit, digesting this, then with a small nod, she rose. She helped Hattie to clear the table and to stack the dishwasher. 'Thanks for the scrumptious lunch,' she said. 'But you should have your rest now.'

Hattie couldn't deny she was ready for a rest.

'And I'd like to take you out to dinner tonight. As a thank you.'

'I'd love that, Flora. What fun.'

Flora nodded, but she looked distracted as she tidied the kitchen, no doubt still wrestling with her decision. 'I might go for a walk,' she said.

'Yes,' Hattie agreed. 'Walking's always good for thinking. And there's a great coffee shop two blocks up, on the left-hand side.'

* * *

Buses, cars, taxis streamed past, bordered on either side by towering skyscrapers, but Flora paid them little attention. She didn't actually need to walk very far. By the time she'd arrived at the corner of the first block, she'd already reached her decision.

It was crazy, really. With a damn good audition behind her and the real possibility of a job here in Brisbane, she suddenly knew with blazing certainty that she couldn't give Mitch up. She had to speak to him again, had to make him understand that she knew the truth deep in her heart – an exciting musical career could never make up for losing the man she loved.

Mitch made her feel centred. Real. Bone-deep happy. And although he had never been prepared to tie her to him with an out-right admission, she was pretty sure that she made Mitch happy, too.

Looking at her situation from every angle, Flora knew she had no choice. She needed to ring the audition coordinator to tell her she was withdrawing her application. She would feel a bit foolish, but it was best to bow out now, before the panel began their deliberations.

Turning her back on the streaming traffic, Flora pulled her phone from her shoulder bag. Ahead of her, a side lane edged by tall office buildings framed a narrow strip of the grey Brisbane River with the QPAC buildings on the far side. When Flora dialled, someone in that distant building – possibly the officious blonde from this morn-ing – would answer the phone and receive her news.

Flora swallowed. *Just do it. It's okay.*

Mitch might be mad with her at first, and her parents would be disappointed, and Hattie would be, too, when she handed the vio-lin back, but everyone would calm down once they understood that this was what she really wanted.

Her thumb hovered over the keys. *Don't think about what anyone else might say. Just do what you know is right in your heart.*

In ten years from now, where did she want to be? With Mitch? Or still playing in an orchestra and heading home each night at close to midnight to a lonely city apartment?

She imagined Mitch's arms around her, warm and strong, and the delicious brush of his lips against her skin.

Just do it. Make the damn phone call.

As she scrolled through her contacts list, her phone pinged, signalling the arrival of a text message. Flora's heart raced as she checked it.

How was the audition? M x

Mitch. Her eyes were so suddenly blurred, she could scarcely see to text back.

It was fine, thanks.

He replied straight away.

You look lonely.

Lonely? How did he know how she looked —?

Flora whirled around, scanning frantically up and down the busy street and footpaths, but all she could see was traffic and strangers. She texted back.

Where are you?

But Mitch didn't answer. Bewildered, she watched as a taxi pulled up a few feet away. The guy getting out of it was dressed in a grey T-shirt and jeans, all broad shoulders and shiny dark hair.

Startled, overjoyed, Flora couldn't move. What was he doing here?

'Floss.'

Her heart thundered as he came towards her. This made no sense, and coming on top of the accumulated tension of the past few days, it was almost too much.

'What are you doing here?'

'I've just been on the phone to Hattie.'

'But why? What are you doing in Brisbane?'

'I came down for an interview, for a new position.'

'In the police force?'

'Yes. I've been accepted as a plain-clothes cop.'

Flora gaped at him, trying to compute this astonishing news. She was conscious of the phone in her hand, the message not yet delivered. On the wings of hope, she slipped the phone back into her bag. 'Does that mean – will you be working here in Brisbane?'

'I will, yes. I'll be a plain-clothes for three years, and I'll have on-the-job training, as well as courses at the academy. And at the end of that time, if I measure up, I can become a detective.'

Flora was sure this was good news. It was incredible news. But somehow, she couldn't allow herself to be excited. 'Is – is that what you want, Mitch?'

Grinning, he nodded. 'It's why I joined the police force in the first place. I'd always planned to become a detective.'

Yes, she could remember him telling her that. 'Detective Mitch Cavello,' she said. It had a certain 'cool dude' ring to it. A beat later, 'But you love Burralea. Your house, the town. Everything.'

'I do.' His dark eyes shimmered. 'But when the bones case came along, I realised I'd got myself into a comfortable rut. I remembered how much I like detective work. And the officer on that job gave me a good reference.'

'That's great.' Flora knew she should sound more excited. Hope and happiness bubbled inside her, but she couldn't quite let go of her fear that somehow this amazing surprise might not be as wonderful as it sounded. 'So you applied for this dream job down here because of a pile of old bones? It had nothing to do with – with me?'

'Don't kid yourself, Floss.' Mitch reached for her now and he smiled at her, letting his dark eyes tell her the truth even before he spoke the words. 'This has everything to do with you.'

Oh, Mitch.

'Burralea will always be there,' he said. 'It'll get by without me, but I can't get by without you.'

She found herself swept into his strong, familiar embrace, and while strangers bustled past them, Mitch swung her round and round, and she clung to him, laughing, giddily, gloriously happy.

Later, when they'd calmed down, they could find Hattie's coffee shop and thrash out details, like whether Mitch planned to rent out his tractor shed, or the kind of part-time work she might apply for if she didn't get the orchestra job.

For now, Flora had the only answer she needed.

CHAPTER FORTY-TWO

The graveyard nestled on a shaded hill, which overlooked a long and splendid view of farmlands stretching to the majestic blue peaks of the Bellenden Ker range in a patchwork of browns, golds and greens.

Joe, ever the gentleman, helped Hattie from the car, and together they went through the gate in the low stone wall, making their way along the rows of tombstones till they found the neat white grave and plaque that bore Rose's name.

Hattie would have kneeled there on the mossy grass if her knees had been up to it. Instead, she set a vase with pink Burralea rosebuds on the grave. These flowers had always been her mother's favourites.

Her mother.

Hattie remembered her turmoil at that time long ago when Rose had first told her the truth about her complicated family history. In spite of this, she'd commissioned the headstone to read:

Rose Bellamy
1915 – 1958

Beloved wife of Stephen
Devoted mother of Harriet
Loved and remembered

At the time, Hattie was sure she'd been right to claim Rose as her mother. Rose *had* been a devoted and loving mother, the only mother Hattie had known. Alone and newly widowed, Rose had made the brave decision to flee the terrible war in Shanghai and to bring Hattie to safety in Australia, to a place of peace and immense natural beauty. To Joe.

Hattie recalled the sea voyage, the little cottage at Kooringal, then the home she and Rose had made together in Burralea. Theirs had been a simple life, but Rose had given her the greatest gift, a safe and happy childhood filled with love.

Now, turning to Joe, Hattie slipped her arm through the comforting crook of his elbow, looked up at him with a shaky, teary smile. 'Rose told me to trust that I would find the right path, that everything would work out in the end.'

She looked down at the vase brimming with rosebuds. In the coming days, the flowers would open, blossoming into delicate and scented beauty.

'Thank you, Rose,' Hattie whispered. 'You were right, darling. You were right.'

* * *

On the day of the wedding, Joe didn't have to wait outside, standing and pacing in the blazing sun. He sat with Father Jonno in the vestry, chatting quietly, while on the other side of the wall, the little church filled with wedding guests and excited onlookers from the Burralea community.

'How are you feeling?' Father Jonno asked him.

Joe smiled. 'Incredibly calm. Not at all like the other time I was married.'

By now, Father Jonno knew the full sorry story. 'You've waited a long time for this, Joe, and I'm honoured to be conducting your ceremony today.'

'It means a lot to me,' Joe said. 'Not everyone is fortunate enough to be given a second chance. It's important to me to make those vows at last. To the right girl.'

'I know. That's why it means so much to me, too.' Jonno gave Joe's shoulder a comforting squeeze. 'It's almost time, my friend. I'll take a peek in there, see how the land lies.'

Joe looked down at his dark suit, brushed off the tiniest speck of lint. He thought of Hattie's happy smile when he'd left her back at the house, being fussed over by Emma and Flora. *Dearest girl.* He wasn't at all surprised that these younger women liked Hattie so much. Her warm and lively spirit transcended generations. Even Janelle was being won around. Slowly but surely.

Jonno called to him in a stage whisper. 'Okay, Joe. You're on.'

An incredible sense of peace descended as Joe entered the crowded-to-overflowing church. The place was transformed with flowers and satin ribbons and smiling guests. His daughters were responsible for the decorations and had dealt with issuing invitations, and everyone who mattered to Joe and Hattie was there. Janelle and Emma and their families, the old cattlemen who were Joe's long-time friends, their wives, and the new friends Hattie had made with remarkable speed during her short time in Burralea. Seth, Alice and Charlie from Kooringal, April from Burralea Lodge, Joan from the post office, Edith Little, Mitch Cavello and Flora, who had both, miraculously, managed to wangle a weekend off from their important new jobs in Brisbane.

Now, the organist struck a familiar chord, one that did not send shivers of disquiet down Joe's spine. At the back of the church, Finn

Latimer hovered, camera at the ready. Father Jonno, who was now stationed at the church's front door, turned to the congregation and smiled, gave a small nod. The organ music swelled and everyone rose, turning to watch, to wait.

Two figures stepped into the arched doorway. Hattie's son, Mark Macquarie, looked handsome and distinguished with a grey flecked beard and a charcoal grey suit. On his arm was the most beautiful girl, in pale cream, carrying an armful of pink roses and white lilies.

Silver-haired and elegant, she kept her eyes on Joe until she was standing beside him. She slipped her hand into his and smiled. At last.

ACKNOWLEDGEMENTS

Once again, I am indebted to my wonderful husband, Elliot, who is my patient first reader and my heartiest cheer squad and who so often, and without a hint of complaint, produces delicious meals at the end of a long writing day.

In researching the exotic locations and historical details for this book, I was fortunate to have several other people who helped. I'm especially grateful to the vivacious Maggie Wang, who took us on a wonderful walking tour of the French Concession in Shanghai and helped me to discover fab books in English about China's history in the 1930s.

When I was writing about police procedure Sergeant Darren Scanlan of Malanda was very helpful and patient in answering my questions.

As for the musical details in this story, I could never have created the character of Flora without the inspiration of my daughter Emma, who is also a violinist and, now, a wonderful music teacher. Thanks for your personal insights, Em!!

And, of course, once the manuscript was completed, I was indebted to the team at Penguin Australia who helped me to polish and refine and produce the finished book, especially Ali Watts and Nikki Lusk, as well as Bethany Patch, Fay Helfenbaum and Ali Hampton.

Finally, I would like to acknowledge Rosie Batty, 2015 Australian of the Year, who so courageously and powerfully raised our country's awareness of domestic violence.